Aut...

As you fall headlong in love with   ...e other characters that I've spent the last fourteen months getting to know, there may be times when their trauma or struggles feel too close to your own. While this book is sprinkled liberally with humor and lively banter, emotional triumph and love, some moments may be distressing to read. I felt it would be a disservice to those who have experienced similar trials if I were to gloss over the characters' painful realities.

With respect to those who want or need to avoid upsetting content, a complete list can be found on my website, https://lauralinn.com. A Wildflower for a Duke contains sensitive topics including: the death of a spouse and miscarriage (discussed), abuse of a child pertaining to the out-of-date and barbaric treatment of autism (discussed), violence and abduction (on the page), grooming and sexual assault (discussed), self-harm (discussed and mildly present on the page), and bullying (discussed). There is also descriptive consensual sex, drinking in moderation, and mild profanity. Oh, and there are goats...very troublesome goats.

Putting this story to paper brought me a tremendous amount of joy, not only in the creative process but also because it provided the opportunity to help others experience a neurodiverse perspective in a neurotypical world. Something near and dear to my heart, both personally and as a parent.

A special thank you to my friends, who are no doubt tired of hearing the ongoing plights of Gabriel and Violet, but still ask how my writing is going without a single noticeable grimace, and my editor, Kate, who endured multiple drafts with a smile despite the fact that I lost my glasses fifteen months ago and couldn't physically see the nonsensical punctuation I applied to the page. And, most importantly, thank you to my husband, Seth, and kiddos, Juliet and Sullivan, for their ceaseless encouragement.

~Laura

For my mom, who kindled my imagination to life with a library card and countless hours of reading. You will always be the voice in my head that says that I can accomplish whatever I set my mind to.

Laura, your lucky penny

Chapter 1

London, England, 1826

Gabriel Anson, fifth Duke of Northam, had always thought of death as a singular moment in time. Now, he saw dying as a slow and steady song that followed him everywhere, coming to climax in unpredictable places that left him breathless.

Emma was dead. And everything in his life had followed her, as if that loss had become the Pied Piper, with all the remnants of good in Gabriel's world falling helplessly in the wake of his hypnotic lure. Gabriel's confidence in the value of his work in the House of Lords, dead. His desire to connect with friends, dead. His devotion to the tenants of his ancestral lands, dead. His interest in romance, also dead.

Staring sightlessly at the gardens below, Gabriel traced the erratic path of one raindrop as it shimmied down its stilted path.

The splintering crack of breaking glass reverberated through the upstairs halls, jolting Gabriel from his thoughts. A cheerful tap at the door followed.

"Are we just going to pretend we didn't hear that, Your Grace?" Keene asked, propped casually against the door frame, lanky as an adolescent cat. Slate grey eyes the shade of a sunbathed rock flickered in the direction of the hallway before settling again on Gabriel.

Another explosion of porcelain sounded, and Keene cringed. "That sounded like the Imari Pattern." His inflection was the same as one might use to announce that a quarter of London's

1

population, along with Prinny himself, had just drowned in the Thames.

"Is that the set that looks like it has bits of pumpkin splattered on the bottom?" Gabriel asked idly, turning back to stare out the window. "And how the hell would you know the sound of one teacup breaking from the next?"

Keene exhaled a suspiciously indignant-sounding puff of air through his nose. "That tea set is soft paste, and I imagine it would make a more spectacular crash than say, the Jasperware. And they aren't blobs, they're orange blossoms. Or, they were." He added the last bit with a grumble.

"Perhaps you would have made a better butler than a valet. Speaking of which, don't you have something to starch?"

The indisputable sound of solid wood colliding with plaster stalled the progression of their asinine conversation. Gabriel stood and lifted an eyebrow at Keene.

"That would be the mahogany tea caddy, I believe."

"Why does my daughter have, what appears to be, tea service for twelve in the nursery?"

Keene spread his hands. "The dolls demanded tea."

Gabriel trudged his way through the door of his study swallowing down his resentment at the interruption. If it were only his future to consider, he would happily lock himself away and marinate in his grief. Society expected him to look to the future of the dukedom, remarry some empty-headed debutante, and produce heirs with all the mechanical thoughtlessness of a chicken laying eggs with the dawn. They could all hang.

What was not in him to ignore was Nora. Eleven years old and equal parts rage and despair. Well, maybe not *equal parts* in this precise moment

He hesitated, one large hand poised to turn the handle, apprehension roiling in his stomach. Uncertainty was an emotion that had never before plagued him. Its burgeoning presence in his life was disturbing. Like tightly stretched skin over a poorly healing wound, it left him angry and chafing.

His Emma had always known what to say, combatting toddler tantrums with light-hearted humour, and, as Nora grew older, soothing hurt feelings with just the right combination of empathy and insight. Alone, he felt clumsy and ineffectual.

It had been almost two years, but sometimes the passage of days seemed laughably irrelevant. All the chaotic emotions rampaging through him were both mirrored and amplified in Nora. *Feelings … my God, she had so many of them.* She shifted from baited badger to withdrawn and inconsolable as fluidly as a river, and he was left trying to follow her changing current like a pebble bouncing across the silt.

But he was trying. And he would keep trying. And Nora would parallel him with a different brand of trying altogether; she'd try his patience, his sanity, and his ability to communicate in complete and rational sentences. *Come on Gabriel. Get your head out of your arse. She's eleven. Stop being a coward.*

With a perfunctory knock, he squared his shoulders and stepped into the porcelain warzone. Broken shards littered the floor, along with bits of something charred. A substance he could only guess was tea was splattered like a muddy rainbow about the delicate, cream-papered wall.

Showered in a ray of sunlight, petite shoulders heaving with exertion, sat Nora. Like an avenging goddess torn from the pages of a book, her back was arrow straight, feet tucked beneath her on the floor. Her defiance was undermined by a slight quiver of her lower lip.

Nora's head snapped around, dark curls bouncing, and she met his gaze without a scrap of remorse. "You can't make me feel bad about chasing this one out. She tossed my animal anatomy book into the fire. She called me names." Nora recounted every moment of the argument, details falling haphazardly like leaves swooping to the ground on the October wind.

Well, that explained the ash, some of which clung to her hair and dress.

"She wants to fill my head with etiquette and watercolours until there isn't room for anything interesting." Nora's hands opened and closed reflexively in the folds of her dress like the steady tick of a metronome, a singular, orderly rhythm in contrast to her otherwise turbulent emotions. "And she insulted Mother. Said I wouldn't be such a heathen if she would have taken me in hand or let the governesses perform their duties. She's horrible. She hates me." Her anger spilled out in outraged splashes, her little body appearing to deflate in gradual intervals until she was left empty.

Into the following silence, his brain dealt out potential responses like a deck of cards. *Okay, so now I know what Miss Makle did, but what did the teacups do to warrant such a swift execution?* Or, *your kaleidoscope of emotional vomit makes my brain throb.* Or perhaps, *will the burning of the books cleanse the prepubescent demons from your soul?*

Gabriel, of course, said none of those things. Crossing the room in small, careful steps, as one might approach a resting butterfly, he dropped to his knees before her and enfolded her soft familiar hands in his own, silently willing her eyes to meet his. When they did, he could scarcely stand the emotion they held.

Every flicker of his residual frustration melted away like candle wax. There was a hopelessness there that he longed to scrub away, to replace with the bright smiles that had been constantly present through her childhood. He wanted to give her strength and peace, but he felt so very empty of those things himself. Plaiting together the frayed threads of his emotional fortitude, he presented what he hoped was passable as a smile.

"When you wage war as the teatime tyrant, you should choose the ugly set the dowager duchess favours. Hideous, beastly little eye sores that beg to be put out of their misery."

"They *are* hideous," Nora said with a sniff.

4

"But since you've already begun the process, we might as well finish off this set." And with that, he seized a forgotten teacup, unfolded himself from the floor, and gave the porcelain a swift execution against the wall. One corner of Nora's mouth tipped up and he felt his own answering smile. "Makes a satisfying smash!" Gabriel exclaimed.

Handing her the last remaining survivor, he bowed. "Your turn, my lady."

She gazed down at the ornate cup, then back to her father. With a disjointed spin and a leap, Nora loosed the cup through the air and into the wall.

"Expertly done!" Gabriel said.

Keene stepped through the doorway, waving a handkerchief like a white flag. Thick hair the colour of wet sand, a cowlick, and deeply-rutted smile lines gave him a youthful, roguish look. His gait was perpetually loose-limbed and insouciant.

"Another successful parenting day I see, Your Grace?" Keene's tone was warm despite his antagonism. He assessed the mayhem of the room with neither surprise nor condemnation.

"Haven't I fired you yet this week?" Gabriel parried with equal mirth. "Come to think of it, I believe there is an opening at my estate in North Wales digging some new drainage ditches. You fancy a more athletic job, Keene?"

"No, Your Grace, you haven't sacked me yet this week, but it's only Tuesday. Still plenty of days to bluster and threaten," Keene replied flatly.

Gabriel ruffled his daughter's hair, "We wasted those cups on the wall. A moving target would have been so much more satisfying. Keene, I believe we are going to need a broom,"

"No, Your Grace, dukes do not sweep."

"Keene, get me a broom, or I will fetch one myself and find another occupation for it."

Keene offered no physical reaction beyond a slight shake of his head. "Go ahead and try, Your Grace. There are nineteen closets, cubbies, and nooks in this labyrinth. Start your search and maybe you will find some ducal dignity or your lost parental skills along the way."

Gabriel let loose a great booming laugh. "I'll ask Mrs Janewood. She likes me better than you."

"Oh no, Your Grace. No one in England likes you better than me. Maybe not even anyone in the world, but I certainly haven't polled any of the citizens of the feral Americas, so it seems presumptuous to make that claim. France and Italy most definitely prefer me. You're pretentious, stubborn, and annoyingly tall."

Nora's voice interrupted their verbal fencing. "*I* will ask Mrs Janewood. She likes me better than either of you."

"Touché," the men said in unison. With that, Nora skipped from the room, all the day's despair temporarily erased.

With Nora safely removed from hearing, Gabriel let loose the sigh of a parent who had used up the last remaining shreds of his parental prowess. "I don't know what to do with her, Keene. This was so much easier when she was little and I could fix all her broken bits by blowing rude noises into her tummy until she squealed."

Picking up a severed teacup handle, Gabriel studied it absently for a moment before dropping it back to join its companions on the floor. "This is all wrong. I'm all wrong." *Dignity, also dead.*

"Don't be a bloody idiot, Gabriel. You're not what's wrong. It's this place that's wrong. Go home." Gabriel sat, dispirited, onto his daughter's bed. Scooping up a cloth doll and toying with the soft fringes of her hair, he resolutely avoided Keene's concerned gaze.

"I am home. All the correspondence here is addressed to me," Gabriel said, mulishly.

Keene responded with a wilting stare. "Estates, Your Grace, not *home.* You've ignored your seat in Parliament, you've skipped so many meals that your trousers would fall off your hips if not for a set of overworked maids with a quick needle and thread, and you've hibernated away like an angry bear. I know it must feel impossible to place one foot in front of the other, but remaining stagnant isn't an option anymore. Nora isn't getting better. If anything, she's worse. Last week, at the flower show, she got into a massive row with Viscount Bainworth's son over the Greek word for hibiscus, something about it being a—"

"Marshmallow," Gabriel whispered.

"Yes, well, when he said that she was wrong, Nora snatched him up by the ear."

Gabriel's eyes trailed to the window, thoughts slipping into the memory of Emma's disbelieving giggles the evening they had read it in a book together.

"And yesterday," Keene continued, "Mrs Simmons told her that she had to wait until after breakfast to sample her new recipe for bread and butter pudding, and Nora threw a five-year-old fit of temper. She never even threw five-year-old fits of temper when she *was* five. Wake up man, it's getting serious! You are a better man than this. A better father than this. It's time Gabriel. You have to go home."

Gabriel's nails dug into the lace of the little doll's dress as he fought to keep what remained of his composure. Keene's disturbingly honest words hung uncomfortably in the air as memories of his ancestral seat swept over him. Like sunlight that would not be contained, it sought out every crack and pierced him. A place that was once synonymous with warmth now scalded his insides, somewhere in the vicinity of his heart. He looked up into Keene's owlish, annoyingly perceptive eyes, then down at the doll, which stared accusingly back.

Inconvenient as Christopher Keene's candour could sometimes be, his friendship was absolutely essential to Gabriel's life. The men had grown up as secret companions, sneaking away and spending many of their free hours building forts in the woods or drawing maps and burying treasure. When he'd been with Keene, Gabriel had felt like an ordinary boy.

During Gabriel's second year at Eton, his father had discovered their friendship and promptly turned both Christopher and his father away from the house without so much as a reference. The old duke might have chosen a different path had he recognised the defining moment for what it was. From that day forward, all the wisdom and training the duke tried to impart to his son became a lesson in what not to do.

After ascending to the title, it took Gabriel nearly six months to find Keene, who had taken a position under a shipwright following the loss of his father six weeks prior. It had been a senseless death, caused less by the minor, easily-treatable wound than by the cruel superiority of a viscount who prioritised his need for a clean shave and a crisp cravat over a man's life. The viscount had insisted that medical attention from a physician be delayed until after his scheduled trip to a country house party.

Keene's father had spiked a fever several days into the journey and was abandoned at a posting inn where the summoning of a doctor came too late. He died alone.

Impotent rage had filled Gabriel as Keene recounted the tale, but from the ashes of that tragedy, the newly-titled young duke arose resolute in his beliefs; unlike his father and so many of the aristocracy, Gabriel would place being a good human above being a good duke. In the process, he found he could be exemplary at both.

Keene came home to act as valet. He was a forthright and balancing force in Gabriel's world, surrounded as Gabriel was by those who served up a steady diet of outrageously sugared platitudes.

"Maybe you're right, old chap," Gabriel conceded with a grumble.

"Of course I'm right. I'm always right."

"Send a footman ahead to give word and prepare for our arrival. We will depart in a week. But if this ends as catastrophically as I anticipate, it's straight to Wales for you."

"Of course, Your Grace. I'll keep my spade at the ready." Keene made no attempt to disguise the flash of a smile.

**

With every rotation of the wheels that brought him closer to home, the squeezing in Gabriel's chest cinched tighter. He was starting to feel like he understood the discomfort of women's corsets. Barbaric. The stagnant air of his lavish carriage smothered him. Scenery rolled past in tangled greens and browns, but he was far too riddled with anxiety to notice more than a blur of colour. He was tense. Brittle. Like overcooked bacon.

Unable to tolerate his body's rising protest a moment longer, he tapped the roof of the carriage and leapt out the door before it had even come to a complete stop. Watching him silently over the edge of her book, Nora cleared her throat.

"I'm fine, poppet. I just need … something." *Air. Solid ground. The insurgence of vaulting tree frogs in my abdomen to desist.* He settled on switching to horseback. Peeling off his topcoat and unravelling his cravat, Gabriel volleyed them into the carriage and traded places with Keene, who had chosen to remain close rather than ride ahead with the other servants.

"I will see you at home." He mounted his horse, Omen, gently squeezed the heels of his Hessians, and attempted to outrun his thoughts.

Despite having been away for several years, the land—every rolling field and copse of trees—was like an old, treasured book. Every line ingrained in his heart. Buttercups peeked shyly through the lush fescue beneath Omen's trampling hooves.

This was a terrible idea. He couldn't quell the anxiety that his already unstable foundation was about to come crumbling down beneath his boots. Emma would be everywhere. The piano bench, where her half would remain forever cold. The ugly, threadbare reading chair in the library that she would never let him reupholster. His bed, where they had made love countless times, and where she suffered endless hours of childbirth. Gabriel could still hear the wails of pain from her final hours, and feel the silence that had been twice as loud. Giving the horse his head, he attempted to pull his cyclical thoughts outward.

The crab apple blossoms should be in bloom up ahead. With less than a mile to the boundary of his park, he tried to relax his body into the steady rhythm of the gallop. The smooth leather reins felt sticky in his damp, un-gloved palms. Abruptly, Omen lurched sideways, and Gabriel careened off-centre before righting himself and settling his startled gelding.

"What the devil?" he exclaimed, dismounting and flinging his reins. Annoyance heaped atop his already abundant emotions, and he marshalled his self-control to avoid releasing them with a tongue lashing that would surely be unfairly disproportionate to the harmless mistake.

A woman stood before him, one arm spinning what appeared to be a glass tube with a bit of rag secured to the end. A wet rag, he concluded, based on the shower of cold splatters landing about his face and waistcoat. In her other hand, she clutched the most ridiculously-oversized, floppy brown hat to her head. She was dressed in an equally unremarkable brown frock, and its contrast to the life and animation she exuded was disorienting.

With one hand protecting his face from the energetic mist, Gabriel watched through the steady hum of his impatience, counting his breaths to quell his exasperation. Her petiteness was exaggerated by the monstrosity of a felt hat and what appeared to be muddy men's boots, giving her the appearance of a small child playing dress up in her father's clothes. A long, straw-coloured, loosely-woven plait swayed with her movements, swishing back and forth across the length of her spine.

"Be with you in the time it takes for a porcupine to peel a potato," she said, pausing to push back the hat brim and examine what he now saw were the numbers on a large thermometer. Cornflower blue eyes snapped to meet his, devoid of the slightest hint of feminine diffidence. Constellations of caramel-coloured freckles showered her face in clusters. Her nose was slightly deviated along the bone as if it had been broken and healed slightly misaligned. Gabriel wouldn't call her pretty in a traditional way, but there was something about her vitality that was undeniably fascinating.

Despite the abundance of more pressing questions about this situation and the woman before him, he couldn't resist pondering exactly how long it *would* take a porcupine to peel a potato.

"Oh I *am* sorry!" she interrupted his thoughts, "I'm afraid I was a bit careless and distracted. Are you well?"

She was a whirlwind of restless activity. As if all her various parts were in competition with one another, each vying to outdo the kinetic energy of the next. Every word stepped on the heels of the one before as she shuffled through papers that littered a nearby rock. Even her eyebrows leapt and furrowed as her finger trailed down a long list of numbers.

There was no logical reason for him to still be standing there. He should be on his way. In a moment he would mount his horse, offer this odd little female a good day, and return to his course. But even as he rebuked himself for dithering, he watched her every movement in anticipation of the next. For days he had been so filled to the brim with dread that there hadn't been space for anything else. Curiosity was a welcome change. and he was loath to allow the lightness to pass just yet. And so he leaned against a tree and crossed his arms, waiting for what she would say next.

"It's to determine the relative humidity." She glanced up, as one would check the time on a clock, then back to the crumpled papers in her fist. "The measure of water vapour in the air. Specifically, it's the amount of water vapour expressed as a percentage of the amount needed to achieve saturation." She paused, then added, "Rain," as if he was possibly too simple to follow the hastily fired-off explanation. Then she continued on because, apparently, it mattered very little whether he understood her or not.

"Generally, as the temperature rises, air becomes drier, making the relative humidity decrease. As the temperature lowers, the air becomes wetter, and the relative humidity increases." The enthusiasm in her voice was unmistakable and strangely contagious. "While it's absolutely fascinating how it pertains to the predicting of weather, it's also applicable to countless other areas of life. Baking, for example, or the storage of dried goods, and even construction, with the swelling of timber or curing in masonry. I began with studying rainfall in regards to animal behaviour, but I am afraid I've fallen down a bit of a rabbit hole."

Her rapidly-expelled scientific exposition came to an abrupt halt, and she took a half step backwards.

He was afraid he may be gaping, staring at her as if she was some bizarre anomaly, like a cow attempting calculus instead of grazing. She bit her lower lip and looked up, her expression slightly self-deprecating.

"We are quite unharmed, I assure you." He offered up his best reassuring smile. "And now, as I travel on my way, I can add a basic understanding of relative humidity to my already abundant vault of unlikely-to-be-required—but still fascinating—information. I'm just migrating home, and I'm afraid my mind was also not on my surroundings, strictly speaking. The fault was as much my own."

He shifted uncomfortably as he recalled his current state of undress. She seemed to either not notice or not care. Based on their five minutes of interaction, he deemed either equally probable.

"I see," she said, suddenly turning her curious eyes on him.

"You see what, exactly?" Gabriel stood a little taller.

"Home should be that one place of predictable steadiness, but it seldom is, is it?" She squinted up at the sky as if proverbs were painted on the clouds. "Like the rain, it can mean the end of a crop-killing drought that saves you, or the flood that annihilates you, washing all your seeds away." He felt those words in his bones.

"Ah, it's the latter." She pressed both palms to her cheeks. "I'm destined to keep apologising. I should just begin all conversations with 'I'm sorry' at this point. Good afternoon. My name is Violet Evans, and I will immediately fill whatever silence you provide with something embarrassing, impertinent, or wildly inappropriate. I beg your apologies in advance, and I recommend you make a polite exit before I take the uninvited opportunity to speak. And there, I've done it again. You see, I am quite the lost cause."

A strangled chuckle escaped him. "No, you're quite right. About home at least." He turned away, partly to gather Omen, who had wandered away to graze, partly because he knew he lacked the energy to hide the messy feelings from his expression. "This is my first time home since I lost my wife." There. He had managed to set the words free without sounding like a lost ten-year-old. Admittedly it was to an anonymous, bluestocking forest pixie, but it was a start. "To carry on with your very apt weather analogy, I've been avoiding the rain." He smiled ruefully at his boots.

"Can't avoid it." The statement was matter-of-fact but not lacking in warmth. "If you try to outpace it you'll only land wet *and* exhausted. Better to just press through it and accept the soaking."

He nodded. "Well, Miss Evans."

"Missus,'' she corrected.

"Mrs Evans, it's been a delight meeting you, and I will leave you to your…" he trailed off.

"To my psychrometer," she offered.

"Yes. Your psychrometer."

She nodded. Giving a hasty bow, he threw a leg over Omen, carrying on at a less breakneck speed along his journey.

Chapter 2

It wasn't the dying light Violet noticed so much as the transformation of the woodland animal symphony that surrounded her. The trilling of blackbirds and the mournful whistle of the collared dove gradually morphed into deep, barking frog songs and rattling grasshopper chirps.

The sun dipped her sleepy head just below the tops of lush, verdant branches, clinging to the horizon like a child insisting she wasn't even a little bit tired. Violet gathered her papers and books, stuffing them arbitrarily into her satchel. A snapping stick alerted her to a presence. The silence it accompanied identified her son Zachariah. "It seems time lost track of me and I missed lunch," Violet chirped.

"Dinner as well," Zach responded gravely.

"The benefit of not being fourteen years old, sprouting like a beanstalk. Unlike you, I'm not hungry every minute of the day."

Violet had tried, and failed, for the entirety of her thirty-five years, to capture and hold onto the awareness of time. Everyone seemed to experience it pulsing through them like blood, rushing and reminding with every thump that a second had passed and they needed to feel that passing. But the moment her mind shifted and latched onto something, those steady beats slipped away, leaving her floating in her own separate space, devoid of time and all of its meaning.

She spent most of her life alternating between feeling guilty for her deficiency and feeling resentful for that feeling of guilt. Neither was particularly productive. But Zachariah would never dwell on her many shortcomings. Acceptance had been at the very heart of their relationship from the day he'd walked into her life. Or rather, rode in, tucked in front of her husband Nathan on his horse. Nathan, with his unshakable sense of right and wrong, particularly as it pertained to those weaker than himself.

Growing up together, she could recall countless instances where Nathan had stepped willingly into the path of certain discomfort in the service of someone less able to withstand the blow. It was quite literally what led them to be tied in matrimony, and how Zachariah had come to be raised as their son.

When Nathan had received word that his brother was sending his "deaf and dumb" son to an asylum, he'd ridden through the night in pouring October rain. He'd returned with a very frightened six-year-old Zachariah, who was, indeed, resistant to touch and mute. Violet still felt hot, percolating anger as she thought of the treatment Zach had endured at the hands of his birth father.

Despite their efforts, those first months were a torrent of rage and frustration for Zach. His wants and needs categorically misunderstood, he lashed out at their every attempt to soothe him, and became increasingly withdrawn.

One day, they woke to discover Zachariah had used a chunk of charcoal to draw on the wall. When faced with discovery, he dove into a wooden chest half-filled with blankets, anticipating fury and fists. Instead, Nathan walked out and returned with art supplies. He cracked open the chest and dropped them inside. Eventually, Zachariah learned to speak. He learned to trust. He learned what it felt like to be accepted, and, in turn, to offer acceptance freely to his family.

That's not to say that life ever came easily for Zachariah. Safety and love were the bare minimum requirements for a child. Preparing him for life outside their secluded home had proven to be a far more difficult task. While he'd learned to communicate his needs quite skilfully, Zach's ability to grasp the subtleties of what others communicated was still a daily hardship.

"I brought you a dinner picnic." Zach passed Violet a cloth sack filled with a jar of cranberry sauce, some crusty bread, and cold chicken.

"Blast. Now you've done it. I was counting on my stomach growls to keep the predators away," Violet jested.

Zach shook his head, as if the motion would dislodge whatever barrier was preventing his understanding and allow comprehension to pop to the surface like a bubble. "What predators? Badgers? Oh," he smiled. "You're joking."

Violet grinned and they sat down to their meal.

It had been a great game of theirs when he was small, identifying various minute facial expressions and decoding what they meant. At first, it was like reading a map to which he had no key, but Violet was a patient teacher and found ways to make it less like a chore.

They even attempted to translate the expressions of farm animals and figures in the clouds. "That cow there, in the field by the woods. See her? Look at the way her eyebrows droop and her tail is held off to the side. Doesn't she look lovelorn?"

Zach would inevitably stare back blankly. "Cows don't have eyebrows," he'd say. "And I think what you're seeing is flatulence." Violet would laugh and muss his hair and he would tolerate it because he loved her.

"I hear the Duke of Northam is back." The sound of Zach's voice shifted her thoughts back to the present.

"I wonder what he will think of our goat shed," Violet said, tapping her fingertips together to form a steeple. Having run out of parchment one day, Zach had painted the exterior walls of the outbuilding. What once was a structure composed of weather-worn, unchinked logs now stood unrecognisably transformed into a mural of wild horses frolicking about a riverbank that slashed through a vibrant, spring meadow. Scattered amongst the majestic animals, cheerful bluebells and daisies nodded gently amidst clumps of late summer grass to the rhythm of a soft breeze so believable you could feel it across your skin.

"I doubt we will ever see him," Zach replied flatly, nibbling a bit of his cheese.

"Probably not, but I think it would be deliciously diverting to see his over-starched reaction to a bit of whimsy. Oh! Maybe he would be so enamoured with your artistic brilliance that he would commission you to redecorate the exterior of all his properties in its image."

Zachariah just blinked at her.

"Or to command the design of an entire line of waistcoats in a similar style, miniature-sized horses chasing one another down his lapels and weaving through the buttons!"

Her vivid imagination was a bit wasted on Zachariah, but she liked to think that some part of him enjoyed her long rambles into the preposterous, even if he remained a spectator to the merriment. He certainly never seemed to mind her forays into the extraordinary, which was convenient since Violet seemed quite incapable of staying to the conventional path.

It had always been this way. While everyone around her seemed to hear and innately match the same, steady rhythm of orderly thoughts and predictable patterns, she found herself constantly swept into the magic of "what ifs."

"No," Zachariah said. "I will be perfectly happy if he leaves us well enough alone."

***

Gabriel's eyes felt hot and scratchy. Grappling with each step, he passed through the grove of fruit trees where he and Emma had picnicked the afternoon he learned he was to be a father. That memory, once among the sweetest in his life, now felt as sour and rotten as fallen fruit left to decompose on the cold autumn ground.

He made his way through the topiaries with an expression of carefully-guarded neutrality that made the aching muscles in his face riot with the need to fall slack. As he approached the three marble steps that led to the front entryway, his mind withdrew to that first day as husband and wife. The memory of her musical laughter, how he had entwined his fingers with hers and raced through the front door, practically bursting with hope and excitement. He stared down at his now empty hand. It had never felt so bereft. Cold sweat tickled down his back, adhering his shirt to clammy skin. His muscles locked in place. She was supposed to be there beside him, to share a lifetime with him. And deep inside his chest, Gabriel's heart fought against every contracted beat he was forced to endure without her.

His gaze swept across his surroundings, desperate for an anchor to ground his whirling emotions. From the open door, Keene watched, his jaw slack, body eerily still in contrast to the swarm of servants scrambling about as they unloaded trunks and prepared for their master's arrival. With a few words, he cleared the garden of servants and came to meet Gabriel on the bottom step.

"It's just me here now, Gabe. We are going to walk through that door like we have done a thousand other times." Gabriel tried to answer but found his throat had grown thick and rigid. He nodded instead, squaring his shoulders, and strode through the entryway as if it was nothing at all. As if it wasn't one of the loneliest moments of his life. Because he was the Duke of Northam with thousands of people counting on his strength. Because he was a father who could not afford to break.

They walked up the grand staircase and down the hallway in silence. Gabriel threw open the door to his chambers and froze as details of the life they'd shared within the walls of that room assaulted him, hammering at him from all sides. There, he crumbled.

"Oh God, I can't do this Christopher. I can't stay in this room. Get it all out. I can't ..."

Keene's arms were around him, his hand resting on the back of Gabriel's head. "I'll clear it out and place it in storage. We'll swap beds with the one from the dower house and settle you in another room until the work is done."

Gabriel clenched his jaw and forced his mind to centre on Keene. It proved to be a pathetic defence against the onslaught of feelings that threatened to buckle his body in two. His breath was coming in short bellows, the corners of his vision beginning to look mottled and grey.

For long moments, Gabriel stayed there. He rested his forehead on the smaller man's shoulder until his breaths came easier and he felt strong enough to raise his head, heavy with the weight of all that he had lost. How could the absence of something feel so heavy? Gabriel was raised to be a god amongst men, but now he swayed under the burden of his own grief. Hot shame began to trickle through his veins. Equally grateful for, and embarrassed by, Keene's presence, he cleared his throat.

"Thank you. I will have a moment in my study, then find Nora." His voice sounded shaky and insubstantial, as if all that remained of the unstoppable aristocrat he had once been was his hazy shadow. Eyes stinging from the effort to remain dry, Gabriel patently avoided the warm and understanding gaze of his oldest friend.

"I know that lofty title of yours makes you feel as if you aren't permitted to cry like the rest of us lowly 'sirs,' but I lost any reverence I had for you decades ago. A few well-deserved tears aren't going to change the way I feel about you, you bloody fool." Keene squeezed his shoulder and turned away.

Gabriel closed the door with a click and splashed three fingers of scotch into a glass, pouring it down his throat with brisk, burning swallows. He stared wistfully at the heavy crystal decanter on the sideboard. Quivering with the need to fill the glass again, to drink until all the sadness and anger and helplessness was buried beneath a warm blur of apathy, he tunnelled his fingers into his hair and squeezed.

Even the blessed, alcohol-induced numbness would fade, leaving space for all that pain to rush over him again. The devastation was too unrelenting—too permanent—for scotch to ever wash it away. He couldn't even imagine feeling whole again. His only choice was to accept the poor imitation of life that stretched in long years before him, and find the fortitude he would need as Nora's only remaining parent. A parent that she required to be present and whole, now more than ever.

After some time to compose himself, he quit the room in search of his daughter, knowing she must be struggling beneath the same mournful fog as he. Traversing the nursery as swiftly as possible, lest he be swept away again, his attention was captured by movement outside the window. Bracing himself against the textured wall, he squinted into the harsh afternoon sun. Surrounded by thickets of roses on the cusp of their bloom, Nora clawed and tugged viciously at the base of a bush. Her mother's flowers.

Alongside Nora, Emma had planted the garden when she had been heavy with child. Gabriel had chastised her for digging, insisting a gardener step in, but she'd stubbornly refused. *Nora needs this,* she had said. Needed time with her before the baby came. It would be their special place, created together. He had yielded to her, as he nearly always had.

Gabriel's feet pounded against the ground with massive, urgent strides as he left the house and crossed the lawn to Nora's special "nursery-view garden." There, he dropped to his knees in the upturned mud and pulled Nora tightly against his chest, absorbing her ineffectual blows as she fought him through angry sobs. After a final flail, she collapsed like a ragdoll in his arms. Gabriel pressed a kiss into her curls.

"It's going to be ok, my sweet. Shh. I know how badly it hurts."

"It's my fault. I killed her and the baby," Nora cried into his shirtfront, growing loud and emphatic as momentum broke away

20

what remained of her composure. "I was jealous and mean and she shouldn't have been digging those holes. She was trying to make me feel better. I made her do it and now she's …" Her words became inarticulate syllables, then heaving gasps. It was the guilt and debilitating sadness of a child who couldn't possibly understand the random cruelty of life. She had taken it all on herself, organising blame in tidy little columns. Applying the logic of youth to a world where logic simply didn't apply. Where sometimes people died and there was no fault to be found.

"No, poppet. It wasn't you or anything you did. Your mama loved you and she built this garden *because* she loved you. She wanted you to be able to see that love outside your window every day." He rocked her, struggling to be the steady presence she so desperately required.

"The baby was in the wrong position in her belly and no one knows why. We don't always understand. Sometimes babies come into this world smoothly and other times they do not, but it isn't anything you did or didn't do."

He paused, then started again. "We don't have to stay here if it hurts too much. Or we can change the nursery …"

"No!" Nora yelled. "If you take it all away, I'll have nothing to remember her by. What if I forget? What if I forget *her?*" Gabriel's chest constricted at her earnest distress, even as part of him thought it would be easier if *he could* forget.

"No love, you won't forget. Not all the important things, like how much she adored you. But we can keep everything exactly as it is, and I can help you remember everything about her." *Even though doing so felt like intentionally rooting through an open wound with a stick.*

He allowed the painful memories to wash over him. "We'll remember how she would race to pick the first daffodil that bloomed because she was so excited for spring. The way she would skip the most exciting chapters in a book because she couldn't stomach the suspense." His head lowered, surrendering to the memories. "How indescribably happy she was the day you were born. We will remember together and it won't always hurt this much." *God how he hoped it wouldn't always hurt this much.*

She nuzzled her sopping face deeper into his shirt. "I ruined her flowers," she mumbled. Gabriel stood with Nora cradled in his arms, then assessed the damage with calm detachment. Bushes were tilted, exposing ravaged roots, and flurries of petals covered the muddy earth below, ripped apart before they had even had a chance to bloom.

"No, Love. They only need a little attention and time."

A gardener leaned against a nearby tree, clearly distraught by Nora's broken-hearted display. "Fix it, please," Gabriel called out. Then he carried her away to the privacy of the guest quarters, where they could mourn together. *Better to just walk through and accept the soaking.*

Chapter 3

In the weeks that followed, Nora found a sense of tranquillity escaping to the meadows and moors beyond the estate's gardens. The house felt suffocating and fleeing was preferable to surrendering to the constant gloom. Her father had buried himself in estate work, her governess had yet to be replaced, and with that relative lack of supervision, Nora could easily slip out of the house in search of adventure. It was precisely the sort of wonderland—thick forests and meandering streams—perfect for capturing the imagination of an eleven-year-old girl.

She collected flowers, searched for unusual rocks, and climbed trees to see how far she could see. She watched deer hidden amongst the thickets and a pair of goldfinches building their nest. As long as she wasn't gone for more than an hour or two, no one seemed to notice that she was gone. One Saturday afternoon she found herself studying a different kind of animal entirely.

She had seen this boy twice before, watching him from a distance as he was sprawled out and drawing under a cherry blossom tree, but this was the nearest he had come to her home and the closest she had come to him. His comfort in the silence, his stillness, and the deliberate focus to his work as he sat cross-legged in a patch of sand by the stream, intrigued her.

The breeze played through his unfashionably long, wheat-coloured hair. A lock had fallen over his face as he worked a stick through the fine grains drawing … something. She had been observing from some fifty feet away long enough to have gnawed an apple down to the seedy core. Absently wiping the tacky juice from her fingers, she crept closer to investigate his activity.

It was an impossible horse. Impossible because patterns of sand could not create such detail. Such life and personality and depth. She shifted closer, expecting the picture to mutate into something less spectacular. It remained unchanged.

"I am focusing. Go away," the willowy artist mumbled without breaking from his task.

"That's beautiful," Nora responded as if she hadn't heard the stranger's cranky demand. He glared at the ground, face scrunching, then continued his work.

"It seems so unjust that the rain will wash it away. Why do you do it knowing the weather will take it all back?" she persisted. Still, the rhythmic rubbing of stick through silt continued, and for a moment she thought he wouldn't answer. As if he could ignore her out of existence.

"I create for myself. What happens after I walk away is irrelevant." His eyes remained fixed on the ground, brows twitching in concentration. "*Now* will you go away?" She didn't, of course.

**

The left side of Zachariah's face felt unevenly hot under her patent curiosity, causing his skin to prickle and itch. He shifted, once, then again, the discomfort from her blatant perusal growing unbearable. Like an ant slowly steaming under the magnification of a shard of glass, he wanted to scurry away as she leaned closer, but he stubbornly ignored his body's thrum of discomfort.

He came here to quiet his mind. Zachariah didn't like people as a rule, and they didn't like him. They didn't understand him and he was happy to remain too "odd" to merit the notice of other boys. That's what he told himself anyway.

He blinked furiously as the facial twitching began. Zach detested this out-of-control feeling, but he was helpless to stop it. He thrust his clay-caked hands over his face. Clutching his hair, he squeezed … hard. The twitches only grew more violent, his muscles stretching taut with the need to contain it.

She would go away. He would simply wait. He could calm his thoughts and travel some place quiet in his mind. Someplace without nosy little girls. Zachariah chanced a peek through his fingers and found she had inched closer, her muddied hem dragging the ground at her feet. But rather than gawking awkwardly or mocking—or worse, feeling sorry for him—she scooped up his abandoned twig.

Turning slightly away from him, she pressed the stick into the sand. With the tip of her pink tongue darting out, she began scratching her own drawing, completely ignoring his present behaviour. Like the tapered end to a thunderstorm, Zachariah's twitching diminished as he watched her enthusiastic scraping. As his coiled muscles relaxed, freeing his brain to reengage, he began to catalogue his observations.

Every part of her looked dainty but a little bit untamed, and he was struck by the presence of so many conflicting details. Her pale purple dress was finely made but wrinkled, with grass stains about the knees that hinted of exuberant play. Dark, curly locks wilfully sprang loose from two identical plaits that fell just past her shoulders, and the remnants of a spider web clung to the ribbon that fastened one. He would guess her age to be ten, maybe eleven years old, some four years his junior. Her eyes were downcast, but he thought they were brown and expressive, bringing to mind a spaniel that had shown up at his home years ago and made a rather successful campaign of begging for scraps. He wanted to sketch her.

"Is that a dog?" Zachariah asked. The words came out as a croak, his throat parched from all the deep breaths he had taken.

"I am focusing. Quiet, you."

He cocked his head sideways. Zach didn't always trust his interpretation of other peoples' humour, but he thought this muddy little sprite of a girl was playfully using his own words against him. He cautiously inched forward.

"And, there! My masterpiece is complete." She whirled the stick with a dramatic finish as if signing her artwork. He looked down at the lopsided stick figure quadruped, then ventured a brief glimpse into her eyes, which were dancing with mock conceit. He liked her silliness. Even more, he liked that it was directed at *him*. Baffled by the sudden receding of his anxiety, he smiled awkwardly at his shoes. Zach's smiles had always been reserved for his family, and it felt strangely out of place using those muscles with anyone else. But it also felt right. *She* felt right. Like discovering a mixture of two shades of blue that blended into a perfect match for the sky.

"A horse I take it? Dreadful." His lips curled experimentally again as he assessed her work.

"Well, it's a good thing I only make my art for my own enjoyment." She threw his words back at him again, and this time he was certain of their intended friendliness.

"I am Nora."

"Zachariah Evans. And shouldn't you be with a nursemaid?" He scanned the surrounding brush for a chaperone.

"Undoubtedly. But Nanny Featherly likes to nap." She shrugged. "Want to see what I found?"

Much like conversing with his mum, no response was actually necessary as she chattered on, bounding to retrieve a small tan satchel and pulling out some kind of animal remains. The forearm from a small mammal, he would guess, covered with dirt and debris but bare of any flesh or skin. Nora reverently offered up her discovery with all the pride of a cat delivering a freshly-murdered rodent.

She radiated enthusiasm, bouncing on the balls of her feet as she waited for him to declare some kind of verdict on her treasure. Zach was cleanly divided in half between revulsion and fascination.

He assumed this was one of those times that he should know how to react but, like a book with entire chapters left blank, he had no idea what he was supposed to do or how he was expected to respond. He settled on scientific curiosity. Reaching down with two fingers, he gently plucked the bone from her hand.

Zach attempted to focus solely upon the severed limb, examining each craggy surface and pit methodically. But Nora was difficult to ignore, practically incandescent with the need to enunciate her findings.

"Look! You can see where some of the meat was pecked and torn away by scavengers in this rough-scored area!"

Because her natural state was so excitable and flamboyant, it served to underscore the way her movements became more cautious as her body moved closer to his. She pointed to indicate the indentations, cautious not to touch him where he held fast to the bone.

Something loosened in his chest at her artless offer of friendship and understanding. Zach had found few friends in his life. It seemed that some differences in people were too much for anyone to tolerate, and when people inevitably left him, the loneliness felt even larger than before they had arrived.

Zach handed the treasure back to Nora, and she tucked it away. Wandering close to a pocket of the stream where the current was calm, she grinned. "Look! Fish! Right there. They look close enough to reach down and snatch up with my hands!" She leaned in closer still, the tip of her finger following their tiny waving fins.

"Please don't. I don't want to have to jump in and pull you out." Zach imitated his mother's best scolding face. Over the years, he had studied his family's interactions, much in the way one might catalogue the behaviour of a different species. He had observed the way their bodies reacted and moved when they joked or became annoyed. When he was younger, he had even compiled a list of his observations to try and arrange them into some semblance of logic. Often, though, what people said seemed contradictory to their movements. Especially his mum's. He had all but given up on understanding her. Apparently, you didn't have to understand someone to love them because while Zach didn't always understand the unpredictable moods of others, he knew love.

Sometimes his mum would insist that she was well, but her shoulders would curve down and her arms would draw into her, as if tucking away. Other times, what she said seemed unkind, but her smile was light and playful, dimple deeply-rutted, and limbs loose. He had decided that it was better to believe the language of expressions and physical mannerisms rather than the words people chose to share. Lying with your body was more difficult than lying with words.

With that foundation established, Zach dedicated himself to studying all the minute shifts that a face could make. How the slight curl of a lip or shift of an eyebrow could transform the entire emotion they meant to convey. At first, he found it dizzying. He wanted to ignore it all and hide, but his family was so determined to draw him out that the only alternative to constant confusion was disciplined study.

He drew hundreds of pictures of faces. Mostly his mum's, but sometimes Hamish's and his papa's as well. He sketched until the language became less disjointed and more fluid in his mind. It still required focus, but it felt less impossible as long as he avoided crowds of people. He couldn't tolerate large groups, with all their voices and expressions. Or strangers, with their unfamiliar movements that made him feel as if he was learning all over again.

Lady Nora had slipped off her shoes, tentatively gliding her feet into the shallow water so as not to startle the fish. "I won't topple over, you silly goose."

He raised one dubious eyebrow at her display of confidence. She watched the sleek minnows intently, fingers wiggling in anticipation. In one clumsy swipe, she plunged her hands into the water, her body becoming unsteady with the abrupt motion.

Zachariah's hand was there in a fraction of a second, grabbing a fistful of the back of her dress and settling her squarely back on her feet. Squeals of laughter erupted from Nora as she threw her head back with glee. She was seemingly delighted in her failure.

"I guess they're faster than they look! You saved me," she exclaimed, as if she had fully expected to find herself face down in the river.

"From seven inches of water," he replied drolly.

"Still. You saved me, so I guess we're friends now."

He looked down to hide the pleasure that bubbled up in his heart at her use of the word. "Yes. I guess we are."

She squinted up at the sky, assessing the passage of time, then scrunched her nose. "I have to go," Nora said with a sigh. "But I'll come back next week. Maybe you can draw a picture for me."

His fear demanded that he decline, that he walk away from the river and deny her a second opportunity to decide he was too different to tolerate. Today had been perfect, and he could hold onto the memory forever, pulling it out and examining it whenever he was feeling sad or lonely. It could be enough. If they met again and it went poorly, it would curdle the joy he had found here. But the pull of potential friendship was too powerful to quell, so Zach arrived early the following week with a pencil sketch of Nora, ankle-deep in the water, trying to catch a fish.

They fell into an easy routine for the remainder of the month, meeting on Saturdays, while Nora's father was engaged in meetings, and on the occasional Wednesday, when Nora was able to sneak away. Zach taught her how to fish with actual poles, and Nora made an ingenious little kite that they kept aloft for over an hour before it snagged on a tree limb and became hopelessly tangled. Oftentimes, they would merely bask in the sun, Zach with his sketchbook and Nora filling every single moment with whimsical stories and friendly chatter.

Gradually, they fell into an easy friendship. Nora learned when to give him space, and he grew comfortable in the moments where she prattled on. She was very much like his mother in that. Nora was adventurous and smart beyond her years, and their age gap seemed to narrow as their hours together grew. Zach found himself looking forward to each Saturday the moment the previous one had passed.

Chapter 4

After his initial stampede of feelings upon returning home, Gabriel devised a system which allowed him to cope with his daily activities. When he felt especially miserable, he allowed himself five minutes to feel completely and utterly despondent. After those moments, he buttoned himself back up and forced his mind in another direction. *Some days it even worked.*

"You missed our appointment for tea."

Five minutes over, then. His mother, the dowager duchess, doled out patience and kindness in doses that would scarcely cover the bottom of a demitasse spoon. Long bent fingers that zigzagged like creeks drawn on a map wrapped around the handle of her black cane with a force that would snap a goose's neck. Her severely-drawn, silver chignon blended with the grey wool of her gown, giving the impression of rainy day fog that buried and consumed any speck of colour that dared to present itself. There was no softness to her, and she allowed for none of it in others. Gabriel was raised in an environment meant to freeze out love, creativity, and compassion. And so he and Emma had provided precisely the opposite environment for Nora.

His parents weren't cruel, exactly. His father never took a cane to him or drank to excess. Prior to his years at Eton, Gabriel's parents employed the very best academic tutors, as well as masters in riding, fencing, and shooting. They provided everything he required as the heir to the dukedom, and not an iota that was not. Attentiveness, empathy, and encouragement were for working-class parents who coddled their offspring and raised weak men. From his parents' perspective, knowing and understanding Gabriel was unnecessary because their sole purpose was to build him into the person they required him to be. When Gabriel was distraught, he would imagine that Keene was his brother, so he too had a father to fish and talk with. A father whose motivation to spend time with him was based upon affection rather than duty.

"I apologise, Mother. My appointment ran late."

She raised one corner of her mouth in a wooden smile and made a three-act performance of looking left and right around the room for any evidence of the "appointment that had run late."

Grinding his teeth together, he forced his expression to remain neutral. "I interviewed another applicant for the position of Nora's governess. Another unsuitable candidate."

Her frown lines relaxed as she considered her granddaughter, whom she presumably cared about in some unrecognisable mutation of grandmotherly affection. Gabriel continued before she had a chance to interject her opinion. "I believe Nora has begun feeling much more herself over the course of the last month. With that in mind, I've decided to allow her a break from traditional education for a time. She can learn the sixteen different curtsies and how to serve tea while balancing a book on her head after she's had more time at home."

The sheer force of the disapproval the dowager radiated could melt layers of skin off Gabriel's bones.

"Lower your hackles, Mother. I am not insinuating that whatever you learn as little girls is inconsequential, but I'm fairly certain that, as the Duke of Northam's daughter with the dowry she will possess, Nora could pour tea down the waistcoats of half the *ton*'s eligible bachelors, and she would still have a dozen suitable marriage offers by the conclusion of her first season."

His mother didn't disagree but neither did her expression unclench.

"In lieu of a decent tutor, I will encourage her to pursue her interests and spend some time with me around the estate. She's a bright girl. I don't want to see her innate talents plastered over by the poppycock society deems more important."

The dowager sneered. "Spend *more* time with her? You could hardly have spent less with her since arriving home."

The most effective attacks were always the ones based in truth. Even if Gabriel could retaliate with an effective defence, it was impossible to emerge victorious from a battle against one's own conscience. Heat rose in Gabriel's face. While his mother's cutting remarks had long since lost their ability to wound, he was keenly aware of the disappointment Emma would feel. His insides shrivelled as he imagined her there, frowning beside his mother. But despite his decidedly insufficient time with Nora, it was obvious that she was rebounding better since arriving home, sans her governess. To his shame, his time and influence had played no part in that recovery.

Gabriel bit back all the perfunctory excuses that threatened to slip out. Instead, he raised his chin and accepted responsibility. "You're right, Mother. I will endeavour to do better." He hoped that by admitting his shortcomings, it would extinguish her impulse to further reiterate her point with twelve other synonyms for the word "failure." *Inept, incompetent, negligent, inadequate.* Apparently, he didn't require her help to come up with a few words of his own.

The look of self-satisfaction she wore made his insides twitch. He was ten years old again, his feelings disregarded as an inconvenient obstacle to the prosperity of the dukedom.

The dowager cut off his self-indulgent wool gathering. "You know, it doesn't have to be this difficult. You are falling short as a parent because you cannot possibly meet the girl's needs."

"As I already expressed, Mother, I will find an acceptable governess when the time is right."

"That is not what I meant." She touched two fingers to her temple, in the only indication of emotional disquiet that his mother would ever give.

"No. I didn't think so." He didn't try to keep the surliness from his voice. As a boy, his relationship with his mother had been no more substantial than that with the cook who had served in their family for years. Less, actually, because Mrs Simmons at least left biscuits out in the kitchen at night in case he was hungry. He hadn't received a crumb of sustenance from his mother, literally or figuratively.

Matters became worse after his marriage. In the eyes of his mother and the *ton*, Emma had little to recommend her as the Duchess of Northam. A pittance of a dowry, a relatively new and unremarkable family line, and, what was ultimately unforgivable to his mother, a failure to provide heirs. The way his mother assigned blame to his wife had made that loss even more difficult to survive, and had further fractured his relationship with the dowager.

"You have been a widower for nearly two years. *Two years*! You're not a woman, Northam. You don't have an excuse for sulking around in widow's weeds. The duchess is gone. Nora needs a mother and this dukedom needs a proper heir ... *your* heir."

Swallowing hard, Gabriel wrenched at his cravat to loosen the knot and met his mother's impenetrable gaze. Neither blinked for long minutes, an entire conversation passed between them in the silence. His futile entreaty for support and understanding. Her callous rejection.

His response, when it finally emerged, was cold and deliberate. Gabriel scarcely recognised himself.

"I fail to see how the presence of a mother would benefit Nora. I've yet to find any benefit in you."

The dowager's lips thinned into a horizon-straight line before she swiftly vacated the room. If he hadn't known it to be an impossibility, he might have said there was sadness in her expression.

***

The sun was tucked neatly behind the clouds, providing minimal light and even less warmth, unseasonably crisp for spring. Zachariah had already arrived and was diligently painting what looked like a tiny row of roosters on a cream-coloured chicken egg. Nora clasped her hands behind her back and tried not to fidget.

"Breathe, Nora." His attention never deviated from his work, but the corners of his mouth tugged up in a slight smile. Given leave to do so, Nora skipped closer and peered around his shoulder. Zachariah shuffled slightly to the side, widening the space between them by several inches.

"It's so lovely, I didn't want to cause you to flinch," she explained unnecessarily.

"It's all right. I'm used to wiggly women. You'll understand when you meet my mum." There was a velvety warmth to his voice at the mention of his mother. After growing accustomed to his matter-of-fact flatness, the sudden metamorphosis piqued her curiosity.

Zach stroked the slender brush against the palm of his hand, leaving a watery trail of red. Then he dipped the end into brown paint, adding spindly legs to the row of roosters. "My papa once said that if you scooped up seawater in a bottle and shook it fiercely, that was her. Sand and salt whirling unpredictably in every direction as if desperate to get out." He cleared his throat and added more paint to his brush.

"She sounds remarkable."

He nodded once in agreement. "What was your mum like?"

Nora plunked down beside him on the obliging rock and rested a cheek in her hand. "She was … happy. She played dolls with me and had a different silly voice for each one. She tucked me in every night and never got angry when I stayed awake to see her. She loved flowers, especially smelly ones. She listened to me talk and was never too busy for me. She loved to sing and play the pianoforte."

Zach lowered his paintbrush and looked at her—really looked at her— for the first time. A long, intimate, assessing gaze that made her feel visible and understood in a way that defied description. "What about your father? What's he like?" Zach asked.

"My father is devoted. To me. To the dukedom. To Mother. He's patient with me, and I know I'm not always easy to live with." Leaning down, Nora plucked a wilting daisy from the ground. She wrapped the stem around her finger until the tip turned a violent red then dropped the flower at her feet. "But he doesn't play anymore. Or laugh often. That part of him just fizzled away when we lost Mother. It's almost like I lost both of them."

Zach abandoned his paintbrush to the grainy sediment at his feet and laid one long arm around her shoulders, tugging her closer to the warmth of his body. He squeezed.

"You're sad," he said, as if the embrace required additional explanation. "I'm sorry I made you sad."

She shook her head then rested it against him for a moment, her temple on his shoulder. He felt stiff beneath her, offering comfort but offering it reluctantly. As if it cost him something to offer it. Was it the physical affection or something that she had said? She mentally reviewed their previous exchange, searching for the source of his discomfort. *Oh, God.* She had been meaning to tell him precisely who she was but … oh she could come up with excuses for her lie of omission all day and it wouldn't make it right.

He finally broke the silence with a whisper, "*Lady* Nora," he emphasised her title, then paused with a sigh. "I suppose I knew you were quality, but Nora, why didn't you tell me?" Zach shifted, removing the comfort of his warm body and retrieving his brush from the ground.

"Mostly because I was afraid you would look at me like that. Or rather, *not* look at me like that."

Zach pointedly fixed his wide blue eyes to hers, undisguised worry and affection patently present.

"I'm sorry I didn't tell you, Zach."

He frowned and returned his gaze to his brush.

"It was wrong. I knew it was wrong every time I thought to tell you and didn't, but I didn't want to lose you, Zach. I guess it felt better to be a liar with a friend than an honest person all alone."

Zach's head jerked up from where he had been staring at his paintbrush. "There's nothing that you could show me—nothing that you could tell me—that would cause me to go if you wanted me to stay."

Nora flung her arms around his spindly bicep, pressing her forehead to his shoulder. He flinched, then softened, covering her other hand with one of his.

Neither child had noticed how the breeze had shifted and cooled. Darkening clouds knitted tightly above, becoming fierce puffs in shades of slate and dove. Like a little brother tagging behind, the rain soon followed with heavy droplets, each racing the one beside it to the ground.

"Come with me. We can make it to the stables before we get washed away." Nora didn't wait to see if he would follow. Grabbing fistfuls of her skirts, she sprinted at a breakneck pace, leading the way to the relatively warm, imposing structure. Despite their speed and their relative closeness to the stable, every thread of their clothing was saturated and ice cold by the time they shoved open the massive stable doors. Nora, thrilled with the excitement, held her sides in giddy laughter, her gasps and giggles startling a nearby horse and attracting the attention of the stablemaster, who delivered a stack of warm horse blankets in a flustered flurry

"Yer father will have me head if he sees you swimmin' in rainwater like a couple of drowned kittens," clucked the withered groom. As if summoned by dark magic, the heavy wooden doors were thrown open, not by a gust of wind, but by her father, hair plastered to his forehead, scowling.

**

37

Having sent his solicitor away earlier than expected to avoid the rain, Gabriel thought he would try again to teach Nora how to play chess. The last attempt had ended abruptly when she stuck a pair of pawns up her nostrils. Gabriel searched all her favourite places but only managed to discover a young maid and a footman engaged in conspicuous flirting, and some freshly baked shortbread, which he pilfered. Neither could he find Nanny Featherly, who, despite his repeated attempts to pension her off, remained a stubborn fixture of the household. She spent most afternoons napping and moved at the speed that a yeast roll would rise, which often left him playing a one-sided game of hide-and-seek with his errant daughter.

One of his nearest neighbours, Mr Cartwright, had surprised Nora last week with a donkey foal that had been shunned by its mother. Nora had taken to helping the stable hands with the creature's feeds. Calling for his coat, Gabriel headed to the door, waving away Keene's insistence that he let a footman go in his stead.

Bennett, who had been his butler since as early as he could remember, attempted to shoo Keene up the stairs. "His Grace made it clear he does not wish for your interference, Mr Keene."

Keene didn't spare the ageing butler a glance. "The rain is torrential! Why do you employ footmen at all if you insist upon doing all your own fetching and carrying?"

"We have to provide *someone* with whom the downstairs maids may shamelessly flirt. How else would they occupy their time if not to vex Bennet with their youthful hormones?" Gabriel teased as he made for the exit.

Out the door and into the downpour, he sprinted across the gardens to the stable. The cold rain dripped down his hair and inside the collar of his shirt, causing his whole body to shiver. He wrenched open the doors and stepped into the warm, sweet-smelling stable. The relief at finding his daughter safe, perched on a pile of hay and buried in coarse brown horse blankets, was immediately superseded by unease as he noticed her unfamiliar companion. Some ten feet away and looking equally drenched, stood a lanky adolescent boy. His fair hair was newly scrubbed with a blanket and standing up on end like a newborn chicken's.

A *boy*. With his *daughter*. God above, he was going to have to throttle this twig of a child. Stretching to the extent of his not-insignificant height, Gabriel flexed muscles in his body that he was certain hadn't existed three minutes ago. Despite the execution of Gabriel's most foreboding ducal scowl, the boy remained detached, as if he could ignore Gabriel out of existence. He cradled an egg close to his body, trickles of red and brown cascading down his wrist and forearm. The other hand held a paint brush.

Perplexingly, the little stripling seemed more disappointed about the muddled paint disaster than terrified of a duke's wrath. Gabriel took a series of deep, slow breaths, uncertain if the source of the roaring in his ears was from the deluge of rain beating down on the roof or his blood whooshing in his ears.

"Here you are, Father." A large, scratchy blanket landed on top of his head. "Oh, I am sorry!"

He struggled to free himself from the wool. *Damn it all, it's hard to look menacing when you're tunnelling your way through a horse blanket*. Freeing himself, his gaze shifted from his daughter back to her guest, who was staring at the opposite corner, looking decidedly pale.

"Father, may I present Zachariah Evans?" Nora said with practised ease. "Zachariah, my father, Gabriel Anson, the Duke of Northam".

Crossing his arms over his chest, Gabriel studied Zachariah, whose eyes remained fixed to the floor as if driven in by nails. One paint-splattered hand rose to his temple and grabbed a fistful of scruffy hair.

"He is … shy with strangers." Noting her father's alarmed expression, Nora rapidly continued her explanation. "We met a little over a month ago and he's been teaching me the most splendid things."

Gabriel's stomach lurched uncomfortably. *I'm sure he has.*

"He's an artist. You should see his landscapes! And he knows about nature; which tracks are made by which animals, how to make a whistle from an acorn, and which birds sing which songs. He even knows about the weather … although, clearly, he has more to learn since he allowed us to be nearly washed away in this nonsense." Nora glanced at Zachariah with a teasing smile, but the jest fell unacknowledged at his feet.

"His mother taught him. She's brilliant! Last week she even tried to meet with the stone mason to show him a test he can perform to help predict curing time. Something about how the …" She looked to Zachariah for help but he remained disconnected from the conversation, the palms of his hands pressed into his eye sockets. "I don't remember. Something about how the humidity in the air can make the concrete fail to harden. Irritating, close-minded man wouldn't even meet with her, simply because she's a woman!"

"Evans. Relative humidity," Gabriel parroted. The memory of another Evans from weeks past sprang to his mind. As Zachariah's identity snapped into place, he found his anxiety ebb, much as the rain was mirroring outside. In his sliver of an acquaintance with Mrs Evans, he had liked her. It seemed impossible that such a cheerful, if endearingly awkward, woman would have a monster for a son.

"I believe I had the pleasure of making a brief acquaintance with your mother." The rhythmic squeezing of the boy's fists in his hair stopped, but that was the sole indication that he had heard Gabriel at all. Despite his initial influx of paternal distress, Gabriel found it difficult to see this sad, withdrawn sapling of a boy as much of a threat to his daughter.

"Come along, you two. Let's move inside to get dry, and then we'll have a carriage hitched to see you home. Zachariah, was it?" The adolescent gave a stilted nod. Nora shuffled a few tentative steps towards Zach, but halted in her approach as he stiffened. It appeared and receded so quickly Gabriel thought he may have imagined its occurrence.

"This is the perfect opportunity to show you my skeleton collection," Nora beamed. Zach responded with one fast jerk of his head to the negative but Nora's smile didn't so much as flicker at his decline. "Yesterday, I found an entire wing from some kind of bird of prey. Buzzard maybe? It's massive. So much bigger than they look from a distance!" Nora paused, but her chattering continued into the silence.

Just as Gabriel was about to insist that his daughter come indoors, Zach's body began to relax by tiny fractions. His eyes searched out Nora's like a plant leaning toward the sun, holding her gaze with such intensity and care that, had they been two adults, Gabriel would have removed himself and the intrusion of his presence. There was tenderness there, genuine intimacy and friendship where communication didn't require words. Zach's gaze lowered to her chattering teeth.

In a barely audible voice, he spoke, "You're freezing. Let's go."

With an approving nod, Nora turned to follow Gabriel out the door and into the last fighting remnants of the dwindling afternoon storm.

Chapter 5

Gabriel peeled off his topcoat, relieved to find that Bennett had already obtained a stack of towels and was awaiting their return. Nora was quick to intercept and offer up the plush material to Zach. Nearby, Keene stared mournfully at the puddles left in their wake.

"Not a word about the blasted floors, Keene," Gabriel growled.

Keene cleared his throat, tugged once on his jacket sleeves, then attempted to shepherd Nora towards the stairs. "You have a nice hot bath prepared, and we'll see to your friend." Despite Keene's coaxing, Nora remained determinedly adhered to Zachariah's side, her stance unmistakably protective.

"I will see him home myself, poppet," Gabriel interjected, employing his softest tone. "Bennett, show young Mr Evans to the library if you will. I understand he has some interest in Nora's skeleton collection; he can examine her findings there by the comfort of the fire." Gabriel inclined his head in Zach's direction. "I will be with you presently." Turning his squeaky leather Hessians on the floor, he swiftly made his way up the stairs, Keene trailing behind.

Dry and hastily dressed, Gabriel entered his library and headed to the sideboard to pour himself two fingers of scotch. Zachariah was absorbed in his examination of the assortment of bones, holding a smaller one up to the light of the window.

"Some kind of rodent?" Gabriel inquired.

Studying the gnarled bone from various angles as he rotated it in his long fingers, Zachariah answered. "No. It's hollow. A part of

42

the wings of a smaller bird. Metacarpus maybe? They're lighter to help them with flight. I'm sure Nora could explain it better."

Gabriel swirled the deep amber liquid around in his glass as he pondered how best to go forward. His much-needed wardrobe change had given him time to consider a few things, and while he was still a bit baffled by the young man's behaviour, it was clear that Nora's attachment was earnest and that he would have to proceed cautiously.

"Would you care for tea?"

"No, thank you."

"How old are you Zachariah?"

"Fourteen, sir." Gabriel watched the column of his throat work with a hard swallow, then he corrected, "Your Grace." Zachariah's attention remained on the bone as he traced the tips of his fingers along the mottled edges, his face pinched with intense concentration. "She introduced herself only as Nora, but I don't think it would have changed anything even if I had known all along that she was your daughter."

Zach's voice was devoid of guilt or even a real spark of recognition that he understood the complexity of this situation. More to the point, the verbal exchange seemed to be background noise to a more interesting private conversation between him and the bone.

Not changed anything? Gabriel was bewildered. "How exactly did you come to befriend my daughter?" It seemed like a safe enough place to start. At this point, Gabriel was considering balancing the bone on his nose like a trained circus animal just to capture the youngster's attention.

"She wouldn't go away." His response was so crisp and unrehearsed that Gabriel felt the corners of his mouth tip in amusement. That did seem very much like Nora.

Experience had taught him that silence was a formidable weapon in inquisition, but the tick of the pendulum was beginning to make *him* strangely nervous while he waited for Zach to continue. Conversely, the passage of empty moments appeared entirely irrelevant to the boy. Zach reverently placed the specimen onto the shelf in exchange for another, then continued his wordless perusal.

"And …" Gabriel encouraged him to continue.

"And she seemed lonely."

The observation plucked at a raw place in Gabriel's chest. *Failure.* His mother's accusations chimed like a gong through his heart. Gabriel continued to allow the silence to fill the room, but apparently, that was to be the extent of the explanation offered. Clearly, a shift of tactics was required. A direct assault.

"I don't know that I should allow my daughter to spend her days gallivanting about with you." *There. Ignore THAT.*

Zachariah's jaw tightened, gaze darting towards the library door like a general overwhelmed on the battlefield and fervently wishing for reinforcements to come over the hill. Gabriel felt a swell of remorse at the naked distress that flared across Zachariah's face. He had cast a stone into Zach's seemingly placid waters hoping for a ripple of response, and blast it, he had caused a tidal wave instead.

Gabriel watched the stricken boy withdraw further, the tenuous thread of conversation snapping entirely. A muscle began to jump on the left side of Zachariah's face, and he covered it with his hand as if to hold it still. The other was white-knuckled, still clutching the forgotten bone.

"I'm odd. I know." The admission tumbled out on a rough exhalation.

Gabriel had to clasp his hands to keep from reaching out. Had Nora exhibited a similarly bedraggled self-worth, it would have torn him in two. This was someone's child, and more than just an anonymous someone. Despite having met Mrs Evans only briefly, he suddenly felt a sense of camaraderie, from one struggling parent to another.

"No." *Well, yes.* "NO," he repeated more emphatically. "You're a fourteen-year-old *boy*. She's an eleven-year-old young lady." For the briefest flash, Zachariah's eyes connected with his, exuding helpless despair in nearly-palpable torrents.

Nora had not been the only lonely one. This young man, who, no doubt, had been mocked and shunned by his peers, had found a friend in his daughter. And she in him. Gabriel's words had been meant to force engagement, but they had inflicted wounds instead. And now he had to do what he could to make it right again.

"You should come *here* to see Nora." The invitation was out of his mouth without a second thought. "You are welcome here, Zachariah." And he found he meant it. "If you want to fish or explore, I will come sometimes. I like to fish. Or, Nora can take a groom. But she cannot go without a chaperone." His voice was low, reassuring, almost … paternal.

Zach offered only a small nod but he had begun to unclench. His shoulders slumped from relief or emotional exhaustion or possibly both.

"Now. Your mother will be worried. Let's get you home, son." He set down his empty glass and held out his hand to indicate the way.

The ride to Zachariah's home was brief, which was a relief since any attempt at conversation was met with a polite but stilted response. The rain had stopped, but heavy grey fog made everything feel thick and murky. Gabriel had grown accustomed to the attention garnered by the sleek lines and imposing size of his ducal carriage. Even in the dreary weather, curtains slid surreptitiously to the side and children ran outside to gawk openly … one of the many reasons he preferred his horse to the grander conveyance.

Pulling up to the residence, he was met by a gaggle of chickens who flocked to him in a chorus of soprano clucks, and a goat who was dining on a flowering shrub. She refused to shift even the slightest inch out of the way, a pink petunia dangling from one side of her furry lips and a patently bored expression on her face, despite the cacophony of activity that surrounded her. Shuffling slightly to the side, she swished her feathered tail, then carried on with her meal as if his carriage and four were easily ignored.

A pair of plump, white ducks also took an interest in his arrival, attempting to waddle their way up the steps and through his carriage door like a pair of entitled dowagers. His driver hastily shooed the nosy little beasts away.

Gabriel was distracted from any other barnyard antics by the most unique structure he had ever seen. Was it a chicken coop? A barn? It was … Gabriel wasn't sure how to classify it. Built into the limbs of two massive oak trees, its uneven stairs climbed up one corner where three more goats were perched like pirate lookouts in a crow's nest. All along the roof, where a gutter might be in any sanely-designed structure, were clusters of wildflowers. A vibrant mural of painted horses raced across the entire east wall.

His gaze swept greedily about, like a butterfly in a blooming garden overwhelmed with too many options for pollen. Dispersed about the gardens were cleverly-constructed rain barrels, some kind of miniature windmill with chicken feed scattered about it, and a broken wagon repurposed with nesting boxes built haphazardly on top. Each item was intricately painted in vibrant blues, greens, and reds.

Even a pile of eggs that had been collected and placed in a hay-filled wooden crate were decorated with the same amazing finesse. Gabriel's memory shifted to the egg from earlier that day, bleeding watery paint down the arm of the young man beside him. "You paint remarkably." He thought of Mrs Evans, with her glowing exuberance and natural curiosity, and it made everything about this place make sense. Its own little universe where everything was upside down and inside out, but somehow exactly right. It made the rest of the world grey by comparison.

⁕⁕

By the time Violet's brain noticed that her skin was soaked, it was well and truly a downpour. Much of her hair had slipped loose of its simple plaited twist, and streams of water followed the course of the waterlogged strands like tiny branching creeks, soaking her shoulders and bodice. Abandoning her work to the English spring weather, she raced back indoors to dry off and find Zachariah.

She poked her head outside the door. "Zach!" Only a goat bleated in response. After several more minutes without a response, worry had begun to seep in. The storm was aggressive, and although Zachariah knew the land and woods intimately, she couldn't quiet the anxiety that rippled through her. Securing Nathan's old brown hat to her head, she ran out into the cold rain.

Violet found no sign of him at the river, the McTash's barn, or in the cherry blossom orchard where he had been painting. As the rain lessened its temper tantrum, first to a drizzle, then to mist, she followed the path toward the road that would lead her home. Stepping through the trees, she watched as a midnight black carriage stamped with an intricate crest slowed to make the turn which would lead only to her home.

Her skirts felt like half-melted cheese sticking to her slippery legs as she increased her pace. In the distance, she could make out Zach's familiar form next to a man who must surely be the Duke of Northam. Their backs were turned to her and they appeared to be examining the nesting box. A broody hen was perched atop, flapping her wings aggressively in an attempt to detour the nosy aristocrat, but he paid her little notice.

Naturally, the Duke of Northam should come by when I'm drenched and covered in mud! She tucked her arms across her chest protectively, recalling all of her flippant jests. Specifically, how she would be amused—pleased even—to see his reaction to their whimsical little corner of his lands. Oh, she would gladly eat every one of those words to avoid whatever was to occur in the next ten minutes! She thought it would be a lark, but what she felt was slightly queasy and threatened. Their safe haven, fanciful and free of judgement or recrimination, was under siege by expensive wool and sardonically lifted eyebrows. She wanted to load the catapults and raise the drawbridge. *Where was a good trebuchet when you needed one? They could hurl chickens …*

Violet cringed as her sodden boots squelched with every step, announcing her approach and alerting the pair, who turned in unison.

Instant recognition seeped cold into her bones. The man from the woods. Embarrassment sparked and climbed up the nape of her neck, only to be smothered almost immediately by a flash of annoyance. Other than the hint of dampness clinging to his dark curls, the duke was every bit the consummate aristocrat.

"You're a mess," Zach stated flatly.

She gave a resigned little shrug. "Yes, well, you know how well the fish-skin cloak worked, and I haven't yet had the time to put the finishing touches on the duck-feather model." Peeling off her felt hat, she wrung it savagely and dropped it, wrinkled and shapeless, back onto her sopping head.

"Hello, Your Grace. How nice of you to mention that you were, in fact, the Duke of Northam last time we met." Grimacing, Violet imagined how blissful it would be if she could simply wash away with the rain. Why did caution and common sense always arrive twelve seconds *after* her impetuous candour?

He flashed an obnoxiously disarming smile. "Fish cloak? You cannot introduce sea life apparel into the conversation and then carry on without explanation."

He removed his topcoat and wrapped it snuggly about her shoulders. Violet had to fight the urge to step out of his reach. It engulfed her petite frame, like using a horse trough as a vase for a single daffodil. Smooth satin and the cosiest wool she had ever touched, still warm from his body, enveloped her suddenly over-sensitised skin. Goosebumps popped up like daisies down her arms as if eager to experience this bizarre decadence. *What the deuce was this man doing? What kind of a duke wraps a goat farmer in his coat?*

Some bewildered, suspicious part of her wanted to thrust the offending garment back into his hands, but instead, she found herself nestling deeper into its inviting softness.

Zachariah's quiet mumble caused her attention to lurch back to the present. "You don't want to know all the materials she's tried," he said before blurting a quick farewell and dashing into the house.

Violet watched her son's retreating form. "Who would figure that fish scales aren't, in fact, entirely waterproof? And they were freshwater varieties, mostly trout. Not that it's relevant to the conversation. And we were discussing your quite intentional avoidance of introductions when we last met." She shot him a vaguely accusatory glance. Despite the edge to her words, she couldn't quite reign in the accompanying dimpled grin that spoke of swordplay with sticks instead of blades.

He parried with a smile of practised ease. Gone was the half-attired anonymous gentleman who wandered the woods, vulnerable and haunted by his homecoming. In his stead stood an impeccably polished peer of the realm, who donned charm and confidence as a second skin. Why he was wasting it on her, she could not fathom.

From his embossed buttons to his polished boots, the man shined with an almost startling perfection. In her youth, despite her family's long gullies of destitution, she'd had occasional contact with a few impoverished peers, but never anything close to a duke. Nevertheless, she would not give his elevated rank authority over her bearing. She raised her chin and squared her shoulders.

The duke seemed to take in her sudden resurgence of pride, and nodded as if he approved. "*You* were talking about my failure to introduce myself," Northam said. "I believe *I* was talking about some kind of smelly and inventive, albeit faulty, rain gear, if I am to understand correctly."

"Your Grace," she sighed impatiently. "Why are you here? I would offer you tea but I never drink the stuff. Terribly un-English of me, I know. I am sure you lock people in your dungeon for lesser crimes." Her eyes kept helplessly navigating their way back to the nearly-reflective shine of his boots. "And really, your boots are beyond distracting. It's like looking directly into the sun." *Belligerent inquisition of his presence, embarrassing, unsolicited personal information, and open hostility towards his footwear … off to a promising start, Violet.*

Apparently unaccustomed to the rapidly-shifting conversations that were commonplace for Violet, he stared at her quizzically.

"I have water. And milk—plenty of lactating goats, so that's never a problem—but I don't believe I am supposed to milk ruminants in the presence of a duke. I'm certain that's an unspoken rule."

Eyes the colour of cinnamon twinkled with mirth as he studied her. "Well, if not, it should be."

After a disquietingly long gaze, he looked away. The moment that connection ended, his relaxed joviality diminished like the sun shifting behind a cloud, leaving a much cooler man in its place. But for that one breathless moment, she had experienced a crackling sort of energy vibrating between them. Something that seemed as if it should belong to two completely different people in a different place.

"I've come to return your son. It seems he has befriended my daughter." *Ah. Back to reality.*

Zach? Her Zach, who melted like hot butter when cornered in conversation with a stranger? She almost snorted at the implausibility. Then his statement and all it encompassed sank deeper into her mind, and even that hint of a smile vanished. *Oh, God. It's a duke's daughter. He really is going to put me in the dungeon.*

"I'm sure he didn't mean any harm. I'll talk to him." She was certain she must have looked unreasonably frazzled. Without the benefit of knowing Zach, the duke would never understand the magnitude of sadness Violet was about to unleash on Zachariah. She was nearly trembling at the thought of having to tell her son, who had been incapable of establishing friendships, that the one child he had finally formed some kind of attachment to was, in fact, completely improper to befriend. Having all of these devastating thoughts while being swallowed ridiculously in this warm—*and, my God, delectable-smelling*—coat, was dizzying. She let the offending item slide off her shoulders and moved to hand it to him.

"Zach won't be any further trouble. I will make him understand." Violet forced the words out.

"No. Stop." He thrust the coat back towards her. "Mrs Evans, wait. I liked it better when we were discussing fish skins and goat's milk. I'm not angry. I was … well, more alarmed than angry. But not any longer." Eyes that had sparked with laughter moments ago were now gravely serious and beseeching. When she offered no response beyond burrowing back into his coat, he continued on.

"I think Zachariah must be good for Nora. She's struggled terribly since my wife …" His voice trailed off. "She has struggled for a while, but recently, she's been happier. More like herself."

Violet played with the buttons on his coat, her index finger circling around and around like the hand on a clock. His eyes dipped down to follow the hypnotic motion, and she immediately halted.

He cleared his throat. "You're wet through and should get changed. I simply wanted to let you know that Zach is welcome to visit. I've instructed him that, should they leave the gardens, they are to take a groom."

"That's very kind of you, Your Grace," she demurred.

"Kindness has nothing to do with it. It's self-preservation." His smile made a heart-stopping reappearance as he continued on, "Life with an emotional eleven-year-old girl is like having an adorable kitten. No one warns you about their tiny needle claws."

"Just so," she responded with an understanding nod.

"You can send the coat back with Zach. Or better yet, I've promised to accompany them on a fishing expedition. Come along, since you are clearly a superior angler. Or was it your husband who collected your materials? Never mind. Let's say this Saturday? I'll send a carriage at eleven o'clock. I'll even instruct my boot boy to ease off the wax for your benefit. They will be positively scuffed for the afternoon."

Northam turned on his heel and leapt into the carriage, his long legs having no use for the lowered step. Two taps to the roof and he was off, careening down the road before she could even begin to invent a polite refusal.

Chapter 6

Violet stood stunned for long enough that a chicken decided her boot would make a comfortable place to roost. Scooping up the hen, she flipped the indignant creature onto its back like a baby, stroking the feathers on its chest. The chicken glared and wiggled ineffectually before settling into her arms.

"I cannot possibly go fishing with a duke. It's absurd. It's terrifying. It isn't done. I absolutely will not go." The chicken blinked up at her. "Well, you're no help." With a resigned sigh, she gently plopped the hen back on her feet. "I guess I'm going fishing with a duke."

After drying and changing her gown, she found Zachariah seated at the kitchen table, string bean body curled about his sketchbook. Reaching for a pile of potatoes, Violet picked one up and began to peel. Moments passed with only the scratching sounds of skins parting and flopping into a growing pile.

"Anything you would like to tell me about, Zach?" Violet grappled with the nearly overwhelming urge to expel all her questions in one breath. Instead, she allowed the silence to hang heavy in the room, broken only by the scraping sounds of the potato. *Peel, plop. Peel, plop. Peel, plop.*

"No." Zach's pencil nub continued to glide across the paper in short, energetic strokes. This was one of those times when Violet wasn't entirely sure if he was unaware of the significance of an event, or if it was simply easier to feign obliviousness.

"Would you tell me about your new friend?" He brought his pencil to the table, tapped it a few times, then balanced it vertically on one end, catching it as it began to wobble.

Violet funnelled her restlessness into potato peeling, casting about for some of the patience that had developed as a result of the many failures and subsequent resolutions to master her impulsivity.

When Zachariah had first come into her life, she found their very opposing personalities to be some kind of a cosmic practical joke. He needed time and space to consider his words, while Violet's thoughts waltzed forth from her mind and into the world as easily as breath from her lungs. When wounded, Zach would brood and retract into himself. Violet flew apart in every direction until her soul was emptied of its turbulence. But as Zach grew, Violet became aware of an underlying sameness between them. While the material of which they were constructed seemed entirely contrasting, they were still more like one another than they were to the rest of the world. A chicken and hawk don't seem very similar until they try to live amongst horses.

She studied the potato in her hands, keeping the persuasive power of her gaze far away from his.

"Her name is Nora." He glanced up, then returned to his graphite circus act. In that half-second, she saw everything. He knew it was momentous, he was overjoyed with his friendship, and he was vastly enjoying toying with her.

"Are you truly going to make me beg for details, you scallywag!" She flung a potato peel at him, and it adhered to his smiling cheek for a long moment before losing its starchy suction and toppling onto his sketch pad below. "I know it's not been easy for you to make friends. You must be excited to have someone to fish and play with. Tell me about her!"

She used the word "play" loosely, as Zachariah had never really played. When he was small and the other boys immersed themselves in imaginative pretend, becoming pirates and highwaymen, Zach could never seem to detach himself from being *just Zach*. It was like music he couldn't hear, and as hard as he struggled to play the notes alongside his peers, he remained three measures behind and syncopated. There were times her heart had bled for him; she could remember the effects of that isolation, how it would burn away every glimmer of self-worth.

As the village boys grew, they became less tolerant of his differences. He was an easy mark for ridicule. Once, when he joined a game of cricket, they had intentionally thrown the balls at him over and over, making excuses for their bad aim as they laughed maliciously. He took ball after ball—to the hip, the shoulder, the knee, the head. They thought, in his reluctance to walk away from the game, that he didn't understand their particular brand of cruelty. He did. And he stayed anyway, stoically enduring endless rounds of physical pain for the slim chance of acceptance. Returning home bruised and emotionally unlaced, he fell into Nathan's arms with haunting sobs.

It only became worse after Nathan died. With no father to accept and encourage him, he withdrew from anything remotely threatening. Unwilling to bet on the cards he was dealt, Zach folded hand after hand until he left the table altogether.

Zach picked up the potato peel and began to study it, stroking back and forth with his index finger. The ever-present solemnity softened on his face, a shy smile growing in its place. Dimples Violet hadn't seen in months made an appearance. So often his expression was shuttered, but when he threw back the curtains and let the sunlight shine through, it was mesmerising. The problem wasn't that Zach didn't feel emotions like other boys. It would be more accurate to say that he felt everything and more, and couldn't always make sense of it all.

"She's a little thing. Silly and inquisitive and stubborn … and nice. She's nice to me. And she collects animal bones. She likes to explore and she climbs trees almost as well as me. She doesn't let being a girl stop her from anything." He threw the peel back at her.

His introduction of gender into the conversation unleashed an entirely different flood of concerns. She remembered how her attachment to Nathan had transformed from childhood friendship into tender adolescent love. Even now, Violet could imagine the ease Zach would find in falling in love with her as they matured … and the broken heart she would be helpless to prevent.

"She sounds lovely." Violet tapped the knife blade into the potato as she mentally floundered about, considering the conversation that—however ineffective it might prove to be—she had to attempt.

"You know, there are some people, some friends, that no matter how much we come to care about them, are destined to remain only as friendships."

"Of course I know that, Mum, and she is only a child."

"Yes, but she won't always be a child. She *will* always be the daughter of a duke."

He nodded his understanding.

"His Grace invited us to picnic Saturday," Violet began, trying for a light tone that she didn't remotely feel. "Would you like to go?"

Zach crossed his arms and resolutely stared at the table.

"The duke is going to have to know you, Zach. If you want to remain friends with Lady Nora, he has to know you."

Zach sighed.

"Oh come now," Violet cajoled. "Today wasn't so bad. You met him and did splendidly."

Zach's mouth pulled tight in a grim expression. "Very well. If that's the only way I get to keep Nora."

Violet was tempted to remind him that Nora wasn't a piece of rose quartz to be kept, but decided it was better to pretend she hadn't heard his comment.

The chicken alarm began squawking outdoors, effectively ending the conversation. "My, but we are popular today. Who now,

I wonder? The queen?" Violet abandoned her potato pile and went outdoors.

Hamish, with his sky blue eyes, peered up from where he knelt at the bottom step of the goat loft. An inquisitive goat sniffed about in his mess of sun-bronzed hair as he nudged at her tickling, intrusive nose. One look into his familiar face, and all her anxiety diminished. Hamish brought the sort of warmth and contentment only present with someone who knows everything about you, and loves you still. After the day's unexpected emotional pyrotechnics, Violet hadn't realised how deeply she needed to unburden, until she found herself at the centre of his scrutinising gaze.

As a child, at an age where being different was the worst possible thing one could be, Violet had befriended Hamish and Nathan, who inexplicably adored her despite—or maybe partly because of—her eccentricities. When her brain became bored by the ordinary and shifted to the implausible, they merrily followed her lead, leaping topics like frogs on a lily pad and considering the fantastic right alongside her.

It had been their love and acceptance that imbued her with the confidence to appreciate her eyes for the colourful world they saw, and to even feel a little sorry for those who drifted through life in shades of grey. The Duke of Northam, who likely thrived on the strangled rules of aristocratic life, was exactly the sort of poor sod she pitied.

"Apple Core got her foot stuck in the broken bottom step again. Do ye have any nails? I'll fix it while I'm about." He returned his attention to the obstinate goat, "Hold still ye smelly beast before I make stew outa ye," Hamish chastised. Freeing the unappreciative creature, he stood and crossed the yard.

"Good afternoon, Hamish. Zach, fetch some nails and a hammer, please." Fiddling with the end of her plait, she waited for him to approach.

"Oot with it, Violet. I've known ye yer entire bloody life. Dinnae ye think I ken when yer itchin' to talk?"

She shuffled through four completely conflicting emotions in the time it took for him to finish speaking.

"Zach made a friend! With the Duke of Northam's daughter … which may be catastrophic … but he made a friend, and I've never seen him quite so hopeful and happy, and … isn't that lovely? Mostly lovely except the duke part." She rolled back and forth on her toes, information tumbling out in a blur of exclamation points.

"Friends with Northam's bairn? Isnae that something? Northam is a widower, isnae he?" Hamish waggled his eyebrows suggestively.

"Oh don't be absurd, Hamish. He's the bloody Duke of Northam and I am Violet Nobody, daughter of the second son of a baronet and keeper of too many goats." She tossed her braid over her shoulder as if it had wronged her.

"If ye think that's what attracts a man to a woman then I have some educating to do." Hamish winked.

"Yes, but we aren't talking about a man at all, are we? We are talking about what attracts a duke to a duchess." She was smugly satisfied with her logic. "And I doubt he finds fumbling scientific loquaciousness all that attractive."

"Aye, I'll grant ye that the English aristocracy is a different sort o' breed entirely, but unwind that cravat and I imagine ye would find a man underneath." His bravado slowed to a simmer. "I just hate to think o' ye all alone." He sighed and tugged at the collar of his loosely-fitted brown shirt. "I've given ye four years to find some charismatic pig farmer or fisherman to land. Ye've already missed oot on so much. I cannae help feeling like some o' that's me fault." His Scottish brogue was thick with remorse and concern.

Violet rubbed thoughtfully at the slight bump along the bridge of her nose, where it had been broken a lifetime ago. "Nonsense. I had years with my very best friend. I was safe and loved. What else could a girl ask for?"

A devilish smile crossed his face, then fizzled away.

"So much more, Vi. You dinnae even know all ye missed oot on. And I want that so much for you. Nathan would have wanted it too. Ye know I'm right." Hamish reached out and entwined his fingers with hers.

"I'm not alone." She squeezed his massive hand, worrying her finger across a callus. "I have Zachariah. And I'm happy. I am. My marriage may not have been," she paused looking for the right word, "conventional … but Nathan brought joy to my life in so many ways. And I have you." She deployed her most dazzling smile.

"That ye do, and ye willnae be rid of me. All right, lass. I'll let off harping ye for now. Where's that lad off to with the hammer?"

Violet wandered away to find the supplies. She hated that Hamish felt responsible for her somewhat lacklustre marriage. Most people didn't get to walk the exact path they would wish, and she refused to allow whatever sacrifices she had made to poison all the good in her life. So she buried those abandoned desires where they couldn't hurt her. She was a mother to a remarkable boy. She was comfortable, with enough food and a sturdy home. She was safe. No one had everything, and what she had was enough. And if those dreams unearthed themselves late at night, when she was alone with only the stars to see her longing, well, she wouldn't blame herself for that occasional falter of her pragmatism.

Violet pushed all the unwanted thoughts aside and continued her quest for the wayward hammer. Nothing was ever in its designated place, but she had only to look to herself for that source of frustration. When one task was complete, or sometimes even when it wasn't, her hand simply forgot the tool where she stood and carried on with the next activity. Zach was much more orderly by nature.

By the time she returned with the hammer—which she discovered by the nesting boxes— and nails—which she remembered having shoved inside of an old boot—Hamish had rolled up his sleeves, prepared to work. He seldom wore a cravat or jacket, decreeing that they were too English, and he often shed even his shirt in outdoor work.

Her closest neighbours were accustomed to his very frequent visits over the years. And so, even with Nathan gone, they didn't remark upon Hamish's perpetual presence, viewing him almost as a part of the family. It didn't hurt that he was a generous and thoughtful member of the community, always among the first to volunteer when help was needed. Not to mention, lethally charismatic.

Hamish ripped off the rotting wood, holding the new stair in place as he began to hammer, missing the nail entirely and almost bloodying his thumb.

"Oh, you are rot with a hammer, Hamish. All muscle and no finesse. Give me that before you injure yourself," Violet laughed.

She dove for the hammer, but he was quick and stayed just out of reach, flashing a grin.

"Och, come now. Ye wouldn't want to injure me masculine pride?"

Violet shook her head with a low throaty laugh. "Oh no. We can't have that." Ceasing her attempts to rescue Hamish from himself, she sat back to watch him work.

"So have ye met him?" The hammer again narrowly missed his thumb, and she winced.

"Who? His Grace? Yes. Twice."

Hamish halted mid-strike. "And, what is he like? What did ye think o' him?"

Oh, God. We are back to that again. "Which part would you like to hear about first? The part where I splattered him with water, nearly unseating him from his horse, or the bit where he returned Zach, and I rambled incessantly while dressed in sopping wet clothing that clung to my body like the skin on a grape? He was so embarrassed that he practically flung his topcoat at me!" She smiled wryly.

Hamish studied her, raking his eyes down her curves in a clinical way, then scratched his forehead with a hooked finger. "And he didnae even steal a glance before doing the gentlemanly thing and relinquishing his coat? Maybe *I* need to meet him!"

"Oh, do be serious!" She swatted him on the arm and he chuckled, massaging his bicep as if gravely injured.

"I made a complete fool of myself. Not once, but twice. Stop making light of my suffering, you cruel man. Zach and I have been coerced into a picnic with him and Lady Nora on Saturday, at which time I am certain to further beat and bloody his opinion of me. You know I am incapable of polite conversation, Hamish. I'll say the wrong things and do the wrong things. Then he'll never want Zachariah around Lady Nora, and Zach's little heart will be pulverised." She pressed her forehead into the vertical beam and sighed.

"Come here lass and let me hug ye." He wrapped a hand around the nape of her neck and reeled her into his massive frame, ruffling the back of her hair as if he was polishing a set of boots. She relaxed into his blundering affection and let her head fall against him.

"It's going to be all right, Vi. You're a wonderful, colourful lass, and if he isnae already scared off by Zach and his unique disposition, a wee bit of chattiness isnae likely to have him running for the hills."

Chapter 7

Despite Violet's prayers for stormy weather, locusts, or a plague of frogs, Saturday burst through with cerulean blue skies and a soft, non-threatening breeze. She dressed in a deep blue walking dress to match the sky and pulled out a seldom-used straw bonnet. Violet may not be able to resist her natural inclination to make a ninny of herself, but at least she could look like a well-assembled lady.

She checked her reflection in the mirror one last time. Oversized blue eyes and pale skin camouflaged beneath a mass of freckles stared back at her. Already, wisps of fair hair fled from their pins.

The proceeds of her milk and goat cheese only allowed for her cook, Mrs Kelly, who doubled as a magician with her unruly hair, to work three days each week. Not Saturdays. This was as good as it was going to get.

The carriage arrived at five minutes to eleven and Zach was nowhere to be found. Hastily searching the house without success, she headed outside and found him perched on the swaying roof of the goat loft with Plum Pit, one of the new spring babies, clutched in his arms. Careful not to step on her hem, she climbed the stairs and bent down beside him.

"Zach, are you ready to go fishing?" She already knew the answer to her question. He released the goat, who looked a bit put out by the rejection, and shoved his hands under his armpits. Every muscle in his body was seized as tight as an overwound clock.

Why did it seem like so much energy in parenting was dedicated to convincing children to do what was best for them, all the while not wanting to do it yourself?

"I've been looking forward to meeting Lady Nora. I saw the picture you were drawing of her last night, the one where she is holding a frog. Did you catch it for her?" Still no response.

"Maybe we'll find some tadpoles." More silence.

One could negotiate and present a rational argument to combat stubbornness, but fear was a different monster entirely. Terror wouldn't barter. Anxiety was too lost in itself to hear reason. He wouldn't budge until he was ready.

When she leaned down to look at the carriage and team that stood placidly waiting, the opportunistic baby goat promptly ripped the untied bonnet from her head, gleefully dancing about with her prize.

Zach made no attempt to assist with the rescue mission as he held his sides, bursting with amusement.

The sacrifice of her best bonnet was a small price to pay to help ease the cinch of anxiety that held her gentle son hostage. Violet dove in ineffectual, exaggerated swipes towards the frolicking goat, kicking up the dust and hay that carpeted the roof. Falling into a melodramatic heap at his feet, she gazed up with a mischievous smile. "Well, now that I am a complete disaster, shall we go?" Violet gently tugged his arm, and, to her surprise, he followed.

Dusting off her dress, which did little more than relocate hay and dirt from one place to another, she walked with her chin held high towards the imposing carriage. The servants were too well trained to show the slightest acknowledgement of the state of her disarray. Amidst the scuffle, most of the pins had escaped her hair, leaving one long, dishevelled plait. *Too late to do anything about it now.* Nestling in the lush carriage seat, she tried her best to appear unimpressed by the abundance of luxury, but she couldn't resist stroking a finger along the fur lap blanket stowed neatly beside her. Violet had no idea what kind of animal possessed such satin-soft fur, but she wanted one in her bed to snuggle every night. The team set off at a cheerful trot.

**

After the carriage rolled to a stop, the driver lowered the steps, offering his assistance before Violet had time to consider scurrying down on her own. The Duke of Northam and a young girl, presumably Lady Nora, sat perched on a boulder at the confluence of the river.

Lady Nora ran at full speed towards them, fishing pole cast aside and forgotten several strides in. At the last moment, she seemed to remember her manners and skidded to a halt, momentum lurching her forward to her tippy toes. Zach reached her in two massive leaps, steadying her before taking equally large steps backwards the moment she was righted.

Violet watched the path of Zach's gaze as he made a quick head-to-toe analysis of Nora, assessing for any injuries from her near tumble.

For years, Violet had recited every prayer she knew, and wished upon every powerless star in the sky for Zachariah to find—and truly connect with—another person, as she had found in Nathan and Hamish. The all-consuming joy she experienced now in watching the evidence of that friendship, transcended all of the more logical concerns about their vast difference in class.

Zach offered no introductions, but the duke was striding quickly behind, amusement rather than chastisement present on his face.

"Nora, may I present Mrs Evans? Mrs Evans, my somewhat overzealous daughter, Lady Nora Anson." Violet dipped into a curtsey, a lock of hair falling over her left eye. She blew it away, only to have it fall promptly into the same place. With a sheepish grin, she tucked it behind one ear.

"I apologise for our tardiness, Your Grace. A spring goatling declared war on my bonnet and I am afraid Zach and I were pulled into the fray. I hope you have saved some fish for us." She explained without the slightest hint of her wounded pride, and she was rewarded with a warm, conciliatory smile that made her chest feel oddly tight. *Oh, but this man's smiles were dangerous.*

"It could happen to anyone, Mrs Evans." He bowed to her as if she didn't look like she had been dragged behind the carriage the entire way there, then offered his arm in a perfect display of gentlemanly decorum. His wool coat was soft under her fingers as they strolled towards a picnic basket and line of fishing poles in the distance. The children had already wandered off to the river and were looking for stones to skip.

"I should have made my invitation clearer. Mr Evans would have been welcome to come as well, of course. I regret to say our paths have never crossed, but I've heard admirable things about him. He was a great deal of help, I recall, when Edward Altford lost his home in a fire some five years ago. By the time my workers arrived, he had already led a team to recover what they could of the Altford's belongings and found temporary housing for his wife and seven children."

"Nathan passed away four years ago. It's just Zach and me."

He didn't turn, but his steps slowed.

"I beg your pardon, Mrs Evans. I hadn't heard. I'm very sorry for your loss." His voice was low and gravelly. After a deep breath, he continued, "Such insufficient words for the loss of an entire life, but there isn't really a better response, is there?"

"No. And thank you, Your Grace."

Despite his kindness and welcoming demeanour, Violet could not subdue the unease that crackled through her body. She hated that she was intimidated by him. Or maybe intimidated wasn't the right word, more that he seemed so flawless and unapproachable, so resolutely self-contained. She was certain life's most insurmountable challenges would burst into flame and crumble to pieces should he command them to do so. *Intimidated was precisely the right word.* Violet tried to remember him as he had been in the woods, vulnerable and experiencing a moment of very ordinary sadness, but the force of nature walking beside her smothered that memory with a presence large enough to blot out the sun.

They continued along in companionable silence until they reached the river. Violet usually struggled to keep her mind dutifully following any one person or conversation when there were so many other tantalising thoughts to distract and captivate her. Now, disconcertingly, her brain only seemed to care about him. The strong set of his shoulders and his graceful stride. The lush curls that fell across his temple. Even his smell, something unrecognisably delicious. The aggravating man altered the force of gravity, embedding himself at the centre. It was extremely vexing.

While the duke busied himself with the poles, Violet knelt, flipping up a rock and sifting through the mud with one finger. "Ah ha! Got you! Sorry, little worm, but it's onto the hook for you!" She looked up at the duke triumphantly, then hastened to school her enthusiasm to a more suitably measured expression. She hoped that her smile said "sedately pleased," rather than "drunk on ridiculously insignificant worm victory." The little creature flipped and wiggled between her fingers. *Oh, well done, Violet. Why don't you go ahead and jump into the river like a feral animal and catch a fish with your teeth?*

He must have noted her flagging zeal, because he cocked his head slightly to the side, bringing to mind one of her baby goats as they tried to figure out the world. Cornered by her frustrating inability to disguise her thoughts, she opted for honesty. "I wanted to make a better third impression for Zachariah's sake." A tiny sigh escaped her as she stared at the worm, still squirming in her grasp. "But I'm a complete disaster with polite society. I dig for worms. While others look to the weather for acceptable small talk, it only exists as a scientific curiosity for me. I missed two consecutive meals last week, absorbed by conflicting theories about what causes one rainbow to shine more vividly than the next. Only once have I been to London, and it left me feeling rather like a pinecone amongst evergreens. I have this terrible habit of doing and saying things before I've considered—even for an instant—where I am and with whom I'm speaking. If you meet me three times or thirty times you're likely to walk away with the very same impression." As she spoke, she stroked the worm with one finger as one might idly pet a cat.

Northam reached out and plucked a stray bit of hay from her hair. His fingertips tickled her as he unthreaded the stalk from her thick frazzled locks. He stared at the bit of debris in his fingers before dropping it to the ground. "Well, Mrs Evans. The first time I met you, I thought you were delightful. I hazard to guess my opinion would remain the same on the thirtieth meeting. And I only accept new friends who are willing to dig for their own bait." Reaching between them, he plucked the frantic worm from her hands, his little finger grazing her palm. Turning away, he put the worm out of its misery on the end of his hook.

Violet looked down at the hand he had touched, half expecting to see a line of fire kindling at the site of the innocent contact. Nathan, and even Hamish, had held her hand countless times, but never before had her nerves erupted in that wild pinwheel of sparks. Squeezing her fist closed, she assiduously pushed the thought away and looked around his shoulder.

"Would you like some help with that?"

He lifted one arrogant eyebrow. It made her want to reach out and tug on the little bushy hairs.

"You're doing it wrong."

"I am thirty-six years old, madam, and have been baiting hooks since before I knew all seven of my titles." He smirked as if that indisputably settled the matter.

"Then you have been doing it wrong for a painfully long time, but that doesn't make you less wrong." She swiftly took the hook and worm from his hands.

"Careful. You'll slice me open, and punishment for mortally wounding a peer of the realm is even more severe than disparaging tea."

She rolled her eyes in answer.

"You dare to roll your eyes at a duke?" he asked with mock severity.

"Well, I wouldn't have ten minutes ago, but I only have a six-hundred-second tolerance for feigning biddability and you are now roughly seven minutes past that expiration." She threaded the hook with expert finesse.

"Look." She held it up on display. "If you go through the middle and down the whole worm without wrapping it twice through the hook, the fish will run away with your bait. And you didn't leave enough waggling off the back to entice him. Are you sure you've been fishing before?" She grinned.

Downstream, Nora had caught a fish and was squealing and wiggling about while Zach helped her retrieve it, indulgently holding out the fish for her to examine it closer.

Violet looked on with approval. "Clearly my son has taught your daughter properly. And it's a good thing. How would she ever be admitted to Almack's without honing her fishing skills?"

The duke let out a low chuckle, then his face became more serious. "Don't remind me. I'm loathe to teach her everything she is expected to learn. Society insists that I cut away every part of my little girl that is unique and endearing so she'll fit into its mould. I never noticed or cared over much until I had a daughter of my own." Gabriel cast his line. "Holding a little girl in your arms has a way of shifting your every opinion of how the world views ladies. The expectation that I should press her into being someone other than herself is something that I will determinedly combat every day of my life." He tugged a bit on the line, then continued. "It's an unpopular opinion, I know. My mother and I fight daily regarding Nora's upbringing. Or rather, we have *non-fights*; she spends her days silently, but not so subtly, brooding and disparaging every parental choice I make, wondering where she went wrong, and I pretend not to notice her disapproving glare."

Violet nodded solemnly. "Not unlike that worm," she said. "They slice you twice through the middle, then expect you to leave just the right amount waggling behind to entice. We women are but worms on a hook."

"An apt, albeit somewhat disturbing, analogy. It gives a unique perspective to catching a husband … and all that's sacrificed in the process. How did you meet your husband? If you don't mind me asking."

"Not at all. We grew up as close friends and neighbours in Hampshire. He needed a wife and I needed a husband. It just made sense at the time to team up against the world. Nathan's family did not approve of the match, and eventually, we retreated to Devonshire"

He made a noncommittal noise in the back of his throat, casting again.

"I met my wife very young also, although not as children. I was an optimistic young pup, not even out of Cambridge, and she was the woman that captured my soul. My family thought I was ridiculous to settle down so young, but she was the only one I wanted. We had an agonisingly long engagement to satisfy them, and I was married shortly after I completed university. My father had died two years prior, so I already had a tremendous amount of responsibility. It was logical to settle into a respectable life, rather than traipsing around the world in search of adventure like so many young aristocrats. I didn't regret that choice for one single moment of my marriage to Emma."

Violet nodded. "Indeed. What's the point of a grand tour if your biggest adventure is right at home? So many people are either chasing after or running from something. I think the perfect moment must be when you find yourself completely satisfied exactly where your feet are planted."

A fish chose that moment to bite Violet's line. Distracted from her pole by the conversation with Northam, it slid from her grip, necessitating a wild scramble of ungainly limbs as she lunged forward, catching it in the tips of her fingers, knee deep in the icy spring water. The fish reeled in easily despite its substantial size. Violet removed it from the hook and tossed the pole to dry land, darting from the cold stream. Unrestrained laughter bubbled from her chest, mingling with that of a much deeper baritone chuckle.

"Well done, Mrs Evans! That was some fancy footwork!"

She collapsed into the lush grass of the riverbank, fish still flopping within the hand that rested on her stomach. Embarrassment began to creep its familiar path up her spine. *He was laughing. Mocking her. Of course he was.* But years of habitual ridicule had fortified her resistance to the accompanying pain. She had grown accustomed to condescension and poorly-disguised sneers. Sometimes not even poorly-disguised.

It never stopped hurting, but she could bury her sadness in a place where only she would know it was there.

Theirs was a world where individuality, competence, or intelligence in a woman were sins practically worthy of the gallows. Those who could not be compelled to hide their eccentricities and conform would suffer the cruelty of isolation for their stubbornness. Remaining Violet had been an everyday, conscious decision: to submit scientific articles in her own name, knowing they would be rejected; to allow her mind the freedom to invent and expand without apologising for her intellect; to fly as high as her own bravery would permit without giving anyone the power to tear off her wings.

But there was a price to be paid, and its currency was counted with a million tiny cracks in her soul. Because all the practice in the world could not completely inure her to the sting of other people's laughter. Steeling herself for the inevitable scorn, she narrowed her eyes and pushed herself up to her feet, stalking in the direction of that deep rumbling laughter. Too late she realised she was still clutching the fish.

Northam turned at her approach, eyebrows raised and an unmistakably genuine smile on his face. So unexpected was that expression of mirth and joy that she almost rubbed her eyes for a second look, stopping when she, again, was reminded of the fish still flopping in her hands. There was not a trace of mocking in his expression, and if she wasn't mistaken, that was respect twinkling in his soft brown eyes. She wasn't even sure what to *do* with respect, having only ever received it from her family and Hamish. And so, she awkwardly smiled back, then turned her attention to ending the suffering of her captured fish.

Chapter 8

As it turned out, Violet was the only one who managed to catch a fish large enough to keep, although Nora sulked that hers was plenty big enough. Violet's playful bragging came to an abrupt halt after she burned her salmon nearly beyond recognition over their overzealous fire. Thankfully, the duke's kitchen staff had packed far beyond what Violet would have expected for a simple picnic. They eagerly consumed hard cheeses, pork pasties, strawberries, cucumbers with mint butter, salted ham, and gingerbread.

By late afternoon, everyone seemed hypnotised by the marrying of pleasantly-filled stomachs and serenading birds. Zach and Nora returned to skipping rocks under the duke's watchful gaze, while Violet reclined on a blanket, making a chain of daisies.

"Today has been lovely. Not nearly the catastrophe I anticipated," Violet said.

Northam lowered to his haunches beside her, his silent observation monopolising all of her senses and disrupting her focus. A warm, agitated flush began to creep up her throat, causing her fingers to slip. Violet grumbled an expletive and dropped her hands to her lap.

"Why do I suddenly regret having befriended two boys as a child rather than huddling together with the girls? Had I known that some twenty-five years later I would be scrutinised and found lacking in my daisy chain skills, perhaps I would have feigned a greater interest in girlish pursuits." She shot him an exasperated glare, which held for only a moment before melting into a wide smile.

Northam eased down beside her, pointedly turning his gaze away. "Nathan Evans was one of the boys, I presume. Who was your other fishing and tree-climbing cohort?"

"Hamish McKenna. He was born in Scotland but came to live here with his uncle when he was young. He's been like a second father to Zachariah, but alas, he never had much interest in daisy chains."

"My wife used to make these with Nora. I've been pulled into the activity a time or two." One expertly manicured hand reached out, pausing in the air midway between them. "May I?"

Violet nodded and watched as his dexterous fingers made fast work of the final knots, forming a brightly-coloured, floppy crown. For a moment, he just stared at the fragile little chain, his expression pensive. There was a heavy, unfulfilled quality to the silence. Thoughts almost shared, then withdrawn at the last moment. He placed the crown atop her head with a wan smile.

"Shall we see what mischief our children are making?" He rose, reaching out to assist Violet, then wrapped her hand snuggly through the crook of his arm. Like a storybook fairy tale, Violet felt as if she had been magically transformed from goat farmer to princess by a crown made of wildflowers and the charm of a duke who thought she required assistance to walk fifty feet. Or perhaps more precisely, not that she *required* assistance, but that she was *deserving of it.*

At the riverbank, the children's chattering and exploration became more subdued at the appearance of the adults. Nora leapt back to dry land from where she had been balancing one-legged on a rock. Zachariah immediately reverted to the nervous, taciturn behaviour that was ever-present in the company of outsiders.

Sifting through the dirt with the toe of his Hessian, Northam bent to pick up a river stone as flat as a tabletop. "Try holding it this way, Zach." He deftly demonstrated without releasing it, then held out the prize river stone.

Zachariah stared for a moment then reached out to take it. "Thank you, Your Grace." Tentatively gripping it as Northam had shown him, he let the pebble fly. And fly it did! Five whole skips. With a puffed-out chest, Zach whipped around, his face lit with euphoria.

"That's the way! Well done!" the duke encouraged, glancing back towards Violet as if to include her in the joy of the moment. Another quarter of an hour passed as all four rifled through the rocks that littered the bank, throwing in turn with a friendly, competitive spirit.

Zach presented one particularly fine pebble to Northam. "Did your father teach you to skip rocks?" Zachariah timidly inquired.

"No. The son of his valet, who remains my closest friend to this day. He can reliably skip a pebble seven times, and he never lets me forget his superiority in the skill."

Zach nodded and launched another pebble.

Stretching his arm back to take his turn, Northam stopped mid-throw, turning to Violet with an inquiring look. "What is it, Mrs Evans?"

"Your valet is your dearest friend?" She squinted up at him in disbelief.

Northam scoffed, "I didn't take you for a snob, Mrs Evans!" He flipped his rock into the air like a coin, but before it could fall back into his hand, Violet snatched it.

"Stealing from a duke is a hangable offence." Northam lunged to retrieve it, but Violet squeaked and leapt away.

"Only if the article of theft is worth more than five shillings," Violet countered, her finger gliding over the surface of the stolen rock. "And while it is a *fine* pebble, Your Grace, I don't believe its value is equal to five shillings."

"Ah, but the value of some items isn't dependent upon what it *is* so much as how it makes you *feel*. And that river stone has brought me far more than five shillings' worth of joy." He held out his hand palm up, and waited.

Some of the levity melted from Violet's expression. "I believe I may owe you an apology, Your Grace."

"I forgive you for stealing my rock," he replied drolly.

"Not for that." She gave him an exasperated glare. "You are nothing like the cold, imperious aristocrat I assumed you to be. I apologise for my unfounded assumptions and rudeness."

Northam looked perplexed. "I don't recall you saying anything discourteous, Mrs Evans."

"Perhaps not, but I thought them very loudly."

The fine wrinkles in Northam's face shifted and became more prominent with the flash of a broad smile. All those distinctive lines serving as incontrovertible evidence of a man who had lived joyfully.

She slipped the rock into his hand.

"I forgive you for that as well," he murmured.

As the day grew cooler, they packed the picnic baskets into the carriage, none of them in a particular rush to end the carefree day.

"We should have ridden horseback. It's a glorious day for it. The stable master and I have been giving lessons to Nora now that we are back in the country and there is more cause to ride. I dare say she's ready for an outing now. Do you ride, Zachariah?" the duke asked.

Zach was back to looking at his shoes. He shook his head.

"Well, that won't do. I'm certain Nora will want to drag you out on some adventures. I have the perfect gelding for you to learn on, a very-sweet natured bay."

That caught the young man's attention. He looked up imploringly at Violet. There were so few things that ignited open enthusiasm in Zachariah, and the sight of it brought a reciprocating smile to her lips. Then as quickly as the excitement flared, it rebounded. "We mustn't take advantage of His Grace's kindness. I'm sure both he and his stablemaster have more important engagements that require their attention."

"His Grace," the duke began with a sidelong look, "offered freely and with heartfelt hopes of your acceptance."

Violet paused, worrying her lower lip.

"Very well then, Zachariah. You may graciously thank His Grace."

"Thank you, sir … Your Grace."

Arriving back at Violet's home, Gabriel jumped out of the carriage and handed Violet down. Zach stammered a thank you and shot off towards the house with a quick wave. Violet watched him retreat.

"I hope you don't think him rude or ungrateful, Your Grace. He struggles with strangers. Even with me sometimes, but I can tell he is pleased by your daughter's friendship and by—"

"No, Mrs Evans. I think he is a fine boy. I look forward to getting to know him better. I thank you for joining us today, even if you did wound my pride with your superior fishing." He added the last bit with a lopsided grin that gave him a youthful, mischievous appearance.

"I hope you'll stop by for some of Zach's riding lessons." The youthful sparkle flickered away. "My mother never had much to do with my brother, Michael, or me beyond a cursory visit to the nursery each night. Before we even had time to organise our thoughts and share the proud moments of our day, she was out the door with a resounding click, off to something more diverting than her two young offspring. I never would have requested her involvement in my activities, but I would have been thrilled for her to find a single moment to watch me do the things I loved. Zachariah is lucky to have you. I thank you again for the pleasure of your company. Until we meet again, Mrs Evans." He bowed over her hands, giving them a gentle squeeze, and was back in the carriage before she could formulate a response. It seemed he had a habit of hasty departures.

***

Zach began his riding tutelage with Nora the following week. To spare Zach the awkwardness of having to meet and work with a stranger, Gabriel had allotted enough time in his schedule to provide instruction for at least the first few lessons, but had found the activity so enjoyable that he continued in the weeks beyond. Mrs Evans accompanied Zach to every single class, smiling encouragingly and offering hardy praise.

Often, Gabriel found his attention drawn to her, ever amused by her constantly slipping focus. Everything that existed as background noise for him captivated her curiosity. One day she divided her attention between her son's posting trot and a colony of little pill bugs that were making their way around the upturned dirt near a freshly-dug fence post. She even built an obstacle course for them, studying their behaviour to learn if they preferred to go around or over a twig from an alder tree.

Later, she added to their maze. Removing a ribbon from her bonnet, she meticulously straightened and flattened the shiny pink road, presumably to discover if they would find the satin too slippery to navigate. Gabriel found her as fascinating as she found her bugs, each of them waiting to see what the object of their interest would do next. Noticing his arrested gaze from across the paddock, she blushed furiously then covered whatever embarrassment she might be feeling with a dimpled grin before returning to her entomological tests. His feet carried him closer, lead rope swinging in his hands. "For your maze." Lowering to his haunches, he spread the rope out in the dirt, adding a series of loops and winding turns. She admired his offering with unabashed enthusiasm. He felt an echo of that joy warm in the pit of his stomach.

After each lesson they spoke briefly about the children's riding progress or joked about whatever had captured her attention that day. The conversations were usually short and light, as he had a perpetually-growing mountain of estate work awaiting him, but he found himself looking forward to those brief moments in her company

"Zach chatted almost non-stop through dinner about his bareback ride last week," Violet told Gabriel. "I had to remind him that his ham was getting cold. I've scarcely seen such an enthusiastic response to an activity from him, beyond his artwork. And even then his comments wouldn't fill an entire dinner and dessert course. He's comfortable with you. Admires you."

"It's Nora that puts him at ease. They are quite the unlikely pair, but he listens to her ramble on as if it were the most interesting sound in the world, and she waits patiently while he finds his words. I had no idea she even possessed such patience. God knows she doesn't apply it anywhere else." Gabriel shook his head slowly. "They bring out the best in one another, I think."

Their fifth lesson was cut short by a sudden and aggressive downpour. With quick action, they managed to stay relatively dry as they all four dashed inside.

"Can I bring Zachariah to the kitchen for a snack? We are ravenous!" Nora said.

Gabriel nodded and turned to Violet. *When had he started to think of her as Violet?* "Mrs Evans, we can either follow the children's example and eat our weight in shortbread biscuits, or relocate to my study and wait out the flood. Do you by chance play chess?"

Violet tapped her chin with her index finger, pretending to give the choice due consideration. "Tempting as eating myself into a stupor may sound, I believe slaughtering you at chess would be superior entertainment."

"Right this way then, madam."

***

As it turned out, their skills were evenly matched. He captured a number of pawns, a knight, and one rook. She had taken fewer pawns, but had his bishop, and managed to capture his queen. The fire crackled merrily, a warm cup of tea in his hand.

Gabriel groaned. "I can't believe I didn't see that! It's this wet coat distracting me. Blasted itchy wool." He grinned and watched her out of the corner of his eye, baiting her to argue.

"By all means, Your Grace. Remove whatever clothes are causing your strategy to be so painfully flawed. This is becoming embarrassing. For you, I mean. I am perfectly content in my triumph."

Gabriel shook his head, laughing. "If you promise not to be too scandalised, I will make myself at home … in my home."

Violet toyed with the smooth circle of the pawn's head. He could feel her following each movement as he peeled away his coat and unwound his cravat.

Glancing at the still-open door, Gabriel pressed and rubbed his fingers into the tingling, newly exposed skin of his neck with both hands. He was never alone and unchaperoned with a woman. Having observed the repercussions of that mistake in the lives of others, it was the one societal rule he followed to the letter. But this wasn't London, and Mrs Evans wasn't one of the title-hungry debutantes who trapped their prey in the gardens during *ton* balls. She was forthright. Kind. Quite incapable of artifice. And the way she stole glances at his exposed body in brief, hungry flicks, well, his heart was suddenly beating like it belonged in the chest of a much younger man. A man who might ignore his better angels in favour of twenty minutes alone with a beautiful woman.

Returning to the empty chair on his side of the board, he narrowed his eyes with a smirk, rolling first one shirt sleeve, then the other, to the elbow. He was flirting. God, it had been so long since he had done it, he wasn't even sure he was doing it correctly. But it felt right. It felt light and freeing and harmless, like riding a horse just a little too fast as a boy.

"If you're trying to distract me by dangling a set of well-muscled forearms in front of the board, then you will find yourself disappointed in my lack of care at your masculine display." The minute the words escaped from her lips, a hot blush rose up her slender neck and bloomed over her cheeks. She covered her face with both hands. *She did have a lovely blush.*

"Why, Mrs Evans, I am wounded that you think I could stoop so low, or that I would even surmise it possible for you to find such things distracting." He pushed his sleeves up another two inches, showing the curve of a slightly flexed bicep, then grinned as if he had already won the game. "Who taught you to play chess?"

There was a pregnant pause before Violet's answer emerged flatly. "My stepfather."

"Well, he did an admirably good job of it." Violet did not respond, staring instead at the board, apparently too intent to divide her attention.

Despite Violet's assertion that she was wholly unaffected by his state of attire, her foothold on victory began to slip; she missed an obvious trap set for her queen, then lost yet another pawn. The pieces were added to Gabriel's collection of hostages.

"Come, Mrs Evans, is that the best you can do?" Gabriel stretched both arms behind his head, interlocking his fingers at the nape of his neck. *She did say I had well-muscled arms.*

Something shifted in her expression, softened like velvet. Eyes he had only ever seen as keen and curious became sensual and intent. They made a slow, meticulous journey down the lean muscles of one arm and across the breadth of his chest, where his shirt had been pulled taut.

Gabriel felt that caress as if it had been her fingers playing across his naked skin. Her steady gaze continued its path, rising to the column of his throat where he worked to swallow, then landing soundly, unrepentantly, on his eyes. *God above, her eyes were so blue.*

His heart pounded, throwing a few extra beats into the chaos of his chest. Releasing a long, uneven breath, Gabriel returned his gaze to the chessboard. He stared dumbfounded at a rook, unable to remember in which direction it moved, let alone what he had planned to do with the piece. Foolishly, he had failed to anticipate that Violet might respond with such transparent female appreciation, or to consider what her response would do to his body.

The remainder of the game was an incontrovertible slaughter, as Violet made fast work of relieving him of nearly all the pieces on the board in rapid succession.

"Check mate." She steepled her fingers, elbows on the table.

"Well played, Mrs Evans, even if you did supplement your chess skills with fluttering eyelashes."

Violet feigned offence. "There wasn't the smallest hint of a flutter. My eyelashes practically became bored to death in their sedentary *un*-fluttering state! Besides, you very clearly started it, putting twelve miles of muscled arms on display. That is undoubtedly an infraction of unspoken chess etiquette!"

"You question my honour?" Gabriel asked, chuckling.

"I question the desperation of your tactics," she parried.

Violet's smiles were contagious, and she offered them freely and often. A moment passed, or maybe several, before he realised that he had grown quiet, admiring that smile.

"Tomorrow is my birthday." He wasn't sure why he had mentioned it. Perhaps he just wanted a friend to wish him happy. The past two years had seen him so far removed from most of his companions; sharing space and smiles with Violet reminded him of what life had felt like before.

"Happy birthday then, Your Grace. Come for dinner tomorrow. You and Nora. We can celebrate together. I'm an above-average cook when it's not fish over an open fire." She turned to set the pieces back to rights. "That is, unless you already have," Violet added.

"No, I don't have any plans. Except…" He trailed off before continuing. "Except would you mind the presence of an extra man at the table? I always celebrate with Keene. I believe I've mentioned him to you before."

"Yes, of course, the award-winning rock skipper. I look forward to making his acquaintance."

Gabriel gave a quick nod. "I will go find our biscuit-stuffed children and have the carriage brought around." He stood, briefly considered his discarded clothes, then left them on the chair.

"Oh, that's not necessary, Your Grace. We can walk. It's not far and the rain has stopped."

"I insist." He left the room before she had time to argue.

Chapter 9

Gabriel glowered, attempting to disassemble the knowing smile that lit up his friend's face as Gabriel declined yet another waistcoat.

"Stop making more of this than it is. I just don't like the brown or that mucus-coloured green," Gabriel grumbled.

Keene's amusement became more pronounced. "Of course, Your Grace. I suppose the olive doesn't bring out the sparkle in your eyes half so well as this royal blue. That silver stitching is quite cheerful."

Gabriel countered with his most *un*-cheerful expression. "I'm the Duke of Northam, and with that highly exalted, ancient title comes the responsibility to refrain from dressing in apparel that brings to mind the sludgy dregs from an algae pond." Gabriel smoothed his waistcoat and turned sideways, inspecting himself in a large gilt-framed mirror.

"You've been drinking too much pond water if you expect me to believe that," Keene mumbled as he turned to retrieve a cravat.

"What was that?" Gabriel's eyebrows rose.

"I said …" He raised his voice with a wicked grin. "That you've been drinking too much pond—" Gabriel swiped the cravat from Keene's grasp and snapped it into his thigh with a resounding crack.

Rubbing his leg through raucous laughter, Keene dodged a second attack, then looked disparagingly at the wilted cravat. "All of my diligent starching, annihilated."

"Serves you right. I wish I had never told you about that chess game." Gabriel tossed the cravat on a nearby chair, sighed, and turned his attention back to his reflection. "I look old. When did we get so old, Christopher?"

"Speak for yourself. I've never looked so youthful or debonair!" Keene stepped in beside him in the mirror, neatening a crease in his own cravat with a satisfied nod before turning his focus back to Gabriel. "Stop fidgeting," Keene said as he created a sophisticated knot, artful with its crisp symmetry and precision.

He nestled a sapphire stickpin within the flawless folds. "And you," Keene said flashing a grin, "look strikingly handsome! Distinguished! Elegantly refined!"

Gabriel snatched his topcoat from the chair and shrugged it on, ignoring Keene's continued rainfall of boisterous adjectives.

"Magnificent! One might even say splendiferous!"

"You're ridiculous. Let's go."

"Formidable! Alluring! Resplendent!"

"For Christ's sake, will you shut up!"

**

Gabriel, Nora, and Keene arrived at precisely five o'clock. The unmistakable aromas of lemon and rosemary hung heavily in the air, along with something sweet. Apples? Violet met them at the door. "Happy birthday, Your Grace. It's a pleasure to see you again, Lady Nora." She smiled at Keene. "Come in, dinner is almost ready. It's only Zachariah and me tonight since I gave Mrs Kelly the night off." She ushered them in and called out to Zachariah.

The house was cosy. Every detail—the stacks of periodicals on the tables, the soft pillows adorning the settee, the handmade knick-knacks interspersed on the bookshelves—felt inviting. Entire walls were painted in boldly-coloured murals. Some of the landscapes were recognisable places that he had been. Others, though equally beautiful, were unfamiliar.

"You invited us to dine with you then gave the cook the night off? As if I didn't receive enough punishment with that chess game!"

Like the transformation from winter to spring, their tumble toward an easy friendship had occurred so gradually that he could hardly mark the moment of that first blooming crocus.

"Actually, I am quite accustomed to cooking. I only hired Mrs Kelly a few years ago, when my herd became large enough that the proceeds of their milk and cheese could sustain extra help. Come sit down."

"But wait, I have been remiss in my duties," Gabriel said. "Mrs Evans, may I present Mr Christopher Keene, my dear friend and terrible valet. Keene, this is the very talented Mrs Evans. Master angler, moderately passible chess player, inquisitive scientist, mother to Zachariah, whom you know, and apparently"—he gave an audible sniff—"capable cook."

Keene's smiling eyes had bounced back and forth between the pair as Gabriel introduced them. "It is my absolute pleasure to meet you, Mrs Evans." He bowed over her hand.

"The pleasure is entirely mine. Now that that is done, let's eat. Mr Keene, how long have you known His Grace?" Violet asked, leading the way to the table.

"Nearly all our lives. I was six or seven when I came to work in the stables. My father was a valet to the previous duke."

Violet nodded and cut a slice of lemon and rosemary chicken. "What was he like as a child?" Doubtless Violet had already conjured up a young Gabriel in her imagination, down to the last vivid detail. He was curious what that picture would look like. Nothing like the shy, careful boy he had been.

"He was a good-natured lad. Responsible. Fair-minded. Very much unchanged in many ways. He made his brother, Michael, and me look embarrassingly wild by comparison. I think he emerged from the womb already having absorbed a preliminary understanding of land stewardship and the Anson family history through the previous six generations. Some kind of in-utero osmosis, I believe."

Gabriel turned his attention to the children whose heads were leaned together conspiratorially. At the onset of the meal, Zach had held himself rather stiffly, elbows tucked beneath him, systematically consuming his food by category. But Gabriel watched in amazement as Nora coaxed him into a quiet conversation with the ease and confidence of a practised diplomat. He felt his throat go dry with pride and respect, and with the sheer joy of having the opportunity to watch her mature. The best parts of Emma echoed on through the character and talents of their daughter. Violet followed the direction of his eyes and seemed to find her interest equally captured. Such an unlikely friendship had kindled between the children.

Gabriel cleared his throat. "It's wonderful to have the children at the table, although I admit it was not the practice in my youth. Michael and I were always cloistered off in the nursery, as is standard in most of the aristocracy."

"Lady Nora has lovely manners. Does she always eat with you?" Violet asked, casting a smile at the young girl.

Gabriel nodded. "When Emma first suggested the unorthodox idea, I was dubious to say the least. Especially through her toddler years." Gabriel's thumb stroked the handle of his fork with the wistfulness of a parent remembering the sort of trial all parents endure. The struggles that, in the moment, feel as if they are unsurvivable, but in retrospect become amusing. "But eventually, Nora learned to put the food into her mouth rather than sending it hurtling into the air merely to test the state of gravity, and it became a very pleasant part of each day."

Violet smiled sweetly, presumably remembering her own bouts of flying peas.

"Tell us, Mrs Evans, what were your dinners like as a child? Did you have a rowdy pack of blue-eyed siblings with whom to engage in vegetable warfare?" Gabriel asked.

Violet dabbed her mouth with her napkin, then lifted her glass, only to return it to the table without drinking. "My childhood was"—she paused—"inconsistent in nature. My father was the second son of a baronet, but he passed when I was quite young, and then there was little in the way of carefree play. My mother remarried a member of the gentry years later. I have but one brother, younger. "

"That would be the stepfather whose chess instruction resulted in my humbling." It would have been impossible for anyone paying the slightest notice to miss the discomfort those memories had brought about. The obvious effort in her smile roused a sympathetic throb in his chest, and Gabriel had hoped that the introduction of their chess game to the conversation would revive her spirits. It did not.

"Yes."

Had they been alone, Gabriel would have acknowledged her discomfort and apologised for being its cause, but given the audience, he found his options frustratingly limited. Before he could determine how best to redirect the conversation, a pea sailed across the table, landing softly in Violet's hair. Every eye shifted to Nora, who sat frozen, spoon perched in her fingers like a catapult. "To make up for your lack of childhood dinner antics," she said with a cheeky smile.

The tension in Violet's shoulders melted away, her smile rebounding with heart-stopping brilliance. When Gabriel could finally tear his eyes away from those deeply rutted dimples, he turned to Nora and gave her the slightest of nods. Not yet twelve years old and she already carried within her the perceptiveness to recognise the discomfort of others and the mettle to deploy whatever antidote would diffuse that pain.

The previous two years had been a blur, every moment distorted by his melancholy until it was all that he could see. Gabriel had remained so impossibly wedged in grief that he had failed to take notice of the little girl whose growth and maturity had continued despite his emotional absence.

Nora's animated discourse filled the remainder of the meal, with only the occasional word or two from Zachariah, who seemed content to listen to her.

"That was delicious," Keene exclaimed. "I don't believe I could eat another bite."

"That would be a shame since I've made an apple pie. Shall we stretch our legs for a while first? I'm afraid I don't keep port in the house, gentlemen." The children popped out of their chairs and dashed to the door, the adults following behind at a more sedate pace.

"Come see the baby goats!" Nora grabbed Keene's arm with an enthusiastic tug. He gave a helpless shrug to Gabriel and was dragged away in the shadow of the bounding children. Gabriel offered his arm to Violet, and they followed a few steps behind. Heavy, low-hanging clouds had gobbled up the sun, alighting the sky in brilliant pink streaks that blazed in every direction. Despite the warmth that still clung to the day, he tucked Violet's hand deeper into the crook of his arm, the soft swish of her skirts teasing back and forth against his trousered leg with every step. A pleasant breeze shifted directions, and with it, the enticing fragrance of spiced apples, rosemary, and the faint smell of crisp plain soap. An odd mixture of smells that should clash unpleasantly, but coming from Violet, it conjured feelings of cosy domesticity, of sanctuary, and of peace. It slowed his racing mind, all his muscles falling slack at the unexpected sensation.

"You are unusually quiet, Your Grace." Her hand tightened on his arm, steps slowing when he did not reply. "I'm a good listener. The goats tell me their woes regularly, and I don't share those confidences with a soul."

His frown deepened. "I'm Sorry, Mrs Evans. I am suddenly very poor company tonight. You will wish that you'd whiled away your evening with those goats instead."

"Ah, but I have already spent too many evenings with my ruminants, and I find that I am enjoying the two-legged company, even if he is feeling a little blue devilled at the moment."

"It's nothing catastrophic. I am just beginning to realise how very much of my daughter's life I have missed while my attention was firmly fixed on my grief. She has grown. My God but she has grown, and I have been absent in every way that matters." He shook his head, thankful for the shield of curls that tumbled over his eyes. "How often did she need me when I was too mired in my own misery to notice?" Gabriel looked away, both embarrassed at his open display of emotion and helpless to stop it. The warmth of her hand disappeared from his arm, but before he could miss its comforting weight, soft fingertips brushed across the angle of his jaw. There and gone in a moment, but encouragement enough to shift his gaze to hers.

"I do not believe our children expect us to be indestructible or flawless, only to remain ceaseless in our desire to give them the best of ourselves. No matter how many times we fail or how impossible it sometimes feels." She encircled his wrist with both her hands and gave it a little tug. "In those years, stripped of your spirit, your endurance fractured, did you give Nora the very best of what remained?"

Gabriel looked down where those tiny fierce hands connected her body to his, then up into her equally determined eyes. "I did. Still, I wish I could have been stronger for her."

"What foolishness. You were—*are*—strong for her. You can be terrified and brave, broken and still resilient. Indeed, any parent raising a child alone is bound to feel all those things and more. Heaven knows I have." Violet released her grip on his wrist to take his arm, and they resumed their stroll.

"Ah, but the fairer sex is permitted, even encouraged to experience the softer side of their feelings. The same cannot be said of men. When I was around six years old, my favourite mare died while foaling. She was a lovely, gentle pony. I had even taught her tricks in exchange for apples," his lip quirked up at the tender memory. "Naturally, I was devastated, having never lost anyone or anything in my life. My father found me sobbing into a pile of hay in the barn, hair standing on end, covered in dust and without the slightest care for my bedraggled state or my father's ire. I only wanted my pony back and the ache in my chest to cease. He hoisted me up by my shirt front and shook me. 'Men do not show their weakness or cry like infants,' he said. 'And Dukes do not *have* weaknesses to show'."

Gabriel looked up at the stars, searching for the constellations he knew, as he remembered that broken-hearted boy. How his tears would not stop no matter how tightly he closed his eyes or how roughly he scrubbed at his face. Gabriel could never quite forget the look of disgust on the duke's face as he'd dropped him to the floor, or how the tears fell at twice the rate afterwards, despair amplified by shame.

When he looked back down at Violet's face there was an unexpected amalgamation of sympathy and rage on behalf of that long-ago boy. Nose scrunched up adorably, she looked ready to do battle—as if she hoped his father would step out of the shadows this minute so she could give him a ruthless set down. She was fierce. Different from any other woman he had ever met. Her strength was neither cold, like his mother's, nor self-contained, as Emma's had been. She was formidable, feisty in a way that made a man feel like he didn't have to hold the whole world up by himself. As if he could admit to being wary and she would dive into battle beside him.

"What despicable behaviour for a father." Her lips were pressed tightly together, jaw set.

"Yes, well, he is long dead in the ground and your kind words and indignant fury have substantially lightened my mood. Come now, Mrs Evans, it is my birthday. Let us talk of something more pleasant. Despite my brief bout of gloominess, it's been a lovely evening. Certainly better than the one I had in mind, which involved overindulging in my finest scotch while taking all Keene's money at cards, then waking with a devil of a headache only to endure poorly-disguised disapproval from my secretary."

"When you put it that way, it doesn't seem all that difficult to top," Violet said, smirking.

He inclined his head in agreement. "Nevertheless, I am grateful to you and to Zachariah for the thoughtful invitation … and for your friendship." He added the last, running his free hand through his curls.

Pausing at the fence line, Violet slid her hand away, wrapping it about the top rail and leaning into the sturdy wood as she enjoyed the laughter and squeals from the antics across the yard. Gabriel's feet shuffled closer of their own accord to eliminate the sudden, unwanted distance.

"Should we rescue Mr Keene?" Violet asked. Nora had merrily shoved a wiggly, newborn goat into the reluctant arms of the valet.

Gabriel chuckled. "Absolutely not." He withdrew from the scene before him, choosing instead to study the little details of Violet, who remained distracted by Keene and the children: the graceful curve of her neck; the dusty gold freckles, softened by the warm glow of the setting sun; the long, lean muscles honed from an energetic love of life; and those irresistible dimples. If he was a different man, in a different lifetime, he would have dedicated his days to coaxing those dimples out of hiding every hour of the day.

"Come on then, you can't possibly be satisfied with simply watching the baby goats from this distance. They really are the *most* magnificently snuggly creatures in the world," Violet said. *He doubted that.* Snatching up the cuff of his sleeve, she gave a little pull towards the gate.

After being introduced to the goats and covering his trousers and jacket with an incalculable quantity of fluffy hairs, Gabriel returned with the others to the sitting room for pie.

"Can I help you with the washing, Mrs Evans?" Keene dutifully asked.

"No, of course not, Mr Keene. You are my guest." He ignored her and began to clear the plates anyway. Gabriel was across the room looking at one of Zachariah's sketchbooks, but more than half his attention followed the pair, who chatted quietly as they tidied. He couldn't hear much of what was said, but their conversation flowed easily, punctuated by Violet's frequent smiles.

His ears perked up several times to his name murmured by one or the other, but the remainder of their sentences were washed away in the ambient sounds of clattering dishes. They looked good together. Comfortable. Right. He found himself unexpectedly bothered by the rightness of it, then irked that he had allowed the flare of jealousy to assert itself in the first place. He would encourage Keene on the ride home to pursue her. Mrs Evans was really quite well matched in disposition to Keene's spirited optimism and dry humour, and she could find no better father for Zachariah.

Keene went ahead to assist a very sleepy Nora into the carriage, leaving Gabriel alone to thank their hostess again and bid her farewell.

Gabriel turned to Violet, taking both her hands in his. "You have fully redeemed yourself from the fish-scorching debacle. It was the best birthday meal I've had in years. Thank you, Mrs Evans."

"The pleasure was entirely mine, Your Grace."

"When is your birthday?"

"February the tenth."

"Then when your birthday comes back around, I shall return the favour. Or rather, I will have my cook return the favour, as she makes the most amazing braised venison cobbler." He suddenly became aware that her hands were still wrapped in his. Sketching a polite bow, he hastily dropped them. "Goodnight then."

Hoisting himself into the carriage, he sat across from Keene and Nora, who was settled into the crook of his friend's arm, eyelids already drooping. Both men fell into a comfortable silence as they set off.

"Happy birthday, Old Man." Keene tucked the sleeping child onto the seat with a lap blanket and stretched out like a melted confectionery, head thrown back and eyes closed.

"Thank you. It was a very nice evening. I'm glad you came. Mrs Evans seemed to enjoy your company as well."

Keene kept his eyes closed and made a noise of agreement in his throat.

"Her husband passed away some time ago, and I can't imagine why she wasn't immediately snatched up after casting off her widow's weeds. I suppose she just hasn't encountered a man who suits her tastes. Someone equally jovial and witty."

Keene's noncommittal grunt was beginning to grate on his nerves. Could he not see how perfect she was? Perhaps Keene was too exhausted for subtlety. Gabriel pushed a little harder.

"You two seemed to share a moment over the dishes."

Keene started to give another murmur of agreement and then halted, opening one eye. Bolting upright, he turned his fully alert gaze on Gabriel, who gave an innocent shrug.

"Are you trying to play matchmaker, Gabe?" Keene chuckled.

"What is it, exactly, that has you so amused?"

Keene's chortling continued.

Gabriel scowled.

Finally, his laughter simmered sufficiently to speak. "Gabe. Are you really so desperate to quash any flicker of romantic feelings that you will marry me off to Mrs Evans?" A moment passed and Keene's face fell into something distinctly forlorn. "Your heart is still there in your chest, Gabriel. Don't be afraid to let it beat. She *is* lovely. But we were mostly talking about you. And I haven't forgotten the bloody nose you gave me for flirting with Lady Mary Elizabeth Seamsbro when we were twelve, and you didn't even like her that much."

Gabriel ran a restless hand through his hair. "I'm not interested in Mrs Evans in that way. I'm not interested in *feeling* that way."

"Nevertheless"—Keene smiled—"my nose isn't taking any chances."

Chapter 10

On the day of the sixth lesson, Zachariah appeared promptly at two o'clock, alone. Gabriel made excuses to himself for the disappointment he felt in her absence. *Surely Zachariah would miss his mother's encouragement in his lessons.* "Good afternoon, Zach. Come with me, and we will get started. Maybe we will start some small cavalettis today. Would you like that?"

Zachariah was a natural in the saddle. He had a confidence which seemed contrary to his debilitating shyness with people. At the completion of Zach's lesson, Gabriel found he was unable to resist asking after Violet. "I hope your mother is well. You did a remarkable job today, and I know she would have been proud."

"Thank you, Your Grace. She is well. A tree fell in last night's storm and crushed part of our goat fencing. She is repairing it."

What the bloody hell is she doing repairing a fence? "If you don't mind, Zach, I would like to accompany you home and make sure your mother has things well in hand."

"Of course. I hated to leave her alone to deal with the mess, but she's bossy. Like Nora." Gabriel couldn't help but chuckle at the astute and frankly-offered observation. Without thinking, he reached out and patted the young man's shoulder.

Zach tensed slightly but made no move to retreat.

"I will tell you a secret, Zach. All the best young ladies are a little bit bossy. So, what do you think? Are you ready for your first ride out of the paddock?"

Zachariah responded with an enthusiastic nod.

"Say goodbye to Nora, and we will be on our way then. Only us men on this particular mission."

From a distance, Gabriel could see two men with axes working to remove tree limbs. One shirtless and the other … wearing Violet's' brown floppy hat. He squinted, widened his eyes, then squinted again. "Is that your mother in trousers?"

Zach smirked up at him with a distinct twinkle in his eye. "Probably."

Gabriel's gaze cut directly to her bottom. Tan men's riding trousers moulded to every single curve of her shapely legs. She had forgone fastening the top buttons of her gauzy cambric shirt and it clung to her breasts, accentuating the long line of her trim waist. Gabriel had grown accustomed to the tingle of interest that brought his body to life whenever Mrs Evans was near. Their lively banter, skating on the edge of flirtation, had felt more playful than overtly sexual, but the lust vibrating through every nerve, thickening his blood and muddling his thoughts, now felt decidedly dangerous. He squeezed his fists tightly, fingernails digging into the flesh of his palms, but it was a paltry distraction for the eager response of his body.

Since he'd lost Emma, the sort of desire that consumes and overwhelms, that lays waste to logic, refusing to be moderated or contained, had been largely dormant. Its sudden swirl to life felt acrid and unfaithful.

As they drew closer, bringing the details of her form into focus, arousal shifted swiftly into annoyance. Pulled to the side by the weight of the too-heavy axe, perspiration staining her collar, Violet paused to wipe a smudge of dirt from her cheek. This was a massive, unwieldy job and she apparently preferred to struggle on alone rather than seek his help. Gabriel surrendered to the swell of anger, a far safer emotion than the carnal hunger that had been rollicking through his insides only moments ago. When he caught sight of the scrap of rag wrapped around one of her small hands and stained liberally with blood, anger flipped inside out to bright, hot frustration. He dismounted and dropped his reins.

"Why are you repairing a fence?" He knew his tone bordered on belligerent. He knew he was overreacting. Knew it was none of his business if she wanted to build a fence or an entire bloody house, but his words tumbled out heedlessly, like a small child rolling down a hill, gaining momentum and speed with each revolution. There was no stopping until he hit the bottom with a resounding *thunk*.

"Don't you have anyone to do this for you? Neighbours? Hired hands? A bloody duke next door who would happily send an army of workers, not only because he wouldn't sit by while a woman bloodies her hands with an axe, but also because you're a tenant on *his* land?"

Gabriel's pulse battered ruthlessly as he closed his fingers around her slender wrist to unwind the cloth. A noise akin to a growl rumbled in his throat at the sight of her pale, tender skin rubbed raw and oozing blood. He stared, incensed and nearly shaking with impotent frustration, into those clear cornflower eyes. He fought unsuccessfully to tamp down illogical feelings of hurt and rejection. As if his body could tolerate no more, his shoulders drooped. All he could do was stand there, motionless, staring at her palm like a bloody idiot, disoriented in the after-effects of his own percolating feelings. While they had undoubtedly built a friendship, he knew he had categorically stomped across boundaries that were not his to cross.

She glowered at him. Brilliant, scalding blue like the hottest part of a flame.

The half-naked wall of muscle that had been working a few feet away was now looming over him.

"Northam." Violet spoke through gritted teeth. "May I make known to you, Hamish McKenna? Hamish, this is the Duke of Northam."

"I dinnae care if ye are the bloody duke." Tenuously harnessed rancour washed over the massive Scotsman's face. "If ye dinnae take yer hands off me Vi, I'll pull off yer flaccid, wee aristocratic arms and beat ye with them."

Here lies Gabriel Nicholas Milburn Anson, 5th Duke of Northam. Bludgeoned to death by his own appendages after throwing a six-year-old fit of temper. The monolith lowered his chin, his hands tightening into fists. Violet leapt between them, tugging Hamish to the side, out of Gabriel's hearing. Both her hands were wrapped around one massive bicep, leaving a bloody print behind as she dropped her hands back to her side. Gabriel looked down at the blood-soaked strip of material in his hand.

Whatever was said seemed to appease the brute, but he remained palpably agitated. The placating smiles and gentle affection she was freely imparting upon her companion evaporated the moment her eyes cut to his. Chin thrust in the air, jaw set, she sliced through the space that separated them in long aggressive strides. Eager for battle.

"Your Grace," Violet growled, "perhaps you would like to come inside with me for a moment while I wash up and get some refreshments."

It was clearly not a request. Having had a moment to rein in his initial impulses, he followed, docile now in her angry shadow.

***

Violet gave Northam her back, ruthlessly scrubbing debris from her bleeding palm. "You—" Grinding her teeth together, she sought to control her blistering rage, but like an ignited stick of dynamite, the eviscerating blast was already set in motion. Anticipation filtered through the silence while the fuse sparked and smouldered. "You have no right to barge in here, berating and demanding, as if you are entitled to have an opinion about my activities." She slapped the wet rag against her thigh for emphasis.

Every word sliced through the air like a lash. "High-handed aristocratic arse. You may own that broken fence and the land it sits on, but you, sir … *Do. Not. Own. Me.*" To combat the searing flush of her skin, she pressed her water-tipped fingers to her cheeks. It was as ineffective as snowflakes falling on a raging fire.

Northam remained silent, accepting her outrage, seemingly aware that he was deserving of every irate word and more.

"Feminine hands may be smaller, but they are no less capable. *I* am no less capable."

"You're right. I was an arse." His voice was soft, repentant in his unqualified surrender.

She cut him off with a howl of pain. "And now you've made me hurt my hand. I hope you're pleased with yourself, Northam." She glared, holding his gaze for a long moment to convey the full extent of her ire before recognising the unjustified blame in this particular instance. She supposed it wasn't fair to hold him culpable for her physical discomfort, but he was well deserving of the rest. She settled into her anger, refocusing on her task.

"Well, *Evans*. If you would stop scrubbing your open wound like it's a dirty potato, maybe it wouldn't hurt so much." His tentative smile flickered, then receded as he began a slow path to her side in small, cautious steps. "I'm sorry. Forgive me, Mrs Evans. I was wrong— terribly wrong—and I do beg your pardon. I was …" She watched his Adam's apple dip as he swallowed. "I was hurt that you didn't think to ask for help … from me. Frustrated to see you struggling. I was stupid and impulsive, and I reacted poorly."

She continued to wash, her strokes growing gentle as if lulled by his earnest apology.

"And a gentleman does not labour in the place of a woman because he believes her less capable. In truth, I have found the intelligence and aptitude of ladies often exceeds that of their male counterparts in nearly every way. Brute strength is our only innate superiority, and applying it in service of a lady is our way of remaining useful. And to show that we care, Mrs Evans. *I care*. I wouldn't see your hands bleed if it could be my hands instead."

Violet felt her surliness begin to melt at his sincerity. "Parliament would toss you out of your nose if you expressed such forward thinking in their presence."

"Then perhaps you would do me the favour of not telling them, as I rather like my nose as it is."

For long moments, there were only the ambient sounds of water sloshing and the slide of leather over skin as Gabriel removed his gloves and dropped them onto the table. He had eased in close behind her. Closer than he had ever been, just a hair's breadth away, both of them staring at the red-tinged water. The hard length of his chest lightly brushed her shoulder, causing waves of unsettling warmth to unfurl in her stomach. Her annoyance washed away like the grime on her blistered palms, replaced by something heady and disorienting

Warm, un-gloved hands settled on the curve of her shoulders, raising goosebumps and provoking the muscles to tense beneath. His fingers gave an answering squeeze in a silent entreaty, but she could not move, transfixed by her body's compelling reaction to his.

"Let me help you … please." Both his words and his breath across her skin were an assault of sensations. The rough timbre of his voice held no resemblance to the distinguished aristocrat she knew, all raw strength and masculinity.

Violet gave a small nod but remained still until she felt the heat of his body retreat, allowing space for her to turn. With a fortifying breath, she extended her dripping hand.

Northam moved slowly, cradling her hand with both of his, the pad of his index finger stroking soft lines across the undamaged skin as he scrutinised her wound. With a growl of disapproval, he released her, removed the bowl where blood and grit battled for dominance, and poured water into a fresh porcelain basin in its place. He washed away every spot of dirt with devastating care. Violet's breath was trapped in her chest. No way in. No way out.

"Breathe. I won't hurt you. I am an expert at this. Eleven-year-old daughter, remember? And she will have no one but me bandage her cuts and scrapes."

I won't hurt you. Hurt comes in so many disguises. But the low rumble of his voice soothed, and she found her breath again, coming easier with every slow pass of the cotton across her hand. When her wound was cleaned to his satisfaction, he moved to retrieve bandages and salve.

The moment he stepped away, the mesmerising anaesthetic of his warmth popped like a soap bubble, leaving the nerves in every inch of her body as raw and screaming as those on her palm. *Oh, no. This is bad. I cannot be attracted to a duke.* Counting her breaths, she tentatively touched around her wound and recited, "yellow horned, alder, gypsey, abrostola tripatia, skipper, corsican swallowtail."

Northam reached for her again, drying the abrasions with careful dabs of a clean cloth. "Why are you listing... moths?" His voice ended with a marked, high-pitched uncertainty.

She cocked her head to the side, unable to completely hide the jolt of surprise at his unorthodox knowledge. "Is there anything you don't know?" Violet realised that her surprise had slipped into a scowl and she tried to smooth the lines from her face, unsure of why such a thing would even irritate her. Except that she didn't need one more reason to like him at the moment.

"Quite a bit actually." He frowned at her hand, continuing to dry as he spoke. "How to show concern for a friend while reigning in irrational hurt feelings, for one. And there is the mystery of why you're naming moths, for another. I'm certain there's more that I don't know, but that's all I can think of at the moment. My education *was* rather extensive. Save me from my ignorance, Mrs Evans. Why the moths?"

"My hand hurts, and I recite lists as a distraction. Also, you have an impossibly large ego if you will only admit to being ignorant of two things." The half-lie and insult came easily. Northam had finished his work, but her hand remained clasped in his. When she found the courage to glance up, his compassionate, honey-coloured eyes were settled on hers, as if he had been waiting for her to meet him there.

"Nearly done now. The worst is over. Nora used to make me compose silly songs to distract her. Please don't say I need to resort to similar tactics with you," he teased.

Leading her to a chair, he pulled another in front and sat on the edge so their knees were touching. Her eyes searched for somewhere safe to fall, somewhere other than the large body that had crowded into her space.

"Next time you have an activity that may lead to bloodshed, please, I beg of you, ask me for help." He leaned close and began to wind long strips of cotton about her hand, his curls sliding down to obscure his face. "I know you have Hamish, and I'm certain he is competent at manual labour, but I have a plethora of servants. Servants that I am willing and ready to call upon should any of my tenants, or more specifically, my *friends*, have need of them. And you *are* my friend, Mrs Evans. Are you not?"

She acquiesced with the slightest nod.

"As an added bonus, it will drive Keene mad to see me slaving away with an axe alongside the other men, making the task that much more enjoyable for me." He finished wrapping her palm and tucked the end in. "There. All better." He dropped a quick kiss to her bandaged skin.

Violet let her hand fall into her lap. "I'm sorry I yelled. You deserved some of it. At least twenty percent of it, twenty-three percent if I add extra points for the volume of your scolding, so I will round off to an even twenty-five percent for efficiency's sake. Even so, you were only concerned for my well-being. And you *are* my friend. I shouldn't have implied otherwise. I'm simply accustomed to being self-sufficient."

He nodded and rose from his chair. "Is it safe to walk out there with Goliath, or should I sneak out the back door?"

Violet opened and closed her hand experimentally, satisfied with the results. "That's Hamish." She glared. "The front door should suffice."

Chapter 11

Gabriel opened the door and took a brief inventory of the destruction. The mighty oak that had once stretched its fingers high into the clouds, serving as a haven for countless wildlife, now lay in a lightning-severed heap upon the earth. As monstrous as the task would be to set it to rights, he had no shortage of able-bodied men at his disposal. Gabriel felt more distraught at the loss of such magnificence. He imagined the thousands of seasons it had seen, the nests of fragile blue spotted eggs and heaping mounds of snow that had nestled amidst its crooked branches. Now it would serve to warm Mrs Evans's home for the coming winter. He held out his arm. "After you, madam."

"Attempting to use me as a shield and disguising it as gentility?"

"You haven't even any skirts for me to hide behind, Mrs Evans." He winked at her.

Hamish, who had paused in his massacre of the tree to stare menacingly in Gabriel's direction, instantly softened when Violet approached. Gabriel dawdled with his horse, tightening the girth and adjusting the bridle while he observed the pair. Violet handed Hamish a glass of lemonade, which he drained in a few massive gulps. He set the glass at his feet, then reached up with one massive paw, covering her shoulder and squeezing it, his fingers coasting down the length of her arm as he walked away to speak with Zach.

Given their long history, it shouldn't have been a surprise to find Hamish equally familiar with Zach—affectionate even—as he ruffled the lad's hair. Hamish adjusted Zachariah's grip on the axe, and Zach remained perfectly relaxed, even as the Scot guided his swing and praised his first attempts with a hearty pat on his back. There was enormous trust there. Nearly a familial connection. It chafed like a too-tight cravat and he didn't care to speculate why.

When Gabriel approached Violet, leading Omen by his bridle, she was gazing wistfully at her abandoned axe … no doubt deciding if she should take it up now or postpone until Gabriel was out of sight.

"I'll be back with men to help you in … the time it takes a porcupine to peel a potato," he said with a half smile. "If I take the time to find proper workmen, you'll be bleeding in six more places before I return, but I have plenty of staff on hand to put this to rights."

Violet looked up with wide, innocent eyes and took a sip of lemonade. "I will be right here when you get back." Gabriel shook his head, mounting his horse.

Omen danced beneath him and he made a tight circle to settle the beast, glancing up one last time. She had already abandoned her refreshment and retrieved the axe. She was incorrigible. She was infuriating. Then she beamed at him and he felt the effects of that smile warm him from the inside out.

**

Gabriel rummaged through his armoire for suitable apparel, piles of rejected options heaped on his massive bed.

Keene appeared in the doorway, hands on his hips. "Should I even ask what you are doing?"

"Do I own a single article of clothing that doesn't cost more than six months of your salary?"

"No, and you pay me rather well."

Keene took stock of the room and heaved a sigh. "Oh, would you stop? You're making a bloody mess. What exactly is happening? Everyone was in a tizzy outside gathering tools. Something about Mrs Evans?"

"I'm shocked there's something you don't know." He shot Keene a goading smirk.

"Only because I was in a hurry to speak with you. I'll find you something appropriate to wear, but why, may I ask, are we dressing in rags?"

"Not rags, just not something from Weston's. Mrs Evans had a mishap from the storm last night. A rather large oak came down on some of her fencing, and the longer we stand here chatting, the more likely it becomes that she will single-handedly disassemble it at the expense of her gloveless hands."

"And you don't think that the legions of servants you have called away from their duties are up to the task?" He paused and rubbed his chin thoughtfully. "Oh, I see, you are playing the hero to her damsel in distress and don't want her showering all of that abundant praise on some strapping young footman."

Gabriel couldn't deny the sentiment entirely. Mrs Evans hadn't even considered him as a potential avenue for help, and he wanted to prove himself beneficial beyond what his title afforded. He wanted her to look to her friend, Gabriel Anson, rather than look to the Duke of Northam. *Look to him as a man?* And if that meant spending the day sweating like a labourer, that's precisely what he would do.

"Are we talking about the same Mrs Evans? I don't think I've ever met a woman less likely to play the damsel in distress," Gabriel said.

Keene gave him a disbelieving look and left, presumably to borrow a set of work clothes in Gabriel's size.

***

"I suppose you thought that was jolly good fun, tormenting His Grace with all that menacing hostility." Violet poked her finger into Hamish's abdomen with all the subtlety and deference of a bull in rut. With the duke gone, Hamish had returned to his usual joviality.

"And really! Rip out your wee aristocratic arms and beat you with them?" Arms akimbo, she made an abysmal mimic of his Scottish brogue.

His face contorted in an exaggerated grimace as he covered his ears. "Dinnae massacre me native tongue, lass."

She yanked his fingers from his ears, attempting to school her amused smile. "And you are an abominable hypocrite, considering that two minutes before his arrival you were chastising me for helping you clear that tree," she said indignantly.

"Aye, but he brought it on himself, lass. Charging in irate, muscles bulging … pissing on everything in sight like a territorial tomcat. I couldnae help toying with him a wee bit. And with all that deliciously untethered masculine bravado?" His eyebrows danced suggestively. "It was too irresistible, Vi. I'm not that strong a man."

"You are insufferable." She swatted him.

"Maybe so, but ye like him. And dinnae try to deny it. I saw your cheeks. Red as summer berries they were, when ye walked out of the house," he said, his voice teeming with mischief. "And it doesna take that long to scrub up yer hands and grab a tankard of lemonade. Yer lucky we Scots aren't so strangled in pointless propriety." A wicked smile stretched across his chiselled face. "I'd half a mind to knock down the door when ye didnae come back."

"I'm a widow. We aren't tied to the same rules of propriety," Violet said with an indigent sniff.

"Och. A widow are ye?"

Violet threw her thick plait over her shoulder, marshalling the twitch of a smile that threatened, and stomped off to retrieve her axe. She tore into the tree, sending splinters of wood showering around her. Beads of sweat trickled down the curve of her neck as she actively ignored Hamish's booming laugh.

Sunshine that would have felt cosy and cheerful in a more sedentary activity, was merciless as she toiled without shade or respite. No doubt her fair skin would pay the price for her stubbornness. Swatting away the intrusive logic, she carried on.

Nearly two dozen men flooded into the yard, some on horseback, others, including Keene, piled into a wagon heaped high with tools. While Hamish paused to greet a few familiar faces, Zach beat a hasty retreat from the influx of strangers after waving goodbye. Despite being dressed like the others, devoid of any scrap of clothing that would denote his station, Northam stood out. He perched atop his horse in artless perfection. There was a confidence in his posture, and grace and authority in his deportment that could not be stripped away as effortlessly as his change of apparel.

He donned well-loved brown trousers that hugged the long muscles of his thighs, bracers, and a cream-coloured homespun shirt. The top two buttons were unfastened, leaving the "V" of his neck, and what felt like acres of well-defined chest, exposed. Cleaving her eyes away, Violet returned her attention to her axe and the delightful cracking noise it made.

As she paused briefly to adjust the weight of the axe in her hand, the familiar hug of her favourite felt hat fell into place on top of her head. She turned then, and Northam's resigned eyes met hers, a pair of oversized work gloves clasped in his hands. He extended the offering with a sigh. *He'd brought her gloves.* She blinked at them.

"I knew you wouldn't stop, so this is the next best alternative." He reached up and shifted the hat brim. "And fair skin doesn't like the sun." *Why did the man have to be so damnably likeable?*

His persistent consideration and charm constantly undermined her valiant attempts to remain neutral towards him. He was picking away at her defences, slowly capturing one chess piece at a time until only her king remained standing, without a single pawn to protect it.

"Thank you, Your Grace." *At least they still had the formality of titles to hide behind.* She turned away to shield the emotions that she knew would pulse plainly across her face and shoved her battered hands into the gloves. The scrape and pinch of cracked blisters against coarse fabric was a welcome distraction.

They were a merry group of workers, chattering and laughing while they sawed and hauled side by side with Northam. While they were inarguably respectful, they also included him in their boisterous play. They genuinely liked and admired their master. Not at all the kind of relationship Violet would have thought a member of the aristocracy capable of cultivating with servants. She had assumed his friendship with Keene was an anomaly, but apparently, that was not the case. He was kind and respectful to everyone. And it seemed this particular duke was as at home on a farm, wielding an axe, as he was reigning over his imposing estate. All the pieces seemed so incongruent with one another, yet here he was, constantly reshaping her views. The more human Northam became, the more fervently she was forced to remind herself that he was not just a man, he was a duke. A duke, she suspected, who was still very much in love with his wife. The thought made her unreasonably grumpy, so she tried her hardest to ignore the blasted man and focus on her task. A feat which was made impossible by her treasonous ears and their refusal to cease their search for the sound of his voice.

She heard him above the crack of wood giving way beneath sharp blades, and over saws ripping through bark and pulp. Periodically, Keene would make some sarcastic jab about sending Northam home to his study where he belonged, which seemed only to make him laugh and work harder. The pair was fascinating to watch. Whole conversations occurred in a smirk and a glance. It was the kind of friendship that took a lifetime to build, which Violet could recognise because she had the same with Hamish.

Violet paused, gazing up at the cloudless sky and vibrant orange sun that fired her skin and caused a prickling sheen of sweat to form. Hamish had stripped down to his trousers, as had several of the other workers. Northam's shirt remained on his back, but he had compromised with the weather by releasing an extra button. Apparently that was as far as his aristocratic upbringing would allow, but it was still four more buttons than she ever would have expected possible. There was no tan line, indicating that in the privacy of his estate, he had occasionally shirked modesty in favour of the sun on his skin. She fought her urge to invent a reason to approach him and get a closer look. *Doubtful such an opportunity would ever present itself again; what would a little peek hurt?*

A throat cleared behind her. "Mrs Evans?"

Violet whirled around so quickly that the toe of one boot clapped against the heel of the other. Northam's arm shot out, wrapping beneath her arm and around her back, steadying her against his *very* exposed, *very* solid chest. He didn't even drop the lemonade clutched in his opposite hand. *Step back, Violet. You should not be here, Violet!* But the soft curling hair on his chest was tickling her cheek, and she could *feel* his heart where it hammered in his ribcage. My God but it was pounding, and hers eagerly joined in the overzealous rhythm. The backs of her eyes felt hot. *What an odd place to feel hot.* Then the hand that rested against the swell of her hip squeezed, and the heat was no longer relegated to her eyeballs. She sucked in a breath and he released her immediately, assuring that her balance was sound before shuffling back.

"Are you? … I am—" He stopped, sighing. "I've brought you some lemonade. Are you well?" She stared at the exposed "V" of his shirt, assailed by an almost overwhelming urge to snuggle back in like some kind of attention-starved feline. A pool of warmth settled in her belly. She blinked several times, then tore her gaze from that spectacularly intriguing place.

"Yes. Quite. And thank you for the refreshments." She folded her fingers into a knot and waited for him to realise that the glass was still gripped in his own hand. A moment passed, then another, as something alive and energetic passed between them. Finally glancing at the lemonade, his eyelids slammed shut, then opened with one swift shake of his head followed by the unmistakable rise of a blush. Handing her the glass, he quirked a half smile.

Violet drank in long unladylike gulps, the sweetness sliding across her tongue. By the time she finished, he had gathered himself and fastened the lower two buttons of his shirt.

"It shouldn't be long now before the last of the tree is cleared away and the fence should be easy work. I sent a footman to procure a late lunch for us. He should be back any moment. We'll break for an hour or so before we finish up." They were rescued from further awkwardness by the arrival of said lunch.

Violet chose a space far from the Duke of Northam for luncheon, having experienced quite enough bewildering emotions for the day. Tucked close to Hamish, she fell into a state of instant contentment. The meal would have been a lovely reprieve if it weren't for Hamish's obvious ploy to inspire some kind of jealousy in Northam. Hamish gave her his undivided attention despite the presence of several friends amongst the group, even going so far as to offer her a strawberry from his fingers. She glared and snapped the ripe berry with her teeth, wishing for all the world that she would miss and nip his fingers instead. For his part, Northam thankfully didn't spare her so much as a glance through the entire meal.

Chapter 12

With the manual labour complete, most of the men returned to the wagon and departed. Gabriel leaned against the newly-secured fence and wiped his brow, assessing the impressive pile of wood neatly packed beneath a newly-expanded shed. Exhausted but invigorated, he let his head fall back, the cool afternoon breeze wafting across his sweat-dampened skin.

Mrs Evans stood beside Hamish, watching the twenty or so goats frolic across the garden. A pair of tan and white does snuffled around where the wagon had been. Another, a stark white spring buck, nibbled a man's discarded jacket. Several others had wandered towards the orchard and were attempting to pluck and pillage from low-hanging branches.

A few of the remaining men were attempting to coerce the goats back through the open gate. Approaching from behind, a burly footman shoved at the rear end of one rotund, sable-coloured doe. Her bottom was raised several inches into the air with every aggressive push, but her front legs remained stock straight and rooted in place. A clump of lush clover hung forlornly from her mouth as she looked over her shoulder, seemingly surprised to see all the activity behind her.

Gabriel scanned the yard for his first target.

"Northam, do ye have any actual experience herding goats?" Hamish's Scottish brogue was thick with amusement.

Gabriel volleyed a surly gaze back. "My valet is an arse and my mother is a stubborn old goat, but that's where my barnyard experience begins and ends. I always thought I would have made a splendid farmer!" He grinned as he stretched his arms, muscles flexing tightly against the supple cotton shirt. Like a child who couldn't wait to challenge himself by shimmying up the highest part of the tallest tree, he vibrated with boyish enthusiasm.

Two goatlings wandered close to the gate, the picture of innocence as they stopped to gaze adoringly up at him. Gabriel remembered them from his birthday dinner, Plum Pit and Apple Core.

"Look at those two little sweethearts. They're practically begging to be tucked up snuggly in their habitat."

Violet bit her bottom lip, apparently struggling to contain her amusement. She failed, as a quick bubble of laughter broke free, followed by a cough.

"Oh, by all means, Your Grace," Hamish said with an exaggerated wave of his tree trunk arms, "return the docile little goatlings to their enclosure." He snorted his amusement, obnoxious brute.

Gabriel walked in slow rolling steps, speaking in a cajoling voice to the adorable babies, arms outstretched as if to offer a tasty morsel. The goats stood stock-still but for their briskly wagging, feathered tails. The moment he stepped within reaching distance, they burst to life in a rousing game of chase, bucking and throwing their little bodies in unpredictable directions as they circled him gleefully. A madcap game of duck, duck, goose ensued, wherein *he* was absolutely the goose. Darting and weaving with unfettered exhilaration, Apple Core zipped between Gabriel's legs at the exact moment he lunged to grab Plum Pit. Tripping over the unexpected hazard, he flopped face first into the grass.

Hamish remained at the fence, holding his stomach through bellowing laughter.

"Oh, my! Are you well?" Violet called out, inching forward..

Gabriel rolled onto his back, laughing and waving off her concern. Fascinated by his suddenly prone body, the babies inched closer to investigate. With one smooth motion, he grabbed a goat in each hand and jumped to his feet triumphantly, a baby tucked under each arm.

"Well, that wasn't so hard," Gabriel said through heavy breaths, dropping the kids unceremoniously over the fence into their paddock. By then, his men had finally hauled the gargantuan tan goat into the fence and were panting with the exertion, scanning the area for their next victim. Gabriel studied the scattered herd. Clearly he had underestimated this pack of ruminants. There was, in fact, nothing angelic about them; they were ingenious, conniving, devious adversaries in cherubic disguise. He would have to adapt his strategy accordingly.

Flexing his fingers, he sighted a medium-sized juvenile and ran directly into her path, arms outstretched to grab a horn. Rather than fleeing as he'd anticipated, she collapsed dead at his feet. Terror gripped his chest. Frantically, he looked back and forth between Violet and the flopped-over beast.

"She's only fainted, Northam." Hamish was leaning against the fence, arms crossed, and casting a sideways glance at an equally entertained Violet.

His words registered in Gabriel's mind just as the goat found her feet. *Only fainted?* He grabbed her by one horn. The gangly adolescent must have sensed the influx of his annoyance as his terror waned. She loped meekly beside him to the gate and freely walked inside. Apple Core, alight with the possibility of freedom, dashed to the opening, but Gabriel was ready and expecting the frontal assault.

"Oh no you don't, you rascal. You have caused enough trouble already," he said with a good-natured pat on her head before he shoved her back in.

A gangly black goat stood with her back to Gabriel near a large pile of straw. Nonchalantly, he crept closer. Sensing his approach, she hopped nimbly up the mountain of straw, glanced back, and gave a mocking goat bleat. *Think I won't follow you, eh?* Gabriel scrambled up behind her, but in his reckless haste, grace and agility abandoned him and all traction was lost. In a riot of flailing limbs, he somersaulted back down in a heap. A loud rip accompanied his descent.

Both Violet and Hamish were standing at his side by the time he recovered and pulled himself up. Concern and amusement warred on Violet's face, as she grasped him by the wrists and combed him for injuries. Hamish, meanwhile, peaked around at his backside, where a large rip at the seams split his trousers. "At least yer not Scottish, aye? Or you'd be giving us a fine show!"

A quick investigation of the tear confirmed that his small clothes had indeed remained intact.

"Good effort, Northam. I'm impressed," Hamish said with a hardy slap to the back that vibrated Gabriel's ribcage. "Care to show the aristocrat how a farmer collects the escapees, Vi?"

Violet walked to a wooden barrel and scooped up a bucket of feed, shaking it as she made her way to the gate. "Come on, ladies. Let's have a little snack, shall we?" Goats of all sizes and colours abandoned their individual interests and eagerly converged, trotting through the gate like a prim line of goslings. She scattered the contents of the bucket on the ground, and fastened the gate.

Gabriel's tongue could not form a single word.

Shrugging her shoulders sweetly, she watched him through her lowered lashes. "You were having such fun, I didn't want to ruin it for you." Helpless to contain his surprise and delight at this situation and all its ridiculousness, Gabriel laughed until he was nearly breathless. He hadn't felt so light since boyhood, and even then his parents had been remarkably efficient at squelching any glimmer of amusement.

"It *was* fun".

***

The sun hung low on the horizon, painting the sky in wisps of hazy peach. Frogs and crickets trilled off-key songs to their mates, and the shuffling sounds of daytime animals in search of their dens gave way to their nocturnal counterparts, rising to melt into the dusky haze of evening.

A slight breeze feathered across Gabriel's skin, raising the tiny hairs across his arms, eager to feel the cool spring air wash over them. The trio leaned contentedly against the fence in a line, watching the goats as one peaceful moment gave way to the next.

Yawning, Hamish scratched his fingertips through his hair. "Well, I best head home before I lose all me light. The trek gets longer in the pitch black." He dropped a kiss to the top of Violet's head and ruffled her hair affectionately. "Northam, I suppose you will be headed on your way shortly as well." He lowered his chin infinitesimally. Any man who had come of age at Eton, where posturing and schoolyard skirmishes were a second language, would recognize that scantily-camouflaged threat. Hamish's casual inquiry contained a clear command: *leave.*

Gabriel pretended not to notice. "Yes. I'll make my way home before Nora retires for the evening." He yawned, then stretched like a cat who knew he wasn't supposed to be on the table, but would leave when he was good and damned ready.

With one last warning look, Hamish turned and disappeared silently into the night.

"You have quite the protector in that one," Gabriel said, motioning with his chin in the direction in which the Scot had departed.

Violet's expression was pensive. "He is dear. I don't know that I would have made it through the loss of Nathan without him. Without someone who loved Nathan and understood the gaping hole he left behind."

Gabriel nodded. "There is a closeness that comes from sharing grief, but no friendship is such that it allows them to truly understand how the loss of a spouse fundamentally changes you. You go to sleep a husband, a lover, a confidant, but when you wake up, you are no longer any of those things. You have no idea who you are or how to be that new person, nor do you want to learn.

You only want to go back to sleep and wake up to a different tomorrow, one where you don't have to navigate this world without her. Nevertheless, Keene's understanding, and his stubborn determination to press life upon me, was invaluable. It still is. I imagine much the same can be said of Hamish."

Violet studied the sky in the opposite direction, her reaction shielded from his view. Gabriel had become so accustomed to her restless fidgeting and chatter that the sudden stillness felt broken and unnatural, like a motionless hummingbird or the way the animals grow silent before a storm.

"He obviously loves you." Gabriel wasn't certain why he'd said it. There was no answer that would satisfy him. If she denied the sentiment or claimed it to be platonic in nature, he wasn't all that certain he would believe her. But if she *did* agree that she loved Hamish, that he was paramount and irreplaceable in her world, well, Gabriel was equally certain that he wouldn't care for that either. He decided it was better not to give her the opportunity to confirm or deny the statement. Better not to know. It wasn't any business of his, and it served no purpose to speculate when he had no intention of pursuing a greater connection beyond the friendship they enjoyed now.

He cleared his throat and looked away, speaking to the emerging stars instead of to her. "It's good that you have Hamish. It's hard to be alone. Harder than I ever thought it would be … although not as hard as thinking about being married to anyone but my wife. Like being desperately thirsty for the one drink you can never have again." He shook his head ruefully as if to break up the large, heavy thoughts into smaller, more manageable crumbs.

"Tell me about Emma." Violet's voice was tentative and soft. Others had tried to ease him into speaking about Emma since her death. Casual acquaintances who had experienced similar losses had probed with gentle questions that only resulted in a visceral recoiling. Even Keene, with his unique blend of humour and understanding, had often elicited a bone-deep reflex to scramble away. Somehow, similar questions from Violet affected him in an unexpected way.

Something in her unlocked something in him. As if she had a magic key that made it possible for all the seized mechanisms and frozen springs inside him to begin to wiggle loose and ease their careful tension. Air that felt as if it had been trapped inside him for years, stale and pungent from confinement, rushed free of his lungs, leaving space for massive gulps of honeysuckle-tinged sweetness to fill and soothe.

Gabriel looked at his boots, then to her.

She waited, giving him time and space to unravel the tangled thoughts.

"Emma was ... kind. Gentle. She was my constant as I grew into a man. Determined, but in a quiet, understated way, although no less unstoppable for her subtlety." Gabriel swallowed through the lump that had grown inconveniently large in his throat. "When Nora was just shy of two years old, Em miscarried a baby. We were both devastated, but she endured, remaining hopeful even as year after year passed and I despaired of ever having another child. She never allowed our loss, or the disappointment, to poison the joy or our marriage. Then she *did* become pregnant again. And the world had never beheld a smile so radiant as the one she wore the day she told me that, at long last, Nora was to have a sister or brother." He let out a tremulous sigh. "And then I lost them both—Emma and my son—to childbirth."

He roughed his knuckles across the fence as he spoke, back and forth like salt water lapping across the rocks in an ancient rhythm. "We were partners, entwined in such a way that it was impossible for her to be sliced from my life without losing chunks of myself in the process ... maybe the best parts." He sighed and turned his attention back to the goats, who were beginning to slow in preparation for sleep. "One day I will have to marry again, I suppose. Sire an heir and a spare. Part of me wants to choose a cold bloodless union like the aristocracy is so fond of, but calling that *marriage*, the same title that joined me with Em, feels like poison to a beautiful word."

Today, laughing and flirting, being caught in Violet's orbit, it was like taking a full breath of air again after seventeen agonising months of shallow pants that had left his lungs weak and groaning with the need to expand. Now, slipping back into those small, strangling breaths again felt unbearable. The cruel reality was that he couldn't release the cord that had tethered his heart to Emma's even now, when the opposing end was left slack and vacant. Even when he was beneath the stars with a lovely, engaging, brilliant woman. A woman who listened, fired his blood, and flooded his very being with life.

He was tired of the gouges left by his wife's departure adding up to be more than the sum of what remained of him. Those long blissful hours of feeling whole again teased like a whisper across his skin, arousing and tantalising, only to fizzle away.

Violet's hands rested on the top fence post beside his as she sightlessly watched the goats. No part of her body turned towards his. They were like two parallel lines with a continent between them in those three empty inches of space.

Her pinkie finger traced the texture of the rough-cut wood, the callus on that delicate finger scratching in hypnotising swirls. How he longed to reach across the space between them and wrap his fingers around hers. To pull her into his arms and bury his face in that mass of tangled hair. To fall in step with her lively rhythm and allow his muscles to remember the tantalising ache of becoming lost in soft, welcoming curves.

But the way his body anticipated the feel of her … it felt like a sin against his own heart. He watched as her hand hesitantly crossed the gap, linking one outstretched pinkie around his. There was nothing lascivious in her touch, only the silent poetry of one soul trying to console another. Nevertheless, all his nerves hummed to life, centralising on that one minuscule point of contact. The way she curled around him, skin hugging skin. His traitorous heart pounded in his ears, wailing for more.

They stood side by side under the cloud-filtered glow of the crescent moon, only their pinkies entwined. He couldn't look at her, too discomposed by the savage war that raged between his heart and his body. "I apologise for my melancholy. It's been such a lovely day. I can scarcely recall the last time work meant something besides reviewing stacks of paperwork with my secretary."

"No. Don't apologise. And it was a good day. It's *still* a good day. Thank you for coming to my rescue." She released his emphatically acquiescent hostage pinkie, and his hand felt instantly colder. It opened and closed reflexively at his side.

"Zachariah rode Clover here. She should be all right in your field for now, if that's acceptable to you. Perhaps next week you could bring her around and we can all go on a ride. I don't think Zach will be happy staying in the paddock anymore. Or if you prefer, I can send a stable hand over in the morn—"

"No. That sounds wonderful. I haven't ridden in years."

"Excellent. I will look forward to it. Can I walk you to your door?" He suddenly felt horribly awkward, his forced cheer like something thick and viscous being piped through a too-small hole. She took his arm, and they walked side by side in silence. It had grown cool, the sun having snatched away all the warmth with her hasty retreat.

Violet shivered, leaning into his warmth.

"I'm sorry I kept you out so late in the cold. If Hamish were here he'd no doubt throw me to the mercy of your vindictive goats," he teased.

"No, I'm only a little chilled. Good night, Your Grace."

He captured her gaze and held it. "Violet. No more of that, please. It's Gabriel. My name is Gabriel. You've seen me with a four-inch rip in the backside of my trousers. Surely that qualifies for a change to Christian names?" Her eyes drifted away but her dimples peeked out beside a slight smile.

"And good night to you … Violet." His next breath quivered from his lungs. Long and shaky and drunk on the sensation of her name on his lips.

Omen was asleep, and no doubt annoyed, when his dreams were wrestled away to carry his master home. He snorted and pawed at the ground while his girth was adjusted. "Sorry, old boy. You will be tucked up in your stall with extra grain soon enough." Gabriel allowed his gelding to move along at a plodding pace without quarrel. He didn't think the backside of his trousers would survive a more aggressive ride anyway.

By the time he arrived home and saw Omen settled, Nora was deep in dreams. A treasured squirrel skull was loosely tucked in one hand. The other arm snuggled about her favourite cloth doll, Lucy, whose hair had been plaited and attire altered since last he saw her. Her fancy lilac dress had been slit up the middle and sewn inexpertly together to form a pair of floppy trousers. He fingered the small row of stitches.

The familiar hairstyle and altered attire squelched the mystery of Zach's disappearance after Gabriel's men had arrived. Zach, no doubt, had doubled back to collect his willing accomplice, then spied on today's activities from a safe distance. How many of her own frocks would be sliced and adapted in imitation of Violet and her unconventional charm? He shook his head, chuckling. That was one way to encourage her needlework.

He gently extricated the bone from her clutches, placing it carefully on the table beside her. Pulling up the covers, he kissed Nora's forehead, stroking back the mass of dark curls with his fingers, and then left her to her dreams.

Chapter 13

Torn between a hot soaking bath and a glass of scotch, Gabriel loitered in the hallway while he considered. The scotch won out. Warm lamplight shone from the direction of his library. Keene looked up from where he lounged in Gabriel's favourite leather club chair, his stockinged feet propped up and toasting by the fire on the matching twin. With a glass of Gabriel's best scotch in his hand and a discarded book in his lap, Keene was the very picture of comfort. It had become a tradition of theirs to end most evenings this way, as friends and equals.

"Good evening, Your Grace," Keene said, without making a move to rise.

"Good Evening, Keene. Isn't it a little late in the day to 'Your Grace' me? I thought the fairy tale had you transforming back into a frog with the setting sun."

Gabriel turned to the sideboard to pour two fingers in his glass.

"Christ! What in the hell happened to your backside?" Keene exclaimed, leaping from his chair and reaching a hand towards the cleaved fabric. He scarcely avoided Gabriel's indignant swipe.

"Get off my trousers, you mother hen," Gabriel groused.

"What *exactly* occurred after I left the lovely Mrs Evans' home?"

"It involved a vicious goat and a pile of hay." Gabriel waved off any attempt at further inquisition and leaned against the sideboard, taking a fortifying swallow of his scotch.

"Oh no, Gabe. You aren't going to evade me that easily!" Keene sank back into the overstuffed chair, oozing into his previous indolent position with all the entitlement of a duke … or a cat, which shared similar qualities, in truth.

Shoving Keene's long, skinny feet from the brocade chair, Gabriel collapsed across from him with a groan. "I'm going to feel every moment of today in the morning." *And relive every moment with Violet.* The way her whole body shook with the force of her laughter … he could hear it, see it when he closed his eyes, remember the way the tiny hairs on his neck stood at attention every time the sound of that musical laugh carried across the breeze. Even in her anger, she had been compelling in a way he could not excise from his thoughts.

"If only your wise and trusted valet had vehemently advised you to leave the work to the actual workmen. But I suppose it would have taken a cricket bat and a sturdy length of rope to keep you from your delectable and distressed lady friend."

Gabriel choked mid-swallow and the liquid ripped a fiery trail down his throat.

"Don't even try to argue concern for a tenant. You would have stayed safely ensconced in your study folding paper flowers out of sheep-shearing reports had it been the pock-faced Mr Jones with a broken fence." Keene stretched his lithe body and crossed his legs at the ankles, face awash in smugness.

"*Are there* reports on sheep shearing?"

"You're a terrible duke, and you're being obtuse."

"She's the mother of Nora's best friend. Her only friend, really. And of course I like her; she's impossible not to like."

Keene lowered his glass to his knee. "No, you *like* those disgustingly macabre pies with the fish heads poking up ogling everyone. You *like* the crusty, hard ends of Mrs Simmons' bloomer bread, which the rest of the intelligent population consider collateral damage for the fluffy inside bits. You *like* the sensation of your foot falling asleep, which, if you weren't the bloody duke, would situate you somewhere on the lunacy scale between your brother's collie that chases his tail all day and that woman in Hyde

Park that likes to pose as an apple tree. What you have for the fascinating Mrs Evans are substantial, legitimate feelings that go well beyond *like*. And don't waste your energy trying to convince me otherwise. I know you, Gabriel Anson."

The tone and temperature of the conversation had suddenly vaulted towards unwelcome solemnity, and Gabriel felt heat radiate up the back of his neck in response. He placed a cooling hand to the back of his neck and massaged, grimacing when he found his palm equally warm. With practised dexterity, he manoeuvred the conversation back towards less shark-infested waters.

"Stargazy pie."

"What?

"It's called Stargazy pie, and if you would open your inflexible little mind enough to try it … the way the potatoes and buttery flakes wrap around the savoury kick from those adorable little pilchards … mmm …" His voice trailed off.

"Jest all you like, but while you let your grief foist you into the role of unattainable, lovelorn puppy, a smarter man than you is going to snatch her up and run. And that stomach-churning Stargazy pie won't warm your bed at night or supply you with heirs."

"Why this malicious contempt towards classically English cuisine?"

Keene sighed his defeat, staring openly into Gabriel's eyes with a knowing look.

God save us from well-intended good friends. The staring continued.

Gabriel tipped up his glass to drink and was surprised to find it empty. Heaving himself from the chair, he moved to refill it, then chased his finger mechanically around its thick crystal lip. "We are to go for a ride this Saturday. Not that it matters because I *am* an unattainable, lovelorn puppy. It's not some fictional self-assessment. It's my reality, however inconvenient. And she's already *been* whisked away. Hamish McKenna couldn't have been clearer in his intent had he thrown her over his shoulder and snarled at me, which he very nearly did. Or did you somehow miss all that posturing today? What would I do in a fight with that brute, threaten him with a papercut?" He threw his head back and stared at the ceiling.

This conversation was everything he didn't want. Every admission he was loath to feel, let alone express. Released from their cage, all those feelings raked across his insides, laying waste to his defences, burning and devouring every pathetic denial in their wake.

Keene's surliness melted into supportive encouragement as he leaned forward and gave Gabriel a slightly overzealous pat on the knee.

"This is why I wasn't going to tell you. You'll skulk around, spying on my every encounter with Mrs Evans, like some hopeful, hungry stray cat."

"Bad analogy, Gabe. You order all the stray cats to be fed. And I seldom skulk"

"I did it to please Nora," Gabriel said.

"Nora was six months old at the time; she didn't know a cat from a rabbit-fur muff. And I'm not suggesting you physically brawl over Mrs Evans' attentions … although I have been at the receiving end of your left hook more than once, and it's far from ineffectual. I merely suggest that you *try* to accept that your love for Emma doesn't disqualify you from caring for another. I've seen the way you look at her, Gabe," he sighed. "What you had with Emma was amazing, but what you feel for Mrs Evans isn't nothing."

Gabriel shook his head ruefully. "She's unlike anyone I've ever met." He attempted to school his face into something less obviously enamoured. "And she's a friend."

"Yes. A friend who makes you want to strip off all your clothes and rub against her like a cat grinding its scent glands into every inch of her sweet skin."

Gabriel could not contain his boisterous laugh, like an over-primed water pump. The relief, however brief, was acute.

"Court her. Marry her. Let your feelings fall where they will when the time is right. You're a duke. Disgustingly rich. A remarkable father. You're even a halfway decent cricket player, and you have that odd thing where your hair still looks attractive when it's rumpled in the morning. Surely that adds up to more than some empty-headed Scottish lout, even if he can rip a sapling from the ground barehanded and hurl it one hundred paces. Besides, it wasn't Hamish she was mooning after all day. What exactly is it that you imagine he can offer that you cannot?"

"Love," escaped his sullen reply. "Undivided, wholehearted, single-minded love. More than the crusty end of the loaf that's left over after everything else is gone."

"Oh, you *are* a hopeless mess, Gabriel." Keene drained his glass in a swallow.

"And if she loves Hamish, I won't stop to distract her away, dangling a gold sovereign in front of her face as if she's a crow." Gabriel ran his hands through his hair, squeezing the curly ends with his fingers. "I like her too much to deny her the chance at finding love again. And she won't find it with me, so why not Hamish if he makes her happy? I won't dazzle her with a dukedom like some cardsharp's sleight of hand." Gabriel met his friend's gaze with beseeching eyes, silently imploring him to stop prodding all the tender places that still actively bled.

"Then just dazzle her with Gabriel. Stray cat feeding, revolting palleted, good man that I love like a brother and frequently want to throttle Gabriel. And for the record, if Emma could see you now, wallowing in your cups, she would kick you in your comically goat-shredded trousers."

"True enough." For a moment, it seemed as if Keene would view this concession as a win and leave well enough alone, but then his contemplative frown reshaped into a mischievous grin, all animated brows and twinkling grey eyes. He leapt off his chair and began to pace.

"Pen Mrs Evans a note to tell her you are looking forward to Saturday. Confirm your plans and settle a time to retrieve her." He paused dramatically, unleashing his fully dimpled smile, then continued his trek back and forth across the thickly carpeted floor.

"Something like this: 'Dearest Mrs Evans, I apologise profusely for all my churlishness and brooding. I am a ridiculous excuse for a duke, as I have more feelings and pent-up sentimentality than my eleven-year-old daughter. Please save me from my own disastrously exsanguinating heart, and know I am counting the minutes until I can whisk you away on horseback. Most sincerely wishing to be yours, Gabriel Anson, obscenely wealthy (amongst a barrage of other equally endearing qualities), Duke of Northam. Postscript, I hope your Scotsman gets dysentery'."

He threw out his arms enthusiastically as if to take a bow.

Gabriel levelled Keene with his haughtiest ducal stare. "Brilliant. I will write it up this very moment. No woman could possibly resist that nauseating bout of honesty. I can't imagine how you've remained unmarried all these years. Now, go earn your salary and refill my glass."

"Sorry, old chap. The sun has long since set, transforming your acquiescent servant into a surly amphibian … and frogs don't have opposable thumbs. You'll have to fetch your own scotch."

**

When Saturday arrived, Violet attempted to remain presentable for their picnic, uncertain of what time to expect the duke. As early morning stretched dangerously close to afternoon, however, she grew increasingly grumpy and frustrated. She detested remaining sedentary.

She stood, staring about her front garden, paralysed by all her warring, paradoxical feelings. She was torn between the desire to delve into all the projects looming before her and an equal desire not to look like an unwashed ragamuffin whenever "His Grace, The

Unscheduled" decided to appear in all his flawlessly assembled glory.

A few gangly wild onion sprouts had pushed up amidst the tidy lines of fledgling pepper plants, taunting her as they waved in the breeze. Her weathervane tilted askew and flopped about on the tiled roof, another casualty of the storm that had uprooted the oak. Dozens of half-finished projects competed for her attention, and she abhorred the thought of wasting another moment.

She tore off her gloves and scooped up a discarded hammer from the ground below. Cold, sticky mud that had caked the surface of the handle transferred to her hands. Casting the offending item away, she growled at her own impatience and stalked away to find a moderately clean cloth for her hands. The grime smeared deeper into the lines of her palms, clinging to her skin as if it was thrilled to be a part of her. *Oh well, that's that then. Might as well accept the inevitable. It's not as if he will turn around and go home if my hands are a little dirty. Will he?* An image of the impeccably turned out Duke of Northam, grimacing dramatically and whirling his horse in the opposite direction, materialised in her mind. *No. Definitely not.* She shook her head, her course decided.

Violet's boots dislodged satisfying puffs of loose dirt as she stamped in the direction of her wooden outdoor table that housed a collection of salvaged gears and springs from an old clock. Rummaging through the rubbish, she found a series of toothy gears and began fitting them together. She settled into her task and allowed the rest of the world to melt away.

The process left her hands gritty and tacky with lubricating oil. One of the smallest gears appeared to be rusted or packed with thick debris between its tiny teeth. Removing a hairpin, she used the pointed end to clear away the space.

The sun had travelled high in the sky, obliterating the last of the morning fog and revealing hints of a pleasant day to come. At last, it seemed as if the rich shades of sapphire and azure would overthrow the opaque grey that had been the prevailing colour all week. She could smell the competing fragrances of hay and clover interwoven with spring flowers and … suddenly, the slight inkling of expensive cologne.

"Will there ever be a time when I arrive and don't have to ask what it is you are doing?"

Like a child careening back and forth on a wooden nursery horse, Violet was unbalanced by rapidly-shifting emotions as they lurched in quick succession between annoyance at being left waiting, and delight at the sight of his warm, interested expression. Then he smiled and she was completely disarmed. Gabriel was clad in a sky blue, superfine wool waistcoat, crisp, snowy-white shirt sleeves rolled to the elbow, and trousers the colour of chocolate. They hugged his lean, muscular thighs like a second skin. There was no topcoat in sight. A few confident, rolling steps had eliminated the distance between them.

She was staring. Her brain screamed at her to find a new occupation for her eyes, but there was some kind of language barrier between her better judgement and her disobedient retinas. *Eyes away! Say something intelligent!* But what came out was, "Did you know that only one-sixth of the eye is visible?" *Abort! Not that intelligent!* Mortified, she reached to cover the blush that burned as it melted into her freckled cheeks. "Hello, Your Grace." A shame she couldn't hide away behind her hands forever …

"It must be an interminable bore for the other five-sixth of the eye, left as they are in both the physical and metaphorical dark. And have you forgotten my name? I'll give you a hint. It starts with a "G" … rhymes with"—he thought for a moment—"nothing. It rhymes with nothing. I'm a poet's worst nightmare." Violet's fingers slid away from where they had been hiding her blush. *And now you've just smeared machine grease on your face. Brilliant, Vi.*

She reached for a discarded rag, but Gabriel was startling in his swiftness. One large, capable hand plucked a handkerchief from his pocket with a flourish. It had been painstakingly embroidered with a lopsided cluster of cheerful, yellow flowers. In smooth, careful strokes, he dragged the soft material across one gently-sloping eyebrow. His touch was leisurely, his lips slightly parted as the linen feathered across her skin. Stepping back, he folded the handkerchief in half and studied the needlework with an expression that could only be described as paternal pride.

"Nora's work?" she inquired.

Observed in introspection, he seemed almost shy and vulnerable. Gabriel folded his hands behind his back and smiled at her.

"Yes. Needlepoint has never been among her preferred activities, but she made it as a gift for my thirty-fifth birthday. So, what are you doing with the eviscerated clock?"

"Nothing, really, just tinkering. I don't wait gracefully. Nathan used to tease that I could bully a pot of water into a rolling boil before science could possibly allow it to occur naturally. He threatened to build a locked gate around the garden to protect the vegetables from my overzealous picking." Violet smiled at the memory as she wandered toward Omen, who was tethered beside a sleek bay horse and a dark chestnut mare. The mare was fitted with a beautiful ornamental side saddle. Violet ran a hand along the chestnut's sleek neck, then leaned in to nestle her forehead against her velvety fur. "She's stunning."

"She is. But she carries a far less distinguished name than she deserves, Mudpuddle. Nora named her when she was a toddler." Gabriel tightened the girths on both horses, glancing up as the children meandered closer. "Where shall we go? We could cut through the moors to the coastal path," Gabriel suggested.

"That sounds wonderful," Violet replied, then froze as she considered how, precisely, she would manage to hoist herself up without throwing her skirts halfway up to her ears. Without the option of a riding habit, she had chosen the dress she thought would provide the most modesty once she was seated, but she had given little consideration to the actual mounting.

Gabriel wordlessly widened his stance and bent his knees, making a step with his twined fingers. When she didn't immediately slip her boot in her hands, he looked up. "I'll see you safely up, Violet. There's nothing to be concerned about."

"I'm not afraid. I'm just considering how much goat excrement these boots have seen."

Gabriel made a disgusted face, then stood. "Onto the next plan then. Come here and I will lift you up." Violet didn't move. "Unless you prefer to scale the nearest tree and jump down, this is your best option." She took one shuffling step closer. "That's the way. I assure you, I'm quite capable." He waited until she closed the remaining distance between them, then eased closer still, placing both hands on her waist. "On three, give a little hop, and I'll do the rest."

"I thought you said you were 'quite capable'," she teased.

"Yes, well, I am a quite capable thirty-seven-year old, not a quite capable twenty-year-old, which means a little hop might decrease the chances of lower back pain tomorrow."

Violet laughed and pushed one of his hands away, preparing to find another plan, but before she had so much as shifted her weight, his grip tightened and she was in the air, then seated on her horse.

"As it turns out, I am every bit as strong as I was at twenty." He gave her a smug grin and politely ignored her attempts to cover her exposed ankle.

"Shall we?" Gabriel asked.

Nora responded with a whoop of excitement, urging her pony into a trot. Zachariah followed directly behind like an adoring shadow.

At the slightest suggestion of leg pressure, Mud Puddle glided into a fast-rolling canter. Wisps of Violet's hair escaped their confines, trailing behind her like the streaks of clouds that painted the sky above.

Chapter 14

Propelled by enthusiasm and with fine horseflesh beneath them, the group reached the pebbled shore with remarkable speed. The moment they arrived, Zachariah shed his shoes and stockings in a haphazard trail and waded into the salty surf. In a moment of remarkable self-containment, Nora looked to her father for his nod of approval before racing off, agile feet bounding like a sandpiper towards the frothy blue ocean.

Violet admired the vast blue of the ocean from horseback, the salty brine alive and pungent, seeping into her lungs. Captivated by the scene before her, she hadn't noticed Gabriel's approach until sure fingers wrapped about her waist and lifted her to the ground. His hands remained there, burning through the layers of her dress, until her balance was restored. But instead of stepping back, he lifted one hand to her temple, tucking a loose strand of hair behind her ear, the callus of his index finger eliciting a curious ticklish sensation down her neck. It was the briefest of touches, and he turned away to his horse almost instantly, but she could feel the ghost of that light caress tingling for long moments after.

While Gabriel collected the rudimentary picnic his cook had packed, Violet struggled to untangle the laces of her boots with uncooperative fingers. Once freed, she strolled onto the beach. The coarse grains flexed and hugged her soles as she sank into their cold embrace. Dragging her stocking-clad toes through the sand, she wrote her name, stopping when a pair of large Hessians occupied the space meant for her "T." Gabriel loomed, a bemused expression on his face, the breeze blowing his dark curls in a mess of wild tangles.

"You, sir, are rudely interrupting my childlike revelry and look terribly uncomfortable in those boots."

Deep smile lines appeared at the corners of his eyes. "It takes every bit of Keene's brawn to get these damnable things on my feet. I am afraid it would be hopeless to try to remove them."

"I never would have imagined you as the sort to cower away from a challenge. The mighty Duke of Northam defeated by two scraps of poorly engineered, overpriced leather. Or are you shy about showing your stockinged feet?" She grinned.

"All right! I surrender. I'll try," he exclaimed, chuckling. Five minutes later, he had wrestled one boot free, but then fell flat on his back with the second still fiendishly adhered to his foot. "Now I shall have to hobble home in disgrace with only one shoe."

"No, foolish duke, you would have to *ride* home with only one boot. Not nearly so plebeian. And I will rescue you from your embarrassment. A man's boots can't be half so stubborn as a woman's corset." Violet scooped up Gabriel's foot, ignoring his wary expression, and tugged with all her diminutive might. She managed to drag him several inches before the boot gave and she collapsed backwards in an undignified heap, the heel crashing into her eyebrow.

Dropping the boot, she threw both hands over her throbbing eye with a groan. When she opened her uninjured lid, he was above her, dropped to one knee and blotting out the sun with his imposing form. "Easy there, sweetheart. No. Don't move too fast. Let me help." The murmured endearment released a rush of warmth as one hand slid beneath the nape of her neck, easing her forward into a seated position.

Both her hands remained protectively over the bludgeoned eye, patched like a little girl playing pirate. He tucked her close, one knee in the sand between her hiked-up skirts, his open palm rubbing slow, tender circles over her back. As the throbbing fizzled into a dull ache, she lowered first one hand, then the other.

"Ouch," she said dryly, her lashes wet with unshed tears. "Is it terrible? It feels terrible." Violet tried for a smile, but it translated into more of a tumultuous grimace.

Hissing his sympathy at the already discoloured swelling, Gabriel reached up to touch her bruise with featherlight strokes of his index finger, as if he could brush away the pain he had unwittingly inflicted.

Gabriel's eyebrows drew together in a frown, narrowing her attention to a smattering of grey hairs that were woven through the dark brown of his brows. She had never noticed them before. They made him seem distinctly human. *Too human. Too attainable. Like a star that had broken from its orbit and fallen squarely at her feet.* His errant finger smoothed down her temple before being joined by the warm, comforting weight of his whole hand as it cradled her face. There was such gentleness in his touch. Almost reverence. Gabriel's thumb traced back and forth across her cheek, each stroke coming closer to the corner of her lower lip, like the gradual rising of the tide.

Violet's breaths had quickened into shallow inhalations that didn't seem to fill her lungs. She struggled fruitlessly to match her breathing to the slow, deliberate rhythm of his sweeping touch. Then the caress tapered away, like the last flickers of firelight before being consumed by darkness.

His hand dropped, but his eyes continued staring openly into hers. Lacerating conflict was evident in his expression, as clear as if it were carved ruthlessly across his beautiful face. He severed their tethered gaze abruptly and closed his eyes.

Easing to his feet, Gabriel took several steps in retreat. "I apologise for my errant boot"— he paused, as if the moment had stolen the fluency of his speech—"and for my familiarity thereafter. I didn't mean ... I feel I may have ... I am sorry." The last was uttered so softly, and with such utter remorse, that she had a sudden urge to comfort him. To smooth her thumbs across the vulnerable greys in his otherwise flawless, brown brows.

Instead, she blinked a few times, both to gather her composure and to measure the level of discomfort to her eye. Finding it bearable, she hauled herself to her feet before Gabriel could offer his hand. "Well, no battle ensues without its casualties. At least we managed to remove your boot without pulling off your foot in the process. As to the latter …" She shook her head to disabuse the entire sentiment.

Gabriel brushed bits of stray sand from his trousers. "Now Hamish will have legitimate reason to dislike me. You're returning from an afternoon in my company bruised and battered." He looked out into the ocean, then back to Violet.

In silent agreement, they walked side by side in the direction of the lapping waves. The breeze was steady but warm, and the children, half-drenched from splashing, were now quietly inspecting a hermit crab.

"Hamish doesn't hate you. He's protective. We've supported one another through some very trying hardships, and that kind of friendship breeds intense loyalty." She paused to scoop up a handful of sand, then let it slide through her fingers. "He and Nathan were inseparable. Hamish suffered that loss as deeply as any man could, and he has accepted responsibility for my well-being in Nathan's stead."

Gabriel nodded slowly once, but he offered no other response. Instead, he bent to rescue something that was tossed about with the waves. He rubbed his thumb across the edges to clear the debris, then extended his hand out to drop it into hers.

"*Cerastoderma Edule*," Violet murmured, exploring the surface with gently prodding fingers.

"Cockleshell," Gabriel mirrored back, a smile in his voice.

"I wonder how far he travelled in his life and where the ocean currents carried him. How old he was and how he died," Violet mused.

"And here I just thought you might like to have a pretty token to remember the day."

"But this is only half of his shell. His perfect match is somewhere out there in this massive ocean. It could be miles away or just there amongst the waves, forever separated and incomplete." Violet looked out into the ocean as she spoke, searching for the missing half in the tumultuous surf, however hopeless the task.

"Or maybe another fortunate explorer found the other half and is wondering, at this very moment, where this half may be."

"It would be kind of bittersweet, I suppose," Violet said. "Two people with such a beautiful prize, but neither ever seeing him whole."

"I wonder if this lad has an heir and a spare out there somewhere to carry on the line." One corner of his mouth rose with his jest.

"How do cockles even make baby cockles?"

Gabriel grimaced at Violet's question. "I can't imagine the endeavour would be very much fun." His cheeks began to look a bit ruddy.

"Maybe the girl cockles simply spew their eggs about the ocean and hope for the best," Violet mused.

"Well, that's just insanity. How's a species supposed to carry on leaving reproduction to such implausible chance?

"I think that must be exactly how it's done. I've decided it's a fact. It makes their existence that much more miraculous."

"Violet, that's not how scientific facts work, you know. You cannot just will them to be the truth because it makes the universe a more miraculous place." He laughed and ran his hands through his dishevelled hair.

"Oh no. Now that I am thinking about it, I believe I read about it in a scientific journal."

She could practically hear him raise his eyebrows.

"Is that so? Which journal? I would like to read about it myself."

"It was the … *Marine Mollusks … British Periodical?*" she stammered.

An undignified burst of laughter rose up from Gabriel's chest, becoming worse with one glance at Violet's feigned seriousness, all drawn eyebrows and compressed lips. The sight completely unhinged his control. When he had finally caught his breath, his smile slipped a little from his face, transforming into something infinitely warmer and more compelling. "You make me wish it was true that the world was just that miraculous." He shook his head. "Don't mind me. The ocean brings out all my un-ducal mawkishness. How about we go see what trouble our offspring are up to?"

The children, Gabriel and Violet discovered, had been busy in their unsupervised play, acquiring a cache of hermit crabs they were attempting to race. Only one was scurrying off in a frantic dash toward the finish line of the water, while the remaining five were tucked into their shells being wholly unamusing.

Losing interest in the sedentary crabs, Zach retrieved a cricket ball from his satchel and tossed it to Gabriel, who snatched it from the air with a smile.

"That's a fine arm you have there!" Turning, he threw a gentle, underhanded toss to Violet.

She caught the ball easily with one hand and then grimaced. "What was that?"

His chin lifted, "A gentlemanly toss."

"Gentleman never learn to throw a ball?" she goaded, pulling her arm back and tearing loose with a whirling fastball.

Stumbling to catch the ball with the tips of his fingers, Gabriel shook out his stinging hand and looked to Zach with an expression of astonishment.

"Who do you think taught me how to throw?" Zach asked.

"I had assumed that Nathan had the privilege."

"Oh Papa did at first, but then he would hardly ever play cricket with Mum and me because she hates to lose."

"More like Nathan hated to lose," Violet retorted with a grumble.

Gabriel turned to Nora and threw yet another "gentlemanly toss," which slipped through the girl's fingers, falling between her feet.

"Oh no." Violet shot Gabriel a vaguely accusatory glare. "You never taught Nora to throw or catch a ball?" With a sigh, she stalked over to a sheepish-looking Nora and smiled. "Quite all right. We will set this to rights in no time." Patting Nora's shoulder, Violet took a half step back. "All right then, show me your stance."

Nora shifted her weight between her feet and shrugged her shoulders, as if to say *this is my stance.*

"Never mind. We will get to that. One of the most important things to learn first is the correct way to grip the ball."

Nora stared at the ball in her hand as if noticing it for the first time.

"Hold the ball in your dominant hand, so that the seam is parallel to your index finger and opposite your thumb. Yes, just like that. Changing your grip can alter the direction of the ball, but we'll get to that another time. Only the basics for today. Stand with your feet shoulder width apart, knees slightly bent."

Stepping behind Nora, Violet helped her find the correct position, adjusting the bend of her knees. "Now, this step is critical. First, you tuck the ball to your chest to keep everything else centred. The next part of the process involves two steps with your feet. When you step forward, you point with your ankle, like so. If you're right-handed, you step with the corresponding leg. Again, this is a critical moment, because if the angle of your foot is incorrect then it affects the swing of your hips and skews the entire direction of your aim. Both hands remain on the ball until your rear leg steps forward. Separating your hands early will affect the timing of your release. As you step forward, you rotate your hips. That is where the power originates, but your whole body is an active participant. Shoulders and torso and arms all working as one. As you release, allow your arm to continue down with its natural momentum to the opposite hip."

Violet moved in slow motion, throwing a few invisible balls to demonstrate the entire process.

Nora watched attentively, then threw a series of her own invisible balls.

Violet clapped her hands with an excited little hop. "Yes, that's brilliant! You're a natural at this!"

Suddenly remembering the presence of the others, she glanced up at Gabriel to find that he was watching her interaction with Nora intently, wearing an expression she couldn't quite place. Almost a reluctant kind of yearning, like when someone surprises you with your favourite dessert after you have already eaten two huge plates of supper. She turned away from the uncomfortable feeling it evoked.

"Catching is simply a matter of practice. Follow the arc of the ball all the way to your hands. Now, throw to your father."

Violet watched with pride as Nora executed a perfectly passable first pitch that landed solidly in Gabriel's waiting hands.

"It's not as if I was intentionally denying her a necessary skill set," Gabriel grumbled, throwing the ball to Zach, who tossed it to Violet. "There simply aren't many moments in life when the daughter of a duke is required to execute a flawless pitch."

"Fiddlesticks, I can think of countless times where the talent would be a boon for any young lady."

Gabriel crossed his arms and lowered his chin. "Oh really? Then you won't have any trouble naming one such instance." He was forced to break from his defiant pose to intercept a ball from Violet's direction. He glared. "I am beginning to understand why Nathan refused to play with you."

"One such example isn't even a challenge."

"Go on then." He threw the ball gently to his daughter, who managed to catch it this time.

"One." She held up a finger. "A lady is accosted by bandits whilst travelling home from a magical evening at a ball."

"I can already anticipate the direction of this outlandish story. Does this imaginary duke's daughter not have outriders to protect her?"

"They are all down with ague."

"Every able-bodied man on his staff at the same time? How unfortunate for him, and for her, poor lady. Go on."

"As I was saying"—she narrowed her eyes—"frantic with fear, she searches about for something with which to defend herself from robbery and worse, but alas! She is alone and without defence! Reaching into her valise, she pulls out her trusty fan."

Gabriel groaned.

Violet began a theatrical pantomime of the exciting events as the story unfolded. "Stepping into the carriage door, she takes aim, channelling all the advice she has accumulated in the art of cricket ball throwing. She hurls the weapon end over end, the pointed tip piercing directly into her attacker's forehead, effectively knocking him unconscious. She leaves without further obstacles, grateful to have only sacrificed her favourite fan in the distressing ordeal."

Nora erupted in enthusiastic applause, and Violet curtseyed with a triumphant grin.

"What happened to the other bandits?"

Violet's head snapped around. *Damn, she had forgotten that detail.*

"Yes." He dragged the word out like a tasty morsel on his tongue, a sly smile flexing into view. "You said bandits in the plural, but our fictional lady is now left to defend herself against … what? Two? Three? More monstrously menacing bandits? And worse"—his voice lowered as if it impart a great secret—"she is now without her trusty fan."

Violet rebounded without further hesitation. "That you even have to ask that question demonstrates a complete ignorance with respect to the character of pirates and highwaymen."

"I cannot wait to be educated."

"Indeed, there *were* three more bandits, but they were so amused by her grit and cunning, so impressed by her tremendous skill, that they were compelled to let her continue onward due to the traditional piratical code of honour."

"And what exactly was it that this code of honour decreed?"

"That if a lady's throwing arm is superior to your own, you must release her without further delay."

Northam's deep, rumbling laugh carried over the others, joyful and relaxed. This was the man he must have been before the loss of his wife, and indications of that man were becoming more evident. He showed moments of lightness, more frequent and longer in duration, like a bear waking up from hibernation, still groggy, but noticing one brightly-coloured flower after the next, the sight of each bloom luring him further away from his sleep.

***

Violet pulled away from the playful pack as the game wound to an end. She was nestled in the sand, clutching a thick reed, absorbed in her task. Her hair fell in a scraggly veil over her face.

"Again I ask, what *are* you working on so diligently?"

She glanced up, then scooted her body away, shielding her project from view. "I will show you when I am done, impatient man. Does everyone leap to answer your every question the moment you ask it?"

"Yes. Did you miss the part where I am a duke?"

She glowered in playful rebuttal.

"You will have to wallow in the unknown for a few more moments. Now be quiet, you're disrupting my concentration."

Ignoring his unsettling gaze, she used the sharp end of a hairpin to whittle away a tiny, matching line of holes and a small "V" at the top, then lifted it to her mouth and played a few high-pitched, hollow notes. As she covered the holes with fast-flickering fingers, the pitch changed.

Gabriel glowed with delighted amusement. "You astounding woman! You magicked up a musical instrument out of weeds and a hairpin." The trilling notes carried across the breeze, alerting the children, who abandoned their play to investigate the sound.

"Is there anything you cannot do? I bow to your ingenuity. *You* should be the duke. God only knows what you could achieve with a thousand tenants and bottomless coffers!"

She beamed up at him, then squeaked out a series of thin, off-key notes.

"I can also fold a paper swan and peel an apple in one long curl, as long as I am ticking off my qualifications for peerage."

He levelled her with some indeterminate expression, then shook his head.

"Well, sadly I do not believe Mrs Simmons packed any apples to allow for you to demonstrate, but shall we sit down and have lunch anyway?"

They ate their picnic at a leisurely pace. Nora commandeered the reed, amusing herself with discordant melodies that echoed mournfully across the empty beach. Gulls swarmed, pecking greedily at scraps of abandoned food as they basked under the waning sun. After rinsing away a small amount of their accumulated sand in the now icy water, they dragged the children, exhausted and happy, back home. Gabriel rode in his stocking feet, his boots scrunched beneath the handle of the picnic basket.

Chapter 15

The clock chimed two, and Gabriel rolled, kicking his legs to dislodge the satin sheet that had wrapped him like a mummy during all his restless writhing. The book he had attempted to read but eventually discarded, poked him in the ribcage. Sliding the massive farming compendium to the plush carpet below, he shook out his pillow and flopped on his back to continue his vigil, staring at the ceiling and trying not to think about Violet Evans.

He had nearly kissed her. *Twice!* His fingers had stroked the soft skin of her cheek of their own volition. They had wrapped about her waist as she dismounted, mere inches below the swell of her breast, stubbornly remaining for long seconds whilst his brain commanded, implored, *rioted* for them to release her. Her eyes had connected with his, so sweet and trusting and full of life, and he had promptly lost all his sense.

Worse still, his hands weren't content to remain idle. They had itched to knead into her like a cat's paws, to pull her close so that his lips could taste hers. Every inch of his eager body had declared war against logic as his eyes drank in the sight of her, with her cheeks pink from exertion and the sunlight dancing through her tousled hair. The battle raged on every moment he was close to her. His judgement had been tied, gagged, and thrust into a corner, setting his body free to lust and fantasise.

Throwing his legs over the side of the bed, he stood and paced, his toes curling into the thick fibres of the carpet. All his nerves felt achingly alive, acutely aware of every sensation, from the rub of the sheets as they cascaded off his naked legs, to his curls tickling across the tips of his ears. Every inch of his skin was sensitised and raw with need.

God, he had touched her ear. Tucked a silky strand of hair behind it. And he hadn't imagined the way her pupils dilated and her lips parted in response. His cock swelled with interest at the memory.

Frustrated at the unwanted arousal, he gave his turgid length an annoyed thwomp with his fingers, but instead of retreating, it surged further to life. His hand immediately wrapped around the girth with several long, slow strokes.

Groaning, he pulled his hand away and stalked the length of the room, pressing his forehead against the cool pane of the window. It did nothing to calm the urgency tingling down his lower abdomen, settling heavy between his legs. When he closed his eyes, she was there. He imagined the little gasp she would make if he allowed his fingers to trail up to cup her breasts, teasing her nipples to hardness, and the delicious purr of encouragement she would breathe into his mouth as his tongue slid across hers for the first time.

In the past, his night time fantasies had featured Emma or some faceless creation of his imagination, not a flesh and bone woman who had burrowed into his thoughts and inflamed his loins.

In one swift motion, he wrenched open the window, letting the cool spring air rush over him in a fragrant gust, but the breeze caressed and compelled, rather than smothering his desire. With a frustrated moan, he wrapped his hand around his cock and gave into his body's unrelenting demand. In his mind she was under him, her legs wrapped about his hips, urging him forward as he sank into her heat with long, delicious strokes, burying himself to the hilt. He spent in a few quick jerks of his hand. His body melted as the tension washed away, leaving his muscles uncoiled with relief. And then the shame hit, tearing through him.

It was Emma he missed. Emma he longed to have back in his arms and in his life again. He recoiled against his own traitorous lust. He didn't want it. Any of it. He didn't want to feel the fluttering in his heart when she smiled at him, or the desire that surged to life every time she was close enough to touch. He didn't want to be astounded by her cleverness, or to react to the sheer gravitational pull of her. It was poisonous to his memories of Emma, but it felt so bloody good.

Distance was the only answer. He had to stay away from her, away from this. If he allowed himself to lean into her warmth, it would tear him in two.

***

Gabriel awoke with an emotional hangover. All things considered, he would have preferred the haze of overindulgence to the sleep-deprivation brought on by unwanted lust.

Nora was also late to break her fast, arriving only minutes before him and heaping ungainly piles of eggs, fried mushrooms, sausage, and toast with jam onto her plate. Gabriel was attempting to gather some enthusiasm for the contents of the breakfast bar when Bennett announced that they had a visitor. Zachariah, pale and shaking, stood in the dining room archway. Both of his hands clutched the hair at his temples, muscles clenching and spasming with jarring force.

Nora leapt from the chair, her spindly legs clumsy in their haste. As she reached to touch his shoulder, he lurched away, tumbling into the corner as if scalded by hot oil. "What's wrong Zach?" Her voice wavered, fingers tangling together. Gabriel was close behind Nora, both hands resting on her shoulders. Suddenly, the smothering aroma of soft-boiled eggs and salty bacon made his stomach threaten to revolt.

He inched closer to Zach and stooped down. Assuming the practised expression of calm steadiness, he forced his breathing into a slow, repetitive pattern. Experience with the young man had taught him that any emotional outburst would only slow the progression of information.

"Is it your mother, son? Is she well, Zach?" Gabriel forced the question through his parched throat. Zachariah nodded, then shook his head and let out an inhuman groan, burying his head in his own hands. Last night, Gabriel had been resolute in his decision to remain as far away from Violet as possible, but now he was desperate to know she was safe, to see her smiling and well. In a matter of moments, all his carefully-assembled plans from eight hours prior came crumbling to his feet. His heart hammered in his chest, jarring his ribcage, his mind vaulting from one catastrophic possibility to the next.

"Is she hurt?" Gabriel tried again.

Zach flung his head back, banging it hard against the wall several times with startling ferocity before throwing himself into Gabriel's arms. His lanky body heaved in broken sobs, nails sinking into Gabriel's back.

"Can't stop it. Can't …" Zach moaned between sharp inhalations.

"Steady there. Whatever it is, I will make it better. Easy, Zachariah. Deep, slow breaths. That's the way." Gabriel laid his cheek against the top of Zach's head, smoothing his hair in slow, methodical strokes. He continued to murmur words of comfort and safety as he held the shattered boy securely in his arms.

"My father is d-dead," Zach stuttered. "They are going to try to take me. Don't let them take me. Don't let them take me. I can't go back there. They'll hurt me." His arms clamped about Gabriel's abdomen with almost painful tenacity. Terror transforming his bones and flesh into an unrelenting steel vice.

None of this made the slightest bit of sense. His mind ran in circles, but every revolution looked the same. "Who's going to take you, Zach? And what's this to do with Nathan's death?" He struggled to make order of the nonsensical wails.

"Not th-that papa. My sire. He's dead now. And they will take me."

146

"No one is going to take you from your mother. You are safe. Your mum would fight every Englishman in rapid succession to keep you from harm. She'd scratch out their eyes like a rabid badger. And so would I."

Nora had crept closer, resting her small hand between Zachariah's shoulder blades. He shuddered visibly, then whirled and buried his head in her lap, curling up like a hedgehog. She settled both arms on his back sliding them up and down as if to roll out a long loaf of bread. After a few endless moments, the twitching eased.

"Nora, Zachariah, I am going to speak with Violet." Gabriel turned toward the doorway. "Keene!" The valet instantly materialised. "I'm going to see Mrs Evans. Stay with the children and see that they are not disturbed."

Keene nodded, lips pressed tightly in a frown.

Gabriel's horse was tacked and ready to go before he could call for it. Leaping astride, he lurched into a gallop. Omen, doubtlessly sensing his master's urgency in every taught muscle, moved as if hell itself was chasing him across the sleepy fields of Devonshire. The ride still felt interminably long.

Questions tumbled upon questions, rolling around his head like a child's game of marbles. *Violet was married before Nathan? Why would anyone take him away?* The violence of Zach's reaction, and the certainty that Violet would greet him in an equally frantic state, caused his stomach to pitch and roll in helpless frustration. Every cell in his body demanded more speed, indifferent to the recklessness.

He called out the moment he thought his voice might carry. "Violet? Are you inside? Violet?"

She burst through the front door, tears defying physics at the speed in which they chased one another down her starkly pale cheeks. "Is he with you? Is Zach—"

He cut her off, leaping from his horse and running to pull her roughly into his arms. Her small frame quivered against him.

"He's with Nora. He's rattled but alright. What in the hell is going on?" Her face was buried in his chest, hot tears bleeding through the material of his shirtfront. Gabriel heaved a steadying breath, one hand sliding up to cradle the back of her head, stroking through her hair with the tips of his fingers. "Forget I asked, Vi. Don't try to answer now. Whatever it is, I am here. I won't let anyone take Zach."

Her hands clutched fistfuls of his shirt. "We can't stay. He'll take Zach, and I won't be able to stop him."

Gabriel pulled her tighter, as if he could absorb all the unabating emotions that ravaged her. "Hush now. None of that. I won't let anyone hurt Zach." After long minutes, her rigid muscles began to ease, and she took a tentative step back. Violet lifted her gaze, her expression lost and hopeless and so completely wrong on her perpetually-smiling face.

"Zach is my nephew by marriage." Her voice was small, without inflection, as if she had no energy left. "Nathan brought him home to protect him from his father's unimaginable cruelty. Zachariah was like a feral animal when he arrived … mute, terrified, and drowning in mistrust and anger. His sire, David Evans, heir to the Baron of Moorefield, had it circulated that the boy died of a fever, and he told us he had no wish to see Zach again. We raised him as our own. In every way that matters, Zach *is* my son." Her eyes squeezed closed, twin tears escaping the corners, falling heedlessly down her blotchy, freckled cheeks. Gabriel ached to wipe them away.

"David died last week in a carriage accident, and now the baron is without an heir." She covered her face with both hands as if to press the salt water back into her eyes.

Gabriel stood silently, waiting for her to restore her shredded composure sufficiently to continue.

"Now that he is without an heir, Moorefield sent a letter demanding to take Zach home. Zachariah found the post." Her lower lip trembled. "Baron Moorefield is a monster. It will destroy my Zach, my poor gentle boy." Her head lolled forward and Gabriel caught her listing body against his again and squeezed, hoping it would convey his devotion when turmoil had robbed him of eloquence. Scrambling for words that would bring her some measure of reassurance, he pulled her to arm's length, hands framing her face. Every freckle stood out in stark contrast to her paleness. "You're not alone in this, Violet. I won't let them take Zach. Neither will Hamish. I will bury them in paperwork, and, failing that, Hamish will bury them in the ground." Settling an arm about her waist, he urged Violet through one unsteady step after the next.

"Come inside. What do tea-hating Englishwomen drink?" He guided her into the kitchen and settled her into a chair before stepping back. He needed distance. He couldn't think, and he couldn't afford to offer her the kind of comfort that was welling up inside him, threatening to tumble out in soft caresses and tender declarations. Nor would he dwell upon those primitive male impulses. It was pointless to examine his feelings under a magnifying glass. The Evans family had come to mean a great deal to him. He couldn't possibly disavow that truth when the mere mention of her running struck him physically ill. But this nearly uncontrollable urge to comfort her body with his own, and the unshakable feeling that he would derive as much comfort from giving as she would in the receiving, well, he was certain that was little more than a reflex. An instinctual reaction to the intimacy of this moment when faced with a painfully distraught Violet.

Gabriel found coffee already prepared in a kettle and placed a steaming mug before her with a grimace. He sat, leaning forward with his elbows propped on his legs. "Now then. After departing I will call on my man of affairs and send a post to my solicitors to determine what legal actions we can find to protect Zach." Falling into the methodical problem-solving that was so familiar cleared away some of the disorienting emotions.

"Without a husband to protect the sanctity of your family, the baron has a solid claim on Zachariah as the only surviving heir to a barony." He leaned back, hands resting on his knees. "Even if you were to marry Hamish, as a commoner, his pull would be insufficient." Her face contorted into what could only be described as horror at the suggestion of matrimony to Hamish. Gabriel chose to puzzle over the violence of that reaction at a later time. "But there must be some loophole. Did he ever sign over formal custody papers? Are there any records to show he wilfully recanted familial ties?" She shook her head, a tear clinging to the tips of her long, spiked lashes before slipping over the edge.

"Well, if legal avenues fail us then we'll resort to blackmail. I will pen letters to every friend in the peerage that might be sympathetic to our cause, every man with deep pockets and a grudge against Baron Moorefield. I've never met the man, but the name has been affiliated with some troubling rumours over the years. Regardless, I won't let him hurt Zach. Or you. I may not be able to whittle a lute from a seaside weed, but I have long arms and a vicious pencil."

"Thank you." She reached out to touch the hand that was covering his knee, and he rotated it to hold hers in a steady, capable clasp. For a moment, a fraction of the distress dissipated from her face, and he felt a senseless surge of masculine satisfaction that he could provide even that brief reprieve from her anxiety. He was her friend, and he would protect her with every weapon at his disposal.

"Now I must leave. I have a lot to do in a short time. I will stop off and speak to Hamish on my way home. I'm certain he will want to be here with you." He swallowed hard. "I won't have you here alone. When Zachariah is able, I will send him home in my carriage."

She stood when he rose from his chair, and he took both her hands in his. They were cold. He didn't want to let them go. "I know it's pointless to ask you not to worry, but I hope you will give some of those burdens to me. Let me take them when I go, and know that I will fight for your family, Violet."

***

Hours of tortuous meetings and Gabriel was in no better state than he had been at the onset. Legally, his hands were tied, and the thought of telling Violet of his failure left him emotionally gutted. He had written and dictated an army of letters, sending them out with riders to be delivered with all due haste. It would be days before he received any replies, and the waiting was already beginning to chip away at his composure. Like an ageing building where all the joists and rafters had rotted away, his walls were on the cusp of impending doom. Exhausted, he retired to his study, sprawling out across a lumpy, striped divan. The clock chimed midnight, but his mind refused to quiet enough for him to sleep. He thumped his lightly fisted hand against his forehead, willing a solution to wiggle free from some hidden corner of his mind, but all he could see when his eyes closed was Violet. Formidable, clever, optimistic, beautiful Violet falling to pieces in his arms. *Thunk. Thunk. Thunk.* His fist continued rapping.

"Get your filthy boots off the divan, you heathen. Who do you think cleans that?" Keene grumbled from the open doorway.

"Not you," Gabriel replied.

"True enough, but you don't want to antagonise the upstairs maids. They can be fiendishly vengeful." He shuddered for effect.

"What am I to do, Keene?" Gabriel sat up and scrubbed his face with his hands.

"MARRY. HER." He enunciated each syllable as if Gabriel was a small child who had repeatedly blown by the most obvious answer to a painfully simple question. "A debilitated drunkard could solve this quandary. Marry her, claim the boy, and crush the baron's testicles under the heel of your ducal boot. Problem solved. Can I have an increase in salary?"

Gabriel groaned. "I don't want her hand to be forced. Marriage shouldn't be some bitter powder she swallows to save her son. I've seen the attachment between Hamish and Violet, and I'm hardly a fit husband at this juncture. I can scarcely make it through the day without falling into a muddled mess in want of Emma." Gabriel stood and began to pace, then immediately turned and sat back down. "There has to be a way I can keep Zachariah safe and maintain Violet's options."

"You're right. I haven't noticed what you claim exists between the Highlander and Mrs Evans, but I have seen the way she looks at you. *Bitter* wouldn't be any of the first one hundred adjectives I would choose." He paused for effect. "Longingly, smouldering, wistfully—" Gabriel hurled a decorative pillow at his head.

"Fine." Keene's voice was uncharacteristically soft and devoid of his earlier humour. "How about fondly, earnestly, loyally? Those are not bad adjectives either, Gabriel. I know you miss Emma. Hell, I miss her, and I wasn't married to her for thirteen years, but Violet is a kind, understanding woman. She wouldn't expect all those years to wash away just because you married her."

Gabriel stared wordlessly into his friend's eyes. His stomach clenched, his mind a tangle of emotions that felt like driving too fast in a curricle that was being pulled by a pair of drunken horses. He sighed. "Tomorrow I will ride out and obtain a special licence, but only as a backup."

"Splendid," Keene said with a satisfied smile as he walked to the door.

"And Christopher, thank you."

Gabriel leaned back onto the divan, allowing the idea to burrow inside of him. What expectations would Violet have of him in marriage? How would he find his equilibrium with her presence in every corner of his life, firing off his emotions like unstable bottle rockets? A cold sweat had begun to form on his brow. But somewhere inside, those same thoughts that fuelled his anxiety also stroked softly across his heart, blooming in places that had remained cold and untouched for far too long.

He thought about her energising presence in every corner of his life, and about the possibility of breaking free from all the turmoil that plagued him. He thought about falling into something sweet and comfortable. He froze under the polarising impulses to simultaneously run from the idea and to curl his body around its warmth. For a moment he let himself want those things, ignoring the sting of unfaithfulness that licked hot at his insides.

Chapter 16

D awn arrived too quickly for Violet. Zachariah had awoken throughout the night in inconsolable fits. She sat next to him, holding him when he would allow it, staying close by when he would not. He finally fell asleep sitting up, sketchbook and pencil in hand.

Violet had long since realised that his artwork offered the clearest image of his thoughts or concerns. Blazed within streaks of paint or shades of graphite, his heart was laid bare. She had felt his loneliness when no peers would accept him, his hopelessness in the months that followed Nathan's death, when it had seemed that joy was irretrievably lost, and the excitement that filled his soul the day he met Nora. His creations spoke for him when he could not.

Violet wasn't certain what she had expected to see on that parchment. Fear? Despair? Perhaps a portrait of Nora? Sliding the sketchbook from his lax fingers, she studied Zach's drawing. Nora was part of the scene he had captured, as was Violet, but in the background it was Northam. Gabriel. His eyes were locked with Zachariah's, and there was a softness there, emotion that held unqualified devotion. One large, capable hand offered up a river stone. Offered friendship and acceptance. There was something in the set of his jaw and the strength of his shoulders that gave him the appearance of invulnerability and safety.

The paper slipped from her fingers and fell to the bed. All night, fear had run unchecked through her mind, like a poem with only one line read over and over again. Powerful images of Zachariah being ripped from her arms mashed and melded with memories from the last time she had felt helpless, until it was no longer one identifiable villain to defeat, but rather a vast and smothering sense of overwhelming doom. As if the world was too large for her to ever find her way again.

But she was not alone, and she would never feel that small again.

***

As Gabriel's carriage pulled up to the Evans's home, his gaze immediately settled upon Violet, who was engaged in savage warfare with her vegetable garden. Clumps of chickweed and crabgrass soared haphazardly over her shoulder in green showers. Wiping her hands on her skirts, she met him halfway, their faces equally sombre.

"I don't have any good news, I'm afraid." Gabriel tried to keep the gravity from his voice. "I'm off to London to pursue some options. It will take two and a half days each way, maybe less if the weather holds and we ride hard. You should expect me in a week."

He passed his hat from one hand to the other, forcing his feet to remain still, to maintain the open space between them. The feat stretched the limits of his control when Violet looked so desperately in need of a pair of strong arms to fall into. But if he came any closer he would touch her, and if he touched her he would hold her, and if he held her, it would make getting back into that carriage—leaving her distraught and alone—more than he could bear. Like dominoes, it would be impossible for one tile to fall without the remainder cascading in rapid succession. She looked from the tops of the trees to her hands to his boots, as if all the places her eyes landed were too unsteady to hold the weight of her worries.

His voice lowered, striving to convey all his affection and comfort, wishing that he could offer more. "Stay strong, Violet. All will be well." He did step closer then, both hands extended to take hers in farewell, but she jerked them away instead, stepping back.

"I'm filthy. You can't." Her lower lip wobbled as she forced a smile, looking over his shoulder at his carriage. And he was done for. The effort of that courageous little smile, like a green lad determinedly facing his first skirmish, laid waste to his resolve.

With one sharp shake of his head and two ground-eating steps, he lifted her up in an embrace so exuberant that her feet left the ground. She held her dirt-smeared hands away for a heartbeat before relaxing into his hold. Her arms wrapped around his neck, taking fistfuls of his overcoat in both hands. "Thank you," she murmured into his ear. He gave himself three seconds, three seconds to offer seven days of comfort and reassurance. He counted slowly, repeating the number three twice, then eased her to her feet and stepped away.

"Be well, Violet."

Turning, he stepped towards his waiting carriage.

"Gabriel!" The use of his Christian name halted his movement mid-stride. It took him a moment to identify the voice as Zachariah's. Zach had only ever called him by his title and scarcely even that. He found that he liked the sound of his name on the young man's lips. Gabriel smiled, inviting him closer and signalling his pleasure at the informality. *Now if only Violet would follow suit.*

Zach moved slowly, carrying a piece of parchment from his sketchbook in his closed fist. Gaze lowered, he presented a picture he had drawn. Gabriel stared at it, transfixed.

The muscles in Gabriel's jaw flexed and bunched as he worked to find adequate words for the tenderly-offered gift. Dropping to a knee to place himself in Zach's field of view, he studied the artwork, his finger tracing the place where his hand held the skipping stone. "Thank you, Zachariah. I will treasure this always." Blue eyes peeked at him from under the cover of long, thick lashes, and the suggestion of a smile tugged at the corners of his mouth.

Gabriel reached into his pocket and pulled out the little pebble that had lived in his coat since that day. "Your mother tried to steal this from me, but I rescued it. I told her that this skipping stone and the joy of that moment were worth more to me than five shillings.

The truth of the matter is this, Zach: that day, and all the days I have since shared with you and with your mother, carry immeasurable worth." He cleared his throat where it had become thick with emotion. "Maybe you could keep this safe for me while I am away?" And like the picture Zach had drawn, Gabriel offered his pebble as a sign of his friendship … and all the devotion and affection that friendship encompassed.

Somehow both members of the Evans family had squirmed their way into his heart, redecorating and rearranging the space as if they had always been there. Gabriel stood and turned away. "I will return as swiftly as possible. Take good care of your mother."

***

The week shuffled along with unnatural slowness, the murky unknown expanding into every moment like poison through blood. Every time the chickens squawked or a carriage rolled past, Violet's stomach dropped and her palms grew sweaty. Her body was exhausted and her mood stormy from the persistent stabs of anxiety. Zach spoke only out of necessity. Gone were his smiles and his confidence, packed away deep down in a place that Violet couldn't even see to reach.

Nora visited often. At first, she attempted to coax Zach out of his shell. She told outlandish stories, her hands gesticulating wildly. She poked fun at him and told silly jokes that were met with stony silence. When all her attempts to distract him proved futile, she shifted to becoming a source of quiet comfort, perching beside him to draw, reading aloud, or practising needlework on a handkerchief … which she promptly sewed to her frock. Her unconditional devotion to Zachariah made the dreadful week more bearable.

Hamish was also always nearby. He chopped already manageable pieces of wood into ridiculously small slivers, took lunch with them nearly every day, and repaired anything he could find that even hinted at being broken. Violet was certain that he had ripped off several roof tiles simply to give him an excuse to hammer them back on. He had known and loved Zach for as many years as had she. While Violet paced and became taciturn, Hamish vented his frustration with large, heavy tools.

The morning of the sixth day, Violet walked outside to find Hamish furiously digging a hole. Sweat soaked his shirt and dripped down his brow, his massive lungs billowing with exertion. His clothes were so caked in mud that she wondered if he had forgone the shovel for a time and dug at the earth barehanded. It was at least three feet deep and two feet in circumference.

"Hamish." He whirled around brandishing his shovel like a sword, then lowered it when he saw who had approached. The wrath that radiated from his body, however, did not lessen.

"What are you doing?" Concern caused her voice to crack.

"I'm planting flower bulbs," he said, then continued to stab and ravage the soil. "Mrs Williams asked me to bring them by and help ye plant them."

"Dearest, you could fit all of St George's Cathedral in that hole along with two or three street vendors. I love you. Stop digging and hug me."

His shoulders sagged. "I cannae do that. I'm a bloody mess."

"Some might argue that's why you need a hug."

Hamish's shovel gave a hard thump as it hit the ground, and he lifted her up into a bone-crushing embrace, clinging to her with all the devastation of a man who couldn't keep his beloved family safe. Her feet were a full foot off the ground, his cheek pressed to the top of her head. "I hate this." The words tore from his chest on an agonised groan.

"I know," Violet replied, relaxing into the silence as he held her. It was unsteadying to watch such a powerful man crumble, and she fought the impulse to melt right alongside him. After a time, he set her down. His shoulders straightened and he dried his cheeks with the sleeve of his shirt, returning to the war he raged against the helpless soil of Devonshire.

***

The seventh day broke cool with pebble-grey skies and thick, foreboding clouds that seemed lodged in place. Layers of silvery fog hung low against the ground, shrouding and suffocating all the brilliant colours of spring. A carriage approached, and Violet was pleasantly surprised at her body's optimistic reaction to the familiar sound. Gabriel would be back, he would have a solution, and they would finally break free from this harrowing emotional limbo. She rushed out to meet his carriage.

Relief flipped into cold dread as the poorly-sprung carriage creaked to a halt. She willed her body to act, to yell out for Zachariah to run hard and fast, but fear was a poisonous paralytic. Terror seeped through her veins, rendering every muscle inert.

Baron Evans' droopy, bulldog face filled the door of the conveyance. An openly-disgusted, fish-faced frown contorted his expression as he fixed his wet, vacant eyes on Violet. The carriage heaved and groaned as he stepped out, three beefy outriders on his flanks as he skulked towards her.

Her eyes darted, searching for Hamish, praying he was nearby to plant this villain in the hole alongside the flower bulbs. But she was utterly alone.

"I responded to your letter. I told you that Zachariah has no desire to live with you. Go away. You are not welcome here." Her teeth chattered, betraying the waves of emotion that threatened to pull her under.

"And I am responding to that correspondence now. He is my grandson and heir to the Barony of Moorefield. He has spent quite enough time making inarticulate grunts and prancing about the shores of Devonshire. Zachariah will come home, where doctors will fix his … condition, and then he will be tutored and attend Oxford like every generation of Evans men." The baron's every syllable was drenched in arrogance and hostility.

"He doesn't need fixing. He isn't a broken wagon wheel." She expected to feel the sting of tears in her eyes, but dread had chased them away. "Please. I am begging you—"

"Don't waste your hysterical female ranting on me. He will come with me today. Now."

Zachariah shot out of the house like a kite caught in the wind, his long legs pounding into the ground, desperate for the safety of the woods. One of the outriders immediately intercepted him, grabbing his neck and flinging him to the ground. Zachariah spun like a child's toy and sunk his teeth into his attacker's ankle. Again, he found his feet and fled. Rage-filled curses mingled with petrified wails as the second outrider grabbed Zachariah by the hair and shook him with hard, punishing jolts.

Violet threw herself on top of Zach's attacker, pounding and tearing at his skin. A vicious elbow drove into her temple before another hard blow to her cheek and a third to her ribs. The force of the momentum wrenched her neck unnaturally, and the edges of her vision began to blur and dim. Even as the dark encroached upon her, she struggled to free herself from the weight that now pressed her face into the cold ground. Her lungs burned with every attempt to expand. Zach was stretched and carried between the two men, still fighting with primal ferocity. "Mum!" he wailed as his bladder emptied. Then there was only darkness.

＊

"Violet! Oh God, Violet. Can ye hear me, lass?"
Hamish.

His hands were on her, touching her temple, her shoulders, her stomach. She tried to pull away. Why was he hurting her? Everything felt distorted and slow, like she was underwater. How did she get here? Then images began to flicker into focus, taking shape in her mind. Zach, terror-stricken and frantic, crying for her, beyond the ability to speak or beg, falling into ravaged animal cries.

160

Violet's muscles twitched and flexed with a visceral need to take action, to cut down and destroy anyone and anything who stood between her and Zachariah. A wailing sound she didn't recognize cleaved from someplace within as she rolled over onto her hands and knees and emptied the contents of her stomach. Then she collapsed into Hamish's waiting arms, drawing in deep, gasping breaths of air that stretched her lungs to throbbing. Her soul, ill-equipped to contain the desolation, released mournful sounds into the grey afternoon sky. Nearby, a crow cawed in an eerie echo of her helpless grief.

Hamish lifted her in the cradle of his arms, carrying her inside and wrapping her in blankets on the bed. Beside her on the wall, the picture of the chestnut horse Zachariah had painted so many years ago stared back. She could not tear her eyes away from it, remembering the boy who seemed to conjure life from his paintbrush, who brought life to her world. A warm, wet cloth touched her cheek as Hamish bathed her face and temples with tender sweeps. Soundless tears fell from eyes that felt as if they had been scrubbed with sand. Violet tried to focus on her surroundings and the sound of Hamish's voice, but her head was throbbing with every constricted beat of her heart. A heavy dizziness began to drag her further away.

Chapter 17

A menacing quiet hung in the air as Gabriel stepped out of his carriage. Not even the chickens made a sound. Goats huddled at the far end of the paddock, geese beneath the repurposed wagon. Despite his exhaustion, Gabriel was instantly alert.

"Violet?" No answer. "Zach?" The hairs on the back of his neck stood at attention as he strode to the front door. Knocking once, he turned the handle. The living room was empty, but the bedroom door was cracked. He walked to the door and opened it further. Hamish sat on the floor, his legs outstretched and his back against the wall beside the bed, staring dazedly at a beam of light that fell across the floor. Piles of blankets covered Violet with only the top of her head peeking out from beneath.

Gabriel paced the room looking for Zach, even as he knew that he would not find him there. Redirecting his attention to Violet, he advanced to her bedside, steadying himself against the fear that knotted in his gut. His open hand hovered over the blanket.

"Don't," Hamish hissed. "She just fell asleep and the day has been hell." Satisfied that her rest would not be disturbed, Hamish's head lolled back against the wall. "They came this morning before I arrived, took Zach, and beat Vi to a bloody pulp."

Hamish's voice was ragged, as if he had been pulled through a gauntlet of unimaginable pain to make it to this moment. He lifted his head, and his red-rimmed gaze dragged over Violet's sleeping form. Tear tracks stained his ruddy cheeks. "My poor lass." The endearment broke in his throat.

Gabriel closed his eyes as rage and grief shredded through him. His muscles locked, lungs working to take in great gulps of air which did nothing to cool the hellfire searing inside him. He opened his eyes and searched for the tell-tale rise and fall of her chest beneath the blanket.

"I've sent Mrs Kelly for the doctor, but it's been hours. Vi's been unconscious more than awake, and when she is awake "—Hamish looked away—"you'll wish she was asleep. I wrestled her down to her shift; most of the abrasions and bruising on her legs and shoulders look superficial, but the blows she took to her face and head must have been …" He trailed away, massive Adam's apple bobbing. "I suspect her ribs are cracked as well."

Violet moaned and rolled to her side, the blankets coming untucked and sliding to the floor.

Christ. Her body was a map of brutality, conveying a story of vicious, unrestrained fists and heavy boots. His gaze settled on her hands, split-knuckled with dried blood pressed beneath the short nails. Despite the futility of any defence, she had fought through the impossible odds, using her delicate body and tiny, ineffectual fists when no other weapon was available. Surely he had never seen anything so courageous, or so absolutely gutting.

The burning jealousy that had flooded his veins at the thought of Hamish seeing and touching her body ran cold with one glance at the ocean-blue bruising that bloomed over her temple and neck. He replaced her blankets, swallowing hard at the sight of the dried blood still clinging to her hairline and the inside of her ear. Gabriel watched the steady rhythm of her pulse and battled to reign in his own.

Where was the damned doctor? He wanted to drag the blasted man away from whatever kept him from her side. He wanted to pull her body into the safety of his own. He wanted to disassemble all the intricate pieces of this messy affectionate feeling he felt for her and cast them in such disarray that they could never be reassembled.

Beneath the covers, Violet's hand began to stir, her eyes opening into unfocused orbs of blue. "Gabriel."

His heart lurched at the soft sound of his name on her lips. Collapsing to his haunches, he reached beneath the covers with both his hands, blindly sliding across soft material and skin until he found her cold fingers. He engulfed her hand in both of his.

Abruptly, she rolled to her side and vomited at his feet.

"She's been doing a lot of that. Me brother once took a hard left to the head and spent two days casting up his accounts." Violet curled her knees to her chest with a moan.

A brisk knock sounded at the door, announcing the arrival of Doctor Higgins, who stepped into the room followed by Mrs Kelly. With a nod to Gabriel and several long strides, he was at his patient's side

Higgins had treated Nora for a series of lung ailments as a toddler. Her petrifying bouts of croup had necessitated countless late-night visits, at which time Gabriel developed a healthy respect for the doctor's competent, unflappable, and compassionate nature. Higgin's forehead scrunched, the only sign that he found the scene before him jarring.

In contrast to the methodical movements of the doctor, Mrs Kelly was a flurry of motherly activity. Her skirts rustled as she bustled from one task to the next, cleaning Violet's mess, settling the blankets about her, and boiling water for tea. Hamish planted himself in the place where Gabriel had been, Violet's small hand enveloped in his. Feeling restless and superfluous, Gabriel fell into a chair by the hearth and leaned his head back.

"Hello there, Mrs Evans." Dr Higgins' voice was a practised blend of empathy and professionalism. "Those are quite colourful bruises you have, and you've been vomiting?" Violet nodded. "Do you know what day of the week it is? And my name?" Rattling off a series of questions, he retrieved a lamp from the table and pushed up the round spectacles that perpetually slid down his hooked nose. He angled the light near her eyes and ears and then handed the lamp to Mrs Kelly. "That cut on your temple may need a stitch or two. I'll try to be gentle." Higgins moved in systematic patterns over her head and along her neck. As his fingers grazed the edge of a jagged cut, Violet whimpered. Gabriel had to clutch the seat of his chair to keep from throwing both men away from her and pulling her into his protective embrace. It was completely illogical; he needed his logic to be steadfast in this moment, but he could find none. He watched her breaths come in short, unnatural bursts, and he slowed the movement of his own lungs as if his steady rhythm could bring stability to hers.

Dr Higgins cleared his throat. "Gentleman, would you be so kind as to step outside while I continue my examination and allow my patient some modesty?" Gabriel acquiesced and rose to leave. Before going, he looked expectantly to Hamish, whose grave expression turned mulish in a way Gabriel had seen on his daughter's face countless times. It would have been amusing if he hadn't been inside out with worry. Hamish rotated the chair with a thump and planted his body back into the seat, staring at the wall without a word. Higgins gave the Scot a resigned smile. "Is that all right with you, Mrs Evans?" Higgins asked.

She must have nodded because Gabriel found himself alone outside. With all the turmoil, he had forgotten his carriage and the team remained at the ready. Thanking the driver and outriders, he sent them home to find their beds. They had travelled at a breakneck pace and were past due for a long respite. It seemed an eternity ago that he had set off for the final leg of his journey. Left alone with his thoughts, he wandered the gardens in no particular direction. The events of the day had irrevocably shifted the course of his life. He would offer for Mrs Evans tonight, but even that realisation felt insignificant beside his concern for Zach and Violet.

Something oval and black nestled amidst the carpet of lush green that swathed the ground caught his eye. Recognition set his feet in motion. Dropping to a crouch, he picked up the river stone, cold and smooth in his fingers. He squeezed his fist closed around it, and Zachariah's trusting expression materialised in his mind. Standing, he slipped the pebble into his inside coat pocket, where it rested heavily against his heart.

Hamish and Doctor Higgins joined him outside a moment later. "I'm concerned. Her pupillary response is sluggish, though she seems lucid enough. In conjunction with the blood from her ear and the swelling around her temple, I worry there's damage we cannot see. We know frustratingly little about the brain and its ability to heal from trauma. One of her ribs may be cracked but most of the bruising on her abdomen seems slight enough to heal without issue."

Higgins removed his glasses, cleaning the lenses with a handkerchief. "She needs rest and supervision. If she has any fits of seizure or confusion, or if her condition worsens in any way, call for me at once. Five days of bed rest, plenty of nourishing foods, and, if luck is on our side, she will be fit as a fiddle again. I've left some powder for the discomfort and a tea that will help her rest. I know I leave her in capable hands." Gabriel reached into his pocket to pay his fee but halted when Higgins shook his head. "Mrs Evans brought over goat's milk twice a week for months when my youngest daughter was colicky as a babe." He gave them a long solemn look and shook his head. "I will be back to check on her." He mounted his horse. "Bed rest. It won't be an easy task after the first few days." He turned and trotted away.

Hamish regarded the bag of tea in his hands. "That should be fun to wrestle down her gullet. I nominate ye for that job, Northam." When Hamish wasn't looming menacingly, Gabriel found it difficult to dislike the fellow. He had a jovial lightness to him that made other people seem to forget their troubles.

"Yes, but I have a daughter whom I haven't seen in a week. She has me trained like a spaniel to be present and engaging." Gabriel felt a stab of unease at the thought of leaving Violet, however unavoidable. "One day, when you have children of your own, you will understand."

Hamish's cheeks grew ruddy. "Not likely. But Zach has always been like me own lad. One that I could avoid when he became sticky with honey or had questions about body hair."

"I'm not looking forward to facing Nora tonight." Gabriel sighed and looked down at his boots. "Children seem to be born with the innate belief that their fathers are an unstoppable force, able to solve any problem. One of the hardest things about parenthood is knowing that there will come a day when you won't be able to live up to that expectation. Still, you can't help but fight like the devil to never prove them wrong."

Leaning against the house, Hamish nodded and crossed his arms. "We'll get him back, Northam. Violet will heal, Zach trusts that we will come for him, and Nora will never stop believing in ye, even if ye crumble a wee bit around the edges."

"You do a decent impression of a father for a man insistent that he will never sire children." A comfortable silence fell between them, a fragile sense of camaraderie forming upon their mutual devotion for the Evans family.

Gabriel looked to the heavy wooden door that separated him from Violet, then back to Hamish. "I require a brief word with Violet … privately, if I may. While I would prefer to wait until she's had a few days to recover, there are some difficult choices for Violet to make, and I want to ensure she has as long as possible to consider those options."

After a long assessing stare, Hamish nodded. "Aye. Have yer talk, Northam."

✳✳✳

Violet was propped up on pillows. Her eyes, clearer now, trailed Gabriel as he approached, but their clarity only made her distress more glaringly apparent. Her hair fell in long, tangled waves over her shoulders. Through the thin walls of the kitchen, heavy, clamouring steps and hushed whispers mingled with the sounds of slicing and stirring as Hamish and Mrs Kelly prepared the evening meal.

Gabriel reached for the small silver-plated brush that sat on her nightstand and shifted his weight from one foot to the other. There was too much to say and emotion stuck in his throat, rendering the already complicated conversation impossible. He ran the bristles back and forth across his palm, watching as they gave and bent with the gentle pressure.

"Nora's curls have always been a miserable struggle. I've grown quite adept at detangling. May I?"

Violet nodded, some of the pink returning to her cheeks.

Watching her closely for any signs of discomfort, he slid the pillows to the floor and gently tucked his large body behind her back, one knee bent. He gathered the errant strands that had fallen forward and slid them into the silky mass of hair cascading down her back. Working in slow, careful strokes, he searched for a place to begin.

"Violet. While I was in London, I obtained a special licence." Having begun, the remainder tumbled out with greater ease, like wind rushing through an open door. "I intended it as a last resort, but if Zachariah becomes my stepson, he will be beyond Moorefield's reach. No court would ever grant a baron grandfather custody over seeing him raised by a duke."

He paused, waiting for the seeds he had planted in her mind to take root. The teeth of the brush found a tangle, which he expertly worked free. "But it's not the only option available to you. Moorefield has made enemies of some powerful people recently by withholding information from his partners in a shipping venture. In addition, I have bought up a great number of his vowels from outstanding debts. We may still have enough coercive power over him with the information I have gathered, but our marriage would be the most expedient and certain means of seeing Zach's safe return." A quick shiver coursed through Violet, but she remained silent.

Grateful for something useful to do, Gabriel pulled the blankets more securely around her, feeling more bashful and ridiculous with every passing word. "I am very fond of you, Violet." He slowed in his brushing. "And while I abhor that Moorefield's actions would coerce you into marriage, I don't believe our union would be a bad one. We have some obstacles … I am still in love with my wife." He lowered his voice. "And I question whether your friendship with Hamish could grow into more. But I believe if we take things slowly, allowing time to heal us as we grow together organically, our marriage of expediency may blossom into more." The silence of the room caused the rhythmic stroking of the brush to feel unnaturally loud in his ears. "And this must be the most awkward, blundering marriage proposal in history," he added beneath his breath.

"Yes." The brush stopped.

"Yes, you will marry me, or yes, I'm horribly awkward?"

"Both."

Laying the brush on his knee, he separated the strands and began plaiting her hair into one long rope. His whirling thoughts were incongruous with the methodical rhythm and familiar pattern of his fingers. Gabriel secured the end and allowed his hands to drop to her slight shoulders. Lowering his forehead to rest on the crown of her head, he sighed. Not seeing her face made all the words easier.

"I'm so sorry I wasn't here to keep you and Zach safe. I'm sorry for the agony you are suffering, both on the outside and within." He made no attempt to hide his despair and regret. "I'm sorry you have to accept my title without holding my heart. But I do care for you … and for Zach. I will devote myself to being a good husband and stepfather." He kissed the hair where his forehead had been resting and stood, helping to rearrange the pillows. Violet's movements were stiff and mechanical, her jaw set. Whether from pain or the prospect of marriage, he did not know.

"It's late. You need your sleep, and Nora is no doubt ready to send out a search party for me. I'll return as soon as I am able in the morning. Try to rest." Tucking her blankets around her one last time, he made his way out the door and home.

***

Hamish returned to Violet's side the moment the front door closed. Unwilling to broach a complicated conversation, she feigned sleep, which did nothing to deter him as he lowered into the chair beside her.

"I know ye'r awake, lass. No point in faking. I also heard Northam offering marriage."

She opened her eyes and stared at the ceiling above, studying a long crack in the plaster shaped like an alligator's snout.

"Are ye all right, love?" he whispered, shifting onto the corner of the bed, one hand resting warm and heavy on her leg.

"I've tried to tell myself it's not the same at all. That he might, one day, come to love me." Back and forth she traced the line of the reptile's nose with her eyes. "That we might be happy. But God, Hamish, it feels the same. It feels hopeless. Another imitation of a dream. And I don't mean to sound selfish or ungrateful—"

"No lass, don't even think it. It's not the same. You'll see. I recognize the look in his eyes when they settle on ye. There is a softness there, and interest. A spark that has the potential to blaze into the kind of marriage ye deserve. The kind of love ye have always deserved. Don't fret Vi, I am happy for ye."

"Oh, Hamish …"

"Move over so I can cuddle ye." She scooted to the side and made space for his familiar form to rest beside hers. Wrapping an arm around her shoulders, he pulled her close, mindful of her many wounds. Violet snuggled her head into the solid planes of his chest and sighed. Hamish had always been a safe space to land, and she loved him for making this all feel more like a choice to be made rather than another moment where survival would dictate the course of her life.

170

Laura Linn

Chapter 18

Nora was still awake when Gabriel reached the nursery. He knelt to accept the crush of her hug. Dropping a kiss on each cheek, he allowed himself to be soothed by her enthusiastic adoration.

"Poppet, there is something I need to speak with you about." Gabriel turned to her, his face communicating the seriousness of the conversation that lay ahead. Nora stilled.

"Zach's grandfather came to take him while I was away."

"No!" Ten crescent-shaped nails dug into the muscle of his shoulders. "You don't understand. They were terrible to him there. It will kill him! We have to get him now, Papa! We have to do something!" She writhed in his arms even as she clung to him, as if her body couldn't decide if it wanted to absorb into him or flee.

"I know, sweetheart. We are going to get him back and he is going to live here with us, he and Mrs Evans. We will keep them both safe so no one will ever hurt them again." She stilled in his arms and wiped her wet sticky nose against his shirt.

"Live here? That's allowed?" Innocent eyes looked up at him through a haze of tears and confusion.

"It's allowed if Mrs Evans is my wife."

Her expression plunged from confusion to incredulity, then settled on something akin to fury.

"No." Her face scrunched up as she planted both hands on his chest and shoved him away. He let her go and settled cross-legged on the plush, pink-and-cream rug that sat by the foot of her bed, tugging idly at the fringes.

He kept his voice low and placating. "You like Mrs Evans, and she likes you. Your mama will still be your mama, but this is how we get Zach home safely." He could tell that the reintroduction of Zach's dire situation to the conversation had shifted Nora's perspective once again.

"And this is the *only* way?" She crossed her arms, her lower lip forming into a pout.

"I love your mama. No one could ever replace her in my heart … or in yours. But Mrs Evans and Zach need us now too. And you'll have a brother."

"Where will she sleep?"

Oh God, please don't make me have this conversation with my daughter now. "In a bed." *Lord, I will do anything if you only make her accept that answer. I will rebuild the parish steeple. I'll bid on every poorly-stitched quilt at the women's auxiliary auction. Please …*

"*Whose* bed?" She forced the question through gritted teeth.

He sighed, reconsidering his pledge to the church's roof fund. "Poppet, there are certain obligations for a duke and duchess to provide heirs … male heirs. But for the foreseeable future …" He cleared his throat awkwardly, fighting the blush that had heated his cheeks. "For now, my role will be that of a friend and protector, and Mrs Evans will be in the duchess's suite."

She seemed to accept this answer and gave a curt nod. "Will she sew a pair of trousers for me?"

***

The following morning, Gabriel rescheduled meetings with his land agent and secretary, attending to only the most time-sensitive paperwork that awaited him before rushing out the door. Violet slept for long hours while Gabriel and Hamish chatted amiably over hands of cards and Nora played with the newest wave of baby goats. While Violet's bruises still looked tender and angry, she seemed more alert and less frantic about Zach now that a plan was in place.

173

Gabriel knocked once on her door, then entered. "I've come with your tea. Now be a good patient and comply, or I will set Mrs Kelly on you."

She made a disgusted face. He found it adorable.

Removing his coat, he folded it neatly across the back of a chair and perched himself on the edge of the bed. Mrs Kelly had helped her change into a clean, white, high-necked nightgown that did nothing to hide the outline of her alluring curves, the tips of her nipples pressing into the supple fabric. Gabriel's eyes commenced a brief but hungry expedition of those two shy peaks before mentally chastising himself and tucking her blankets higher. "Lean forward." He urged her closer with one arm as he reached to rearrange her pillows with the other. "Slowly there, sweetheart. That's the way. Now just rest against me; this will only take a moment." Two insignificant layers of finely-woven fabric were all that separated the electrified nerves of his skin from hers. He was utterly disgusted at his undisciplined mind, like an untried youth's rather than a mature, experienced man's. *They are nipples, Gabriel. You've seen them before.*

Yes, but not those nipples, his lower anatomy argued mulishly.

Violet's groan of discomfort promptly halted his baser thoughts. Redoubling his efforts and his focus, he gently eased her back onto the pillows.

"That's done. Now time for your tea, little lamb," he cajoled.

"You are enjoying this far too much." *Oh, she had no idea the level of sweet torture.*

"In four days, you will promise to obey me for as long as we both shall live. Start now. Drink."

She took a small, assessing sip, then coughed and gagged.

"Oh, it's terrible! I can't drink this!" She thrust out her cup to the extent of her reach, as if even its proximity to her lips was unacceptable.

Gabriel laughed at her extreme reaction to the bitter brew, like that of a sullen toddler who refused to eat peas, deeming them inedible after touching a single one to the tip of her tongue.

"Oh, give me that. It can't be *that* bad." He took the cup from her hand with mock annoyance and swallowed a long flaunting gulp. His chest lurched as pungent bile bubbled up his oesophagus. "I stand corrected, madam, it is *exactly* that bad," he said through coughs and sputters.

She hid her smile behind her hands.

"Since getting better isn't nearly enough motivation to drink that pig swill, how about we make the deed a little less unsavoury with a game of sorts." He glanced thoughtfully into the contents of the cup, then handed it back to Violet. "We are very soon to be husband and wife, and I would wish for you to be comfortable …" He looked away, then back again, "That is to say, I'm sure you have questions. Questions about me and what our life together will look like. I will answer one question—any question—for every sip you take."

She considered, made a resigned face, then nodded. He watched her expectantly while she took a tentative sip.

"That's a good girl," he praised.

Gabriel took a breath, steadying himself to be laid bare, picked clean like a carcass by scavenger birds.

"What's your middle name?"

The breath he had been holding escaped in a whoosh, and he grinned. "*Any* question, and that's what you choose? I was named Gabriel Nicholas Milburn Anson. I would have given you that for free!"

"All right then." Apparently, she took his remark as a challenge, a little frown of concentration forming between her brows as she suffered another choking gulp.

"How did you meet Emma?"

He looked down at his knees and rubbed his palms against the buttery soft material of his trousers. "She was having a picnic outside the grounds of Cambridge my second year. I was setting off a rudimentary model rocket with friends, and she was eating strawberries, reclining in the sun. I became so distracted by her that I burned my hand with the liquid propellant, and she rushed over to offer water from her flask. I was immediately smitten."

Another sip.

"What kind of timeline …" Spots of colour bloomed at the curve of her cheekbones. She began again. "For heirs. What kind of timeline did you have in mind? I'm not a *young* woman, I realise, but I'm just not certain—"

Gabriel laid his hand on her blanket-covered knee, and her words trailed away. "I have no desire to press either of us into more than whatever we find mutually agreeable. A year? Six months? I don't know, Violet." His hand tightened infinitesimally on her leg. "I won't lie and say I am not attracted to you. But I'm not a beast. Nor am I a lad without an ounce of self-control." *Unless your nipples are on display, apparently.*

She watched him over the cup as she took a long swallow. It felt absurdly intimate the way she drained a mouthful of that hot liquid, her heavy-lidded gaze seared to his as her throat worked. Gabriel shifted and found an interesting picture on the wall to study.

"Do you have room on your staff for Mrs Kelly?"

Gabriel felt some of the tension leave his spine at the reprieve from complicated questions. "Yes, of course. My staff is extensive, but I'm certain we can find placement in whatever capacity she desires." There was a long pause as she fiddled with the handle of the teacup.

He had no idea what this next question would be, but he could say with absolute certainty that it would be a more intrusive subject than his household staff. Violet's chin lowered and her arms wrapped around herself, giving the impression of a kitten tucking into a ball to avoid the rain. Suddenly, he didn't care how uncomfortable the question, he simply wanted to put her at ease. To soothe away those worry lines and restore her confident smile.

"There is nothing you cannot ask me, Violet."

Her uneasy gaze grappled with his reassuring one for a tense moment before she nodded. "At the beach. Did you want to kiss me?"

Christ! Except that.

Gabriel's insides twisted as he stared into the cornflower blue of her eyes. Reaching for her cup, he noticed that it was empty. He could tease, make light of her attempt to pilfer extra answers and cheat the game. But there was bravery in that question, and seeing her summon the courage to ask it felt akin to watching someone inch, with tiny shuffling steps, to the edge of a precipice and look down. She was nervous and self-conscious, and he would accept his discomfort if it lessened hers.

No, evasion was not an option.

Gabriel set the cup on the table and took her hand in both of his.

"Did I want to kiss you at the beach?" Raising her hand, he tipped her palm to his mouth and kissed the soft centre. "On the beach." His lips lingered, brushing her skin as he continued to speak. "By the goat fence." His bravery fled, eyelashes drifting closed against the sight of her parted lips and the sensation of her soft skin pressed into his hand. "Right now." Gabriel's heart thrashed against his ribcage. What he had intended as a reassuring declaration had become a flare of unguarded intimacy. Lowering her hand to the counterpane, Gabriel opened his eyes and stood. "I am going to see about your lunch." He turned and walked away before he could fillet himself open any wider.

***

The following day was a disaster from the start. Less than a second after entering, Gabriel realised he had stepped into a hornet's nest.

"I need a bath. Water and a cloth will no longer do. I require actual, honest-to-goodness soap that lathers. I need to wash my hair. I need—"

Hamish loomed with stony-faced patience, but Gabriel could see a blood vessel begin to pulse in his temple. He sliced through her ranting, enunciating through gritted teeth. "What ye *need* is to stay in that bloody bed until the doctor tells ye it's safe. Last time I carried ye to the privy at yer insistence ye nearly fainted. I'll not have ye drown."

She literally growled at him, throwing her hands up into the air. "I could not possibly drown in six inches of water. You're being ridiculous."

"That's true. Ye cannae. Because ye aren't getting in that blasted death trap," he yelled, white-knuckled fists on his hips.

"For heaven's sake, Hamish. I'm starting to smell. I'm offending myself!"

He stomped across the room to her bed, shoved his nose into her neck, and took a long audible inhalation. "Ye smell like a daffodil, now stop yer bloody arguing, woman."

Violet closed her eyes, presumably praying for the patience not to throw something at Hamish, then opened them, visibly calmer. "Gabriel." She turned her gaze, soft and imploring, on him. "Tell him I need a bath."

Gabriel's eyebrows stretched to his hairline. "Oh no. I was a happily married man for thirteen years and I have a daughter. I'm not an idiot."

Her face fell.

Concluding that a more tender approach was required, he closed the space between them and reached for her hand. Drawing small circles with his thumb, he coaxed away some of her stubborn frown lines. "Sweetheart. We just don't want to see you hurt. Is it so bad to smell like a goat for a few short days to ensure your recovery?"

"See! He thinks I smell like a goat!" She wrenched her hand away, pulled the covers up over her head, and groaned.

Well, maybe that wasn't quite tender. He chuckled despite himself.

"How did you stay happily married for thirteen years?" Hamish muttered.

With a burst of determination, she threw back the covers. "If you won't help me, I will do it myself." Both men moved to intercept her at once.

Narrowing her eyes, she prepared to stand.

Gabriel settled her immediately back to the comfort of her bed with a defeated sigh.

"Hamish. Put water on to boil. I'll fetch the hip bath." Ignoring Violet's look of smug satisfaction, he set about to complete his task, then returned to Hamish who was in the kitchen waiting for the water to heat. He met Gabriel with a glare that straddled the line between accusatory and resigned. "Mrs Kelly is visiting her sister on her day off. Vi's gonna need help. She may be stubborn as an arse, but she's weak as a kitten."

Gabriel glanced at the closed door where Violet was no doubt growing impatient. "You've known her longer. She's more comfortable with you." The minute the words were out of his mouth, he wanted to find them, haul them back, and stuff every one of them back into his idiot mouth. As uncomfortable as this would be for him, the thought of Hamish helping her undress, standing twelve inches from his wet, soapy fiancée made him want to gouge out both the man's eyes.

"Oh no. Ye'r the one that buckled under the pressure of a wee temperamental lass, and ye'r marrying her. Ye get to make sure she doesna die." Hamish put his hands on his hips, a knowing smirk sliding across his face.

Once the tub was filled, Hamish stepped into the kitchen and closed the door behind him with a click.

Clinical. You can be clinical about this. Artists draw naked women without embarrassing themselves. You can handle this. He adopted his most ducal tone. "I'm going to keep my eyes closed or averted as much as I can, Violet. You just make sure I don't bump into anything"

She gasped. "No, you can't stay in here." Her voice dropped to a whisper as if to impart a secret. "I'll be naked."

"Yes. That's generally the way of it. I stay or no bath." For a moment, he thought she might abort the mission and remain abed, and he couldn't decide if the flip-flopping of his stomach was a result of disappointment or relief, but before he had time to consider further, the blanket slid away and she turned to place her feet on the floor.

"Nice and slow then, let me do the work for you."

Reaching beneath her arms, he eased her to stand, pulling her flush against his body as she winced and threw a hand across her middle to protect her ribs. They remained still for a moment as she adjusted to the discomfort, the length of her pressed against his chest and abdomen. *Clinical! Be clinical!*

"Ready?" Gabriel murmured.

"Don't peek."

She turned, and a pink blush crept like a sunrise up the nape of her slender neck. The tub was close enough that once undressed, she could travel the few steps on her own. Climbing in would be easier than out. Gabriel took a deep steadying breath and reached to unhook the row of tiny pearl buttons. *One million tiny buttons.* A teasing wisp of a sleeve slid down, exposing her shoulder, and she quickly moved to right it. Considering that he was about to remove the entire nightgown, her shy response to three inches of exposed skin struck him as oddly endearing.

Closing his eyes, he reached down to grasp the hem and, with one swift movement, slid the garment up and over her head. He listened to the careful patter of her feet across the wooden planks followed by a slosh of water and a groan of pleasure. *Oh, God.* He bit back his own guttural response.

"Are you all right?" Turning back to the tub he moved a chair close but angled it away.

"I'm better than all right. This is heavenly." Gabriel smirked at her choice of adverbs as he had fallen into the polar opposite location … a sweet sort of hell.

Gabriel waited for the minutes to pass, trying to ignore the sounds of soft sighs and trickling water. His teeth ground together with the Sisyphean effort *not* to consider the exact path of those meandering rivulets, but his body had become too familiar with hers. His hands knew the shape of her, and his vivid imagination was all too happy to invent what remained unfamiliar, the soap gliding over her heat-flushed skin and a light smattering of bubbles clinging to the tips of her breasts.

He shifted uncomfortably and adjusted the placket of his trousers. It had been nearly two years since Emma had passed, and while there had been plenty of offers from willing widows, he couldn't bring himself to touch another woman. But he was marrying Violet, and any hot-blooded man would react to the sensual assault of a naked Violet twelve inches away. *This was the longest bath in the history of baths.*

A violent splash of water and a squeak galvanised Gabriel into motion without the slightest regard for modesty.

"Gabriel!" Unable to decide what to cover first, Violet's hands sprung to her face first, then between her legs, eventually settling on her breasts while she crossed one leg over the other. Her eyelids slammed shut. Gabriel's body had catapulted into a state of panic at the sound of her distress. Even after raking his eyes over her from head to toe then back again, and confirming that she had not caused herself further harm, he struggled to calm his skin-prickling alertness.

"For Christ's sake, Violet, I can still see you with your eyes closed. Are you well?" he groused. "I nearly jumped out of my skin when you yelped." Hastily grabbing a bath sheet, he spread the length across the surface of the water. Her eyes remained shut with comical vehemence and sympathy for her modesty had begun to rub away at the brusque edges caused by worry. Gabriel lowered to his haunches.

"Sweetheart, I'm thirty-seven years old. I have seen naked women before." Technically, only within the last thirty seconds could he claim to have seen naked *women* in the plural, but he suspected that if Violet knew that, it would make this situation more awkward. It was better if she presumed him to be some devil-may-care rake who'd seen as many naked breasts as scrambled eggs in his salad days. He could be nonchalant about this; she didn't need to know that he had skipped the entire salad course. Besides, thirteen years of happy monogamy *had* offered him as many opportunities with the naked female form as any rogue. "Besides, with all those bubbles I could scarcely see a thing. Have you even any breasts under there?" He forced lightness into his tone. *She did. And they were spectacular.*

Violet opened first one eye, then the other, sinking as deep as the small tub would allow. "I was rinsing the soap from my hair and my ribs—"

He nodded succinctly. "Lean forward then." He kept his movements methodical, his touch gentle but impassive. Tilting her chin up with the tips of his fingers, he used a cup to pour water over her long tresses until it ran clear. After fetching a dry bath towel, he forced his body to relax and waited. "Are you ready?"

She gave a quick nod.

Looking away, Gabriel groped for the space beneath her arms to lift, his fingers making contact with dripping skin that was decidedly not the consistency of an arm.

She inhaled sharply but said nothing. Once Violet was safely out of the tub, he turned while she dried and slid on a fresh gown.

"Would you do the buttons?" she asked.

Gabriel was embarrassingly aroused and clinging to the unlikely chance that she hadn't noticed, which was ridiculous. Any married woman, presently or previously, couldn't miss the massive erection he was sporting. He slid the buttons through their maddening eyelets as quickly as his fumbling fingers could manage, and turned to look out the window.

Watching the geese splash in an old tin wash tub, his mind travelled to the last time he had been so blundering and awkward at the prospect of his hands on a woman's body. Emma had been his first, and on their wedding night they had both been clueless, unrefined, and desperate not to leave the other disappointed. His brother, who was two years his junior but twenty times more experienced with women, had needled him relentlessly to find an experienced courtesan before the merry event, but Gabriel stubbornly insisted that he would have no one but Emma.

So lost was he to Emma's touch that his untried cock had raced to the finish line before he had even entered her body. He had wanted to dig a hole and bury himself for the waves of shame that washed over him. But Emma—perfectly lovely Emma—had soothed his pride, and, after a distracting few rounds of cards, they had stumbled their way through a brief coupling.

Moments ago, running his fingers through Violet's soapy hair, his jaw falling slack at the sight of the translucent bubbles that spilled down and disappeared between her breasts, his body had rioted with need every bit as strong as that first coupling with Emma. And yet, here he was, minutes later, remembering his wedding night.

His shoulders drooped. Was this what the coming months and years would bring him? A constant tug of war between lust and his stubborn heart, where there could be no winner. Where memories of Emma would crest and spill over like salty waves into every moment with Violet.

For a moment, he allowed himself to consider what it would feel like if he could find peace in her arms. What *she* would feel like—look like—spread out before him like a banquet when he didn't have to pretend his gaze was occluded by an inconsequential inch of frothy bubbles. Returning his mind to the present, he counted goats.

Chapter 19

On day three, Gabriel had estate business to attend to that kept him away from Violet, and day four was blissfully uneventful. By the fifth day, Violet was churlish and grumpy from confinement, the need to see Zach home and safe pushing her into a state of near-frantic desperation.

Gabriel couldn't imagine the strain she was under without his stomach roiling. Had someone taken Nora, they would have a devil of a time keeping him abed, even if his life depended on it, as was the case with Violet.

"I don't think the doctor meant for me to be chained to the bed. I only want to stretch my legs."

Gabriel looked for support from Hamish but he was nowhere in sight.

"Oddly, I think that is precisely what Doctor Higgins meant when he said 'keep her in bed and let her have plenty of rest and nourishment.' It's difficult to misinterpret such a plainly made statement."

Violet's eyes narrowed, then took on the tell-tale shimmer of imminent tears.

"One more day, Violet," Gabriel murmured. "Tomorrow, the doctor will reassess you, and we will be married and on our way to Zach. Soon he will be back in the safety of your arms, and all this will be in the past."

A tear trickled down her cheek and she turned her face away. Gabriel lowered himself onto the bed, his hands clenched in his lap. "You have been impossibly strong, but you don't have to be."

Stretching out his long legs on top of the floral quilt beside her, he laid back, gently sliding an arm beneath her neck, urging her to tuck into his chest. She remained rigid for a heartbeat, then curved her body into his, releasing hot, silent tears. "There, Love. Have a good cry. That's it." As if she'd been waiting for leave to do so, Violet's restrained trickles became deep heaving sobs before eventually tapering to soft sniffles. Temporarily emptied of her grief, she fell into an exhausted sleep.

Gabriel lay unmoving, watching her eyelashes flutter in dreams and allowing himself to enjoy the feeling of her soft curves tucked tightly against him while she filled the room with quiet, rhythmic snores. In sleep, she had thrown one arm around his abdomen, and he played lightly with the tips of her fingers. It had been so long since a woman had wrapped herself around him in any capacity, and he felt a primal sort of contentment from being the source of Violet's relaxed body.

So many of his feelings these days were enormously conflicting, and he found himself exhausted under the weight of his own shifting emotions. A part of him hoped that it wouldn't take long for their marriage to progress to intimacy. After the days of close contact, it would be difficult to revert to polite distance. He just wanted to stay here, in her sweet, trusting arms, where everything felt safe and uncomplicated so long as she remained lost to faraway dreams.

The front door closed and he heard Hamish's distinctive, heavy gait in the kitchen alongside his daughter's chattering. Careful not to wake her, he dropped a kiss to Violet's forehead and slid out of her lax embrace.

"Good afternoon, Nora. Hamish, where have you been off to?" Gabriel inquired.

"Hiding from Violet. She's in a mood today." While he'd made the same remark in his own mind hours before, it chafed to hear the words from Hamish. Like rubbing a dog in the opposite direction of its sleek hair growth. Gabriel's spine straightened, his expression turning hard.

"She has every right to be as grumpy and churlish as she feels at the moment. It's an impossible request to expect Violet to be sedentary under the best circumstances, and these are very nearly the worst."

Hamish smiled.

"Aye, I think you'll do quite well as her husband, Northam." His words were genuine. Emphatic. Approving. Gabriel felt some of his offended haughtiness slip away under Hamish's satisfied gaze.

"Thank you, Hamish." He cleared the emotion from his throat. "I have an idea …"

By the time Violet awoke, they had gathered six baby goats into the house. Two were asleep on her bed, one was perched in the middle of the kitchen table, and another nosed curiously at Gabriel's throat, balancing atop his lap. One particularly mischievous fluffball was trying to chew the cover off a book as the last pranced about the kitchen, nipping at the hem of Mrs Kelly's skirt. Mrs Kelly assessed the disaster with a forlorn frown while aggressively slicing a loaf of bread.

"Oh, my goatlings!" Violet exclaimed from the bedroom with obvious delight.

"We picked ye some flowers too but Apple Core ate them already," Hamish said as he ruffled the silky head of a sleeping goat.

"I know it's been difficult being cooped up, so we brought the outside in." Gabriel hadn't felt so bashful since he was in short-pants. Until that moment, he hadn't realised how desperate he had been to restore the happy ring to her voice.

"Thank you. It's perfect."

And so was she.

"I think I will knit a little sweater for one!"

"Only ye would waste good wool to cover an animal that's already wearing a coat," Hamish said through the twitch of a smile.

The remainder of the day was peaceful, quiet but for the soft clicks of Violet's knitting needles and her occasional squeals of delight about how adorable Apple Core would look. Nora had joined Violet on the bed with a set of knitting needles. Every few minutes, Nora would drop a stitch and groan. Each time, Violet patiently set aside her work and repaired the damage with gentle encouragement. After dinner, however, Violet's restlessness began to return.

"Shall I read to you from *Frankenstein*?" Gabriel suggested. He pulled a chair close and casually propped one stockinged foot on the bed. "Where were we? Oh yes: 'As I stood at the door, on a sudden I beheld a stream of fire issue from an old and beautiful oak which stood about twenty yards from our house; and so soon as the dazzling light vanished, the oak had disappeared, and nothing remained but a blasted stump. When we visited it the next morning, we found the tree shattered in a singular manner. It was not splintered by the shock, but entirely reduced to thin ribbons of wood. I never beheld anything so utterly destroyed'." He paused when he noticed the pained expression she wore.

"Violet?"

"What if this time, he's too broken? When he came to us, it took weeks for him to heal physically, and months before he would respond with anything but fear. The things they did to him, Gabriel, it was torture."

He was helpless to assuage her fears. Reassuring her would be unfair, even if he could find the words, when her concerns may very well be justly founded. "Tomorrow all the unknowns will vanish. We'll do everything in our power to drive out whatever fear remains, and together we will love him through the damage that has been done."

Gabriel did not reach out and Violet made no move to beckon him closer, but her eyes, soft and grateful, met and held his. Her shoulders relaxed and her hands unclenched, as if his words were made of more than just letters and syllables meshed together. As if they had the power to soothe her anxiety and shelter her heart. It made him feel indispensable, relevant and vital to her life, like a child's favourite blanket that held the ability to transform the world into a less overwhelming place. He had almost forgotten the warmth of that feeling. To be that person for Violet, it astounded and humbled him. It left him hungry for more.

He lifted the book and continued to read, and when her breathing became slow and regular, he skipped ahead several pages.

"I'm not sleeping," she mumbled through sluggish, drowsy lips. "And you are doing that thing parents do when they think their children are no longer listening … leaping to the last paragraph of the chapter."

He smiled at her over the cover of the book. "You caught me."

She shifted, "I can't sleep. Every time my mind starts to drift, my imagination conjures every nightmare scenario possible for Zach."

"Perhaps Frankenstein is a little too engaging for a bedtime story. When Nora is restless, I let her curl up in my bed while I play the pianoforte."

"You play the pianoforte? And you have one in your bedroom?"

"Yes, now hush. You're supposed to be getting sleepy. Tomorrow will be tiring, and your body needs the rest." Gabriel walked to the pile of scattered books, immediately finding what he sought and returning to his post by Violet's bed. He shuffled through the pages until he landed upon the desired verse … a tragic ending, but the middle stanzas would do. Glancing up, he smiled, then returned his attention to the page and read aloud:

> I met a lady in the meads,
> Full beautiful—a faery's child,
> Her hair was long, her foot was light,
> And her eyes were wild.
>
> I made a garland for her head,
> And bracelets too, and fragrant zone;

189

She looked at me as she did love,
And made sweet moan

I set her on my pacing steed,
And nothing else saw all day long,
For sidelong would she bend, and sing
A faery's song.

***

As weddings went, this one was rushed and unremarkable … if you ignored the noteworthy fact that the groom was a handsome, sought-after duke marrying an unknown woman from the country without pomp, circumstance, or even an adequate number of witnesses before the last-minute arrival of the duke's valet.

Hamish was there, of course, bright and beaming like the summer sun.

All Violet could think about was getting past the vows and into the carriage so that Zachariah could be retrieved. Later, she would think about the fact that she was marrying a man who didn't and possibly couldn't love her … again. And that again, she had fallen into marriage because of some life-threatening circumstance. But not now. Gabriel's attentive and gentle demeanour through her recovery had begun to chafe at her conscience. With his unswerving chivalry, he had prioritised Zach's needs over his own, and he was too fair-natured to show even a flicker of resentment.

Violet had always considered brown eyes to be mundane and common, but his brought to mind all the shades of October melted together. Like crisp amber leaves and roasted chestnuts, his eyes were warm and compelling and fixed on her as if she was the only person in the world.

"With my body, I thee worship, and with all my worldly goods, I thee endow." He squeezed her hands in his, and, in a whirl of words, they became man and wife. A gratingly enthusiastic Keene herded them from the picturesque village chapel to the waiting carriage, their trunks already loaded.

Hamish walked just behind them and paused as a footman opened the door. Violet threw her arms around him and he leaned close to whisper into her ear. "Oh, how I love ye, Vi. It's going to be all right. Better than all right." Hamish stepped away and took a hold of Gabriel's hand in what looked to be a crushing grip. "Take good care of her, Northam." Then his grip gentled and he smiled. "Off with ye now. Bring our boy home."

Gabriel helped her into the carriage, then chose the seat beside her. She had grown so accustomed to seeing him in his shirt sleeves over the previous week that she had almost forgotten how elegant he looked wrapped in his satin-lined wool topcoat and his sleek waistcoats with their dashing designs. She wanted to trace the silver embroidery with the tip of her finger. His only ornament was a simple, black opal stick pin tucked smartly into his crisply-tied cravat. He was magnificent in his simplicity, every inch the untouchable duke. She suddenly felt awkward next to him, as if she had accidentally stepped into the wrong carriage and he was too kind to just drop her off on the street.

Violet fiddled with the new ring that adorned her second finger, a clear, immaculately-cut sapphire bracketed by a pair of iridescent pearls.

"If you don't like it you may choose another. The blue reminded me of your eyes, although it lacks their warmth—"

"No," she stopped him. "I love it. It's beautiful."

His posture relaxed slightly. "I'm glad you like it."

"How long will it take us to reach Southampton?"

He tossed his top hat to the opposite seat and stretched out his legs. "We will ride most of the day and stop over in Dorset for the night. We'll arrive before lunch tomorrow, at which time I will seek an immediate audience with the local magistrate. By the morning after, we should be on the road home with Zachariah."

His confidence assuaged the sharp edges of her anxiety, and she settled into the opulent seats of the carriage. Deftly, she untied the ribbons of her dark purple bonnet and sent it off in a flurry to join Gabriel's top hat. Immediately, she regretted the choice, acutely aware of her own unsightliness. The bruises had faded to a putrid yellowish-green, clashing with the incalculable number of freckles that dusted her face. She ran a finger across her temple self-consciously.

Mistaking the direction of her thoughts, Gabriel reached up and gently cupped her cheek, sweeping his thumb across her bruise in featherlight strokes. "Is it hurting you?"

His question was simple, almost casual, but the obvious undercurrent of concern in his tone and touch caused something warm and soft to bloom in her chest. "No. It hardly hurts at all now. Only my vanity remains wounded … and my ribs from time to time."

A smile tugged at the corners of his mouth. "You're beautiful … even adorned with skin the colour of algae."

"With such a silver tongue, how do you keep the ladies from swarming?"

"Lucky for me the droves of admirers should abate now that I will have a lovely, albeit polyphyletic, duchess at my side." His eyes scintillated with mischief.

"Duchess! Oh goodness! I know that is what happens when one marries a duke, but I really hadn't considered it until this moment. I have no idea how to be a duchess or what to do with servants to peel my potatoes and button my gowns. It seems preposterous. I garden in trousers, for heaven's sake. And what will become of my goats!"

A strangled laugh escaped Gabriel. "Easy, sweetheart. My valet is my childhood best friend. He spends as much time undermining my authority and drinking my best scotch as he does tending to his duties." Gabriel's hand slid across the seat and covered hers. "Don't worry yourself over the servants. They are so overjoyed at the prospect of a new duchess that you'll dazzle them even in your floppy brown hat and trousers. Feel free to peel as many potatoes as you like, but I intend to procure a new wardrobe for you that will require a lady's maid. As for your diabolical goats, I could fit their current paddock four times over in just my rose garden and still have extra space for ducks and chickens. Not that I have any intention of allowing them to cut loose in my rose garden." He flashed her the boyish grin she was becoming so fond of. "I am certain we can find a corner of the estate where they will thrive."

She stared at him blankly. "You make it all sound so simple. How do I fill my days?"

"It *is* simple, *Your Grace*." He kissed her hand. "Go riding. Have non-tea beverages with friends. Tinker to your heart's desire. Spend my money. Buy an actual, functioning rain slicker or continue brainstorming ridiculous alternatives. I am not an autocratic man by nature, and I have no desire to extinguish your natural vivacity. I would beg your assistance to find a suitable governess for Nora, as I've had abysmal luck in my recent attempts, but beyond that, I would simply like the pleasure of your company—often, if you can tolerate me." Colour rose on his cheeks and she was certain his ears would be red beneath the curtain of his curls. "Walks. Picnics. Chess."

Her own skin began to prickle as she realised the way his words could be interpreted … and the haste with which he had clarified. A dull ache settled in her chest. Gabriel may be attracted to her, but he did not want her company in *that* respect. He had all but said it.

Violet had always lacked the ability to hide her feelings. It was a heinous trait, often impelling her to explain feelings she wished she didn't even have. Compounded by her tendency to expel her thoughts at a speed race horses would envy, it left her stewing in embarrassment an alarming amount of the time. When she tried to redirect her attention elsewhere to disguise her clamorous emotions, her unnatural quiet attracted even more unwanted notice. Was it asking too much to be permitted to marinate in her own emotions without having to unscramble and explain them?

She shifted her attention to the window and instantly felt his concerned, analytical gaze burning into her back. His voice was soft and cajoling.

"I beg your pardon, Violet. I think that must have sounded different to your ears than what I had intended."

She shrugged her shoulders with an air of indifference. "The carriage ride is making me a bit sleepy. I think I will rest for a while." It was churlish to be hurt by something that he had always made abundantly clear, but she couldn't tamp down the childish response. She drew her hands up and held herself protectively across her chest, leaning her head against the window.

Violet knew if she spoke one single syllable now, she wouldn't be able to stop the hundreds that would heedlessly follow. This man married her to save her son. She wouldn't let her own feelings of inadequacy injure him; he hadn't meant to hurt her. You simply hear what you expect to hear, and the words "unwanted" and "undesirable" throbbed down to the very marrow of her bones.

"No. Don't do that. Seeing you withdraw is as unnatural as watching a lioness sprout a turtle shell and crawl inside." As he spoke, he turned and reached for her, tucking her petite frame against his body. Like spoons fitting together, his chin rested on the top of her head and he sighed.

"Of course I want you." The admission seemed to pull from somewhere deep in his chest. "Beyond the opposing sides of a chessboard. You are ..." his grip tightened around her as the moment stretched out. "Enchanting. Distracting. Beautiful. Compelling in a way that makes me want to know more. To *see* more. To become so lost in the magical world you weave that I merrily disregard the fundamental fact that I am just not ready. It wouldn't be fair to you to slap strips of cotton over a bleeding heart and call it healed. I want to be unbroken for you." He tightened his arms around her and she relaxed. Unsure if she was more grateful for his reassurance or for the fact that he understood without her having to bungle through an explanation.

Tipping her head up, Violet gave a quick kiss to the place where his chin curved to his neck, then settled back into his embrace. It was a mockery of a first kiss, but her lips tingled where they had touched his slightly abrasive chin.

"Thank you, Gabriel … for explaining. And for always being honest with me."

Chapter 20

Gabriel's laugh filled the confined space of the carriage. "No. You can't be serious."

"He left me no choice! I couldn't handle Nathan's chiding about how I would strain my eyes with poor lighting for one more moment. He was such a mother hen. So I waited until he was away with Hamish and scattered the entire house with as many glow worms as I could catch."

"Oh, that's famous! He must have wanted to throttle you!"

"No doubt, but he took his revenge by stocking the bathtub with live fish while I was out in the garden. He found me toiling away, covered in grime, and told me he had prepared a bath. An entire school of carp were circling about, and there was Nathan with a great big smile on his face. I tried to push him in but apparently, I am predictable. You can guess which of us ended up splashing about with the fish."

"It sounds like your marriage was filled with laughter."

She tried and subsequently failed, to keep her smile from dimming. "It was that. He was a good man."

"How did you come to marry?" he asked, crossing his ankle over one knee.

"He saved me from an unpleasant situation," she answered cryptically.

Gabriel nudged her leg with the toe of his boot. "Oh come now, Vi. I bared my soul to you and you throw me scraps that wouldn't satisfy a starving hound."

Considering how best to shuffle the conversation forward, she settled with a version of the truth. "My stepfather, John, was not a kind man." Gabriel instantly sobered and shifted upright. "I was trapped in an impossible situation with no way to escape. Nathan made a door." Gabriel leaned in slightly, reaching out to run his index finger down the slight bump in the bone of her nose.

Uncomfortable in his intense scrutiny, she answered the question before he had the chance to ask it: "Yes. John gave me this. Amongst other scars. He's dead now, and I try not to remember." The dichotomy on his face was clear—thunderous hatred and desolate sadness.

"I wish I could bring him back to life so I could kill him again for you," he said, looking away.

There had been a time when she had adored her stepfather. He took her fishing and read her books that her mother deemed too masculine—murder mysteries and war stories, books that glorified horse racing, and grand pirate adventures. She had been ten when her mother married John. Although her father had been the son of a baronet and Violet's early years had been carefree, there were long years after his death when their only focus had been obtaining necessities. Suddenly, they didn't have to ration candles and could purchase flower-scented soap that didn't cause her tender skin to rash. They ate beef again. Her stepfather had represented safety, which only made his behaviour that much more reprehensible.

Her younger brother, Samuel, was the only member of the household who seemed to notice her stepfather's shift in attention as she developed into a young lady, but at four years her junior, he was powerless to stop it. The shame and impotence he felt for her suffering melted him like honey under boiling water.

When she could take no more, she left, found Nathan at Oxford, and unravelled in his arms. They were married, and she spent every day trying to forget. Like so many cruel men, her stepfather had damaged her as much by what he had taken away from her as by the scars he left behind.

A Wildflower for a Duke

***

They arrived at The Horse and Hound at a quarter past six. Despite the relatively smooth conveyance and their regular stops to stretch, Gabriel's body felt as if it had been tied in knots from the long day's travel in a cramped conveyance. While the same aching muscles must also have plagued Violet, she appeared instantly invigorated and intrigued by her surroundings.

It was a respectable, tidy little inn connected to a public house that thrummed with excitement. A crowd of rowdy men were shouting bets and laughing amongst themselves … one was vomiting into a patch of azalea bushes. Gabriel looked about for assistance and wrapped one arm about Violet's waist to pull her closer.

"I've stopped at this inn in the past and its patrons aren't usually quite so … colourful. If this makes you uncomfortable, we can ride on a bit; there is another acceptable coaching inn about ten miles further." He looked down to gauge her comfort and smiled at her obvious curiosity.

"No. This is wonderful. What do you suppose is happening over there?" She took a step towards the crowd, but he caught her around the wrist and eased her back to his side.

"Some kind of tournament perhaps." He was interrupted when the vomiting lad, who was apparently the stable hand, greeted them with a sheepish smile.

"A bit shorthanded we are tonight." He was chipper despite the effects of his overindulgence, blue eyes twinkling beneath a well-worn brown cap. "The proprietor's at the bar if you'll be needing a room."

Gabriel nodded and ushered Violet into the taproom, which was charged with cheerful chaos. Nearly every table was packed, tankards of ale flowed freely, and the aroma of heavily seasoned venison stew tickled his nose, causing his mouth to water. Someone plunked out a merry Irish melody on a grossly out-of-tune pianoforte in the corner. Violet's toe began merrily tapping along.

"Oh! Good evening, Your Grace!" The proprietor was a boisterous fellow with deep smile lines and springy, greying hair that stood up in every direction, as if his natural energy exploded all the way to the tips. "Will you be needing a room tonight?"

"I will. We were wed only this morning, and it has been a long day of travel. Her Grace will require a hot bath, and we would like dinner brought to our room as soon as possible. Is the suite available?"

"Congratulations! Congratulations! I wish you all the happiness that my Edna and I have shared these thirty years. Unfortunately, with the tournament both our suites are in use, but we have a single available and we will bring up some of Edna's stew, fresh buttery rolls, and a helping of jam roly-poly. The custard will melt in your mouth, just you wait. I probably have a bottle of that scotch you like so much around as well! Mary will show you to your room, and I will send Harry up with your trunks."

A maid materialised, and they followed her to the adjoining building where private sitting areas and most of the rooms to rent resided. As they walked, the noise began to fade away until they reached an oak door at the end of a long corridor. The maid handed him the key and stepped to the side. "Will there be anything else, Your Grace?"

"No. Thank you, Mary." He gave the maid a brief smile before turning to unlock the door, holding it wide for Violet to proceed him. She didn't move and, instead of surveying the room, had turned her keen gaze on him, head cocked adorably to the side.

Gabriel cocked his head in the opposite direction. "Is there something you wished to say, Your Grace?" He found he enjoyed addressing her by the new honorific just to watch the subtle way it flustered her each time.

Violet glanced toward the maid who was turning the corner, then back to Gabriel. "Only that you are the most un-ducal duke I have ever met."

Gabriel stepped closer, mimicking her light-hearted grin. "Met a great many dukes, have you?"

Her chin tipped up in challenge. "Not exactly, but it's common knowledge that they are all imperious and self-important, intractable in their opinions, and loath to exist amongst the lower classes, let alone *smile* at them and address them by name. You are kind and respectful regardless of station. You, Your Grace, are downright charming."

Gabriel grinned at his shoes. "I can be imperious and intractable when the situation requires. But my uniformly courteous manners became somewhat of a habit of my youth, born of my determination to irritate my father. He was a wholly disagreeable man, setting unreasonable expectations for everyone around him and thriving on opportunities to make others feel insignificant. He viewed basic human decency as an inconvenience unworthy of his time or exertion."

They walked in, closing the door behind. "After he sent Keene and his father away to sever our friendship, I made it my primary objective to act as his exact inverse. He belittled the servants, and I would apologise to them. He threatened to evict tenants for overdue rents, and I found ways for them to barter with neighbours for the balance due. It enraged the old duke like nothing else I could have possibly devised." He shrugged. "Eventually it just became who I was, and in the process I discovered that benevolence motivates far more effectively than intimidation."

Violet tucked her arm through his and looked up, "What a remarkable man I have married." After holding her gaze for a moment, he turned his attention to the room.

It was small but acceptably clean. In his past travels, Gabriel had only ever stayed in the two-room suite, and he had planned to rest on the settee in the sitting area. Instead, the only remotely inviting furniture in their room—apart from the bed—was a pair of George Smith armchairs that looked a bit rickety. Violet hadn't moved beyond the entrance to the door. Her gaze trailed him as he surveyed the space, running his hand across the arm of the chair and then sinking into the overstuffed abomination. It was every bit as uncomfortable as it looked.

"I apologise, Violet. I should have brought along a servant to act as lady's maid so you could have the comfort of your own space. I didn't think—"

"No. It wouldn't have done to stay in separate rooms on the first night of our marriage. Titbits like that tend to find their way to the gossips. And that's not at all what I was thinking. It's only that …" She looked to the door as longingly as if it led to a room piled high with strawberry pies, then back to Gabriel.

His entire body relaxed, concern shifting to amusement. "You cannot stand to be jailed in this room with all the excitement of the tournament calling to your adventurous spirit."

She grinned her response, dimples making a full appearance.

"What are they playing? "

"It's a game called Skittles. Players compete to knock over small pins on a board by spinning a top connected to a long thread. They wrap the line around the top, then, with a quick tug, it sets loose in a whirl to knock over as many pins as possible. I used to play it with my brother, Michael, when I was a boy. If I'm not mistaken, they host a tournament here every year, though I wasn't aware of our collision course with the night's event. It's mostly an excuse to drink in excess and spend time with neighbours after a long winter packed away at home. Normally it takes place in very early spring. I'm unsure why it's occurring later this year."

"I'm really not tired, Gabriel. I could just tuck down there to watch for a few minutes while we wait for our dinner."

Crossing to her, he rested a hand on her shoulder.

"Duchesses do not tuck down into tap rooms alone," he whispered, a slight frown tugging at his mouth.

"I've only been a duchess for twelve hours! Isn't there a warming-up period, like water on a kitchen range? Duchesses may not scurry off alone to watch tournaments, but widowed goat farmers relish the activity!"

The woman was incapable of retreat, down to her adorably tenacious bones. She batted her eyes at him, and he instantly felt his resolve begin to deteriorate.

"One day into wedded bliss and I can already see you are going to be a lot of trouble, Your Grace." He submitted with a nod, smothering a smile as he offered his arm, but Violet remained still, staring as if perplexed.

"Well?" he asked. "I can't very well set you loose on a tavern full of foxed Irishmen. They couldn't possibly handle you, poor chaps." Looping her hand through his arm, she gave him the sunniest smile he had ever seen. No clouds. All beaming light and warmth.

For a time, Violet seemed satisfied to watch from the outskirts of the room, but like a bee circling wisteria in bloom, she inched closer to the activity. He inched closer to her. A cheer erupted as a robust red-headed man knocked over an impressive series of pins. Violet squealed with enthusiasm, clapping her hands with open delight. The competitor turned to Violet with a too-friendly smile. "Have a turn, darlin'. I'd be happy to show ye how."

"I'm sure you would," Gabriel mumbled under his breath. Violet shot him an exasperated look, but Gabriel's menacing stare did not wither in the slightest. "Thank you for your gracious offer but the lady would prefer to watch."

Violet bounced on her toes with unrestrained excitement. "No, she wouldn't. She definitely wouldn't. She wants to play!" Like a dog resigned to sleeping on the floor, Gabriel gave a curt nod and stepped forward with her, his eyes sending stabs of warning to anyone whose body leaned a little too close to his wife.

The Irishman handed her the top and angled himself close, as if to begin an explanation of the rules. Gabriel coolly inserted himself between the pair. "I would be happy to explain the technique. Thank you for your kind offer."

Violet moved around both men as if bored by the masculine posturing. "I think I've got the gist of it. I just pull this little cord and knock down all the pins."

The Irish bloke took a healthy step out of Gabriel's reach and answered. "Oh, it's harder than it looks, but give it a try."

"And what do I get if I knock down more than you?" The pub erupted in amused snickers.

"Well, you would win the purse for the evening, as I currently sit in the lead."

"I have no need of your money, but my husband and I would prefer to be resituated in the suite. Would whichever one of you is currently residing there care to place a private wager?"

The room quieted as a rangy brunette staggered forward, his skin liberally sprinkled with freckles that gave him the appearance of being younger than he likely was. "That's me, but what'll you give me when you lose?" A row of straight white teeth flashed into view. "How about a nice big kiss?" he slurred.

Gabriel's head shot up, his shoulders squaring, but before he could utter a word, Violet rested a light hand on his forearm, stilling him.

"How about a dance?" she countered with a flirting twirl of her finger through a tendril.

The room erupted in cheers as he nodded his agreement. "That'll do. Although I'd prefer the kiss."

Violet stepped up to the game board, stretching her arms and flexing her fists open and closed, playing to the riveted crowd. Then she deftly set the top spinning with the practised ease of an experienced player, crowing with delight as it toppled every pin save one. Shocked silence followed by deafening cheers exploded from the men who encircled her.

Gabriel threw his head back, chuckling in surprised delight. "You little imp!"

"I never said I didn't know how to play. That will teach you to underestimate me."

"You have never been at the slightest risk of being underestimated by me." He pulled her close and dropped a kiss to her temple. "I believe a change in rooms is in order, and then we will bid you gentleman goodnight. But first, I would like to dance with the victor." He glanced down to Violet, "If your ribs can tolerate the jostling." She nodded, eyes sparkling under the golden glow of the taproom lanterns.

"Good, then. Will you do me the great honour of joining me in this dance?" He bowed low, as if they weren't in an overcrowded public house surrounded by drunken Irishmen and other assorted locals, and she curtsied with a giggle in response. Stomps and claps shook the room as other partners came together to join them in a rousing country dance.

The spirited melody reverberated through the room, but his focus narrowed to Violet. The revelry and clattering, the pungent medley of rich food and closely packed men in tight quarters … they all fizzled from his awareness until all that remained was his wife. Her brilliant smile. The expressive little lines that crinkled the corners of her eyes as she twirled around him with an effervescence that would have had her thrown bodily from Almack's. She was enchanting. Her musical laugh and unchecked delight stripped away the reserve that had been pounded into him since birth, and he matched her enthusiasm while performing the intricate steps with ease.

As the last notes faded away, one of his hands remained clasped with hers while the other gently caressed the line of her hip. Violet remained still and pliant in his arms, her cheeks pink with exertion.

"Claim your kiss, Duke!" the locals chanted, joined by whoops of mischief and whistled cat calls from all around them. His gaze dropped to her soft, inviting lips then returned to her eyes.

"Sorry, lads! You'll have to find your entertainment elsewhere. I don't perform for an audience … and I need to get my duchess to bed." The mention of bed only further encouraged the intoxicated crowd, but he ignored them, squeezing her hand and then tugging her close to loop an arm around her waist.

Chapter 21

Settled into the larger, more comfortable rooms, they ate a leisurely dinner. Once the fastenings of her gown were loosened, Violet skittered off bashfully to the sitting room to enjoy a hot bath. Gabriel managed to wrestle out of his dreaded boots, then stripped down to his shirt sleeves and trousers. He found an extra blanket and set it to the side to take with him to the settee after Violet finished bathing.

Thirty minutes later, she emerged clean and languid, her wet hair saturating the material along her delicate collarbones. The nightgown, which did nothing to hide the shape of her body beneath, clung damply to her skin. She looked content. So touchable and welcoming that his blood began to zing beneath the surface of his skin, his pulse patterning an erratic little song. Gabriel approached to bid her goodnight, his feet gliding across the threadbare rug. The friction against his bare skin sent frissons of delight through his arches and up his calves.

"You know, this bed is large enough for the two of us to share," Violet said.

Hesitantly, he reached up, resting his hand on one shoulder and playing with the lacy fringe that ran about her collar. The heat from her bath had turned her skin to pink, obscuring the sweet smattering of freckles that dusted her face and neck. His breath escaped in a slow, steady exhale.

"It's kind of you to offer." Sliding the tips of his fingers down the soft cotton that covered her shoulder and arm, he lightly clasped one hand, staring at her dainty fingers wrapped within his own.

"I had better not, Violet … besides, you snore."

Her jaw dropped. "I do not snore, you great bully!" He squeezed her hand with a cheeky grin.

"Thank you for winning a more comfortable sleeping place for me. I will steal my kiss now, if you will allow it."

Violet began to nod, then stopped and tilted her head.

"Wait a moment. I won. Shouldn't it be *my* kiss to steal?"

Gabriel's heart stopped entirely, then started again at twice the rate of speed. He was prepared for a moment of intimacy that was his to control. Something brief and insignificant. With one logical little sentence, she had stripped away his command and left him floundering. "I suppose that's true."

"You suppose? Such enthusiasm," she mocked playfully. "I won't hurt you, Your Grace."

He forcibly relaxed his shoulders, "Very well. I'll have my kiss now."

Violet tipped on her toes, but no amount of neck straining or extending of muscles would bring her lips any higher than his chin, which was apparently not her destination. Gabriel remained stretched to the full extent of his height, smiling as Violet gave a little hop, landing again on the balls of her feet.

She gave an annoyed "harrumph."

"You are a terrible thief," Gabriel said.

"Well, it's not as if you're helping my endeavour!"

"If I am to play the damsel, I don't believe it's my job to make your thieving especially effortless."

Violet's hand shot out, tightening around a fistful of his shirt front and easing him well within reach of her lips. "Not such a terrible thief now, am I?"

What she had stolen was his ability to breathe.

As she listed closer, he forced himself to remain still, his nerves firing off a trail of pyrotechnics that followed the path of her hand, which slid from his chest up his neck and settled against his jaw. She turned his head with the brush of her fingertips and touched her lips to his cheek, unbearably soft as they lingered. Her thumb caressed the space behind his ear with teasing little strokes even after her lips had left his skin. Gabriel straightened, dizzy from the sensation of her touch.

"I retract my accusation. You are a quite proficient thief," he dazedly murmured

Stepping away, she turned and handed him a pillow off her bed and the blanket that was laid out for his use. "Goodnight, Gabriel."

"Have pleasant dreams, my duchess."

***

Gabriel counted backwards from twenty for the fifth time. Their travel had been slow, the roads caked with sticky mud that rocked and jostled even his well-sprung carriage. Not that it would have mattered, as physics and engineering had not yet invented a speed that would have been fast enough for Violet. She was a coil of anxious energy, and sharing a confined space with her fidgeting had all but driven him to run beside the carriage.

He understood her feelings; as a parent he more than empathised, but it didn't make the behaviour easier to endure. After the seventh time she asked when they would arrive, he reached over and encircled her wrists with his hands. Her squeak of alarm caused his grip to ease. Gently turning her body to face away from his, he laid his palms on her shoulders, the tips of his fingers grazing the exposed edge of her collarbone.

"Relax," he ordered with mild sternness. She stiffened further. "That's not relaxing, Violet," he chided with a low, rumbling chuckle.

"I'm not accustomed to, that is to say ..." A blush rose up her neck like steam from a hot bath as his fingers began to massage in tight circles, easing the knotted muscle beneath her skin.

"Well, you will have to become accustomed to it. I may not be ready for marital intimacies, but I am affectionate by nature so you will have to learn to appreciate some innocent physical contact." She let out a little sigh as her head lolled forward. His thumbs stroked beneath the neckline of her dress, easing the tension along the top of her shoulder blades.

She let out a contented groan. "Don't stop." Finally, he felt her spine and shoulders relax under the gliding pressure of his fingers.

"As you command, Your Grace," he said through his smile.

Arriving, Gabriel hardly had time to hand Violet down before she leapt from the carriage. Although she took his proffered arm, the length of her stride was so vast that she practically dragged him forward. He knocked only once at the door of the county magistrate's office before being invited in by the clerk. Gabriel handed the young man his card.

"Your Grace, if you would like to wait here, it will be but a moment." Gabriel turned to offer Violet a steadying smile just as the sound of his childhood courtesy title brought him to attention.

"Barnet? My God, it *is* you!" He was pulled into a quick, crushing hug. "Or I suppose I am to call you Northam now?"

Gabriel shrugged to indicate it made little difference to him.

"It's great to see you, Denslow. What are you doing out this way? Last I heard you were blazing your way through the London gaming hells, and now a magistrate! Quite a leap there, old chap!"

"I married my Abigail and she tamed me. I have a son now, you know! But enough of that. Since you didn't know whom you would find behind this desk, clearly this is not a social call."

The happiness at seeing an old friend fell from Gabriel's face. "Indeed. We have quite a lot to tell you. But first, Vi, this strapping, handsome fellow is Stephen Denslow. He used to be the most pathetic string bean in our class, and I spent the whole of my first year beating down bullies on his behalf. Denslow, may I present my wife, Violet Anson, Duchess of Northam?"

"It is an absolute pleasure to meet you, Your Grace." He bowed regally. "Please, join me in my office and have a seat. I will ring for tea and you can explain how I can help you today."

Twenty minutes later, Gabriel had conveyed the pertinent parts of the story and a plan was in place.

Denslow leaned back in his chair and steepled his fingers. "I don't mind telling you that depriving Moorefield control of his heir will bring me a great deal of satisfaction. I am convinced the blaggard tampered with my curricle in last year's Statefield race, though I could never prove it. And will you be needing a second? I assume you plan to call him out for the damage your duchess is still sporting."

"No!" Violet lurched forward and grabbed Gabriel's arm. "No, I don't want that. I want Zach, and then I want to leave as quickly as possible."

Gabriel held her gaze for a long moment before nodding, his lips pressed together in a frown. The trio rode together in Northam's carriage the short distance to the Moorefield estate. It was small by comparison to Gabriel's sprawling, Jacobean-style manor, but well maintained.

As they passed through the broad, open wrought-iron gate and up to the circular drive, Gabriel covered Violet's hand with his. "Remain here."

"No. I need to go to Zachariah. He needs me."

Gabriel took her hand in both of his and brought it flat against his chest. "And I need you here. I cannot have you within fifty yards of Moorefield or his men." He lowered his voice but the vehemence remained. "If he touches you, I will kill him."

She settled back in her seat without further argument.

"Thank you, Violet. I will take care of this. Trust me to take care of Zach."

Denslow, who had been attempting to camouflage with the seat in the presence of their private interlude, wrenched open the door and leapt to the ground. Gabriel nodded and stepped away. Approaching the door, Gabriel reached for the brass knocker.

An expressionless butler loomed in the entryway, gnarled, thick-jointed fingers wrapped around the handle. Despite the lack of greying hair or wrinkles, he had a defeated, battle-worn look about him, along with stooped shoulders and a flat, cold gaze. It would take very little to convince him to allow their entry, and indeed, he admitted them without question.

Before the butler could request a card, Denslow stepped forward, expression imperious. "I am the Honourable Stephen W. Denslow, Magistrate Judge, appearing with His Grace the Duke of Northam on urgent business. We will see your master at once." His tone brokered no argument, and the butler stepped hastily away, exiting through a side door.

Not a minute later, the servant returned and showed them to a large formal sitting room. Every detail spoke of excessive opulence. It was the kind of affluence accrued through generations of barons who had squeezed their tenants for every farthing they had.

Moorefield appeared in the doorway. "Gentlemen, I am afraid I'm not accepting calls this afternoon, as I am on my way out to a meeting that cannot be rescheduled. Perhaps you would be so kind as to return tomorrow to attend to whatever business brings you here." Haughtiness rolled off him in waves. "I would have sent word with Jones here, but one does not simply turn away a duke without acknowledgement, does one?" His plump lips curled, revealing a greying smile and one snaggle tooth that crossed into the space of another.

"I will be quick then, so you can return to your schedule." Gabriel's jaw lifted, challenging the self-important prig to deny him the time he demanded.

Moorefield visibly deflated.

"I have come to relieve you of the care and responsibility of Zachariah Evans." Moorefield's face purpled, his chest puffing in barely-contained outrage, but Gabriel continued on without acknowledging his ire. "I have recently married Mrs Evans, now the Duchess of Northam, and your *attention*"—he snarled—"to my stepson will no longer be necessary. Or welcomed. In *any* capacity."

A guttural groan sounded from the vicinity of an upstairs room, and Gabriel shot off at a sprint, conquering the steps three at a time. Throwing open every door in the hallway, wood crashing into plaster, he searched for the source of the ravaged cry.

Zach was submerged in a large copper tub, writhing and flexing to escape the vice-like hands of a burley footman who struggled to contain him in the water. Zach's wrists were tied together with strips of cotton. Dried lines of blood stood out starkly along his nearly translucent skin, gouged in deep, angry trenches that covered his forearms in criss-crossed patterns. Zachariah's frantic gaze connected with Gabriel's as he plunged his arms into the bath to wrench Zachariah free. Needles of ice-cold water assaulted his skin as he pulled the saturated youngster tight against his heaving chest.

"Stop at once! You are interrupting this boy's treatment. He is a danger to himself and everyone around him," yelled a small-statured man dressed in unrelieved black. He wheeled to approach but froze as Gabriel's eyes cut to his.

"You are about to learn an entirely new definition of danger," Gabriel hissed. He wanted to drown that bastard in his own ice bath. Adrenaline burned through his veins, a primal need to rein down with punishing fists until the water ran red with blood.

The chatter of Zach's teeth, punctuated by unholy sobs, tore him back to more logical and immediate needs. He wrapped Zachariah in a blanket, tenderly tucking him close, and then stormed down the steps. Gabriel didn't pause or acknowledge the baron's furious protests as he bolted out the door, trailed by a shocked and silent Denslow. The driver opened the carriage door and Violet lurched halfway out of her seat, falling back as she tried to pull Zachariah into her lap. He reached beneath the seat to a hidden compartment and retrieved a sheathed knife, using it to slice efficiently through the binds that held Zachariah's hands. He stared at the weapon for a split second before dropping it onto the seat.

"This will only take a moment," Gabriel ground through tightly clenched teeth as he turned on his heel and pounded back up the drive with purposeful strides, his greatcoat flapping behind him like the cape of a vengeful wrath. Slamming his way through the large door, he flew at Moorefield. His fists hammered with blinding force without regard for precision or control. Three punishing strikes into flesh and bone and the baron was reduced to a weeping puddle on the cold marble floor. Wiping his bleeding knuckles onto his trousers, Gabriel turned without uttering a single word.

Gabriel leapt into the carriage and tapped twice on the roof to signal the driver forward.

He struggled free of his greatcoat, placing it heavily across the quietly sobbing boy. Gabriel's body shuddered violently, as if it had no idea how to contain the uproar of tumultuous feelings inside him.

As the carriage lurched forward, he opened his arm in silent invitation. Violet buried herself in his chest, pulling Zach with her. He secured both arms around them and held tight.

"We will stop off at the next available inn to rest and summon a doctor to see to Zachariah." Gabriel's throat felt dry and abraded, as if he had swallowed a handful of finely ground glass. "You're safe now, son. No one will ever hurt you again, I swear it." He made no attempt to hide the tears that made their way down his cheeks, disappearing into Violet's hair.

Chapter 22

Denslow had ridden up with the driver, and Gabriel was thankful for the privacy as his emotional control disintegrated. After depositing Denslow back at his office, they travelled swiftly and silently to the Red Crow Inn which, blessedly, was only a few miles down the road. But even the short ride felt laden with unexpected trauma; every bump of the carriage brought forth a startled whimper from Zachariah. He was like a wild animal who had been stalked and tormented into a state of anxious exhaustion. Despite the heat from Violet's fierce hold and Gabriel's well-insulated greatcoat, Zachariah's teeth chattered for every moment of those three miles.

Even after they arrived and Zach was dry, dressed in one of Gabriel's shirts, and settled under countless blankets, his intense distress remained. He stared blankly at the wall, and any attempts to touch or comfort him ignited a panic-stricken frenzy of flailing limbs. He had flipped a chair on its side, broken a table leg, and knocked a painting askew in his desperate efforts to avoid physical contact. All recognisable signs of the boy Gabriel had taught to ride, who had so gently befriended his daughter, had vanished. Zach was like a rose whose petals had been savagely ripped away. All that remained were thorns.

They had decided that most of the bodily damage was superficial and that the presence of a doctor would cause more harm than good. Gabriel procured coffee for Violet and ordered oxtail soup which was left untouched by both mother and son. Gabriel choked down half a bowl, if for no other reason than to set an example.

With Zach finally asleep, Violet slumped into the chair where she had been maintaining a silent vigil. It was positioned as close to the bed as Zach would tolerate, which Gabriel suspected was not nearly as close as she wished to be. Wary from inactivity and impotence, Gabriel quietly approached Violet, dropping to his haunches at her feet, his palms resting on her knees. All her feelings were laid bare before him—frustration, desolate sadness, fear, rage. He saw it all.

"Let me take care of you, sweetheart." Gabriel lifted her into his arms, her head flopping listlessly to his shoulder, and carried her into the sitting room, where a crackling fire and hot bath waited. Setting her on her feet, he began to slip the line buttons of her dress free. The act that had set his body into raging arousal just days before, now felt like the words of a quietly-murmured prayer. The moment he loosened the last button, her gown slithered to the floor. He turned away while she continued to undress and immersed herself in the steaming water.

"I'll sit with Zach. Take your time. Please eat when you are finished."

He could hear her convulsive sobs from his place by Zach's side, barely muffled by the thin walls that separated them. He felt her sadness as if it had been his own.

Zach's eyes flew open and darted around the room like a cornered rabbit until they settled on Gabriel's still form. "Violet is just in the other room. You're at the inn, safe with your mama and me." The word "safe" had become a chanted mantra. Over and over they had both reassured him, willing that word to find meaning in the chaos of his mind.

"I married your mama." Like sounding a gong in a field of chattering birds, the statement seemed to split through all the background noise that clamoured through Zachariah's mind. His body stilled, his gaze settling somewhere near the third button on Gabriel's shirt.

"I see you understand what that means for you, smart boy. No one can take you away from your mother and me ever again. You will be safe in Northam Hall, with Nora to badger you every day and all the art supplies you could ever want for. You can choose a horse from the stables as your own,. Or if you like, we can look for one elsewhere. Your mother's goats are being relocated to a massive paddock as we speak. You'll see it's filled with lush fescue and clover, and we can build them a perch like the one you had at home. We'll take trips together to the ocean and fish in the stream. From now on, Zachariah, you and Violet are mine; I will care for you and give you all that I have."

As he uttered his assurances, Zach's eyes drew closer, rising incrementally until they caught and held Gabriel's. "You are safe," Gabriel repeated with as much emotion as he could pour into the simple promise. Zach gave the smallest of nods and relaxed into his pile of blankets.

"Can you eat something for me?" Gabriel asked.

Zachariah looked suspiciously at the lukewarm bowl cupped in Gabriel's hands, and his mouth drew into a frown.

"Just a few bites will help your mother rest easier," he cajoled. Zach reached for the bowl, inspected it, and took a hesitant taste.

"That's it. Not half bad, is it?" In a few short moments, Zach emptied the bowl of every drop. He had lost weight, dramatic on his already lean frame. His collarbones were sharp angles and his cheekbones appeared more hollowed.

"Good lad." When Zachariah was finished with his bowl, he returned it to the table and leaned back against his pillows. His eyes began to shift to that unfocused stare, and Gabriel scrambled for a topic to reel him back again.

"I didn't bring any books, so what shall we talk about? Art? Do you know much about Leonardo da Vinci?" Zachariah peeked up from beneath his lashes. Leaning back in his chair, Gabriel searched the corners of his mind for everything he had ever learned about Leonardo.

"Well, he was born out of wedlock … bit of a stilted start, really. His mother was a beautiful peasant and his sire, a wealthy Florentine. I don't actually know that she was lovely, but it's more fun to see her that way. He didn't have much formal education as a lad. He was curious and self-taught with arithmetic and reading. He even learned Latin on his own, which was the language of academics of his time. It still is, though not to the same extent." He shifted in his chair, pausing to measure Zach's interest.

"He was left-handed, like me and all the most brilliant men. You have a dominant left as well, if I'm not mistaken."

Zach nodded.

"When historians studied his notebooks, they were surprised to find that often he wrote in 'mirror script'—backwards from right to left—which baffles me to think about, but must have been tied to being a 'southpaw'."

Zach lifted his left hand and stared at it. The action drew Gabriel's attention to the lad's fingers, where blood and skin were jammed beneath his jagged nails. He thought of the scratches that ran down the length of Zach's arms and suppressed a shudder. The child had gouged his own flesh. Gabriel forced himself to continue.

"While his brilliant paintings are synonymous with his name, Leonardo only painted seventeen works of art that we are aware of. He dedicated much of his time and his clever mind to scientific and engineering discoveries. Many of his theories and drawings are the foundation for what we know today." Zach snuggled deeper into his pillow, then turned on his side to face Gabriel.

"He participated in over thirty dissections of the human body to satisfy his curiosity about the mechanics of human anatomy. He and Nora would have been fast friends. I imagine Di Vinci would be particularly interested in her collection of skeletons, although perhaps not, because he was known to have a passion for animals and wildlife. He contemplated the morality of their treatment, and some speculate that he refused to consume meat."

"He had a wild imagination, not unlike your mother," Gabriel said with a smile. "There are drawings of everything from a machine that flies to a rapid-fire gun. Who knows what future generations will use and apply towards technological discovery."

Zach yawned and burrowed down further in his blankets. "I will be in this chair, right beside you all night long. Rest easy, son." Reaching into his inside pocket, he retrieved the river stone and set it on the nightstand. Zach picked up the stone the moment Gabriel's hand moved away, clutching it in his hand and bringing it beneath the blankets.

***

Gabriel knocked lightly and opened the door a crack. The sitting room was quiet.

"You can come in, Gabriel." Violet was dressed, her robe drawn tight and her arms wrapped around herself.

"Zachariah would want you to know he ate all his soup. Will I be equally delighted when I look inside your bowl?"

Violet made a guilty face.

Walking to the sideboard where the innkeeper had left some rolls, he raised one to his nose with a sniff. "Not as good as Mrs Simmons's, but tolerable."

He eased closer to her, the scent of clean skin and something uniquely Violet filling his nostrils as he approached. Exhaustion and sadness had pulverised every hint of the innate joy that was a rudimentary part of Violet. He could imagine how, immersed in that shallow, lukewarm bath, she had drowned her own worries and steeled herself to annihilate every one of Zachariah's. She stood tall despite the unimaginable emotional burden she carried upon her shoulders. Witnessing her strength and competence, however, did nothing to assuage his desire to crush every one of her worries into dust. In that moment, he had never wished more fervently that he was free to love and comfort with his entire body, heart, and soul. He looked down at the roll pressed into his fist. Gabriel couldn't *be* that husband now, but he could see her fed and he could listen to her. Those things he could do.

"How about this much?" He tore off a literal crumb and handed it to her.

She looked down at the speck which had slid into one of the lines in her palm and frowned at it. "I don't know if I can handle such a mouthful." She popped it into her mouth with a ghost of a smile.

"And this one?" He tore off a blueberry-sized crumb and set it in her palm. She touched her tongue to the fragment of bread so it would stick to the tip, then brought it into her mouth and swallowed.

He watched her mouth with far too much interest for a long moment, then returned his attention to the bread. "This one should be no challenge then. Grape sized." Rather than placing this bit in her palm, he held it up to her mouth, and she hesitantly opened for him. He set the titbit on her tongue, then his fingers made a hasty retreat. Holding up the remaining plum-sized chunk, he waited as she assessed the roll, bit into it, and took the remainder from his grasp, consuming it in smaller portions and licking the crumbs from her fingers.

Gabriel cleared his throat and shuffled backwards. "There. That wasn't so difficult. Shall I tuck you in, or would you care to sit for a while? I will sleep in the chair by Zachariah."

She yawned and scrubbed her fingers through her hair. "I think I could sleep."

They walked side by side to the settee and stopped, his hand falling away from the small of her back.

"When I think of today, and what would have become of Zach had it not been for you…" Violet began, then stopped. She ran a restless hand through her damp waves, dislodging a droplet of water that shimmied down the open "V" of her robe. He blinked a few times, struggling to reorganise his thoughts. It had been an impossible day, and his restraint was clearly the first line of infantry to fall under the siege. He returned his gaze to her face. It was a catastrophic mistake. Violet's eyes were wide and watery, bright with barely-contained emotion that pulled at him like the current of a river. His desire to comfort her with his entire body was nearly irresistible.

"We owe you so much. How can I ever thank you?" Violet said with a sniff.

Gabriel tried to break away from her intense gaze, but he was hopelessly ensnared in that brilliant blue. Thunderstruck. He had always thought the declaration "my heart skipped a beat" was just nonsensical poetry and fodder for romantics with overactive imaginations, but damned if his did not. The palms of his hands felt hot and itchy. He rubbed them against the thighs of his trousers and licked his parched lips.

"I am humbled by the opportunity to protect you and Zachariah, and I am grateful to be entrusted with that occupation for the rest of my life. You owe me nothing. I care about you, Violet, and I care about Zachariah." Gabriel's hands stilled, allowing those words to stand on their own without distraction.

No amount of reassurance eased the troubled lines from her face or relaxed the tight clench of her jaw. He imagined soothing those bunched muscles with his fingertips … with his mouth … coaxing her worries away. The two steps that separated them felt absolutely imperative to his self-control, and in the flicker of a second, she eliminated them, hurling into his embrace like a locomotive.

Pushing those images out of his mind, he held her. His cheek fell to the top of her head. Gradually she relaxed in his arms and the peace she found gave rise to his own. Breaths slowed; muscles surrendered. He could have stayed in that space indefinitely, protected from conflicting emotions and the uncertain terrain that stretched out before them. But her head grew heavier against his chest, and he realised she was falling asleep on her feet.

He smiled into her hair. "Come here, Vi. Time to sleep horizontally." Guiding her heavy limbs, he tucked her into the settee, her hair fanning out like a halo around her.

As he pulled up the blankets, she caught one of his hands in a gentle clasp. Frowning at his split knuckles, she kissed one. Gabriel rubbed the backs of his fingers against her face in a gentle caress. "You are impossibly sweet."

Her warm breath tickled against the thin skin of his wrist.

"Good night, Violet."

Chapter 23

If Violet had found the ride to Zachariah interminably long, it was only because she had yet to experience the nauseating anxiety of returning "home" to a foreign place, after being transformed into an entirely different person, and accompanied by an upended fourteen-year-old boy. She had never travelled well, and her muscles twitched with the need to escape the stagnant carriage and move by her own momentum.

Gabriel tried his hardest to engage them, but both she and Zach were lost in their own worries, which only seemed to multiply as the space between the carriage and home grew smaller. While Zach appeared more connected to his surroundings today, he still hadn't spoken. The gaping unknowns of his trauma left Violet feeling as if she'd been tasked with rebuilding a clock where half the pieces were missing or damaged beyond repair. When compounded with the terror of becoming the world's most inept duchess, melancholy had begun to loom. Gabriel cleared his throat, startling Zachariah from his dazed stare at the embroidered ducal seal that was stitched into the seat.

"When we arrive, Zach, I can show you to your bedroom. You don't have to see anyone unless you want to. Even Nora … although I admit I'm at a loss for how to keep her away. Your clothes and effects will already be unpacked, as I have overzealous servants. For the time being, I will alert the staff that they are to refrain from visiting the upper floor, with the exceptions of: Keene, whom you know; Bennett, my butler; and Mrs Janewood, the housekeeper. Your mother will also require a lady's maid, but her visits will be limited to necessity. You can take your meals wherever you're comfortable, and I will be available to you in whatever capacity you require."

He had thought of everything—designing a plan down to the smallest details—to set Zachariah at ease. Blast him, he was impossible not to love. She had to put some distance between them before she started composing ridiculous sonnets to the man. She had always been rot at poetry.

There was once a duke from Devon
Who may have just fallen from heaven
The duchess fell hard
She sang like a bard
And the duke ... oh hell, what else rhymes with heaven? "Became *annoyed with her calf-eyed flirting and moved into the stables to avoid her,*" didn't seem to fit the stanza.

The entire length of Gabriel's body had been pressed against hers for the last hour. He seemed happy to pretend that the fourteen inches of space to his other side didn't exist. Each time that he spoke to her, one of his fingers stroked across the back of her hand, and to her acute embarrassment, her nerve endings fired off angry cannonballs of protest each time that teasing wisp of contact fell away. This was madness.

Midnight approached as they arrived at the sleepy house. Zach and Violet followed Gabriel to the second floor. He stopped briefly to discuss arrangements with Keene, who welcomed Gabriel home with a jovial slap on the back, then carried on down the long hallway whistling. Even in the semi-dark, the estate was breathtaking. Plush Turkish rugs ran down the wide halls, flanked by elegantly-papered walls and intricate moulding. While she had seen the main rooms and library before, they appeared grander and more intimidating now that the home was to be hers. Gabriel opened a door.

"If anything is not to your liking, Zach, we will change it. The next door down is your mother's, followed by mine. Nora resides in the nursery around the corner to the right." Zachariah nodded and stepped inside, closing the door behind him. Within a few short steps, she and Gabriel had reached the next door. Her door. He swung it wide and extended an arm.

"The duchess's suite. I ordered it to be redesigned after my wife … after Emma … I can't speak to the decor. I left it in the hands of the dowager duchess, but she's renowned for her impeccable taste. As I told Zach, we will change whatever is not to your liking. I want you to be happy here." His voice trailed off with a vulnerable lilt.

She would have readily feigned excitement over residing in a horse stall if it meant he would be reassured. An un-mucked horse stall, with moulding hay and a flatulent donkey. But, as it happened, no feigning would be necessary. A massive, plush bed stood in the centre of the room, adorned with a navy velvet canopy, which swept down in rich folds to the floor. Every detail was flawlessly coordinated with soft creams and silvers. A gilded mirror hung on one wall and a landscape of the sea on another. A sitting area with matching chairs, a tea table, and a chaise lounge sat adjacent to massive French doors that led to a balcony.

It was exquisite. The opposite wall housed a set of imposing double doors. She paused for a long moment, considering what lay on the other side. There was an unnatural stillness to Gabriel's body as his eyes followed the path of hers, and it fed her flustered urge to fidget.

She wandered back to the doorway. "It's lovely, but I'm a little afraid I may sink so deeply into bed that you'll have to send in a fleet of maids to dig me out."

She tried to smile at her own quip, but something in his expression had shifted, changing the quality of the air between them. Perhaps it wasn't the air that had changed, so much as her ability to take in enough of it. Breathing was something largely ignored when your lungs were expanding and contracting with ease. She forced her disquieted body to still. His gaze didn't linger, it burned as it clung to her. As if the effort to tear his eyes away was something you could die from.

"As luck would have it, I have just such a fleet of housemaids at my disposal," he murmured. There was no humour in his voice, as if only a fraction of his brain was engaged in the conversation, and it wasn't enough to attend to expression or tone. He was close. Close enough to touch without even extending her arm fully. She didn't.

"Would you like to come in?"

Gabriel took a half step backwards. "No, Violet. I shouldn't."

She nodded and turned away, "Good night, Gabriel."

Before she could take a step, his hand shot out and grabbed her roughly around the waist, pulling her against him, her back pressed flush with his chest and stomach. One muscular arm wrapped around her abdomen and his hand splayed across her ribs, fingers stretched as if to touch as much of her as possible without moving an inch. His other hand remained in a tight fist at his side, stalwartly refusing to engage.

He exhaled in short, ragged breaths against the little hairs that had fallen free from the messy knot at her nape. With a muffled groan, his head dropped to nuzzle her neck, the rough friction of a day's growth on his face sending sparks of pleasure down the length of her spine. "Don't turn around … Please." The desperation in his gravelly voice caused something hot to uncoil in Violet's stomach. His lips traced a path across the exposed curve of her neck. Not a kiss, just a dancing caress of his lips as they explored the texture of her skin like they were searching for something. Then his forehead fell against her shoulder and he remained there for long, measured moments. "Goodnight, Violet." Then the warmth of his body disappeared.

Violet made it two steps into the room before her legs failed her. She stood immobile, attempting to reunite her pendulous body with her racing mind. Gabriel had mentioned a lady's maid named Agnes, but the thought of having to speak in coherent sentences was inconceivable. Thankful for her choice of dresses, she contorted her body sufficiently to escape the garment and stripped down to her shift. Sinking into bed, she stared at the ceiling.

Violet attempted to herd her thoughts in a less dangerous direction. She wondered how Zach would adapt to the massive changes, whether her goats would be comfortable in their new space, how freeing it would be to have her own horse to ride again. She jumped from topic to topic, but nothing could distract her mind from its wilful pull back to Gabriel. Back to the feeling of his mouth on her skin, leaving trails of heat everywhere they touched, and the pleasure of his body surrounding hers. She had never felt more alive with anticipation, more hungry for one moment to stretch endlessly on, or more terrifyingly tantalised by hope.

In that moment, she couldn't tamp down the certainty that their union would become more than the selfless gesture of a man to save his daughter's closest friend. At the very least, the desperation with which his body wanted hers was undeniable. She settled into the ridiculously large bed and sighed.

As she studied the glow of moonlight that stretched across the rich, navy canopy, the first soft notes of a pianoforte floated through the air and wrapped around her. All her feelings of lightness trickled away as those first softly caressed notes transformed into the mournful melody of Chopin's *Nocturne in C Sharp Minor*.

Every keystroke thrummed bittersweet and desolate. Every note of his broken melody laid bare the feelings she had been helpless to interpret on his face. This was not a man who shared her optimism and anticipation. His song spoke of longing for another. It carried a palpable desperation to annihilate unwelcome lust. She ached for him. Not to have him, but for the devastation he felt. Tomorrow, she would have to begin closing off parts of herself or risk bleeding out. She would learn to be happy with what he gave her. And he gave so much. Not only protection, but friendship, honesty, and loyalty. She had found satisfaction in that life before, and she could do it again. She would not hurt him, or herself, by pushing for more. But God how it ached to be here all over again, and to feel such optimism only to have it crumble away.

As the final notes lingered around her, she fell into a fitful sleep.

***

As it happened, Violet needn't have worried about creating distance between herself and Gabriel during the following fortnight. While Gabriel was every bit as thoughtful and attentive as always— even politely affectionate when he was present— he spent the bulk of most days locked alone in his study with the mountain of estate work that had been ignored over the previous weeks.

Violet found very little to like about being a duchess. Overwhelmed by the responsibilities of managing a grand household where everyone seemed to be competing for scraps of her time, she daydreamed about the privacy of her quaint home and the simple life it represented. Gone were the long afternoons of becoming a willing captive to her curiosity, of burying herself in the unanswered questions that only the trial and error of experiments could satisfy, of rambling through the woods and keeping company with her goats.

At Gabriel's insistence, she was measured for a new wardrobe. She forced herself to make all manner of pointless decisions, from menus and refurbishing the guest quarters in the east wing, to choosing which linens should be rotated out and replaced. While Gabriel exerted no pressure for her to engage in such activities, she felt doing so was an important step in gaining the respect and approval of the servants. She found herself furiously guarding the remainder of her free time to allot for hours with the children. Their combined duties allowed for very few moments that necessitated a cool head and neutrality towards Gabriel.

With any unscheduled hours, Gabriel prioritised playing with Nora and finding ways to reassure Zachariah. He had ordered the beautiful east-facing morning room stripped and reallocated as an art studio, filling it with blank canvases, brushes of every size and texture, and an assortment of rich, vibrant paints. He often took tea there, poring over account ledgers while Zach painted for long hours. Each night, Gabriel absconded to his office until Violet retired for the evening, and she fell asleep to the haunting sound of Gabriel at the pianoforte.

Zach also struggled to find his footing. His appetite had returned but his sleep was often broken with nightmares. Invitations to play with Nora were ignored, and his moods remained unstable, cascading between fits of violence perpetrated against the plaster, and melancholy. He still hadn't uttered a word to anyone, and he refused to take a proper bath. Two weeks of adolescent sweat had begun to have dire effects.

On the fourteenth day since arriving at the estate, the fragile quartet settled in to take their midday meal in the informal sitting room on the second floor, as had become their habit with consideration to Zach. Bennett arrived to serve their main course of salted ham and small porcelain boats heaped with roasted rosemary potatoes.

The moment the meal was placed before Zach, his face grew pale and mottled. He lurched forward, shoving the bowl or potatoes with such aggressive force that it sailed across the small table, ricocheted off Nora, and shattered at her feet. She yelped in pain and alarm, clutching her arm protectively.

Zach was a jumble of frantic feet, falling over himself to get to Nora's side, reaching for her arm with both hands outstretched. "I'm so sorry Nora … let me … oh God, Nora." As his feet squished into a potato, he lurched upright and stumbled out the door onto the balcony, where he wretched repeatedly into a potted plant. Violet stood to go to him, but Nora was faster to her feet. "Let me. I'm fine. I was only startled." Not waiting for a response, she bounded out the door and closed it softly behind her.

"What do you suppose that was about?" Gabriel asked, puzzled.

"I have absolutely no idea," she said, watching the door through which Nora had fled. Then she looked up to Gabriel with the smallest hint of a smile. "But he spoke."

"He did." His expression mirrored hers.

They watched the silent play through the glass. Nora leaned close to Zachariah, offering comfort as he continued to cast up his accounts. Then she wrapped her slender arms around him, leaving no space for argument as she pulled him into an embrace. Zachariah's arms hung limply until she reached down to each wrist and secured his arms about her, adorable little bully that she was. A thin smile tugged at the corners of Zach's mouth in response to Nora's insistent hug. Thanks to a recent growth spurt, he towered a full head above Nora and had to practically fold himself in half to hold her. They remained locked in an awkward embrace, conversing in short spurts. There were several moments where it appeared that Zach would disengage, but Nora clung to him doggedly. Eventually, Zach sagged against her small frame and rested his chin against the top of her head.

After a few moments, the children meandered around the corner and down the steps, disappearing to the gardens below. Violet felt the heat of Gabriel's eyes shift their focus to her. She squirmed in her seat, willing herself to remain unaffected, but some fiendish self-sabotaging sliver of her heart preened under his intent gaze. After two weeks of polite distance, she welcomed an alternative to that aloof detachment with an eagerness that bordered on embarrassing.

Gabriel had the innate ability to make the subject of his attention, whether a kitchen maid, Nora, or—devil take him—*her*, feel as if they alone captivated and delighted him. As if they were the only person in the world. Even Davies, the head gardener, whom she'd been convinced would go from cradle to grave with a perpetual scowl on his face, twinkled to life when on the receiving end of Gabriel's lethal charm. She steadied her thoughts and redoubled her efforts to resist him. Escalation was dangerous. *This* was dangerous.

Gabriel was a fool to dangle his feet in shark-infested waters just to cool his toes, and she would not rip off her metaphorical stockings and wade in beside him. No matter how blasted good it would feel. He was as devoted to Emma now as he'd been when she was alive, and Violet would not engage in some mad game of tug of war with a ghost.

Bennett appeared with warm slices of blueberry pie, but Gabriel's attention never so much as flickered in the butler's direction. Bennett darted a quick glance between them, then he quit the room as briskly as he had arrived. Violet felt an itchy warmth begin to creep up the back of her neck. To keep from placing her hand across her nape to cool it, she speared a bite of pie and popped the warm fruit into her mouth, allowing the sugary sweetness to melt on her tongue with delicious distraction.

She skewered another few bites and looked out to where the children had vanished from view.

"Is there a reason you are looking at me?" *Well, that was direct!* She glanced down at her plate to discover that she had consumed her entire slice.

His head cocked to the side. "Because you are actively *not* looking at me."

Violet raised her chin and faced him with exaggeratedly wide eyes. "I'm not *not* looking at you. I'm just not … Oh this is insane! I was simply more interested in the children and my pie at that particular moment. I like blueberry pie." She returned her gaze to her woefully empty plate and frowned.

"Mmm. I see. You mean the children who have since exited the area?" A smile tipped the corners of his mouth. "So your not *not* looking at me has nothing to do with avoiding me after a certain moment in your doorway a fortnight ago?"

Damn his equal directness. She heaved a sigh. "I wouldn't know what you're talking about," she sulked. "I just like pie." She eyed Zach's slice covetously.

"And does Zach like pie?" His words were laced with humour. Blasted man had read the exact direction of her thoughts, and she could feel her embarrassed flush grow in equal measure to her traitorous, pie-thieving thoughts.

"Yes." She recalled her eyes back to her plate, chastened.

Gabriel unleashed the full gale force of his smile on Violet. "As it turns out, I'm not terribly hungry and would be delighted to sacrifice my pie to such a worthy cause."

Lord, but he was irresistible. It wasn't even his looks, precisely. Although with his broad shoulders and thick, deliciously-touchable hair, he certainly wasn't an eyesore, his appeal wasn't limited to physical attraction. He was just so open and approachable, so freely giving of himself, as if he could only be completely satisfied when the people in his world were glowing with contentment.

And she could feel those metaphorical stockings glide off her feet—*threat of sharks be damned*—completely helpless to withhold an echo of his bright, beguiling smile.

She rose and crossed to the chair beside him, pulling it closer. The outside of her thigh brushed against his beneath the table. Gabriel's lips parted at the sudden contact, as if he was just as in tune with her every touch as she was to his. That sudden feeling of equilibrium bolstered her confidence.

Taking up Gabriel's fork, she helped herself to a hearty bite, giving him a mischievous closed-mouth smile, like a chipmunk with its cheeks full. Deep lines crinkled at the corners of his eyes. Gradually, his amusement ebbed and fizzled away until a completely different kind of moment suspended between them

"You have ..." His rumbling voice trailed off, replaced by the light touch of his thumb gliding across her lower lip, warm and slightly rough, sweeping with determined slowness. His gaze followed his finger's path as if it wasn't *his* thumb at all. As if he was unsure what it would do next. Completely transfixed, his lips parted. "Blueberry …" The single word resonated from some cavern deep in his chest. Her tongue darted out to capture the bit of fruit sauce smeared across the pad of his thumb. With a slow inhale and a double blink, Gabriel slid his chair backwards, the wooden legs tearing across the parquet floors, and strode several steps away. With his back to her, Violet could only guess at his expression, but both of his hands ran roughly through his hair, squeezing the tips of the curls. He didn't turn, and when he spoke, the sound was so wrought with distress, so unsteady, that her stinging pride and annoyance immediately dissipated.

"Violet. Christ. I'm so sorry. I …"

The door creaked open, and the children—momentarily forgotten—re-emerged. Zach quietly excused himself from the room. Nora took her place at the table, stepping over the potatoes that littered the floor. She was unusually silent. Both adults watched her as she chased cold squares of ham around with her fork.

Shoving all thoughts of Gabriel to the side, Violet studied Nora, waiting with as much patience as she could muster.

Nora looked up, then down at her plate again. "The only food they offered was potatoes, which was some quack doctor's version of a 'cure' for his behaviour. When he refused them, they forced the potatoes down his throat. They starved him. They beat him. Tormented him…" She stabbed at her meat with a fork. "How could anyone do that to Zach?"

Gabriel opened his arms to Nora, who eagerly soaked up the comfort he offered. When Violet rose from the table, Gabriel shook his head. "Let me. I have an idea." As they swapped places, Violet stepping in to comfort Nora, he held her gaze for a moment, his lips parted and then pressed together.

"It's fine. Forgotten. Go," Violet urged quietly.

Laura Linn

Chapter 24

Gabriel found Zachariah in his studio, sitting against the wall with his knees tucked up, charcoal and sketchbook in hand. Zach didn't acknowledge, him but his long strokes grew short and agitated.

"I didn't mean to hurt her."

"Of course not." Gabriel sat down beside him, his legs stretched out and crossed at the ankles. "And it would take more than a bit of porcelain to scare off an Anson; we are made of stronger stuff." Zach's hand halted its strokes, head flopping back like a mushroom with a stalk too lean to hold its cap upright

"Zachariah, I won't pretend to have any understanding of the hell you have endured. I'm not sure how you find your way through that kind of darkness without absorbing some of it inside you, but I do have an idea for an outlet. A means of mastering some of that fear and anger. I've found that physical exertion helps. We will have to wade through some servants to get there. Do you think that's something you can tolerate?"

Zach considered for a moment then nodded slowly, as if not entirely sure himself.

"Come then."

They walked side by side in silence, down flights of stairs and through corridors, until they were close to the kitchens. Gabriel opened a door and threw back three sets of heavy drapes, filling the room with warm afternoon light. He watched as Zach surveyed the equipment. A hanging bag filled with sawdust, focus pads for pugilism, a hanging rope with knots secured to the beams above, and assorted medicine balls filled the room. Gabriel deftly removed his waistcoat, cravat, and shirt. Approaching the bag, he took several swings. Each landed solidly, causing the heavy bag to sway and groan in protest.

He tossed a pair of padded leather gloves to Zach. "To protect your hands. If I return you injured to your mother, we will both have hell to pay. Do you know how to make a fist? Yes, just like that. Thumb always on the outside or you'll break it. The bag is weighted, so it likely won't budge. You may be thrown off balance as you strike, so focus on keeping your feet beneath you and your weight centred. Go ahead, son. Give it a go."

Zach threw one hesitant punch, then another, gaining confidence and momentum.

"Good, son. Keep your hands up to protect your face."

Over and over, for long minutes, Zach's fists pounded the bag of sand until sweat and tears mingled and dripped down his face. Then he fell in an exhausted heap on the floor, lungs working hard as they heaved with great shuddering breaths. "Am I crazy? They said I was. I know I'm not like other people. Not like Nora."

The sadness in Zachariah's voice nearly split Gabriel in two. "If Nora is the standard by which we measure our sanity, then we are all in a great deal of trouble." He sat down beside Zach and then laid back flat on the floor, staring at the rafters. "You are different, but different isn't a bad thing. I quite like you as you are." He silently counted the rafters that stretched across the ceiling as he searched for words.

"Before Nora was born, Emma and I had been married for a long while without children. Month after month, well-meaning friends and family offered near-constant reassurance that one day we would have our heir. Then she arrived … a she."

Zachariah looked indignant on Nora's behalf.

Memories of that downy-soft, perfect little girl swelled in Gabriel's heart. "The announcement of her sex brought forth waves of sympathy, which I beat back with all the fervour of a father desperately in love with his child. I would never let her be seen as, or feel like, a disappointment. And there has never been a time when I wished she had been born a male, but that's not to say that there isn't room in my heart for a son. I am proud to be your stepfather. And anyone who thinks my stepson is anything but uniquely delightful can answer to me."

From the corner of his eye, Gabriel watched as Zach's lower lip began to quiver. He threw one arm across his face, hiding under his spindly bicep.

"I will always be here for you, Zach. I know you must miss your papa terribly. I am not trying to replace Nathan, but I think he would be relieved—grateful even—to know that another father will love you and take care of you when he cannot. I know I would want that for Nora."

Gabriel ached to hold the gangly, sweat-soaked boy, to dry his salt-stained cheeks and ruffle his hair. But despite the trust that had formed between them, there were still myriad bulwarks separating them, defences Zachariah had set in place and was not yet prepared to remove.

A pang of guilt stabbed at Gabriel's conscience. However difficult it had been for him to watch Zachariah's self-imposed isolation, the preceding weeks must have been torture for a nurturing mother. While endeavouring to avoid confronting his feelings for Violet, he had largely abandoned her to cope with those feelings on her own. He sighed, forcing the guilt away to be examined at a more appropriate time.

"Shall we have another round at the bag?" Gabriel tossed the boxing mitts back towards Zach and extended a hand to help the boy to his feet. Zach stared at his hand for a moment, then allowed himself to be hauled upright.

Gabriel meant what he had said. He loved Nora to distraction, but it was a privilege to help Zach grow into a man, and he intended to fulfil that role faithfully. One day Zach would inherit a barony, and Gabriel would ensure that the young man possessed the knowledge and confidence to fulfil that role with excellence. And, even more importantly, that he would come to value his own eccentricities. Until that day, he would settle for small steps. Today, pugilism. He bestowed abundant praise, gave recommendations on Zach's stance and follow through, and even offered up a few unguarded moments as they sparred, allowing the boy to land a glancing blow.

"Well done, son. That's good for now. We can come back tomorrow, but for now, I have another athletic endeavour in mind."

Gabriel picked up a bar of soap from beside a basin and two towels from a stack. Not bothering with his discarded clothes, they made their way out the door of the service entrance, past the winter garden that was adjacent to the newly-constructed goat paddock, and to the nearby pond. Gabriel sat on the ground and began to wrestle his Hessians off. Again, he managed one and made little headway with the second. Zachariah reached down and wrenched it free.

"Thank you. I'm happy you fared better with that than your mother. I'm beginning to think my left foot is bigger than my right." Gabriel shed his trousers and shirt, tossed the bar of soap to Zach, and dove into the water. He glanced back at Zach. "Come on then. It's not a tub, it's a swim … with a bar of soap."

A loud splash followed. They swam in long laps until Gabriel's muscles burned pleasantly. After washing, Zach tossed the bar of soap to the side and dove underwater, popping up like an otter in front of Gabriel. He heaved both arms back and forward, causing a massive wave to rush over Gabriel's face. With a waterlogged chuckle, Gabriel dove playfully toward the youngster, dodging and splashing without physical contact until they fell into an exhausted truce.

Zachariah's attention locked in on something behind Gabriel. Turning, Gabriel lowered in a clumsy aquatic bow to Violet and Nora, who were watching from behind the goat fence.

Nora was already skipping over. "Zach! Come and play chess with me! I almost beat Violet last time."

Sinking into the murky water up to his neck, a flush spread across his cheeks. "All right, but I need my towel." He looked imploringly at Gabriel.

"I believe what our young man is saying is that he requires a few moments of privacy before he joins you." Nora released an exasperated sigh and turned her back. With a glance at Violet, who was seated in the grass and busying herself smoothing non-existent wrinkles from her dress, Zach scampered out, snatched up his towel, and wrapped it around his waist. Nora gave a quick wave, and the pair loped off toward the house.

**

Violet did her best to feign indifference to the half-naked man splashing twenty feet away as Gabriel sliced through the water in long, powerful strokes towards the shore. Pausing once he was able to stand, he shook the water from his hair and grinned. "Care for a swim?"

Violet slid back several inches, "Oh no. I will stay on dry land, thank you very much. There's only one remaining towel. Besides, I would sink to the bottom in these skirts."

"I wouldn't dream of taking the only towel! The children have gone, you wouldn't have to swim in quite so many layers."

"No, thank you," she repeated, keeping her voice light.

Rising from the lake in rolling steps, with water dripping down the long lines of his sun-kissed chest and abdomen, Gabriel looked like a young Poseidon emerging from his salty domain. His nearly translucent small clothes clung to his legs and the bulge where they converged, making him the embodiment of confidence and unchecked virility. She turned her head away, resting her cheek atop her bent knee as he approached.

238

Unwilling to be ignored, Gabriel plunked down beside her, oozing with self-assured swagger. Crowding close enough that she could feel the chill emanating from his skin, he spoke, his intonation velvet-soft with a hint of something that felt wicked. "There's no need to be bashful, Vi. I don't mind if you look. It's not as if you don't know what's under a man's small clothes. We were both married, and men's bodies are largely the same," he teased.

She buried her face further into the skirts draped about her knees. "I mind." What had begun as embarrassment over her body's reaction to his state of undress, and her own relative inexperience with men, was rapidly reorganising into annoyance and resentment.

Violet turned, her eyes flashing hot with unchecked frustration. "I've been giving you the time and space you requested, and here you are, putting yourself on display like some stud horse waiting to be bred. You may be content to tease and flirt while remaining largely out of bounds, but I'm beginning to get vertigo from your emotional indecisiveness."

She worked to moderate her voice, her shoulders slumping in defeat. "I care about you, Gabriel, and I don't mind waiting, but I'm not a toy to be played with one moment and discarded the next."

He remained silent through her verbal barrage, neither defending himself nor apologising. His expression was devoid of emotion, and it was that mask of ducal indifference that served as flash paper for the outrage that had been looming just beneath the surface of her composure.

"I am going to visit Hamish," she spat.

"Violet, please don't leave like this." He reached for her, but she snapped her arm away.

"I will return after dinner."

"Violet."

She retreated in the direction of the stables, careful to keep her footsteps light and self-contained in contrast to the fury that rolled through her insides.

***

Violet leaned into her horse's muscular neck. The animal's hooves beat a steady rhythm, tearing up clumps of soil in their wake. The force of the wind stung her eyes and dried her sticky tears against her cheeks as she ripped down the path to Hamish. Frustration with Gabriel, embarrassment over her outburst, and persistent worry about Zachariah had woven together like a thick blanket to smother every ounce of Violet's optimism.

She rioted against her heart's stubborn inability to remain unmoved in the face of Gabriel's fluidly shifting levels of intimacy. She had spent an entire marriage not only accepting, but *grateful* for a completely platonic relationship. Why did returning to that life within the confines of this marriage feel like an unbearable compromise? Having a tiny bit of Gabriel felt worse than having none of him at all. She refused to spend her life in a constant state of wishing and wanting.

Hamish was outside when she arrived, and he pulled her up into a tight embrace before her feet had even touched the ground. She pressed her face into his broad, sturdy chest and breathed. He smelled like pine trees and horses and … safety.

"What's the matter, lass?"

One unladylike sob escaped, followed by a hiccup. God, how she hated crying.

"Which of the men in yer life is causing ye to leak enough salt water to fill an ocean?" He ran two fingers down the curve of her cheekbone and gently lifted her chin. His face pinched in feigned revulsion. "Och, ye *are* a mess. Red-rimmed eyes like an archery target, skin as puffy as a newborn duck. And that bit of mucus that's stuck to yer cheek? Very attractive."

He untucked his shirt and wiped her face with the tails. "There, I cannae honestly say that's better, but at least yer face is mucus free. Now are ye gonna tell me what happened or leave me here to poke fun at ye all afternoon?"

She slipped free of his embrace and unhooked Mudpuddle's girth, sliding the saddle from her back. "It's Gabriel. Or me. I don't know. It's like playing a game of chess where he keeps rotating the board every few turns. He says he's not ready for love, but that doesn't seem to stop him from …" She faltered. "There have been moments where it feels like … It seems like … Oh, I don't know. " She kicked the ground with a frustrated *thwomp,* causing chickens to glare and scurry.

His 'Ips stretched in a wicked smile. "Like he wants to drag ye into the hay loft and cause the wee goats to blush?"

"Must you be so crass?" she huffed, removing her horse's bridle and turning her loose in the paddock.

"Och, lass. It's lust, and it isn't logical or sensitive to feelings. It's passionate and needy. His brain may know what's good, for him but it doesn't sound like that particular part of him is steering the carriage."

Violet pursed her lips, glaring, then huffed when she realised she likely looked about as threatening as an angry bunny rabbit. "I think I could tolerate that. It's more like his brain and his—"

"Cock," he supplied as he dodged her swatting hand.

"Yes... *that.* It's as if they are taking turns at the reins and have spun in so many circles that I've gotten dizzy."

Hamish crossed his arms and lowered his chin challengingly. "Do you even know what happens between a man and a woman?"

"Yes. No. That is to say, I think I get the basic principle. I do own a great many goats who aren't shy about procreation. And I shared a house with Nathan for nearly half my life and caught unintentional glances." She could feel a prickling warmth rising up the back of her neck.

"Of his cock," he said drolly. Another swat, and Hamish crowed with laughter. "Well lass, if ye plan to get up close and personal with one, ye should at least be able to say the word. It's not so hard. Rhymes with rock … which is stunningly appropriate considering what happens when ye *do* get up close and personal with it."

He gave one cheek a patronising pinch at her puzzled grimace. "Och, this *is* famous. I wish Nathan could be here for this. Surely there's no one more categorically perfect to give the 'virgin-bride-on-the-night-before-the-wedding' talk than me. Grant you, my experience has been a bit more ... diverse than what ye might find on your first physical encounter but—" His face was ruddy with restrained laughter.

"Stop right there, Hamish. Not one more word or I'll knee you in the ..." She lost her nerve at the last minute.

"COCK! Come on lass, ye were so close that time." He could hardly breathe through his riotous laughter. Violet shot him what she hoped was a menacing scowl as he wiped tears of mirth from his bright eyes. After finally catching his breath, he considered her thoughtfully then pulled her into a one-armed hug and began to walk beside her. "Love, I spent enough time with Gabriel to know that all this problem needs is wee bit more time. He may not love ye but he certainly feels more than a passing fancy. And more than just lust too or he wouldn't be fighting so hard to contain it. He's a good man, Vi. Talk to him. Be patient with him. He's lost the love of his life." His voice cracked with the last words, the muscles in his throat working hard as he swallowed. "No matter that he's found a remarkable partner in ye, he's got to find his own way, reconcile his own feelings."

"Well, *you* are a terrible friend Hamish McKenna. You're supposed to take my side."

"This *is* me being a good friend, lass. I'm offering sound advice and teaching ye about male anatomy. What else could ye possibly ask for in a mate?" He threw one arm around her neck, pulled her close, and mussed her hair. "Now. Let's get you out of those clothes and have some good physical exertion." He waggled his eyebrows suggestively

Chapter 25

Gabriel tried to carry on as if nothing had happened, but he was terrible with unresolved conflict. He couldn't shake his slight nausea as her words replayed over and over in a dizzying loop through his mind. Her hurt expression was permanently etched on the interior of his eyelids, and the defeated quaver of her voice haunted his heart like a persistent fog that followed him wherever he moved. It grew worse after dinner, when every maid scurrying through the course of her duties and every creak of a door had him leaping to his feet in anticipation of her return.

After the twelfth leap to his feet and subsequent plummet, Keene hauled him up by the elbow and dragged him, stumbling sideways, out the door and down the hallway. "Enough. You're like some deranged jack-in-the-box, and you're starting to make *me* anxious. She will come home when she is good and ready, and throwing yourself at her like an overzealous puppy the moment she does will not do."

Gabriel wrenched his arm free with a growl, eliciting a defeated sigh from Keene.

"Gabe, there are only so many times you can catch and release the same trout before she stops biting."

Gabriel crossed his arms, baulking at the annoying way Keene had given voice to the exact sentiment that had been stomping through his brain. "I know it isn't fair," Gabriel admitted grudgingly. "I keep bounding after her until my very short tether snaps me backwards, but I can't seem to resist the impulse to stretch right back to the end again." Gabriel ran his hands through his hair. "She's not the only frustrated one," he added with a grumble.

"Why not simply ease your tether to a comfortable length and stay there awhile? Accept and enjoy the physical intimacies that are within the bounds of your own self-imposed rules. I never expected you to be so damned romantically inept, Gabriel. Court her. Kiss her. There is a world of options between ignoring her and throwing her bodily into your bed."

Gabriel leaned against the wall, his arms falling to his sides. "I don't know if I can do this, Keene. You saw me after I lost Emma. You've seen me every day since." His head lulled against the wall. "Why can't I be like every other man in England, swiving anything with breasts without assigning the slightest bit of emotional attachment to the act?"

Keene grinned, laying a hand on Gabriel's shoulder with a squeeze. "You missed your opportunity to be a scoundrel, my friend. The key is to sleep with as many women as possible before you grow mature enough to acquire a conscience. Had you found your pleasure with untold numbers of dairy maids and willing widows, it would be less of an act of love and intimacy than one of biological necessity. Like brushing your teeth so your bicuspids don't rot out."

Gabriel rubbed his forehead, frowning.

"Just stop overthinking everything, Gabe. And for Christ's sake, even if you don't sleep with her, then at the very least find some path to mutual orgasm. I've never seen two people as sorely in need of release as the pair of you. You've been wound up tighter than a spool of thread for weeks."

Gabriel glared, then laughed.

Keene whacked him on the shoulder with an enthusiastic pat. "Come now. You can funnel some of that unspent lust into pummelling me for a few rounds," Keene offered wryly.

After exhausting himself with endless bouts of friendly sparring, Gabriel felt marginally better. He was headed up the backstairs when the door to the servants' entrance opened, revealing a dirt-encrusted, bedraggled Violet. She wore dark grey wool trousers rolled at the cuffs and an oversized men's shirt that had likely, at one time, been white. Her hair was tied in a messy knot, but the bulk of it had come unbound, falling loose down her back. Dirt was smudged on her cheeks and ground into the slope of one delicate eyebrow.

The apology he'd planned wiped clean from his mind.

With insolent, stilted slowness his eyes raked over her body. "I distinctly recall you attired in a different wardrobe when you fled." His voice was cold, an octave lower than it normally was. "High-waisted and indigo, I believe. The kind that requires the services of a lady's maid. Has Hamish taken to employing one of late? And now you are skulking like a burglar through the service entrance."

The story she told within the lines and curves of her face shifted from embarrassment to consternation to unadulterated fury. "I don't need to explain myself to you." She thrust her nose in the air, the smudges of dirt lessening some of the desired haughtiness, and quit the room, every inch the duchess that she was.

Gabriel stalked after her. "Violet!" he snapped. He stifled the urge to grab her shoulders and force her to face him as they made their way through the front foyer and up the main stairs. "Violet," he tried again, louder. Keene watched surreptitiously from a doorway and banged the palm of his hand against his forehead in a series of comically exaggerated blows. Gabriel pierced him with a wordless threat and continued to trail his wife towards her room.

"Damn it, Violet. Stop running away!" Something inside of him stretched to its limit and snapped as she made to close the door.

He threw his arm into the opening just as the heavy wood hurtled to close. "No," he hissed through clenched teeth. "We will talk now." The autocratic demand rumbled in his chest as he let himself into her room, rubbing his arm where the door had mashed into his muscle with bruising force. The throb was a welcome distraction from the pulsing rhythm in his temples.

Violet continued to walk away. "Suit yourself, but I am taking these filthy clothes off and there is nothing under them."

He chafed to call her bluff. To stand there and see if she *would* peel those thin layers of clothes from her skin while he gawked openly. Even as his imagination painted the slide of wool trousers down the curves of her behind, he felt himself retreat. "Give me five minutes. Five minutes is all I ask." His voice took on a pleading edge.

Violet looked equally beaten down. She reached back with one hand and massaged the base of her neck. "Fine. Five minutes." She beckoned carelessly for him to enter, although he already had.

Gabriel knew he had to make the best of his three hundred seconds, but he suddenly felt exhausted. "I'm certain there is a reasonable explanation for your wardrobe change and a logical reason why you look as if you've been freshly tumbled under a tree in the woods. I know you've assured me that your relationship with Hamish is platonic, but I can't seem to quell the feeling that he is the man better equipped to offer you the things that you need. I feel"—he paused, running a hand through his hair, leaving it mussed—"irrationally angry at the possibility of losing you before I've even had the chance to have you."

She stared for long tense moments. "It sounds like you are jealous."

He scoffed. "I'm not jealous. I only wish you would run to me with your feelings instead of him."

"That's jealous." She glared.

"I know," he grumbled. "But I'm a man. A powerful one. And there is something decidedly pathetic about a duke who is jealous of a Scottish sheep farmer, especially when I know in my heart that he doesn't have eyes for my wife, and she has given me no reason to question her loyalty." He stared despairingly at his boots. "I *am* sorry Violet. Truly. I shouldn't have yelled, and I shouldn't have been so thoughtless in the first place. I'm having a difficult time … Every time I am alone with you … But I feel conflicted and frustrated and

… But I know it isn't fair to you when …" He gesticulated wildly, then dropped his hands to his sides with a sigh.

He felt, rather than saw, when her feelings softened. Like a summer storm blowing away with the shifting clouds, all the electric charge dissipated into calm stillness.

Inching towards him, she took both his hands, entwining her fingers with his. "I was gardening. I borrowed some of Nathan's old clothes. That's all." Her voice was light and reassuring, soothing to the rough edge of bitterness that had been scouring his insides.

"I believe you. But I still don't like it," he brooded. "His hands unfastening your clothes, even in a perfectly innocent capacity …" Gabriel trailed away.

"Gabriel, look at me." He grudgingly raised his eyes. "There is something you need to know. I probably should have told you before we were married, but it wasn't my secret to share even though I have played a part in keeping it. When it comes to Hamish, *you* would be much more at risk of being ogled while undressing than I." Gabriel frowned in confusion.

"Hamish likes men. More specifically …" She took a steadying breath and held it for a moment. "More specifically, Hamish loved Nathan."

Violet continued on as if she hadn't just flipped his entire perspective upside down in the course of a single sentence. "As I've told you, Hamish, Nathan, and I grew up together. I never had much interest in feminine pursuits, as you have probably surmised. I found the company of other girls my age stilted and superficial. Children in general were not kind to me, and I was a particularly sensitive child." Her lips twisted into a self-deprecating smile. "Rather than clawing my way into acceptance with peers with whom I had little in common, Hamish and Nathan became my closest companions. For once, I could share my ideas without being laughed at. Rather than mocking or simply tolerating my outbursts of enthusiasm, they would join in with the schemes, helping me build and dream. Nathan was brilliant with tiny mechanics and understanding the way everything fit together. He's the one that taught me about clockwork mechanisms, although I've never had the eye for it the way he did."

She tilted her head to the side as if she'd just noticed he was still standing there, gaping at her. "Should we sit?" she asked rather brightly. "I feel like when your wife tells you that she is a virgin who spent half her life married to a man who was in love with her best friend, it's something you should sit for."

Gabriel nodded. "Yes, I think it makes the list of conversations best absorbed from the seated position."

"Oh, drat. I can't sit. My clothes are all muddy. They will ruin the settee."

Gabriel looked incredulous as she began to brush some of the dirt away from her trousers. "Violet! Forget about the damned upholstery and sit." Gabriel sighed, head lowering, then reached out to touch her wrist. "I only mean that what you have to say is more important than a bit of dirt on the furniture."

Gabriel looked to the ceiling in exasperation as she ignored him and covered the seat with a towel before sitting daintily on the edge. Her back was arrow straight, knees together and slightly angled to the left, her fingers clasped gently in her lap. Had she been wrapped in layers of muslin and lace, she would have been the classic picture of grace and deportment. In trousers, she was provocative. Downright erotic.

"You're staring. I know this all must be a shock."

"No. Well, yes of course it is, but it's not that. I've just been reminded of how lethally seductive you are in trousers." He shook his head.

"Well, eyes up, Your Grace. I can't remember my place in the story with you drooling over my shapely limbs."

Mention of her legs did nothing to draw his gaze back to her face.

She raised one eyebrow in chastisement. "You better pay attention. There may be a surprise exam at the end of this lecture, and it won't be about the curve of my thighs." Then she began again, despite his clearly divided attention. "Nathan went off to school, and I missed him terribly even though he was home for every school holiday. When I was thirteen, I developed a deeper attachment to Nathan … and told him so. I can still feel the heat of embarrassment. He tried to soothe my fragile juvenile heart, assuring me that he loved me more than nearly everyone else in the world. He told me how special I was and how much he wished his feelings for me were of the same sort. Naturally, I believed he was just placating me with lies, and in a fit of humiliated indignation, I declared that I never wanted to see him again."

"Yes, I can imagine." Gabriel shot her a look, considering her explosive anger when he had been the target.

"That's when Hamish stepped in. He surmised the swarming beehive he had stumbled into and explained that Nathan couldn't love me because he was already in love with him. Suddenly, a lifetime of moments made perfect sense, like watching so many tiny streams converge into one rushing river. I still remember how completely overcome I was witnessing the open adoration between them, and suddenly knowing it for what it was. When Hamish reached down and took Nathan's hand in his, the truth in their eyes was indisputable." She paused to assess Gabriel's attention, then carried on without a word.

"From that moment on, when we were together in private, they made no attempt to mask their affection for one another. It may not have been the kind of love I was raised to accept, but it was no less powerful. In many ways, it was like being the middleman in any relationship. They both tried to pull me to their side of lovers' squabbles. I watched them support one another through life's trials. They were affectionate and playful and, well, very much in love." She broke off quite suddenly and made to stand. "Do you need tea? Maybe this is also a conversation that requires tea?"

"No, Violet. No tea. Carry on." Gabriel took her hand to offset his abruptness and stroked the back with his thumb.

"When Nathan started at Oxford, Hamish moved closer to be with him when they could. They both wrote to me regularly and returned home for visits, but less often. That's when things began to unravel at both ends." She stayed silent for several minutes, watching his thumb draw a path across her hand. Gabriel guessed that somehow this tied into her troubles at home. She had, in the past, mentioned the abuse of her stepfather, and Gabriel was loath to be the reason she had to remember all the things she clearly preferred to leave buried.

"My stepfather, John, had always been the ideal stand-in for a parent. He made time for me, supported my interests, and even helped me rebuild an old, broken music box I found in the attic. Life was wonderful for a while, before the boys left. But with Hamish and Nathan gone, I spent more time in John's company. As I began developing a woman's body, he started to make comments. At first, it seemed that he was just complimenting me."

Gabriel's jaw clenched.

"He would say that my shape was irresistible to men, that he loved the way a certain gown hugged my bodice. And I *was* pleased with my new, more grown up appearance. But the longer his comments continued, the more uncomfortable they made me feel. One Sunday I stayed home from church because I had taken a fall from my horse that morning and scraped my knee quite badly. Once we were alone, he told me to sit on the sofa and lift my skirts a bit so he could apply liniment to the scrapes. I thanked him and assured him that I could apply it without trouble, but he insisted that it may become infected, and that he knew what to look for in a wound. I didn't want him to touch me, but he argued my mother would be upset if my stubbornness caused me to miss another week's church services. So I slid my skirts up, exposing my knee."

Gabriel kept the hand that held Violet's gentle. The other was clawing into the threads of the fabric with silent violence. He didn't want to hear what came next. The idea of anyone, especially a trusted family member, hurting her in such a vile manner made bile rise in his throat. He struggled to swallow it down, silently praying for her to stop her story there, to spare him the torment of hearing of all the things that he would give anything to have protected her from. But however impossible it was for him to hear those words, to feel that agonising helplessness, he would make himself listen to every devastating word if she needed to share it.

"He started to rub the oil into my cut, his circles growing larger as he slid under my dress. I winced and pulled back. He told me that he could tell it hurt a lot and that he was going to do something to make me feel better." Her voice broke. She heaved a great shuddering breath and looked away from Gabriel as she continued, her eyes fixed on some unknown place behind his left shoulder.

"He reached into the slit of my drawers and … touched me. He cooed disgusting things about how he knew this would make me feel good. But it didn't feel good. It felt terrible. Before that moment, I didn't imagine that kind of terror even existed. The betrayal I felt … the helplessness …"

An incalculable number of tears were streaming down her face. Gabriel reached into his pocket to extract a handkerchief, glaring disdainfully at the inadequate offering.

"Mama came home then, and at the sound of the door, I escaped and hobbled off to my room, hiding there all night. She assumed my leg was bothering me and left me alone. I remember being cold. So cold that no amount of blankets would halt the shivering. Like the cold came from the inside, and I would never be warm again. My brother knew something wasn't right. He had noticed things, but he was so much younger than me and powerless to stop it."

She blew her nose and dabbed her reddened cheeks. "I tried, after that day, never to be alone with him. But sometimes I couldn't find a way to escape, and it was more of the same. I told him I would tell Mama. He shrugged and said that Mama would believe exactly what she wanted to believe, and somehow I knew he was right. Then, one weekend, my mother and I went to visit an aunt about two hours from home. By this time my brother had been sent away to school."

"When the carriage pulled up we learned my cousin had scarlet fever. My mother had a mild case as a child. I had not, so I was promptly sent away. Ironically, that was to protect me. She stayed to nurse my aunt back to health and I returned home in the carriage. At some point during that nauseating carriage ride home, I decided I would do whatever it took to make sure he could never hurt me again. This was my opportunity to flee. I could run to Hamish and Nathan, and they would protect me. I prayed over and over that he wouldn't be home when I arrived, but he was, and he cornered me immediately. He was sneering this disgusting wicked smile, as if Christmas had come early and he knew he would have everything that he wanted." A sob broke in her throat, but she slowed her breathing and continued. "There was something in the look of certainty on his face that terrified me more than all of his groping and leering before. I tried to get to my room and close the door, but he was faster. I kicked and thrashed, but he grabbed me around the ankle and I lost my balance. My nose hit the edge of the table."

She rubbed the small bump on her nose absently. "I kicked as hard as I could as many times as I could, and then I ran. I jumped back into the carriage and told the driver to go. He saw all the blood and assumed I needed the doctor, but once we were away, I instructed him to take me to Oxford."

"I found Hamish first and told him all that had happened. He wanted to kill John, and I would be lying if I didn't say that a part of me—a big part of me—wanted to let him. But I couldn't stand the thought that Hamish might be punished for protecting me, so I managed to convince him of another idea. Around that time, unwanted speculation had arisen about the relationship between Hamish and Nathan. Someone had found a love letter Hamish had written to Nathan. Nathan and I managed to convince everyone that the letter was from me. Thankfully, it was left unsigned. We let word spread that we had long been in love but had kept it a secret due to his father's disapproval. I shared the same story with my mother by letter. Nathan and I married almost immediately."

"Years later, after John died and Nathan had finished at Oxford, we returned home. I tried to tell my mother what had happened with John, but she wouldn't listen. She said I was blaspheming the dead and told me to leave and never come back. So I did. I foolishly thought that since I was expecting that response, it wouldn't hurt quite so much. But it did. Nathan's parents never approved of our match and he was all but cut off, but his aunt mentioned the possibility of taking over a tenant lease from a friend in Devonshire."

"Hamish eventually followed and found adjacent land, but more often than not, he stayed with Nathan and me … and then eventually, with Nathan, Zachariah, and me. The life I shared with them, while unorthodox, was happy. My marriage to Nathan brought safety to us all." Gabriel remained silent, watching her.

"Nathan—and even Hamish, to an extent—always felt he had robbed me of a life of love. But from the day we married, I was *always* loved. And, honestly, after everything, I was more than content to spend my life with a man that I knew would never touch me."

Violet looked down at his handkerchief in her hands and traced the embroidery with one small finger. "So, you see, having Hamish release twelve buttons down the back of my dress was truly the most inconsequential thing in the world."

It was the most heart-wrenching understatement Gabriel had ever heard.

Chapter 26

He was trembling. Not the small, polite shivers that come from being cold, but the whole-body spasms of overwhelmed muscles pleading for some kind of action. He wanted to beat something bloody for her. He wanted to rip away all the hurt and smother the horror she'd been forced to survive.

What he wanted most of all was to pull her on top of him and wrap his arms and legs around her to keep her safe, so that nothing in the world could so much as tickle her in an uncomfortable way again. But he didn't know how she'd endured the few physical advances he had made, let alone if she would welcome the intimate way he longed to cradle her. And so he sat trembling and raised his arms so she could tuck her body close. She was limp against him, as if the effort to push all the words out had vanquished her ability to do anything but remain breathing. They sat like that for a long while, side by side.

"Your heart is pounding," she murmured.

"I know."

"You're trembling."

"I know that too."

"You haven't said a word … beyond 'I know,' that is. Sometimes I have so many words to say that they bicker over which one is to go first. Like there's a fire in the theatre and everyone is pushing like a mob to be the first one free. Is it like that?"

He nodded stiffly.

"Maybe I can do some of the talking for you. Eliminate a few of the squabbling people so the rest can get out more easily." She turned her body towards his and rested one hand on his stomach. The violence of those already painfully embarrassing tremors abruptly increased. Having her close only made the need to drag her closer and bury his face in her hair that much harder to disregard. She started to pull her hand away.

"Bad?" she asked, so much vulnerability in that one little word that he felt inside out with self-loathing to have put it there.

He squeezed his eyes closed and emphatically shook his head. He could feel the tears stinging at the backs of his eyes. She settled her hand back against his abdomen. He wanted so desperately to comfort her, but he had no idea how.

"When Nathan first heard … everything, he was afraid to touch me. But I wasn't afraid of Nathan, and Gabriel, I'm not afraid of you. Do you want to touch me?"

"Please." It came out as a groan while his frozen muscles broke free, like icicles shattering against cobblestone. In one fluid motion, he wrapped his arms around her, pulled her onto his lap, and squeezed her as tightly against him as he possibly could without hurting her. He fisted the loose fabric on the back of her shirt, and, after a moment's hesitation, he gave into the impulse that had been screaming inside him and buried his face in her neck. "Oh, Violet."

Memories of every asinine comment, every thoughtless, possibly frightening action he had unwittingly inflicted upon her, flooded Gabriel's mind. He had been so wrapped up in his own internal struggles that he hadn't noticed the right details or asked the right questions. She had certainly hinted that her marriage to Nathan was based in friendship, but he had never thought to ask *why* Violet would have accepted a passionless marriage. It was equivalent to reading the last chapter of a book, and realising the abundant foreshadowing you failed to recognize was really quite obvious.

She said she'd been happy to marry a man who would never touch her. He'd spent weeks alternating between panting over her, which likely terrified her, and refusing to let her in at all. And, *for the second time*, she had found herself in a marriage with a man who was in love with someone else. This time, not even a *living* someone else. Two separate marriages where attaining the love of her spouse was either utterly impossible or, in his case, must have felt hopeless.

The cruelty and injustice Violet had suffered was inconceivably and utterly unfair, and he hated himself for his small part in it. Still, he could not speak. It was too much. Everything he was feeling was too much.

Violet began to rub up and down his spine. "One terrible man betrayed my trust in the worst way possible. I think it might have been easy to believe that *all* love could lead to betrayal, and to deem the possibility of something safe and enduring, unworthy of the risk. It *might* have been easy to believe that had I not witnessed a lifetime of selfless, unwavering love between Hamish and Nathan. Watching them year after year was undeniable proof that the betrayal of one man didn't mean that all men betray."

Gabriel's shuddering body had finally relaxed, his fists partially unclenched. His nose was still tucked in her neck. So much of what he felt didn't have a strong enough spoken equivalent. He didn't want to say that he was sorry for all the hurt she had suffered, when what he felt was so much more than sorry could ever be. But there was one thing that needed to be said. He raised his head and looked into her clear blue eyes.

"Violet, before we married I told you I hoped our relationship would eventually lead to the natural progression of heirs. But you know I have a brother, Michael. A kind brother that would take good care of the tenants and be a fair and capable duke. You married me to save your son, and you have had enough options taken from you. I'll be damned if this will be another. I will be whatever kind of husband you need me to be. If you want a platonic relationship, I will take care of you and be that friend, without so much as another salacious comment. If you decide you want more …" The pad of his thumb began to slowly stroke her cheek, still red from tears. "If you want more, I am going to court you, and kiss you, and move so slowly that my feelings have plenty of time to work themselves out, and you have all the time that you need to become comfortable with my touch. You don't have to decide today or tomorrow or the day after that. You have every option available to you, Violet. And no matter what you choose, I will never let anyone hurt you again." His muscles ached. Even the small amount of space he had created between their bodies so he could see her was too much. He longed to pull her close to him again. He felt the pull of her as if he were yarn around a skein of Violet, helpless to do anything but wind towards her gentle tug.

She wrapped her arms around his neck and kissed the tip of his nose. "Would you …" She looked suddenly unsure of herself.

"Yes," Gabriel said. "Whatever it is, the answer is yes." He snuggled her close to his chest again.

"You don't even know what it is. I could be asking for ten more goats."

He smiled despite himself. "Even if it was fifty more goats, still yes."

"Will you stay tonight … just for a little while I sleep?"

"That's far better than fifty more goats. I need to go and check on the children, and then I will return directly."

***

Gabriel found Nora perched on her bed, reading with a blanket over her head like a cape. "I think he's going to be all right," she stated without removing the blanket. "Zach, I mean. And he doesn't smell like old pig slop now! That was a brilliant idea to take him swimming, Papa!"

Gabriel lowered himself beside her, stretching his feet out to the end of the bed. "Yes, and he has you to help him." He watched and listened as she rambled on with all the lightness of a child who was blissfully unaware of the darkness lurking in the world. He knew he couldn't protect her from everything, and that was the most terrifying part.

257

Gabriel kissed her forehead. "You know you can always talk to me about anything, right? If anyone ever tries to do anything to make you feel"—he scrambled for an appropriate description—"scared or uncomfortable. You're always safe to come to me. I will always listen, and I will *always* believe you."

She appeared puzzled by his words, spoken without any context to anchor them. She nodded, watching him as though trying to decipher his expression.

"Good. That's all. I'm going to check in on Zach. Goodnight, poppet. I love you so much." He kissed her again, and she went back to reading her book before he had even left the room.

He knocked twice on Zach's door and cracked it open. Zach was fast asleep, sprawled out on the bed fully clothed, with his head at the foot and his boots on his pillow. Gabriel grabbed a blanket and tucked it around him, careful not to jostle his sleeping form.

Finally, Gabriel stopped in his own bedroom, but Keene must have been waiting for him in the library. He shed his boots and clothes, changing into looser-fitting trousers and shirt sleeves.

***

Gabriel crossed the room and opened the connecting door to the duchess suite, where Violet had already prepared for bed and had her blankets pulled up to her chin.

"Are the children asleep?"

"Zach was." He stood propped against the doorframe, watching her. Everything about Violet now made him cripplingly unsure. His own emotional upheaval regarding Emma felt insignificant compared to the anxiety and confusion Violet must have endured.

Gabriel glanced between the chair by her side and the bed, trying to decipher where she might want him. She answered the unspoken question, sliding her body towards the centre to make space for him. Nodding, he approached. When Violet pulled back the corner of her blankets, he stalled again. Her face fell, and he immediately regretted his hesitation.

"The chair is all right too. I realise that what I said doesn't change anything. I wasn't trying to … That is, I didn't mean to make you feel uncomfortable." He ignored her offered chair and pulled the covers back, peeled off his socks, and dropped them on the floor.

"Of course it changes things. But it doesn't change the fact that I want very much to hold you, Violet."

Slipping into bed beside her, he curled his body towards hers. Violet rolled to face him, knees tucked up, and, like two bookends sharing the same pillow, they stared at one another. Their noses nearly touched, but their bodies remained apart.

Neither said a word as they adjusted to the closeness. Then he felt her toes touch his calf under the blanket. He watched her face as she encouraged his leg to cross to hers, her toes flexing and curling into the material of his trousers. Pressed flush together, from their knees down to where her bare foot draped across his ankle, their bodies formed a lopsided heart. Her toes continued to stroke and nuzzle at his calf, and one of her hands crossed the distance between them to twine her fingers with his. He glanced down at the bump where their hands clasped beneath the counterpane, then back to her face.

"More?" he rasped.

"More."

He disengaged their hands and slid one arm beneath her neck, settling it gently on her shoulder. His other hand travelled to rest on her hip, the soft material of her nightgown bunched beneath his palm. Like a small mammal seeking heat, she shifted her body closer to his, her head tucked to his neck.

When the tips of her breasts touched against his shirt front, and a few scant inches separated the remainder of their bodies, he squeezed the curve of her hip gently, silently willing her to stop moving closer. "Enough?" he asked in a croak, fervently praying that it would be. He wouldn't deny her whatever closeness she required, but he didn't want the slightest risk of his body misinterpreting her need for physical touch. Gabriel had never been happier to be a thirty-seven-year-old man in control of his own base needs. This was about comfort; nothing more.

"It's perfect," she replied on a sigh.

He dropped a kiss to her hair.

"Will you stay?" Her sleepy voice was breathy against the slope of his neck.

"Yes."

Within minutes, Violet's breathing was steady and deep. Throughout the night, Gabriel fluctuated between profound contentment and unwanted arousal. Asleep or awake, his body remained acutely aware of her soft, sleepy form instinctively wrapped around him. Sometime during the night, he awoke painfully stimulated, as the thigh she had unknowingly hiked up and stretched across his unwelcome erection shifted and ground against him. His cock throbbed against the heavy weight of her leg. Biting back a groan, he carefully extracted his body from beneath hers and rolled onto his side.

Eased from slumber, Violet followed him, rolling to her side and laying her palm against his shoulder blade. "Are you well? Did I hurt you? When my brother was small he used to steal into my bed at night. He always regretted it, claiming I kicked in my sleep." She kneaded her thumb into the muscle of his shoulder as he gritted his teeth, willing his erection to subside. When he didn't respond, she tried again. "Gabriel. What's wrong?"

He had never been so annoyed with his own traitorous body, "It's nothing. I just need a moment."

"Won't you tell me what's bothering you?" The tender concern in her voice redoubled Gabriel's efforts to think of something—*anything*—to quell his painfully obvious problem. He did not want to plant the idea in her mind that men could not control their bodies. *This man would control his, goddamn it!*

Gabriel's breath caught in his chest, every muscle becoming rigid as he felt her supple thighs slide against him and cradle his buttocks. He bit his lip and threw an arm over his face. Her retreat was immediate.

Cold replaced the space where her body had been as she scooted away nearly the full width of the bed. "You don't have to stay."

The almost unnoticeable quaver in Violet's voice, shimmied into his soul and tore. "No Violet. No." Thankfully, his cock had finally receded to half-mast, and he rolled to look at her. "It's nothing you did. And God help me, it's nothing I meant to do. It's an automatic reaction that happens …" He could tell she had absolutely no idea what he was talking about. Ignoring his cowardly impulse to hide his explanations in the safety of shadows, he fumbled to the nightstand and lit a candle. He needed to see her and ease the sting of his unintentional rebuff. And he thought that once she *did* understand, she may be frightened in the pitch black. By now it was safe to draw her near, and he was eager to do so.

"Come here, little love. No, don't hide from me over there. I am sorry. I will explain. Just come here." She reluctantly scooted closer and he pulled her closer still. He ground his teeth, searching for the most clinical explanation he could find. "Sometimes, if there is friction against a man's penis, it … stands up." He struggled not to sound like the clumsy, ridiculous oaf that he, at this moment, very clearly was. "Other times it stands up for no reason at all, and I understand it has something to do with blood circulation. It also reacts similarly when aroused … when a man anticipates a woman. But I swear to you, that's not the case tonight," he added hastily.

Gabriel chanced a glance at her face to see if more explanation was necessary. Instead of the fear or disgust he expected to see, Gabriel was met with deeply rutted dimples and an impish grin as Violet fought to contain her laughter. "And you already know this." His cheeks aflame, he covered his face with his hand as relieved laughter bubbled up.

Violet peeled his hand from his face.

261

"Not all of it, but I do have livestock that make babies in the spring."

Gabriel relaxed. "When you were sleeping, your leg … you were shifting in your sleep. I didn't want to scare you so I pulled away until it was no longer so obvious."

Violet sighed. "I do understand the basics, but I have no doubt there are differences between ruminants and men. I probably shouldn't have refused Hamish's 'wedding night' talk. Now I'll just have to ask you."

"Hamish? He seems an interesting choice for an education of this nature." More laughter escaped, the knot in his chest loosening. "But I suppose in lieu of an older sister or mother, a close friend with experience is the next logical choice."

"Indeed." Her voice was smiling now. "He called it a different name. Quite crude sounding, really. Then he made an endless series of jokes I didn't understand pertaining to how it rhymes with 'rock'."

"Cock."

"Oh! You know it!" She sounded oddly delighted, as if she had been admitted to a secret club, and he couldn't help but grin at her unorthodox curiosity and enthusiasm.

"Yes, love. It's quite common vernacular." The hot rush of embarrassment returned, but the glimmer of her customary zeal left him hungry for more.

"Are there other names for it?" She sounded downright giddy with interest now.

"Yes. Loads. Manhood, member, shaft. People in the 1400s frequently referred to it as a man's 'pin,' which seems like an excellent way to terrify the fairer sex. In the 1600s it was commonly called a 'plum tree shaker,' which, while comical, does bring to mind a kind of aggression that I would prefer not be implemented on my plums." This evoked a quizzical frown.

My God, she was innocent. He carried on, attempting to dance around the follow-up questions the plum tree shaker would no doubt evoke. "For a while it was referred to as a 'knick knack,' which I can only guess stems somehow from the word knickers. Then, in the early 1700s, someone took to naming it the 'silent flute.' I'm not going to hazard a guess as to the etymology of that one." Gabriel prayed his red face did not betray the blatant lie. "I think my favourite may be 'the shaft of delight,' but even *I* admit that it does have a certain unhealthy arrogance to it."

The bed shook with the force of her giggles, and, inappropriate as the conversation felt, he couldn't resist the urge to encourage more uninhibited laughter

"There's also 'rudder,' 'pike,' 'maypole,' 'noodle,' 'standing wire,' 'spigot,' 'fiddle,' 'spindle,' 'cranny hunter,' 'Captain Standish'—"

"No. Now you're just making these up."

"No! I swear it."

"Wait. Who *is* Captain Standish? And if his name has become synonymous with a penis, does it mean that he was well liked or hated? Men do seem rather fond of them. And…" She began to fidget, as if the need to ask all her questions at once compelled her body to squirm in tandem with her rapid mind. "How do you even know so many names for it? Did they have an entire class at Eton on what to call your manly bits? How did you have any time to learn Latin or calculus with that list? Oh! Was it part of the end-of-year examination?"

"Slow down! I will answer all your mad questions!" He laughed and playfully tapped her on the head with a pillow. "I have no idea who Captain Standish was, but I would guess he was well liked. Although, I am not sure if I would appreciate it being called 'the Duke of Northam.' I will have to give that one more careful consideration. Most of the names, I imagine, were invented by adolescent boys who think of little else besides girls, their penises, and where they want to put their penises. If there *was* a class at Eton, I can assure you I would have passed with high marks."

"It still seems ridiculous to have so many names for it. I don't have a billion names for my …" Her voice trailed away.

"Oh, don't worry. We men have given it enough names to make up for the fairer sex's obvious oversight." He smiled wickedly

"NO! You haven't!"

"By far the oldest and most popular over the years is 'cunt,' which I have never much cared for myself. It sounds so harsh. There is also the ever-popular 'purse.' That's stood the test of time dating back to the 1500's. Some lesser-used names are 'bookbinder's wife,' 'treasure,' 'altar of Venus,' 'honey pot,' 'quiver,' 'cunny hole,' and the very bizarre 'two leaved gate'." A smug smile curled his lips at her flabbergasted surprise.

She promptly wiped the smile off his face. "And, what do *you* call it, Your Grace?"

He pretended to consider it for a moment. "I've always been partial to 'pussy.' A velvety word for the softest part of a woman. Certainly brings to mind better images than two leaved gate …"

"I will never be able to look at a cat the same way again."

He grinned. "Indeed."

"Pussy." It slid from her lips as if she was testing the feel of the word. Gabriel's lips parted with a slow breath.

"Yes, I see you *do* like that word. You're blushing, Your Grace."

"Impossible. Dukes do not blush."

"What hogwash. You blush all the time. And you have completely distracted me from my questions." She cut him a look, then grew contemplative as if pondering some great philosophical enigma. "You said it stands up. With a goat, it's kind of tucked away until …" She gestured with her hands. He would have laughed if not for her earnest expression. Why did society insist upon keeping unmarried women from understanding basic physiology? It was maddening.

"I'm certain you've seen statues. Artwork. That's the way it looks most of the time, more or less." He smirked. "But when it's … agitated, or ready to couple with a woman, or, as I mentioned, sometimes for no reason at all, it rises like this." He held up one small, unassuming finger and uncurled it so it stood erect.

Understanding lit her face. "Well that makes sense since it wouldn't work with a woman if it was floppy. That would be like threading a noodle through a needle." She grinned as if she had just been awarded the Copley Medal for her brilliant deduction. Then her expression softened and she reached for him. "And you pulled away because, after what I shared, you thought I might be afraid of you? Or were you embarrassed?"

He squeezed her hand, enormously relieved that she understood. "Mostly the former. A bit of the latter," he said, sheepishly

"Gabriel. I *am* nervous about what will happen, of being touched and all that comes after. But I am not afraid of you. I know you'd never hurt me, or force me, or lose control of your moral compass because of a little influx in blood circulation. He was a monster. You are the man who saved my son. Who respects my individual choices enough to give me work gloves when you would rather me watch from the side. Who has never been anything but gentle and patient with me." She paused for a moment, biting her lower lip. "Everything about being with a man intimately is either petrifying or totally unknown." Her lashes lowered. "I've never even been kissed before, so the list of possibilities that intimidate me would fill three sheets of parchment. But if things do eventually progress between us … and I hope they will," she added shyly, "I trust that you will be considerate and tender with me while I work through every single fear on that list. I will feel safe with you. Hamish and Nathan told me that with the right person, there isn't any reason to be afraid, and so I believe that."

He pulled her close and laid his chin on her head. "I *am* going to kiss you, Violet, but not tonight. And when I do, the only thing you will feel is how absolutely cherished you are. We will cross off one line at a time from that list until the experiences that remain don't seem so scary anymore." She hugged his calf with both bare feet and smiled at him.

"But for now, we need to sleep. And hopefully my Captain Standish can refrain from waking us both again. My mother returns from London tomorrow, God help us both. We shall have a full day of attempting to avoid her. Luckily, she'll only be around for the day before leaving to harass my brother for another fortnight. Gabriel stretched out and Violet immediately snuggled close, resting her cheek against his heart as if they had slept that way a hundred times. Keene's advice from earlier that evening flashed through his mind. *Think less*. With everything that had been said between them tonight, he would have expected his overwrought brain to spin like a top, but oddly, the opposite had occurred. Perhaps the tangle of his thoughts felt so insurmountable that his mind had opted to abandon introspection altogether. Like finding a skein of hopelessly knotted yarn and casting it back into the basket to sort through another day. Regardless of the cause, he was thankful for the chance to simply enjoy the weight of her in his arms and her soft breaths wafting across his chest.

"I like this," she said.

"I do too."

Chapter 27

Gabriel stepped into his private rooms to find Keene already present and debating between two shirts that appeared completely identical, at least as far as Gabriel could tell. "Hiding from your mother?" Keene inquired, abandoning his shirts to pour himself a cup of tea.

"No, I'm not hiding. Thank you for the tea." Gabriel confiscated the cup and set the saucer on a nearby table. "And for your information, she hasn't even arrived yet."

Keene frowned and poured a replacement cup for himself.

Taking a scalding sip, Gabriel coughed. "Is it your goal to burn my oesophagus to cinder?"

"Oh, I *do* apologise, Your Grace. I mistakenly assumed you *wanted* your *hot* tea hot. I would say you must want your tea lukewarm like your love life, but the upstairs maids report your bed was made this morning when they arrived to clean." He raised his eyebrows and jabbed Gabriel with a playful elbow, causing him to spill some of his tea.

Gabriel filleted him with a glare. "How do you know I didn't make my bed this morning?"

Keene gave a snort of derision. "Probably because you wouldn't have the slightest clue that the sheets and counterpane are folded down precisely sixteen inches, and you can't even put on your own stockings. You're as helpless as a baby lamb."

"I can too put on my own stockings," Gabriel muttered.

"Also, you left those aforementioned stockings in the duchess's room …" He paused, as if building anticipation before he dropped an ace on the table. "Next to the bed."

"My God! You are a nosy arse!" Gabriel chided with no real heat to the insult.

"I prefer to call it well informed. I had my doubts yesterday when you stormed after her like a moody twelve-year-old, but it appears you have more prowess than I gave you credit for. Well done, Your Grace."

Gabriel rubbed two fingers up and down his temple trying to find a balance between sharing his worries with the person he trusted most in this world, and not betraying Violet's confidence. "No. We talked. We slept. We talked some more."

"If there was giggling and hair plaiting involved, then it sounds exactly like when my cousins came to stay with my sister when we were children." Keene smiled over his cup.

"She had a series of very bad experiences with a man many years ago. She told me about it last night and—trust me when I say this—even if I wanted to remove more clothes than my stockings, it definitely won't be occurring for a while."

All the good humour vanished from Keene's face. "Damn. I am sorry, Gabe."

Gabriel stared at the unlit hearth. "Why does it always feel like the worst things happen to the best people?" He took another sip of his slightly cooler tea.

"Probably because when bad things happen to the worst people, we don't care enough to notice. Does the dowager know that there is now a duchess?"

"Yes, I informed her by letter the morning we arrived home, but I'm certain she'd already read the announcement by the time my letter arrived." Gabriel pointed to one of the two identical shirts and stripped off his nightshirt,

Keene nodded absently as he turned his attention to the task of readying Gabriel for the day.

Gabriel smoothed a non-existent wrinkle from his shirt. "I am aware that I cannot keep her from my duchess forever, but I'm dreading the moment of their introduction. You know Mother; she's rigid in her expectations and incapable of appreciating a unique mind. All the qualities that I value in Violet will be irresistible targets for the dowager's vicious tongue."

Keene remained silent while he examined various pairs of trousers, then held up a pair. "Our duchess is stronger than she looks and leagues more cunning and perceptive than the dowager. In truth, Violet is very much like her namesake, a wildflower. They're resilient and enduring, vibrant and surprisingly charming. They will adapt and grow no matter the changing environment, and are more interesting than any hothouse flower. It's only through random chance and the asinine opinions of society that the delicacy of a rose is considered more desirable than the wildflower's untamed beauty. Your wildflower will fare just fine, Gabriel." Keene Glanced at the door. "Speaking of your mother, I hear terrified maids, so she must have arrived. Let's get you dressed and ready to conquer the world. Or at least one ageing, cantankerous aristocrat."

***

"Eliminate this atrocious flower arrangement and find one less akin to being olfactorily assaulted by a bawdy house girl." The dowager had cornered a young maid and was assailing her with a list of all the unacceptable details of his home.

"Welcome home, Mother." Gabriel kissed her proffered cheek lightly. "I see you haven't wasted any time bullying my servants. Need I remind you that you have your own set of servants to terrorise?" He gave her a warning glare, then turned to the trembling maid. "You may go, Abigail, thank you. And please leave the flowers."

"My, you are feeling combative today," his mother tsked.

"Not at all. I just happen to like those flowers. They have yet to say anything rude or offensive to me. Did you have a pleasant trip?" he asked, already knowing what the answer would be.

"No. Every mile was an abominable torment. I am convinced the driver intentionally swerved to hit potholes along the road, none of the inns were remotely acceptable, and I was forced to let my companion go the day before I departed, so I had absolutely nothing to occupy the hours."

"Dare I ask what the poor girl did to offend?"

"Everything about her was offensive! She had an unbearable habit of swinging her arms when she walked, as if she was trying to doggy paddle across the Thames; she made an abominable racket of clicks and clacks while knitting; and she was always underfoot."

"Isn't it a companion's job to be underfoot?" he inquired without the slightest hint of sarcasm. He made a note to reach out to the girl and see that she, at the very least, had a character reference.

"Don't be insolent, Northam, you know I cannot abide it."

"Of course, Mother. Perhaps you would like some tea before you retire to the dower house for a repose?" Gabriel indicated that she should lead the way to the drawing room.

"What I would *like* is to meet the Duchess of Northam. You spirited her in the back door and married her the moment I left, and I'd like to determine if there is some rational reason for the unseemly haste. For instance, the sort that results in the arrival of an heir in seven months' time."

Gabriel halted mid-step, turning about slowly. "She is unavailable at present. You will meet the duchess at her leisure, and when you do, you will, I trust, be the picture of politeness. As to how and why our nuptials came about, you shouldn't trouble yourself with those details. Come. Let's have tea. You can describe those cathedral-sized potholes in greater detail."

"Where's my granddaughter? Off frolicking in the fields dressed in a potato sack, no doubt."

He increased his speed. The faster Gabriel could choke down a cup of tea, the faster this would be over and he could join Violet for a picnic and to gather strawberries from her old garden. She would likely be in the goat paddock waiting for him by now. Certainly those stubborn old goats were preferable to this one.

"She is with the duchess, wearing a sky blue frock with a bit of lace about the collar. All the potato sacks are being laundered at the moment." He settled on the settee across from his mother, then immediately rose to tug the bell pull. *Please, God, let the tea be ready.* A maid entered promptly with tea for two and a broad assortment of scones and biscuits on a three-tiered silver tray.

"Thank you, Mary. Would you care to pour, Mother?"

"I will never understand how you learn all their names. Or why you bother. I daresay it embarrasses them to have that kind of attention."

He lifted a scone and sunk his teeth into it aggressively. "It's politeness, Mother. And I don't know *all* their names." He did, actually.

"Your duchess …" She stared at her tea as if it had wronged her in some way. "I understand she is the widow of one of your tenants, and not a young widow." Her forehead wrinkled on the word *young*, as if she had discovered an insect crawling inside a bite of fruit. "I'm told she is the impoverished daughter of a baronet? I cannot fathom how she fell so far as to find herself a tenant farmer. What were you thinking? You have a dukedom to consider. A dukedom that requires a lady of childbearing age to provide you with an heir and a spare. That is her principal duty as your duchess. Did you learn nothing from your last abysmal attempt?"

Of all the mornings to have this conversation. His fingers froze on the handle of his cup as the scone in his mouth turned dry and crumbly, abrading the inside of his throat. "I believe I was thinking that I wanted to marry her, Mother, and that my decisions are not contingent upon your approval. Your reference to Emma and Violet as if they're broodmares is tasteless, and I will not have it." His tone hadn't altered in the slightest. Gabriel had been raised to remain unflappable in the face of antagonism, but he felt himself toeing the limits of his self-control at the thought of his mother causing Violet distress. He took a gulp of tea to soothe his throat, then continued. "I would joyfully welcome children of either sex, but I rest easy knowing that Michael is a competent heir." Ruefully he examined the still half-filled beverage. *Damn it. Why hasn't it emptied?*

"I hear she has a son. A troubled boy," she prodded.

"Zach is a kind, perceptive, brilliant artist. He and Nora are very close, and I am gratified that he has been so accepting of my guidance as a stepfather. I have enjoyed getting to know him." Gabriel took a massive gulp of tea and skewered his mother with a glare. Fragile from the evening prior, he felt ill-equipped today to catch the daggers his mother so thoughtlessly hurled. Not that the dowager cared about his emotional well-being.

Gabriel's needs as a human, rather than a title, had never warranted his mother's notice. Although he had tried to hold tightly to the moments where her behaviour hinted at maternal care, those flashes had been fleeting and few. As a boy, he'd searched for crumbs of connection from her and always returned hungry. He wondered in passing why he still bothered trying to appeal to warmth she didn't seem to possess. And yet, here he was again, searching.

"I care about them, Mother. They make me happy." The admission emerged quietly, hesitantly. Like a wild rabbit showing its soft underbelly to a fox, knowing he would soon be gobbled up for his poor choices. It was a final plea to the mother who must have been buried beneath layer upon layer of impenetrable dowager. He waited for the lash of her words, confident they would come.

"It does not signify. You're flesh and bone, and will one day be dust. The dukedom will carry on for generations. Every choice you've made has been utterly and unequivocally selfish."

His insides recoiled but he didn't flinch. Instead, he looked into his cup. With overwhelming relief, he found it empty. "I have a busy schedule today, Mother. Thank you for the tea. You may see yourself out." He bowed respectfully and fled with practised calm.

***

Having finally collected all the ingredients necessary for her task, Violet settled onto a milking stool behind a long, craggy oak table in the goat stable. Beside her, the rusty hinges of the door groaned. She turned, expecting Gabriel, but found a stoop-shouldered Nora instead. Her feet dragged as if the motivation to complete the journey had trickled off somewhere along the way.

"Good morning, Nora!"

"Good morning." Nora echoed back identical words but with none of the enthusiasm. Like a pencil-drawn replica of vividly painted artwork.

Violet set down the knife she was preparing to use to decapitate a fish, and turned to give the youngster her full attention. "You look like a raincloud, little one, what has your water vapour so suspended and heavy?" At Nora's questioning glance, she rephrased the question: "Why so sad?"

Nora picked up another stool, set it across from Violet, and plunked down with a grunt. "It's nothing important. Hardly worth bothering with."

Resting her elbow on the table and her chin in her hand, Violet gave the statement consideration. "I beg to differ. If it has the ability to make you upset, then it *is* important. Little bothers have the annoying tendency to turn into big bothers if we ignore them and let them grow."

Nora scrunched her skirt in a fist, then let it go, smoothing the little creases with her fingers. "I was with Zach, and he was attempting to show me how to draw a chicken."

"Ah, Zach can be a difficult act to follow when it comes to art. I once tried to draw a boat, and he thought it was a sea monster. Zach doesn't understand the concept of pretending to be impressed when he is not."

"It's not that. I don't care all that much that I can't draw, but I wish I was really amazing at something, *anything*, like Zach is. Naturally good at it, like I was made to be that way."

Violet picked up the knife and balanced it on its tip where it hovered for an instant before crashing down with a *plunk*. "I'm not sure I would wish that for you."

Nora frowned.

Turning away from the table once again, Violet scootched her stool closer. "When you are born as a sword, and it's obvious that's what you are, you seldom consider that you might enjoy being something else. And so that becomes your identity from the moment you are created. If you're lucky, you actually enjoy it, like Zach. But either way, it's hard for a sword to ever imagine being anything different."

Nora made a considering expression and leaned forward in her seat.

"But, if you are born a stick, you might try your hand at being a sword one day and part of a tree fort the next. Maybe you will decide to be a fishing pole, or a cricket bat, or the handle of a paintbrush… or all of those things during the course of your life. My point is, a stick is only limited by its own imagination, while it takes a great deal of courage for a beautifully crafted sword to transform into something new. And the world will always consider him to be playing at a person he is not."

Nora sat up tall in her seat, a thoughtful smile playing across her face. "That makes sense. Like Father. His lot in life was etched in stone before he even wet his first nappy." She giggled. "Grow up. Treat everyone beneath you with cold disdain. Marry someone equally rude and have a house full of snobby children to do the exact same thing all over again for the next generation."

Violet laughed. "Exactly so."

"And instead, he falls in love with a bluestocking goat farmer, drinks scotch with his valet every night, and raises a daughter who gets to be a stick instead of a sword."

Violet swallowed hard at the introduction of love to the conversation, but nodded eagerly anyway. "And had he been born an ordinary man himself, no one would ever question those choices. But he is a duke, and so a great deal of bravery and stubbornness is required to make, and to live by, those choices each day. You may be whatever you wish to be. You may be a thousand different wonderful things in your lifetime. Your father and I will support you as you explore exactly who it is you *want* to be. Yes, you will always be the daughter of a duke, but that's not *everything* that you are. Create poorly drawn chickens merely for the joy of it, discover what you excel at, and then, from those things, choose only those that also excite you. Maybe in doing so you will encourage Zachariah to see beyond the end of his paintbrush as well."

Nora beamed. "I'm so glad I came to talk with you. I suppose I could have sought out Papa, but … somehow I knew you were the person who could help me feel better."

Violet blinked to keep the tears from swimming up in her eyes. "I'm glad you came too."

Nora threw herself into Violet's lap, choking her with an enthusiastic, bony-armed hug. Violet happily returned the embrace. "Now, would you like to help me with a little fish dissection? We can talk about the organs and bones as we go along."

Chapter 28

Gabriel felt certain his mother would suffer apoplexy if she knew his "important business" involved "field labourer work" and basking in the company of his wife. Knowing it would vex the dowager made an already pleasant task that much more enjoyable. Like a soggy dog shaking off water, Gabriel actively shook off the sadness his mother had inflicted and hurried off with eager, jaunty steps.

A putrid aroma, rather than his beautiful duchess, greeted Gabriel as he approached the goat stables. Grimacing, he fought to restrain the urge to tie his cravat about his nose and mouth.

"Violet?" he called out. "What is that God awful sm—" His voice cut away as he discovered Violet perched on a stool, elbow-deep in a tub of disgusting, gelatinous soil. She looked up at his approach, her expression warm and teeming with unabashed joy. Gabriel took half a rolling step back and covered his nose with his hand despite feeling completely charmed by her greeting.

"Oh, hello," Violet chirped. "Isn't it wonderful!"

"Is this your way of maintaining some physical distance?" He laughed and shook his head, only then noticing Nora nearby with a pile of fish bones. She was crouched, with a look of deep puzzlement on her face, as she attempted to reassemble the skeleton into some terrifying hybrid beast from her imagination.

"Good morning, Nora," he added with a nod.

"How was your mother?" Violet asked, returning to her rudimentary and somewhat savage hand mixing.

Gabriel glanced at Nora. "Every bit as snide and disdainful as you might imagine. And I have a healthy respect for that imagination of yours."

His brief glance, and the promise of further boring adult conversation, were sufficient encouragement for Nora to gather her bones within a makeshift pocket of her skirts and make a hasty exit. "I'm off to see if I can tempt Zach into a ride this morning."

Gabriel nodded, watching her leave, then returned his attention to Violet.

He forced himself in the direction of her repugnant concoction. "The dowager terrified every member of my staff, belittled helpless flowers, and somehow managed to imply both that you trapped me into marriage by becoming pregnant *and* that you are too old and barren to be of any real use as a duchess. I didn't bother to point out the impossibility of those two statements being true simultaneously." Picking up a wooden spoon, he stabbed at a glob of wet, murky soil. "And that was all before tea." He forced a smile, dropped the spoon, and shifted directly behind Violet, placing his hands on her hips and peeking over her shoulder into the cauldron.

"Oh, she sounds deliciously ruthless! Like a great, powerful cat who toys with a mouse before slitting it straight up the centre with a claw. Except you're not much of a timid mouse, are you?" She tipped her head back against his chest with a mischievous twinkle in her eye.

"I can be mouse-like," he whispered in her ear, enjoying her nearness now that his nose had adapted to the stench.

Gabriel had come to the conclusion that constant, gradually-increasing physical contact with Violet would be the ideal way to ease them both into the idea of intimacy … like the incremental rise in the water temperature of a lobster pot, except with a less macabre result.

The collective *ton* deemed it gauche to show any affection toward your spouse in public, but he had always disregarded that reigning opinion with Emma, and he was finding that it came every bit as naturally to disregard it with Violet. Casually gliding his fingertips along the creamy inside of her arm, stroking the pad of his thumb across her wrist, seizing every opportunity to press his hand to the small of her back … It would be no hardship to allow his fingers free rein of all the acceptably benign but lovely parts of her body. That is, when she didn't smell of fish entrails. Gabriel intended for his touch to become as familiar and welcome to her as the breeze across her skin. Hopefully Violet would invite him back into her bed tonight, allowing him another opportunity to demonstrate his unflappable restraint and his devotion to the respectful care of her body.

Gabriel's thoughts stuttered to a halt. *Fish guts. That's what I'm smelling.* Why was he surprised? God knows, nothing she did should surprise him by now. His lips remained close to her ear. She squirmed a little, but her smile never faded, and she made no move to step away.

He spoke into the curve of her neck, allowing his warm breath to tickle across the delicate skin hidden beneath her escaped tendrils. "All right, Violet. I have assuaged your curiosity. My turn. Why are you playing about in fish innards?"

Such a grotesque topic of conversation shouldn't be arousing, but everything about her— from her backside snuggled close to his thighs to her delight in the most unexpected things— made her completely irresistible. Sometimes inconveniently so. Even the stench of fish guts was not enough to discourage his body's hum of awareness in her presence. In fact, it had catapulted enthusiastically past awareness directly to blatant lust as he watched the rapid rise and fall of her chest. His height and position allowed for a delicious view down the front of her bodice.

Gabriel's first instinct was to put distance between his obvious erection and the small of her back, to shy away from the feelings she so easily induced. Especially considering last night's education, staying close behind her felt like a gamble. But he wanted her to feel the full extent of his wanting and to see that he would remain respectful of whatever boundaries she erected.

Trust had to begin somewhere, so he would allow the lobster water to warm a bit. "Your fish entrails …" he prompted, dropping a brief kiss to her collarbone. He could see the rapid flutter of her pulse, but her body remained pliant in his embrace. "You are using them for …"

"Fertiliser," she whispered. He kneaded his fingers into her hips urging her closer.

"Some of Emma's roses are struggling."

He stilled. She was helping Emma's roses thrive. She was providing the sustenance to heal what was broken with her own two hands, just as she nurtured the damaged pieces within him. "Thank you." Gabriel found he had trouble speaking beyond the lump that had swelled in his throat. "For …" He sighed. "Thank you."

She gave a little nod of understanding, relaxing a bit as he stepped in beside her.

"It's haddock. Cod is better suited, but this is what the kitchen had available."

Gabriel crinkled his nose.

"As the fish breaks down, it increases the soil fertility by providing the primary nutrients necessary for the roses. It offers a source of burn-free nitrogen, along with phosphorus and potassium." She glanced up at him, her ears beginning to pink around the tips. "But in its undiluted form, you would have to be very precise about the time it's allotted contact with the roots. This way, I can make the appropriate mixture, providing for the roses without damaging them."

"Hence the noxious pig swill you're concocting," he finished.

"Hence the noxious pig swill I'm concocting," she mirrored with a satisfied smile.

"Have I ever told you how delightful you are, and how that scientific brain of yours inflames me?" His eyes performed a slow exploration of her body, catching her gaze with his best attempt at a rakish grin.

Violet flushed. "I'm not delightful. I smell. And I have sticky bits beneath my fingernails that are the furthest thing from arousing."

"And yet, I still find myself completely captivated." His voice dropped to a silky baritone. "And decidedly aroused, sticky bits and all. Come on, my odoriferous duchess. Let's scrub you down and pick some of those strawberries you promised me."

**

Twenty minutes later, Violet declared herself to be as clean as possible and they were on their way, having made the choice to walk and enjoy the pleasant weather. Violet looped her hand through the crook of Gabriel's arm, and he promptly readjusted the grip to twine her fingers in his. Given their plans to berry pick, he had forgone gloves, and the intimacy of her hand wrapped skin-to-skin with his made him intensely glad for the excuse.

Violet smiled down at her feet as they walked. "You know, your hand is likely going to smell putrid. Soap can only do so much to combat fish goo."

"It's a risk I'm willing to accept for the opportunity to hold your hand. Who knows, perhaps I will learn to love the aroma of rotting carcasses because my brain will associate the stench with a vision of you." Gabriel winked.

She looked away and sighed.

"You shouldn't say things like that," Violet murmured.

"Whyever not?"

"Because you wouldn't have said it a week ago. Or you would have said it and then dashed away like a frightened canary. You sing your enthusiasm then flit off into the trees, tucked away for another fortnight. You're motivated now by sympathy for my situation,

Gabriel, not by some sudden influx of my irresistibility. I don't need your pity compliments." Her lips stretched into a weak smile.

"Pity compliments? Wait, Violet."

She dropped his hand, her pace and stride unbroken.

"Violet, stop!" He ran to catch up, reclaiming her hand. She let him and slowed, but didn't meet his eyes. "Vi, no. Of course I'm sympathetic. But if I seem freer with my feelings, it's because it has become abundantly clear that stifling them is impossible... and that trying to do so hurts us both. Although your frightened canary analogy is fairly accurate, I am endeavouring to be more pigeon-like in my approach."

A soft stroke of his thumb against her knuckles caused Violet to slow her steps further.

"You didn't have a sudden influx in irresistibility, you have ever *been* irresistible." Gabriel sighed and halted abruptly. "When you left to visit Hamish, it occurred to me how unfair I've been. The greater my effort to maintain command over my feelings, the more they seemed to surge out in unexpected ways. You smile, or play with Nora, or make dead animal fertiliser, and I topple helplessly under the force of my affection for you."

Gabriel's eyes dropped to his boots. "Sometimes I can scarcely breathe for how my heart thrashes and I ache with the need to just let go, because everything about you feels so bloody right." His breathing had become rough. "But I can't so much as think of love without being inundated with memories of Emma. And then she's there, in my head and in my heart, and I remember all over again what a complete mess I am. I don't want to hurt you with those complicated feelings, Violet. But I'll be damned before I let you go a single minute believing that what I feel for you, and what I say to you, isn't genuine."

There was a long pause and she released his hand. *He wanted it back.* Then her palm touched his cheek, warm and perfect … and smelling faintly of rotten fertiliser. And all he could think was that he may *actually* learn to like that smell.

A lively sparkle gleamed in her eyes, a prelude to her clever, scientific mind engaging. "Did you know that caterpillars turn into gelatinous globs before emerging as butterflies?" Her tone was gentle. Understanding. More than he deserved.

Gabriel waited for her to continue, centring himself on the sensation of her fingertips tickling across the angle of his jaw.

"It's true. A caterpillar release a substance that liquefies his entire body, essentially turning him into caterpillar soup. It's from that mess that a butterfly emerges. I think it must be a painful, harrowing process for the poor creature. How disorienting to be reduced to sludge! Especially when he's loved every day of his existence, exploring the world on sixteen active legs and squirming about in the sunshine. But then, if luck is on his side, he emerges from his cocoon into a completely new existence. Not better than his previous one, but different." Her fingers wrapped around a curl in his forelock, stretching and releasing it to watch it hop back into a coil.

He swallowed hard and leaned his cheek into her palm.

"And I am the caterpillar."

"You are indeed." She came up on the tips of her toes and set her lips to his jaw. She was there and gone in a second, and then she had his hand, tugging him forward again.

The day was one idyllic pattern of laughter and berries and innocent caresses.

***

The following afternoon they attended a sheep shearing at a neighbouring farm. Violet lasted exactly twelve minutes before she was waist-deep in the river helping to flip and swish uncooperative, woolly ruminants.

"Violet. Oh, for God's sake, be careful. Those rocks are slippery." Gabriel trudged into the river after her, wincing as the cold water rushed down the tops of his boots. "Keene is going to have my head." His expression froze, then fell into devious delight.

Many of the ewes had already given birth to their lambs, complicating the process, but the presence of the adorable, cloud-like youngsters seemed to lighten the laboriousness of the task.

"Gabriel, we really do need sheep," Violet said matter-of-factly.

"Need them, do we? I already *have* sheep. On one-third of my tenant farms."

"That hardly counts. You cannot snuggle them when they are so far away."

"No sheep, Violet."

One burly man jabbed another in the ribs with his elbow, speaking in an exaggerated whisper: "It sounds like our duke is gettin' him some sheep." The men surrounding him broke out in hardy laughter.

"No sheep," Gabriel reiterated, but he was unable to keep a stern expression on his face, which only led to further snickering. It wasn't long before they were all laughing and taking friendly jabs at Gabriel for his obvious softness towards Violet.

There had always been a sense of loneliness that came with his title, of being set apart. Even when he joined the locals, their desire to remain deferential isolated him. But Violet had been one of them for years, and he soon found that their ease with her extended to him, providing a sense of inclusion he'd never had before.

Big Jim, who was aptly named, had pulled Gabriel, stuttering and waterlogged, back up to his feet after Gabriel had lost his footing thanks to a hard kick from a particularly affronted ewe. "Back up ya go there, Your Grace." Jim slapped him on the back. "Despite your little tumble, you really are getting the hang of it. Won't be long before you're as good with sheep as our Violet here. Helps us every year, she does. But my Susan won't believe me tonight when I tell her that *you* were soaked down to your skivvies in the river with the rest of us blokes … and lady." He nodded at Violet. "How come you never came out and helped us a'fore?"

A younger man, Harry, chimed in, "Because you're not half as pretty as Violet. He's here courtin' his girl, can't you see? Any ol' duke can give his wife jewels, but it's a fine man that will wallow with her for sheep bathin'. That's devotion there, that is."

From the corner of his eye, he watched Violet peek at him from overtop of the newborn she was holding,

"How much for the lamb and her mother, Big Jim?" Gabriel asked.

"Devotion indeed," Big Jim whispered with a covert grin. "Nothin' says I love ya like a baby lamb." He elbowed Harry in the ribs playfully then proceeded to give Gabriel an exorbitantly high price, which Gabriel accepted without argument.

The next day it rained, and they took turns drawing silly portraits of one another, enjoying Zachariah's attempts at diplomatic artistic advice. The ewe and her lamb were delivered that afternoon and introduced to the goats, who met the "odd-looking goats" with reluctant curiosity.

Gabriel found Violet that evening in the goat shed, cross-legged in a pile of hay with the lamb in her lap. The baby's eyelids were half closed, chin stretched out and resting on Violet's thigh. Gabriel watched her from the entryway then shuffled closer and sat down beside her, giving the sheep a scratch behind the ears. The lamb didn't budge. "I don't blame you, little fellow. If I had such a comfortable pillow, I'm sure I would never care to lift my head again." His hand trailed down the sheep's neck … then further to her thigh, before stilling just above her knee. Gabriel looked up and waited for her slight nod, then nodded back. He kept his caress light, one thumb back and forth across the outside of her leg. They remained perfectly still but for that one timidly-exploring thumb.

"Do you like that?"

There was a lengthy pause.

"Yes."

He added his four fingers, brushing up and down and in slow gentle circles. His palm remained still. "And that?" Her response emerged slightly breathless.

"Yes."

Gabriel gave a quick nod.

"What will you name your new herd members?" When she didn't respond, he withdrew his hand and stroked the lamb instead. Violet cleared her throat. "I'm not sure. Have you any ideas?"

"I was thinking Cumulonimbus and Stratus since you think they look like clouds."

She covered his hand with hers and squeezed. "I like that very much."

Gabriel wasn't entirely sure that she was speaking strictly about the names.

Chapter 29

Over the following fortnight, most evenings ended with Gabriel testing the strength of his self-control, sleeping harmlessly beside Violet in the duchess suite. He didn't kiss her, but neither did he run from her. And while Violet seldom initiated physical contact, she met his attentions with glowing smiles and warm glances. And there had been many such opportunities, private moments where he had cautiously tested the boundaries of their mutual comfort.

One night, after plaiting her hair, he had left a series of slow, lingering kisses on the nape of her neck. Another evening, while reading out loud on the settee, he had encouraged her to sit between his outstretched legs, leaning back into his chest. He wrapped an arm around her as he read, his hand resting harmlessly on her stomach. When he shifted to turn the page, she turned it for him so that his hand could remain in place.

They fell into a comfortable routine. Gabriel spent every spare moment enjoying Violet, enjoying his family.

Zachariah had also begun to test his limits. He visited the stables and rode on his own without Nora to speak for him, even occasionally exchanging greetings with the servants along the way. He extended invitations to both Gabriel and Keene to join him in rounds of pugilism and stopped by the kitchens to pilfer cookies from Mrs Simmons. One evening he suggested they take their meal in the dining room. Gradually, the servants were allowed to resume their work on the second floor. Zachariah even struck up a brief, somewhat stilted conversation with a hall boy of similar age. The effort he put forth was obvious, and although it sometimes resulted in a retreat into solitude, he seemed determined to find comfort in his new home, however overwhelming.

One sunny Sunday, Gabriel awoke in his own bed, his head groggy after a gruelling evening poring over shipping ledgers. He hadn't wanted to wake Violet, but instead he'd spent a restless night wishing that he had just slipped quietly into her bed.

Gabriel consumed a hasty breakfast, then set forth towards the goat paddock, where they had planned to construct a loft. Violet hadn't seen Hamish in weeks, and when Gabriel had suggested that they extend an invitation to him, she'd responded with an embrace so enthusiastic that it nearly toppled him from his feet. Gabriel assumed that her absence from breakfast was due to Hamish's early arrival.

Violet's incredulous exclamation carried across the paddock. "You *really* knew *all* those names for a man's bits?"

"And more, actually. Just because I land mine in a different place than Gabriel's, doesn't mean we don't utilise the same age-old list o' names for our tool. See? There's another one he forgot! And I don't like the word 'bits.' It implies smallness which, frankly, is insulting to a lad me size."

Violet's sunny smile greeted Gabriel at twenty paces.

"Good morning, Hamish. It's a pleasure to see you again. I appreciate the help as I am afraid I'm sorely lacking in experience with goat habitats." Gabriel let his hand glide down the length of Violet's spine and then rested his palm on the small of her back. "Hello, Violet," he murmured.

"Hamish will be more of a hindrance than a help with his carpentry skills, but I always appreciate his engaging company," Violet said

"I'm glad to be here, Northam. When Vi told me … I was worried that …" Hamish shifted uncomfortably. "My whole life, Violet and Zachariah have been the only souls to know about Nathan and me. It's hard for me to even imagine another friendship where I dinnae have to pretend to be something I'm not." His voice was uncharacteristically solemn. "I appreciate yer discretion and yer acceptance … and I promise to keep the ogling of yer rear to a minimum."

Violet, ever incapable of containing her thoughts piped up brightly, "Well that last part is definitely untrue as I have observed plenty of surreptitious ogling. In fact, I believe *you* were the first to note his—"

"Shut it, lass. Ye'r making the lad blush."

"Considering all you have done for Violet, I think I can ignore a little harmless ogling." Gabriel chuckled and walked towards a pile of supplies they had collected. He turned as he heard Violet approach.

"I missed you last night," she said

A burst of warmth suffused through Gabriel at the admission. "You could have come to me. It's only a short fifty steps between my bed and yours."

"I didn't want to intrude"

Gabriel abandoned his search for a hammer. "Your company is never an intrusion. I missed you too." He reached for her hands, tipping one up to kiss the inside of her wrist, then scowling when he found that it was concealed by heavy work gloves. "Kiss armour."

"I suppose you will just have to find a different, less fortified place." Violet leaned incrementally closer, watching him through half-lowered lashes.

"Would you like me to kiss you, Violet?" His hand came up to stroke her cheek.

She gave the slightest nod and her eyes slammed closed, opening again when he didn't move.

"Not here, love," Gabriel chuckled, utterly delighted by her enthusiasm. He raised his other hand to frame her face. "Tonight, when we're alone, I can kiss you properly." His voice dropped to a silky whisper. "Although I'm not entirely sure how I'll make it through the motions of an ordinary day when my every thought will be of kissing you. When I am working beside you and my hand brushes yours, when you can feel the warmth of my gaze from across the paddock, look at me and know that I am imagining the sweet little quiver of your lower lip as I have that first taste of you." His thumbs began a slow caress. "That I am counting the seconds and milliseconds until I can feel your heart thundering against my chest, knowing mine will be pounding every bit as desperately."

"Violet!" Hamish yelled from across the garden. "Quit yer lollygagging and bring the nails!"

Gabriel let his hands fall to his sides. "We'll continue this conversation later. Come along, this architectural monstrosity isn't going to build itself."

"How am I supposed to work after *that?*" With a deep breath, Violet threw her braid over her shoulder, and stomped towards Hamish. Gabriel followed in her wake.

"We can't all stand around batting our eyelashes at Northam," Hamish chided, then winked at Gabriel.

"I was busy." Violet gritted out through gnashed teeth.

"Aye, I saw how busy ye were. And then I thought about all the times a certain girl interrupted Nathan and I when we were equally busy, which led to my urgent need for nails." He grinned.

As it turned out, Violet was quite correct in her assessment of Hamish's carpentry skills. After doing more damage to the surrounding wood than actually hitting the nail, Gabriel wrenched the hammer from his grasp. "Give me that. You're going to give the goats splinters with that masticated wood."

"Goats dinnae get splinters, ye oaf. Care to show me how a duke pounds, then?" His double entendre hung between them for a moment, Hamish's lips pinched together as he tried, then failed to contain his laughter. Gabriel toyed with the hammer, smiling at his boots.

"I take it this is another conversation only understood by those who were once fourteen-year-old boys?" Violet stared at each of the men in turn.

Catching his breath, Hamish spoke. "I swear it, Northam. I only meant hammer in the most literal way." Unconvinced but amused, Gabriel shook his head and reached for a handful of nails.

"For your information, Hamish, dukes don't hammer. We pay generous wages for others to hammer in our stead. But for my duchess, I'll make an exception." He turned, allowing his expression to echo the soft sentiment of his words. "Also, I believe you're making it look harder than it is." Gabriel rolled the hammer in his hands, feeling its weight. Holding a nail in place he gently tapped at the head, making gradual but steady progress.

Violet peeked around his shoulder, observing the technique with scholarly seriousness. "You have excellent finesse for a novice, but your grip and swing are all wrong." She covered his hand with hers and slid his palm several inches down the shaft of the hammer. "Let the hammer do the work for you. And less elbow, more wrist." Her hand cupped his wrist and rotated it within her gentle clasp. "Better." She nodded approvingly as she stepped back.

Within a few short hours, they'd built something resembling a loft and had begun work on a set of stairs. Nora and Zach had joined them, and Nora was zipping back and forth between badgering Zach, who sat apart working on a drawing, and offering up outlandish ideas for goat entertainment. A board atop springs for bouncing, for example. The list grew more ludicrous from there.

As the day turned hotter, Keene arrived bearing lemonade and dainty cucumber-and-ham sandwiches. He lingered with the exhausted group as they rested in the shade.

Studying their construction, Keene gave a complimentary nod. "All those skills you mastered designing and constructing forts with me as a boy seem to have found a valuable outlet, Gabe." All eyes closed in on Gabriel, who smiled sheepishly.

Sauntering over with bouncy steps and a wide-eyed expression, Violet cornered Gabriel against an aspen tree. She clasped her hands around his bicep and gave a playful shake. "Why you little imp! You had us all believe you didn't know which end of the hammer to hold!"

Keene chuckled as poured himself a glass of lemonade. "Oh, that's grand. Northam made a two-story knight's castle out of repurposed barn lumber one summer. It's still standing, last time I checked."

"Looks like I'm not the only one adept at swindling people!" Violet said.

Gabriel leaned closer so that she would be the only one to hear. "Not at all. I just knew I would enjoy your private tutelage."

***

Violet could hear footsteps and faint activity beyond their connected door. With her current rate of indecisive flip-flopping, the fresh Shrewsbury and Cornish fairing biscuits on the plate she carried would grow stale before she managed to cross the entrance to Gabriel's room.

A soft rap jarred her thoughts to a halt, and the door opened three innocuous inches.

"Violet?"

"Yes, I'm here. I was about to knock." *If one could define "about to" as staring at a door for twelve minutes.*

He looked at the plate of biscuits, then back to her, waiting with a wisp of a smile tugging at the corners of his mouth. Apparently, an unacceptable amount of time had passed while she stared at him clutching her offering.

"Are those for me?" he prompted.

"Yes!" She startled at the exuberant brightness of her voice, then took several slow breaths to combat her racing heart rate. "We missed you at dinner and I thought you might be hungry." *Yes, because what a grown man would really like is a plate full of sugary biscuits for his evening meal.* She thrust the plate towards him, supremely regretful that she had not included more practical choices.

He accepted it with a wolfish smile, but instead of crossing over through the doorway as had become their routine, he took two rolling steps backwards, indicating that she should enter. Setting the plate on a nearby table, he snatched up a biscuit in each hand and chomped a bite of each.

Amusement at his childlike enthusiasm temporarily distracted her.

Gabriel remained near, watching her watch him as he devoured a startling number of biscuits. This was a man who could effortlessly assess and ease the concerns of others. Sometimes she forgot that those skills had been fostered in him since birth. That he had been raised and trained to debate in parliament, to mediate and resolve conflicts with tenant farmers, to navigate complex problems and the equally complex people who relied upon him.

Unlike many ostentatious peers, Gabriel's skill at controlling his domain was a covertly wielded weapon, an understated advantage. Gabriel's keen perceptiveness wrapped around him as surely as the signet ring on his smallest finger. It would be a lethal quality in a less benevolent man.

His bites turned to lazy nibbles as he studied her through deceptively disinterested eyes, his body responding to the minute shifts of hers

"I did have a plate sent up to my study, but there wasn't a single biscuit in sight." He sucked the sticky crumbs from the pad of his thumb. "I apologise for abandoning you during dinner; I was distracted by some ongoing issues with the local fishing boats. Many are urgently in need of replacement cod traps and hand lines, but this winter was a difficult one and the blasted men are too proud to accept assistance beyond what they feel I am obligated to provide. I've been encouraging them to embrace some changes—sturdier materials and simple innovations—but many of the men have been fishing for generations, and they are hesitant to explore even the slightest adaptation to the traditions taught by their fathers and grandfathers before them. Even something as minor as using a locally-owned, fledgling manufacturer instead of the previous distributor."

"I would prefer to invest money back into local industry." He shook his head and sighed. "Then there is the growing problem of runoff from copper mining affecting our local waters. I've been working with a neighbouring county to restock fish, create artificial spawning beds, and make alterations in the process to protect those remaining, but, again, change is slow and frustrating. I apologise for losing track of the time."

He scrubbed his open hands up and down his face, then his arms dropped to his sides. For a moment, she could see the effects of those burdens in his troubled expression and the worry lines that etched into his brow and bracketed his mouth. Then his eyes closed and his body stilled. When he opened them again, they were fixed on hers, his worries shuttered away. It was in that moment that Violet realised she was still lingering in the doorway. Apparently, he noticed as well.

"You can come in, love, or I can come to your room if you would be more comfortable. I've been looking forward to seeing you without the chaperonage of a Scotsman, two children, and a field of curious goats."

Gabriel eased backwards until the width of the room was open between them. A queen and a king, staring from neutral territory across the broad expanse of a vacant chess board. She had been comfortable, eager even, to be alone with Gabriel throughout all their shifting and escalating intimacies. She had wanted him to kiss her ... had been waiting with almost breathless anticipation. But as she approached the waters that she'd been so eager to explore, Violet felt timid and ungainly. The lure to be close to him, to bask in his undivided attention, had been so all encompassing that she'd forgotten the inconvenient fact that she hadn't the slightest idea how to swim.

"No." She pinched the bridge of her nose. "Not no, I won't come in, but no, your room is fine. So is mine. Either really. Any room."

Violet sighed audibly.

As she stumbled over her own clumsy words, Gabriel began to narrow the space between them in careful strides, until he was near enough to touch, posture relaxed and palms outward as if to indicate complete harmlessness. He had beautiful hands, accomplished in everything from consoling his daughter to swinging an axe, capable in all the masculine ways that seemed antithetical to his station. Those long fingers looped in a warm, velvet clasp about her wrists.

She couldn't have met his eyes for all the Shrewsbury biscuits in the world.

"There's no reason to be nervous, Violet. It's the same as yesterday and the day before. The same as every evening of the previous fortnight. You can leave whenever you like. You choose how much distance separates us, a barleycorn or a furlong. I'll never ask for more than you wish to give." Baritone and mesmerising in its softness, his voice raised the little hairs along the back of her legs as if they were reaching for more.

"It couldn't possibly be a furlong if we were to stay in this room. While it *is* a formidable suite, it's a far sight shorter than the measured two hundred and twenty yards that define it." She braved a glance to his face and watched as his smile lines flexed into view.

"You would know the exact distance of a furlong."

Violet glowed in the warmth of his unique praise, feeling the knot in her stomach uncoil as they fell into familiar banter. "What I don't know is the length of a barleycorn, but it sounds more applicable to the size of this room."

"Just over four centimetres." His thumb passed in slow strokes across the inside of her wrists, evoking little zings of sensation.

All day, Gabriel's knee-weakening seduction had been shuffling through her thoughts like an agitated hedgehog. Now, as she imagined all that could happen in a barleycorn of space, her nervous hedgehog was reinvigorated.

Gabriel's hands coasted up the length of both arms, his fingers wrapping around her shoulders. With the finite pressure of one single finger, he coaxed her closer, to where the heat of his body lingered in the diminished space between them.

"Somewhere around this much space."

His murmured words were soft petals that seemed to touch her everywhere all at once. Tentative fingertips coasted up the line of her shoulders to her neck. Every fraction of a movement he made was measured and unhurried, as if his lungs wouldn't so much as exhale without first assessing her comfort. Following some invisible pattern in sweeps and curls along her neck, Gabriel's touch soothed her even as it fed some silently-expanding hunger.

"Violet." It felt impossibly unfair that his voice sounded so steady when the nerves of her skin were clamouring, alive with activity in every place his body made contact with hers. "Violet, love," he repeated when she failed to respond. "I need to know you are here with me, making choices. Focus on my voice, not on my fingers."

"If you wanted me to be able to focus, you wouldn't be doing that thing with your fingers on my neck," she chided playfully even as she shifted, trying to relieve the awareness fizzling over her skin.

"Fair enough." His fingers ceased. "Better?"

She felt bereft as the sensations stopped. As if he had been playing a sonata and fell silent mid-measure, leaving the room thick with something unresolved.

"Violet. I *do* very much want to kiss you. Is that what you want?"

God yes. Please. She nodded again.

"Words, please. I need to hear you say it."

An unsteadiness had crept into his voice, a yearning that refused to be shrouded by his steely composure.

"Kiss me, Gabriel." She was proud of the certainty of her tone, so light and steady that it could have been a request for something as inconsequential as tea.

A delighted smile curved his lips, his deliciously busy fingers resuming their play at her neck as his body drifted into the open space between them. His breath tickled the sensitive skin just below her earlobe, lingering, then his lips touched where his fingers had been. It wasn't a kiss. More an inquisitive nuzzle, a gentle brush of his mouth as if he was trying to absorb her scent into the soft skin of his lips.

Violet's head lolled to the side, hands instinctively reaching to grip his waist. She felt his muscles flex and bunch at the sudden contact. His lips dragged across to her cheek, leaving a trail of feather-soft kisses to the corner of her mouth.

"Still a yes?" Every syllable rumbled in his chest. There was effort in his posture, conscious restraint. She knew without question that if she offered the slightest wisp of hesitation, he would stop.

"Yes." Her eyes fluttered closed.

Gabriel's warm, impossibly soft mouth touched hers, tasting and retreating in a series of slow, gliding caresses. With each light pass of his mouth against hers, his coaxing rhythm became more certain. His fingers burrowed into her hair as he placed wet open kisses against her lower lip, each a flirtatious little caress that lingered sweetly until he pulled his lips away, resting his forehead against hers.

Violet inhaled short, unsteady breaths that did nothing to appease her lungs, as if he had taken away something vital when he severed the contact between them, more necessary than air. He, conversely, appeared relaxed and content. She would have thought him completely unaffected if not for the slight quiver of his hand as it stroked the curve of her shoulder.

"Breathe through your nose. Breathing is necessary for kissing."

"I think I need more practice." Her smile was shy despite the daring invitation.

This time there was no hesitation, no soft opening notes to a rich, unfolding melody. It was all vibrant, complex chords with every finger on a key. His mouth was on hers, hot and greedy and devastating. He nipped at her lower lip, then ran his tongue across the seam of her mouth. Making a vaguely frustrated noise in the back of his throat, he eased away just far enough away to murmur against her mouth.

"Open for me, little love. Let me in."

She allowed her mouth to ease open, following his guidance and her body's demands. Gabriel let out a guttural groan as his tongue passed against hers in slow, rolling sweeps. Excitement sparked and burned within her like dry autumn leaves, but when she gasped at the wicked thrill of his kiss, he jolted backward, tearing his mouth from hers. He reached to frame her face with his hands, every suggestion of desire banked and replaced with concern.

She shook her head vehemently and hurled herself back into his arms, her fingers kneading his shirt into bunches at his sides. A gust of air whistled through his lips in a short exhale and he captured her mouth again. With every nudge and stroke, a delicious, unquenchable need infused through her like hot steeping tea. His hands skated down the curve of her shoulders, grazing the sides of her breasts with the pads of his thumbs, then settled on the small of her back to urge her closer.

She had no idea kissing was like this. So intimate and hungry, like feeling the hot licks of fire and wanting to dive into them. Dizzy like spinning in circles but never wanting to stop.

His mouth broke away, but before she could protest, he buried his face in the curve of her neck, searing her skin with delicious friction as he sipped and tasted at the place where her pulse hammered erratically. She was vaguely aware that her hand had wrapped itself around the nape of his neck. *More. God, she never wanted him to stop.*

He teased the sensitive skin of her neck with his breath and lips, nipping and sucking in unhurried, deliberate passes as if he was browsing for the most succulent fruit at the market and pausing to try each one. "You're so sweet here," he murmured appreciatively as he sampled languidly. "And here." He laved at her collarbone. She arched her neck into his mouth. She wanted to grab his hair and press for more delicious friction, but the more she writhed, the more leisurely he became. Kissing his way back to her lips, he gentled and remained there. His hands began to move in slow circles on her back.

"Easy, Violet. That's enough for tonight. Slow breaths."

"Again." As the breathy word escaped, she knew she should be embarrassed, but places on her body she had never even considered, tingled madly for more. She lifted onto her toes and dropped a line of soft, unsure kisses along the tight tendon of his neck. He made an almost pained sound in the back of his throat and she felt an answering shiver run down her spine beneath his hand.

"God, you're so perfect," he said on a groan. "So soft and eager—" He gasped as she touched her tongue to his flushed skin. "I want to touch you everywhere. But I don't want to rush this. Rush you. I need to keep my head, sweetheart."

Her lips stilled and she dropped her forehead to his chest. "That's it. Just give it a minute." Gabriel's voice was steady, but his hand shook almost violently now where it cupped the nape of her neck. With her head rested against him, she had an unobstructed view of where he strained against his trousers.

"I guess that's what you meant by 'agitated' that night."

"Something like that. My body isn't at all in accordance with the plan my brain has put into place." He smiled into her hair and continued to sooth her with his touch. "Why don't you ring for a bath and prepare for bed? Then we can sit in those two widely-spaced chairs over there while you tell me about the governess interview. Wasn't that this afternoon?"

Violet made no attempt to reply, knowing that whatever came out would be a befuddled jumble of embarrassing sentiment … or worse, more lusty begging. Her pulse still pounded in places where she had never before considered the presence of arteries.

She had chanced upon Nathan and Hamish in romantic embraces over the years, but she'd had no idea about the emotional and physical explosion that accompanied such an act. How did people go about life in an ordinary way knowing this indescribable convergence of touch and tongues and breath existed? How could they think of anything else? *How was she going to think about anything else?* Gabriel wanted to talk about governesses, and all *she* wanted was to melt into a puddle for him to lap up.

Disengaging with a quick squeeze to her shoulders, Gabriel crossed the room to the abandoned plate and picked up a biscuit, only to drop it back down a moment later. Even from this distance she could see his lungs work in an uneven cadence. His struggle to slip back into calm normalcy, to master his passions, was patently evident in his every stilted movement. She wasn't alone in these overzealous feelings; he felt them too.

"Thank you, Gabriel." She sought his gaze and told him with her eyes what her lips would not. Could not. That his patience and gentleness were changing something inside of her, soothing old wounds and rebuilding a space in her heart where only he could reside.

Chapter 30

Violet tried not to feel guilty over the number of trips it had likely taken to fill the massive copper tub, given she did not want to be in the bath at all. Sinking into the steaming water, her hair floated to the top like a lily pad. Agnes had sprinkled the water liberally with sprigs of lavender, which seemed to somewhat counteract the nervous urgency to scrub herself clean and jump from the tub. The poor footmen went to all the trouble of filling the monolith, the least she could do was sit there until the water was cool.

Maybe not cool. Lukewarm? She washed her hair efficiently, then scooped up water in her cupped hands to see how long she could hold it captive before it trickled through the cracks. She reached a record of two minutes, fifty-eight seconds. Next, she spent an inordinate amount of time remembering all the places Gabriel's mouth had been before abandoning her bath and dressing for the evening in her favourite pale pink nightgown and robe. Cheerful white daisies trailed down the hem to where it swept the carpet below.

Violet rang for Agnes who brushed and plaited her hair neatly down her back, wrapping a long satin ribbon four times around the end and securing it with a floppy bow. The young maid bid her goodnight and disappeared, leaving Violet alone to repeat her twelve-minute stare at the door. Eleven minutes in, she knocked.

"Come in, Violet." Gabriel had draped himself casually across the settee with one bare foot propped up, the picture of an indolent aristocrat. He wore a sapphire-blue brocade banyan she'd not seen before. The asymmetrical swirls of golden thread embroidered into the fabric reminded her of what a tempestuous storm might look like if you could see the wind. His curls fell in messy disarray, giving him a soft and approachable appearance. Supremely touchable. Despite his jest that they sit in chairs divided by four feet of empty space, she took a place on the settee beside him. The warm weather earlier that day had dissipated, leaving a crisp chill in the house. A lively fire burned in anticipation of her arrival, and she stretched her legs out, toes wiggling and reaching towards the cosy glow.

"Are you cold?" He reached for a blanket that had been thrown casually over the settee's sturdy arm.

"A little."

Laying the blanket across her, he tucked the edges in.

"How was the governess?" Gabriel asked, settling back into the settee.

"Miss Lioni. She will do very well, I think. She's Italian, her father was a professor of botany. Her mother passed some time ago, and her father more recently. I wonder at how long she has been on her own. She's thin, Gabriel. Terribly so. But she's clever and interesting, and more than adequate with her knowledge of literature and foreign languages. She's studied some higher mathematics and has a love of all the natural sciences. Best of all, she seems to respect individuality in children. Nora took to her immediately. And you might be interested to know that Keene practically clawed past the line of servants who volunteered to give her a tour of the estate. When Bennet decided to take on the task himself, Keene snatched up a broom and threatened to run him through. Mrs Janewood was forced to intervene!"

"Oh, that's delightful. I can't wait to return the favour and meddle in his romantic endeavours."

"Gabriel Anson, behave yourself!" He dodged her playful swat, swooping in for a kiss to her cheek before falling back into his half-reclined position. "There's not a chance in hell of that occurring. He was like an eleventh plague in my courtship with you, falling somewhere between livestock pestilence and locusts. But even aside from the unexpected bonus of tormenting Keene, she certainly sounds a fair sight better than Nora's last governess, who literally set fire to one of her books. Anatomy, I believe."

Violet gasped. "No! Poor Nora."

"Yes, poor Nora. And poor tea setting that she sent careening into the wall in the anger that followed." Gabriel chuckled and rubbed his forehead. "She's had a hard time of it these last few years. Befriending Zachariah has done a lot to lighten her heart. Certain people seem to have that effect. They help you to see the sun again." The words suspended in the air between them for a moment, then he pointed to where her toes peeked from the blanket, flexing as if to stretch the muscles.

"Are your feet hurting you? You seem to have some very active lower digits."

"A bit. My new half boots aren't quite broken in yet, and they pinch at my little toe. All that time in the paddock today has my legs and feet displeased." She shrugged to indicate the discomfort was inconsequential.

"Poor abused toe. When Emma was pregnant, both with Nora and with … our son, her feet would swell like cooked sausages. I was smart enough to deny it emphatically when she would bring it to my attention, but it was true nevertheless. She even took to clunking about in my house slippers the last month, refusing to have larger shoes made. She was certain her feet would return to their normal petite shape after the babies were born. They never did, but I ordered all her favourite shoes in a bigger size. She pretended she didn't notice the exchange, but I am certain she did."

He watched the fire dance as he opened up his memories to Violet, his eyes reflecting the empty space his wife had left behind. Then, as if closing the book of history that had been written on his heart, he blinked several times and the wistfulness disappeared, his full focus returning to Violet.

Standing, he turned—his body blocking the warmth of the fire—and slowly sank to his knees. "I became quite adept at foot rubs. May I?" His hand lingered centimetres above her feet, which had suddenly gone still. She gave the smallest of nods. The heat of his hands enveloped one foot. He didn't move, only sat, studying her face, one palm cradling her heel and the other splayed across the top.

She let out a long, slow exhale.

Gabriel nodded as if he had been waiting for her to breathe again, then began kneading the ball of her foot in deep, slow circles. He found every sore place and coiled muscle, stroking and soothing until they uncoiled under the gentle pressure of his hands. She groaned and pushed her foot farther into his hands.

"Good?"

"Oh, so good. I think I would have married you just for the foot massages if I'd known." He continued to work each muscle for long minutes until they relaxed and surrendered beneath his fingers. She watched him through heavy lids, her lips parting as her body sank deeper into the plush settee.

A featherlight touch of his index finger travelled along the curve of her instep. With exacting diligence, he stretched and caressed each toe, tugging and squeezing until the joints fell loose and limber. He gently laid her foot on his bent knee and moved to lift the other, treating it to the same tender ministrations. Her head lolled to the side, suddenly too heavy to hold upright. Both his hands encircled her ankle. With languid sweeps, his hand began to wander up and down her calf.

Like being violently jolted from sleep, every muscle lurched and retracted as she mashed her body into the settee to escape the invasion. Gabriel fell onto his bottom to move away, wrenching his hands back. She worked to slow her breathing and focused on the details of his face. *Gabriel's face.* Only then did she realise he had been talking to her.

"Oh God, Vi. I'm so sorry, love. I'm so sorry … I didn't think. Christ, I'm such an idiot." His eyes were frantic, hands fisting the material of his trouser knees.

"No," she said, her voice quavering with the effort to speak. "No," she repeated, more calmly. Scooting down onto the floor in front of him, she took his hands in hers and pressed them hard into the muscle of her calf where her nightgown had slid up. He moved to wrench them away, but she held fast. This was Gabriel and he would not hurt her.

"Touch me."

He shook his head violently but did not retreat.

"Please."

Gabriel's face twisted in a pained expression..

"A fortnight ago when I woke up to you rolled away from me, you told me your body's reaction was involuntary. This was my involuntary reaction. I trust you. Let me trust you."

He exhaled long and slow, then lowered his eyes to where his hands still encircled her leg.

"I don't want to frighten you," he whispered.

"You won't."

There was a long stalemate before he nodded. "Take off your hair ribbon." He moved one hand to indicate her plait. Perplexed, she followed his direction, releasing the silky strands. Holding it out to him, she waited, but he gave one short shake of his head.

Wrap it around your leg and tie it wherever you want me to stop, and I will. You will know exactly what to expect. No surprises. I won't cross the line."

A soft smile curved her lips. She slid her thumb back and forth across the silky ribbon, then raised her nightgown and began tying it just below her knee. Changing her mind, she loosened the bow, slid the ribbon three inches higher and secured it.

When she looked up, he was smiling at her, shaking his head ruefully. "My fierce duchess. You are remarkable, Violet. Are you ready?" He sat with one knee up and the other leg tucked in, his expression suddenly grim. Gabriel set both hands on her ankle. Watching her face for any hint of alarm, he began to massage in slow, tentative strokes around her ankle and lower calf. She relaxed into his touch as he eased the bunched muscles.

There was nothing salacious in his touch, only tenderness and caution. Although it mirrored the onset of her childhood terror physically, it was emotionally the opposite. She was in control. Rather than existing as the powerless paint forcibly splashed across the canvas, she was the artist. Every decision, every stroke of the brush, was placed squarely in her hands.

A low purr emerged from the back of her throat.

"Right there?" Gabriel asked.

She nodded.

Gabriel never came close to the ribbon, and she hadn't felt a moment's more anxiety. Instead, she felt treasured and cared for, as if he was the safe place that her soul had been silently longing for. Their intimacy hadn't magically erased her memories of violence, but Gabriel's touch was so far removed from that of her stepfather's as to feel categorically unrelated. His tenderness was the very antithesis of John's brutality. When he had finished both legs, she was boneless and content. His cheek rested on her knee as he stared off into the fire.

"To bed now," he said, dropping a kiss to her knee. "Will you stay with me, Violet?"

"Yes. If you will play for me? I had grown accustomed to hearing you while I fell asleep, I've missed it."

While his gaze remained locked with hers, she could feel him drift away. It was like watching a handful of snow melt into droplets and slither off in every conceivable direction.

"Of course."

He walked beside her to the bed, arranged the blankets into a cocoon around her, then settled himself at the pianoforte. His head hung low, staring at the place where his fingers rested unmoving on the ivory keys.

She'd had no life experience equal to his loss of Emma, but every evening when he was alone, she listened as he discarded the exhausting burden of trying to return to a life without her, allowing himself to feel the full weight of his despair. With no one watching and dissecting his words and actions, Gabriel freed his sadness to breathe within the unchecked elements of the night.

Violet waited for his haunting melodies to wrap around her. What emerged was something entirely different. He played hesitantly at first, as if his fingers had forgotten the emotion carried by that particular sequence of notes. As if they were reaching for something that had been so far away, for so long, that he had to remember how to call it back. And then he melted into the music.

The notes of Bach's *Air on the G* vibrated through the room. With every caressing note and soulful crescendo, he shared a part of himself that was hopeful, like a fragile seedling determinedly reaching for the sun. A caterpillar fighting to escape his chrysalis. An answering hope swelled recalcitrantly in her chest.

She watched through heavy eyelids as he played his heart for her.

Chapter 31

Gabriel eased into wakefulness just as the first hints of dawn began to creep through the windows. Awareness of Violet's presence in his bed, her softness pressed against the length of his body, made the blood in his limbs feel thick and heavy. One adventurous hand had found her breast, claiming it in sleep. His fingers reflexively kneaded into the inviting swell, saturating him in a warm rush of desire.

He would have enthusiastically forfeited every one of his unentailed properties for ten more seconds of that delectable breast in his palm, but his base desires were inconsequential compared to his need to be unwaveringly deserving of her trust. Even as he glared at his mutinous hand, her nipple pebbled beneath it. He would not permit years of abstinence to overpower decency and logic. She sighed. He couldn't tell if she was awake, but it was past time for a strategic retreat.

Gathering every thread of self-control, he began sliding his hand towards neutral territory. Instead, he found it trapped in place, wedged beneath her slender fingers. He froze, his mouth watering at the deliberate press of her full, tantalising breast into his palm.

"Violet. My hand." He tried to keep the request light. Then his name escaped her lips on a breathy little sigh that had him mentally reciting all the surnames in the House of Lords alphabetically. "Sweetheart, there's no rush." Despite the obnoxious logic exiting his mouth, his nose had somehow nuzzled into her hair, lips following a line of freckles behind her ear.

"Touch me." The gentle command was breath without sound, but it vibrated through him like a roar, catapulting from his aching loins to his racing heart and every space in between. There was confidence in her voice, certainty and trust that caused the careful declination that hovered on his lips to melt away. Her faith fed his fortitude.

She felt safe, and he would yield to her demands without sending her through a flood of violent memories in the process. He could kiss her and touch her without losing his head. He could do that. *He could.*

Experimentally, he played the pad of his thumb back and forth against her nipple. She turned in his arms to pull him closer, but he stilled the action, settling her in place and pressing a quick kiss to her clavicle. "Just relax there, love."

Propping himself on one elbow, he watched his hand as it teased and encouraged her growing arousal, the material of her nightgown sliding across her skin beneath his exploring fingers. He gently pinched her nipple between his thumb and forefinger and she whimpered, pressing into his hand. Bloody hell, she was responsive. He turned away from the erotic sight, lowering his mouth to the curve of her neck. With determined focus, he clung to his control as she sighed and writhed, her inhibitions melting as he sucked and swirled his tongue over a particularly sensitive place. "Gabriel." She drew out his name on a long sound, a delicious amalgamation of a sigh and a groan.

Stretching onto her back, her nose bumped against the side of his and she looked up with a lopsided, bashful smile. Intimacy and affection roiled through him as if an arc of lightning had passed between them. Longing asserted itself and surged in the form of a heavy, warm ache that spread through his chest. Her eyes were fixed on his as if gravity itself held them there and no force from man or the universe could strip them away. Christ, he wanted to tether himself to the feelings those eyes inflamed. Gabriel kissed her hard, covering her body with his and her arms immediately wrapped around him.

He would give himself one moment … one moment to cast off his restraint and revel in the passion she evoked. *No. Before today, Violet's only experience with a man's touch was violence.* He squeezed his eyes closed against a rush of pleasure as Violet chose that moment to slide her hand around his backside and squeeze. *Half a moment,* his lascivious bits bargained. *No.* He gentled his mouth against hers and the little minx nipped his lower lip.

There was no question he had carried this too far to gracefully guide her back the way they'd come, but if he touched her … intimately... His cock leapt even as his soul recoiled. He couldn't live with himself if he caused her fear.

"Sweetheart." Gabriel's lips grazed the satin of her flushed cheek, his words landing in warm puffs against her skin. "Tonight, you are going to be my hands." Her confused, unfocused gaze met his, and he wanted to melt into her all over again. "It's all right, Vi. We'll figure it out as we go."

Easing his head to her breast, he grazed his cheek against her cotton-covered softness, allowing the friction of his unshaven face to rake across the thin material.

"I can't … I don't …"

He paused hovering in place. "Stop?"

Her fingers wrapped around his nape and squeezed. "No," she groaned.

"Shh … Easy, Vi. I've got you. I'll take care of you."

Turning his mouth to her nipple, he lingered there with the slightest touch, more breath than contact. He watched, mesmerised, as she tossed her head to the side, pressing her forehead into her arm. She was lost to sensation and so beautiful. His lower lip trembled as he took her nipple into his mouth, worrying the wet material with his tongue and working in long pulls.

When she arched, offering herself up to him, he shuddered, straining against the flood of lust that rushed over him. Her nails bit into his shoulders. Gabriel had to get control over himself, had to bring her to release before he was turned inside out with the desperation to bury himself inside her. God above, it had been so long. Loss and sadness had drained his desire for years, like a creek bed made dry by the force of unforgiving sun and drought. But she was here, so blessedly good and right in his arms, and he was overflowing … drowning in her.

His hand slid down to catch her chemise and raised the hem to uncover her softly-rounded stomach. There he paused, palm resting across her belly, still and heavy. Violet's dazed eyes met his, a shadow between her brows as she puzzled over his sudden hesitation.

"I feel …" she started in a breathy whisper.

"I know. You ache. And I will help you, love. I want to show you what it feels like when you're not afraid. At night, when you are alone, have you ever touched yourself there?" A blend of curiosity, embarrassment, and confusion played across her face.

"My hands will remain safely on your legs and your stomach, nowhere else. You will do what I cannot tonight. Can you trust me, love?"

Her cheeks flared rosy pink but she nodded.

He began to move his flat hand in circles across her stomach as he alternately nipped and soothed at the hollow below her ear. In long, slow strokes, he travelled down the outside of her thigh and her knees fell helplessly apart. "That's it, Vi. I will never hurt you and I will always stop at your slightest indication. You will always be safe with me."

Gabriel forced himself to take a few long breaths. The sounds she made were more intoxicating than an entire bottle of his best scotch. "Do you want to slide your drawers down, love?" He had intended for his tone to be light and relaxed but it came out so bass it was nearly a growl. Violet wasted no time in shedding the garment but covered herself modestly with a hand.

What she had intended as an act of shyness put her fingers exactly where he wanted them to be. His own hand retreated to her chin, and he captured her mouth with deep, searching kisses. Violet met his methodical slowness with unchecked urgency. She countered the gentle caress of his tongue with feverish intensity as she edged towards a climax she didn't understand, nipping again at his lower lip when he refused to match her flaring arousal. Easing away, he raked his gaze down her body until it rested on the hand that still rested between her legs.

"Touch yourself, Vi. Slide your index finger up and down your pussy nice and slowly." The crass word fell from his lips, further inflaming him. "Yes. That's it." She obeyed without hesitation and he watched as her fingers nestled through the golden curls at the apex of her thighs. A gasp escaped as she explored her intimate places.

"There's a bud of nerves a little higher. Find it with your fingers." His hand skated down and clung to her hip bone where, by God, it would stay. She moaned and her hips arched greedily towards her glistening fingers. Gabriel closed his eyes, grappling with conflicting desires to watch every moment as she came unravelled and bury his face in the pillow with a frustrated roar. His mouth had gone dry as he panted along with her little mewls of pleasure.

"That's perfect. Good girl. Just like that." He continued whispering a string of encouragement into her ear as she chased sensation. Gabriel locked his jaw like a vice, his muscles contracting as if to hold his willpower in place. He was mad with arousal, drowning in it.

Turning his focus inward, he watched her wildly skipping pulse. His fingers may not be the direct source of her pleasure, but he was the voice that guided her, that would show her intimate touch could bring more than just fear and disgust. The magnitude of the trust she'd placed in him funnelled his focus to a pinpoint, casting everything else into an inconsequential blur. Her ecstasy was all that mattered. All at once his muscles relaxed, eyes locking with hers.

"Run your finger around that little bud and follow your instincts. That's good. So good. Just how I would touch you, love. Just relax and listen to my voice." Her breath came in short gusts, knees opened like a butterfly and quivering. "You're so close to climax now. All of that urgency throbbing through you will converge and crest in a wave of pleasure like you've never known before. Rapture so acute that you'll never want it to end."

Suddenly her hand shot to the side and clamped over his, guiding him to her centre to replace her touch with his own.

He required no further invitation. Resting his thumb on those delicate nerves he began to circle, dipping and gliding gently through her satin folds. Christ, she was so wet and hungry and delicious. The sensation of his textured fingertips turning slick with her desire left his cock pulsing greedily against the prison of his trousers.

Later he would teach her about a slow build to release. For tonight, he was already walking a razor's edge and had to end this delicious torture before his carefully contained lust reasserted itself. Her eyes widened, deep blue and unsure as her climax approached. "No Vi, don't be afraid. This is as it should be. It won't hurt. I promise you, love, just let it come."

She pressed her face into his shoulder, her body taut as a bow string, and let go with a groan. How he longed to be inside of her, to feel her squeeze around him. But she needed to learn to trust this feeling and anticipate the pleasure he could bring before any part of him would breach any part of her.

She fell limply against him, flushed and docile in his arms, and he couldn't imagine anything more lovely. Or anything more tempting. He reached down blindly and pulled the counterpane around them. They remained silent for long moments.

"Have I actually managed to quiet that mind of yours, or are your words simply incapable of keeping pace?" Violet looked up, her eyes filled with wonder. She snuggled into his arms.

"That was … well, I don't know what that was, but it was … remarkable." Then she gave a little hiccup of a gasp, her expression wracked with concern. "But you. I will admit to my ignorance but you … You're …" She trailed off as her gaze wandered down to his rudely outspoken erection beneath the blanket. He rested his lips against the soft crown of her head, drinking in the clean smell of lavender and the carnal perfume of the pleasure she had experienced at his hands.

"No, sweetheart. I'm fine. Better than fine. That was perfect." And he *was* fine. The aching need to couple with her had subsided under the satisfaction of having conquered something together that weeks ago felt insurmountable.

"Rest a while, love. It's early yet." He found that his suggestion was unnecessary as sleep had already begun to cradle her in its warm embrace. The house was still silent but for the distant shuffles of servants as they prepared for the new day.

Tracing the lines of her body beneath his fingertips, protective devotion pooled inside of him. He felt a sense of rightness and tranquillity that a younger, less experienced man might take for granted, but he recognised it for the fragile miracle that it was. A moment to be savoured and tucked away inside his heart. Contentment, and hope, and awe came together to form a word that he hadn't used to describe himself for so long that it almost felt out of place. He was happy. Happy with his marriage and with Violet. Happy to just be happy.

But slipping in amongst all those welcome feelings were thoughts of the last woman he'd held in his arms. Emma and the lifetime of joy they'd shared, memorising every curve and angle as they travelled the years together The quiet moments of reassurance after Nora was born and Emma had tried to hide her beautifully-changed body beneath the sheets.

He loved Emma—painfully still—and he wanted to reach in and rip those tender feelings out of his chest for how they intruded on this moment with Violet. Shame and frustration, for all the emotions he was helpless to relieve, seared through him. So much of his heart still clung to those memories as the last remaining pieces of his wife.

Gabriel had known—been certain—of the destruction that would slay both him and Violet if he allowed himself to be swept away before he was ready, but his undeniable affection for her grew more every day. His need to combat Violet's fears, to deny her nothing after she'd spent a lifetime surviving on crumbs, was overpowering. He felt helpless to withhold himself from her. He didn't *want* to withhold himself from her. Violet's thick eyelashes twitched in her sleep, and her nose wiggled like a little rabbit's. He stroked the bridge of her restless nose with an index finger.

He would simply have to bury these warring feelings deeply enough that they could not hurt Violet. He longed for the simplicity of what he'd had with Emma, but it seemed that the past would always be there, circling like a vulture, colouring every experience he shared with Violet. His arms tightened around her; and even in sleep, she responded, wrapping herself around him.

***

An impatient rap at the door sliced through Gabriel's slumber. He hitched a leg atop Violet and pulled her closer. "Ignore him."

The knock came again, accompanied by Keene's cheerful voice through the cracked door. "Rise and shine, sleepyheads."

Violet shimmied out of his grasp, donned her satin robe, and opened the door wide in invitation before sinking into the settee. The dark, permeating aroma of coffee assaulted Gabriel's nostrils, and he wrinkled his nose with distaste.

"It's not for you. It's for Her Grace, who isn't lollygagging in bed all morning." He offered the coffee to Violet and placed the teacup out of Gabriel's reach.

"I don't know what will drive me faster from this bed, that acrid smell or you withholding my morning tea." Gabriel gave an exaggerated shudder.

"Neither would be enough to drive me out of bed with such a lovely woman," Keene purred charismatically.

Gabriel stretched and flexed his stiff muscles, not bothering to glance up at Keene's playful flirtation. "If you recall, I did suggest you marry her. You've missed your opportunity now, old man. A fact for which I am deeply grateful. Besides, your arrival already drove her from my bed. Devoid of my beautiful wife and my tea, it's entirely lost its appeal." Gabriel turned to Violet, but she was watching Keene over the rim of her cup with a curious glint in her eyes.

Keene grinned. "It's nothing. Gabe, in his infinite wisdom, thought I might have taken a shine to you on his birthday. He graciously offered to promote me as a possible match for you."

"How kind of you, Your Grace. Keene *would* be a fine prospect for a husband."

Possessive heat unfurled in Gabriel's belly, surprising him. He wanted to kiss the saucy grin off her face and remind her whose hands had coaxed her to climax just hours before. It was a pointless, primitive impulse and Gabriel stuffed it away as quickly as it had surged to life. "Yes, well. Is there a reason you are dragging me out of the aforementioned bed.?" Gabriel threw his legs over the side and stalked to retrieve his cup like an annoyed child.

Keene regarded his display with a bored expression. "I overheard talk between some of the kitchen staff and Jessica, the new upstairs maid. The dowager has returned from your brother's and is most impatient to pounce upon your lovely duchess. Naturally, I am doing everything in my power to foil her plans."

"We have a new maid?" Gabriel took a sip of scalding his tea, eliciting a cough and a glare in Keene's general direction.

"Don't tell me you haven't noticed her!" Keene shot him a disbelieving grin. "She has the most remarkable set of …" He glanced at Violet, remembering himself at the last minute and tugging at his wiry, cowlicked hair. "Ears," he finished lamely. "She hears everything. Damnedest thing."

"Oh, you mean the fair-haired one with the large bosom?" Violet asked.

Both men chuckled, quietly goading one another on with impish glances. Gabriel was the first to recover, his juvenile bit of fun soured by the reminder of his mother's presence.

Their meeting was inevitable, but the prospect of subjecting Violet to the dowager's calculated viciousness turned the tea bitter in his mouth. Violet was strong and resilient, but he lamented that so much of her life had required her to utilise those attributes. He would not stand idly by while his mother endeavoured to dismantle her confidence.

"We will be away most of the morning. Mrs Hartford, who is one of our closest tenant farmers, lost her husband several weeks ago. Violet and I made arrangements to look in on her and her boys." Gabriel took another sip of tea. "And how will you fill your hours whilst we are away, Keene? Perhaps you'll be attempting to broaden your mind with some … *private tutelage?*"

Keene jerked his head around, pinning Violet with a comically accusing gaze. "You wound me with your gossiping tongue, Your Grace. I thought we were friends."

"If we were friends, you would call me by the Christian name I have repeatedly given you leave to use. Here. I will show you how it's done. I call you Christopher, and you call me—"

"Disloyal Traitorous Duchess who has thrown me to the metaphorical wolves."

"That's closer, I suppose, but it starts with a V. Like this Vi—"
"Villain."

Laura Linn

Chapter 32

Gabriel rushed through his morning ablutions such that three-quarters of an hour later they were picking through a basket of muffins when the dowager swept into the room.

Gabriel turned, dipped in a respectful, albeit stilted, bow and turned to Violet with rote introductions. "Good Morning, Mother. Violet, may I present the Dowager Duchess of Northam? Mother, my duchess." Violet offered a demure smile, something Gabriel wasn't even aware she was capable of. Apparently his duchess was determined to make a favourable first impression. He rested one large hand protectively at the small of her back. Duchess and dowager locked eyes. Silence prevailed for only a moment before Violet's smile bloomed, brilliant and irresistible in its lure, like the first warm day after weeks of thick, foggy rain. "I am very pleased to meet you, Your Grace, and delighted our paths have finally crossed. His Grace has occupied much of my time of late, helping as I adjust to my new role. I must beg your pardon in not seeking you out for an audience."

The dowager's eyes narrowed, as if studying a slab of meat to decide where she would make her first cut. He was not going to wait for the opening slice.

"Unfortunately, Mother, now is not a good time. We were just stepping out to visit a grieving tenant, and I am afraid we really must take our leave." He laced his fingers with Violet's and inclined his head to the dowager.

Flawlessly sculpted twin brows lowered infinitesimally. "I am afraid you will have to conduct your business without the duchess as we have much to discuss."

Gabriel widened his stance and replied without inflection, "My tenants. My home. My schedule. And *my* duchess. If Violet is amenable, we can see you for tea this afternoon. I bid you good morning." The dowager sniffed and looked away.

Violet dropped his hand. "Oh, Gabriel. I was going to bring a few books for Mrs Hartford's boys. I thought they might be a welcome distraction. I'll be but a moment." With that, Violet turned and fled, leaving him alone in the frigid company of his mother.

The dowager wasted no time. "She seems …"

Gabriel clasped his hands behind his back and waited. In other people, he might consider such a pause to be a sign of careful word choice. A moment of reflection to discard sharper comments in favour of kinder, more diplomatic statements. In regards to the dowager, however, he had no such illusions. Her pauses were dramatic, designed to ensure the listener was attentive so that she could skewer them to greatest effect. Any glimmer of hope that she cared enough about his feelings to curtail her opinions had long since been disabused. He shifted, choosing an apple from the basket and biting into the mottled red fruit.

"Painfully lacking in nearly every requisite way."

He worked to swallow the mealy chunk of apple that had become lodged in his throat. Marvelling at the similarities between its sour tang and the woman standing before him, he coughed, discarded the repellent fruit on the table beside him, and maintained his silence.

"It's clear why you have been secreting her away. No visitors, not even an introduction to your own mother. She hasn't the slightest trace of the social aptitude required for a duchess. No elegance. No breeding. No poise. I have met cordwainers with more culture." She glanced at the breakfast selections on the sideboard disdainfully. "What I don't understand, Northam, is why you

319

married her in the first place. I'm certain you could have helped her out of whatever debacle in which she had entrenched herself without having to flex a fraction of your ducal authority, let alone marry the chit! You are one of the most powerful men in England. Greatness is your birth right, but you condescended to marry a nobody. I am completely befuddled."

Gabriel watched the dowager with an air of carefully sculpted indolence, waiting for her to run out of breath. Apparently, she had a second set of lungs stowed away in that cold cavity of a chest.

"Northam, for two years you've wandered around in a pathetic, lovelorn stupor over Emma's death. I won't pretend to understand the human heart, but surely you cannot expect me to believe that you were magically healed by the love of some freckle-faced goat farmer!"

Gabriel crossed his arms, awaiting the next onslaught of criticism to emerge. When nothing seemed forthcoming, he began, his voice no less lethal for its softness.

"I am sorry your life has been so devoid of love that a feeling so central to being human remains completely foreign to you." The dowager gasped as if he had struck her. He couldn't help but soften in response to her pain, but he forced himself to continue regardless.

"It's true I could have found another way to help Violet, but this was the most efficient means of resolving a catastrophic problem. I do not regret marrying her. On the contrary, I grow ever more enchanted by her each day." His eyes trailed away to the door through which Violet had quit the room.

"I liked her from the start. She abounds with kinetic energy and curiosity, like a forest pixie. If not for a simple twist of fate, I would have continued on with her always on the outskirts of my life. And without all the brilliance she exudes, my world would have remained colourless." Despite having opened his heart to the person in his life least likely to possess the organ in question, his smile remained. Not even the dowager's contempt could compete with the pleasure that invaded him at the slightest mention of his wife.

When he looked back to his mother, an expression oddly like satisfaction crept across her face. His face pinched in consternation, unable to reconcile the glimmer of maternal gladness with the woman who raised him. He blinked twice and looked away, perplexed.

"You're right about one thing." His voice was little more than a murmur as he looked down at his boots. "I will always love Emma, and she's never far from my thoughts. A part of my heart will be faithfully reserved for her alone. The closeness we shared isn't lessened by time or affection for another." He picked up the discarded apple and began digging his thumbnail absently into the flesh.

Those words had been burning inside him like corrosive poison since he'd married, but confessing them aloud felt like even more of a betrayal to Violet. Fascinating, delightful, vivacious Violet. Intelligent, guileless, loveable Violet.

He pressed his sticky fingertips to his temples where a headache was threatening, then looked up to his mother, having almost forgotten she was present as he unburdened his feelings. Beside the dowager stood his wife, unblinking. He watched as she pulled a shaky breath of air into her lungs and reassembled her composure, an achingly determined smile stretched across her face.

Something inside of him snapped in two.

"I'm sorry," Violet whispered. "I didn't mean to intrude. I'll be outside when you're ready, Gabriel." She vacated the room with brisk, even steps.

"Shit." The apple fell from his hands with a *thwomp*.

"Exactly so," his mother responded with a curious lack of venom.

"Mother, if you will excuse me—"

"Yes. Go. You'll probably have to buy her a second herd of goats to make this right." He glanced at his mother, startled by the uncharacteristic lightness, then followed after Violet.

With his long economical strides, Gabriel caught up to Violet less than halfway to the stable. She didn't turn to look at him, only continued on with those quick, rigid steps. He shortened his stride to match hers and searched her face for any indication of the extent that he had wounded her. *How long had she been present?* Violet's brows were furrowed, but her eyes were dry. *Thank God.* He didn't think he could survive making her cry. She marched along, the silence hanging heavy between them.

Gabriel wanted to crush her in his arms and apologise. Wanted to offer up the words to ease the sadness he'd caused. Instead, he found himself completely and frustratingly inept. She was twelve inches away and suffering, and he was suddenly unable to communicate with even the slightest semblance of intelligence. He was drowning in sentimentality. She had become the sun in his sky, and he couldn't bear it if the darkness in him dimmed that glow by even a fraction.

He was broken, and he was breaking Violet right alongside him. But what could he do or say that would make this better? He *did* love Emma. That wasn't ever going to go away, and he was destined to watch helplessly as emotions that had always been beautiful in one marriage, turned to poison in the next.

As he entered the stables, he could tolerate the silence no longer. He didn't care what kind of impotent, muddled begging emerged from his mouth. Anything was better than the heartsick uncertainty that churned in his stomach.

"Leave us, please." His clipped tones prompted a cacophony of rapid shuffles as busy stable hands abandoned their work and fled. Gabriel's fingers tunnelled through his hair. "Violet," he rasped. She didn't look up. Instead, she appeared uncharacteristically pensive. But unlike her usual curiosity about the world around her, this seemed to originate within. He reached out and touched the sleeve of her dress, and when she did not step away, he captured the fabric in his fingers like an uncertain child might cling to his mother. She lowered her eyes to his hand, raised them to meet his gaze, frowned, and then took his hand in hers.

"You're hurt." His gravelly voice broke on the word.

"No."

"Angry?" he whispered.

"No."

"Desolate?"

"No."

"You feel in—" *God, he couldn't even say the word.* "Inadequate."

"No," Violet sighed.

"Disgusted?"

"No, Gabriel."

"Frustrated, then." His hand tightened on hers.

"No."

"Well fucking hell, I am."

Her head jerked up, and one corner of her mouth lifted.

"Disappointed?"

She shook her head. Apparently the single word answers had become tedious.

"Shocked."

"Not even a little."

He threw his head back and stared at the rough beams that crossed the roof.

"Hopeless."

"Isn't that the same thing as desolate? It seems like synonyms would be a bit of a wasted question."

"Well, Vi, I've run short on my supply of emotional adjectives. Boys are only taught eight, so now I'm going to have to keep offering synonyms until you take pity on me."

Her eyebrows rose. "Maybe dukes are taught eight. Most of the males in my experience suffer through life on an average of six, so you are well ahead of the curve."

He ignored her attempts at levity, determined to make this right. "I'm sorry." His voice hitched on the last word, and his grip tightened as if she might slip away. He began again before she could speak. "I'm sorry I can't be the husband that you deserve. I'm sorry my heart is such a fragmented wreck. I'm sorry if I've ever made you feel anything but cherished and desirable and perfect, because you are all of those things and so much more." As the words tumbled out, Gabriel's hand slid up Violet's arm, clasping the nape of her neck.

"I'm sorry I'm not the kind of man that can stop loving once I've started. I wish I could. If only to spare you the ... well ... the whatever the hell you're feeling in this moment. The last thing I ever want to do is hurt you, Vi. The very thought of it breaks me in two." Violet's eyes began to swim with tears and he groaned.

"Please say I can hold you, because this is torture."

She fell into his arms, and he crushed her trembling frame against his chest.

"Christ. Please don't cry, love."

"I'm crying for you, you idiot man."

It made absolutely no bloody sense. He wanted to look into her eyes, but his arms would not—could not—let her go, so he gave up fighting with himself and relaxed into her embrace. Only then would his lungs inflate fully. His exhale came on a shudder, and she tightened her grip in response. After a moment, she pulled away, but only so far as to see his face.

"I'm crying because you have tortured yourself so unnecessarily, and for the scorn you've felt towards your own heart, for doing something I would never wish to change." She shook her head. "Of course you love Emma. Of course you will always love Emma. When you're struck with pride at the person Nora is becoming, or you see a nest of Emma's favourite birds, or when a million other ordinary things make you look for her beside you, wanting to share the moment ... only to find she isn't there."

"You can be sad that she isn't here *and* happy that I am."

She paused, gently tugging on a curl that had fallen over his forehead as if to chastise him. "You've somehow forgotten that I met you the day you returned home. I saw the undisguised longing on your face, as if every forward movement of your body hurt without her. And I've seen it a thousand times since. Heard it in your voice and in your music." Her tug transformed to a gentle stroke through his hair. "Did you think I would hate you for it? Feel resentful?"

Well, actually yes. Exactly so. And he felt like an idiot. Albeit an intensely grateful idiot.

Of course his sensitive, empathetic, intelligent wife would understand his unbreakable attachment to Emma. The alternative seemed utterly preposterous when he thought about it. He had beaten himself bloody over feelings that were, apparently, completely reasonable.

Annoyance at his own stupidity washed over Gabriel. How had he doubted Violet? Then, something that felt suspiciously like love for the woman clutching his shirtfront rioted through him, followed by indescribable relief that he hadn't hurt her. Because of all the pain that he could suffer, that was the one thing he couldn't survive.

He felt as if he'd been holding his breath, red-faced and desperate for air, and suddenly his lungs were assaulted, inundated with beautiful, life-giving oxygen. He felt free.

Gabriel took her face in his hands, pressing his forehead to hers and fervently hoping she could feel all the declarations that he didn't know how to say.

"You," he said. And then nothing, because she made all his words feel insufficient, too small and subdued for the overwhelming joy that crashed over his soul, melting into him like the light from a thousand twinkling stars. And then his mouth was on hers.

Chapter 33

Gabriel's kiss was fierce and uncivilised, piratical in its single-mindedness. He couldn't gentle his mouth while his pulse pounded so violently in his ears. He felt off kilter, like a listing ship, and touching her—kissing her—was the only thing that could right him. Violet met him with equal ardour, plunging both hands into the den of his coat, frantic fingers pulling at the material until her cool fingertips met with a sliver of skin at the small of his back.

Then her fingers stilled. A puff of air pressed through her lips at the contact, sounding something like the unfurling one felt with the first bite of food after a stomach-gnarling fast. A fleeting moment to relish the relief before diving in to devour. Her fingers strained against the tightly tucked material, stretching for more contact until, with an irritated mumble, she jerked both hands free and began wrenching at the buttons of his waistcoat. With an efficient jerk, she ripped his shirttails loose, then clung to his skin like moss to a rock. The few orderly thoughts still lingering in Gabriel's mind evaporated at the contact, singed away by the sensation of those ten little fingers pressed into his muscles.

Her tongue mated with his, awakening his length with prickles of jealous desire. There was no finesse to their movements, just frantic eagerness to connect. To soothe and be soothed. His cock struggled to press closer through the layers of fabric separating him from her sex.

Words of nonsensical encouragement tumbled from Gabriel's mouth between breathless, inelegantly tangled kisses. His hips had begun a steady rocking rhythm against her abdomen, his erection unapologetically heavy and eager for contact. It wasn't enough. The soft curves of her belly only teased and inflamed him, offering no relief to his desperation for warm, squeezing friction.

His body clamoured for her, clamoured to taste all the places he couldn't reach—the delectable satin skin beneath the high neck of her riding habit, the inside of her thighs, and higher up to her sensitive nub. Sweet Christ, he could smell her arousal.

He knew that eventually they'd meet a hard boundary, and their adventure would have to stop, but he needed her now. Needed to be close to her. And he would communicate with lips, tongue, and touch where words had failed him.

One of Violet's hands had abandoned his back and begun a shy exploration of his thigh, like a wallflower trying to summon the courage to circle closer to a gentleman. Their galloping speed settled into a more deliberate rhythm, becoming a shared, steady cadence. Every nerve ending in his body focused on the fingers that traced across the tense muscles of his thigh.

Gazing up through half-closed lids, she searched his eyes. He gave a slow, emphatic nod. "Please." His voice felt hot and raspy in his throat. Her teeth sank into her kiss-reddened lower lip, eyebrows furrowed. "It's all right, Violet. You can touch me."

"How?"

"Anything. Everywhere. Please … just please." They both watched her hand as it hovered above him. He was going to implode from the wanting. His cock leapt toward her outstretched palm like some overeager puppy begging to be stroked. He should have been embarrassed, but he was too desperate—too hard—to feel anything but throbbing need. She smiled as his length twitched eagerly.

"I didn't know it could do that!" Amusement trickled in through the steel of his desire and a hoarse chuckle escaped, giving way to a guttural groan as her palm grazed the length of his shaft through the thin barrier of his trousers. She sucked in a startled breath of air and pulled her hand away. Shaking his head in dazed reassurance, he rested his hand atop hers and guided it back.

"I didn't hurt you," she murmured. It was a statement more than a question, but he answered it anyway.

"No, love." She paused after each stroke as if to catalogue his reaction, running the tip of her index finger down the length of him, then cupping him with a tentative squeeze. His jaw was beginning to ache from the teeth-grinding restraint. Every coiled muscle in his body bellowed with the need to thrust into her hands, but he remained motionless as she explored.

"Can I see you there?" She was already reaching for the falls of his trousers, and he could only nod. It shouldn't have surprised him that curiosity would percolate through Violet's lust, leaving him a boneless puddle at her disposal while she investigated and analysed. His cock sprang free and Violet's hand slowly dropped to her side.

"You don't have to, Violet. I can tuck back in and we can go."

"As if we could get that back in your trousers. It would take a pulley, ropes, and a draft horse to pull your fall flat enough to fasten." She smiled mischievously.

"I assure you, I can put it back," he responded drolly and began to do just that when her fingers wrapped about his wrist.

"No." She released his wrists and ran one finger from root to tip. Gabriel's eyes drifted closed, and a long guttural moan escaped his lungs. It was a whisper of contact, but every nerve fired along the path of her teasing caress. His skin was fever-hot, every muscle riveted and strung taut save for his heart, which bounded fiercely in his ribcage. If she was aware of his response, she gave no outward indication.

"I didn't expect it to be so soft. Like the underbelly of a baby rabbit." He cracked one eye open incredulously. Soft was not how he would describe his current state of being. But before he could utter a word of disagreement, she had taken him between both her warm hands and begun sliding down the length of him. His arm shot out to brace against the wall as a jolt of sensation ricocheted through his limbs. She pressed one thumb to his sensitive head and rubbed in soft lazy circles.

"So good." The words rushed out in a hiss. He wrapped one arm around her shoulders, resting his forehead in her hair, and inhaling the soft hint of her honeysuckle soap. He watched, transfixed by her exploring hands. She pumped in slow tight strokes, and the first twinges of a familiar tightening began to pulse through his abdomen and below. Wrenching his hips away, he reached down to take both her hands in his.

"Sweetheart, we have to stop now." He took her mouth with deliberate slowness.

"Stop?" Her voice was husky and distracted, and she squirmed in his arms, attempting to free her busy hands from his grip. He chuckled despite his rampant arousal, holding her fast.

"Yes, love. I don't want to spill in your very capable hands. Nor do I want to deflower you in a pile of hay while the horses watch. You deserve better, Violet, and frankly so do I. It's been a long time and I want more for us. I shouldn't have gotten so carried away." He softly touched his lips to hers while he tucked himself away, closing the buttons against his emphatically disappointed parts. She glanced down at his trousers ruefully.

"That doesn't look comfortable."

"Kiss me better then?" he murmured against her lips. He kept his mouth gentle, struggling to limit his focus to the tender feelings welling up inside of him with every featherlight stroke of her lips across his.

The door creaked on its rusty hinges then. A wide-eyed Nora stood blinking up at them, Zachariah trailing behind.

"Come on, Nora," Zach said, attempting to lead her away, his hand curling about her wrist with an ineffectual tug.

Nora's face scrunched up, her chin quivering as a single sob escaped. In a whirl of knee-length skirts, she bounded away. Gabriel lifted Violet's hands to his lips. "I'd better—"

"Of course."

Strolling to the open door, he cast Violet a smile over his shoulder before setting out in search of his daughter.

A pair of stable hands and a gardener milled around a cluster of daylilies, pointedly avoiding Gabriel as he laboured to thread his second arm through the sleeve of his coat. He was untucked, rumpled, and, he noted ruefully, he had misaligned the buttons of his waistcoat. Keene was loping in his direction, scattering curious servants as if he were a gale force wind. They reassembled some fifty feet further in the distance, stagnating about uselessly like a flock of scratching chickens.

"See? Helpless as a kitten." Keene plucked the buttons free, straightening and securing them deftly with dexterous fingers and a self-satisfied smirk. "Mauled by an overzealous donkey? I warned you not to keep the carrots in your trouser pockets." Gabriel smoothed at his wrinkled shirt, actively ignoring his friend's goading.

Arching away to survey his work, Keene grimaced. "No. You still look like you've been tumbling your duchess in the hay loft," he clucked with mock disparagement. "There's nothing to be done for it, Your Grace. Please at least tell me some actual tumbling occurred. Shall I send out Agnes to tend to Her Grace?"

"Stop fishing, Keene. Her Grace is perfectly assembled."

"Oh really! Then what *did* you have in your pocket that made the donkey so excited?"

Gabriel signed and scanned the horizon for hints of his daughter's whereabouts. "As much as I would love to stand here and regale you with tales of my manly prowess, I have a distraught eleven-year-old to contend with … Come to think of it, I have no desire to discuss my manly prowess with you at all." The hint of a cocky grin pulled at his features, undermining his words to Keene. He had to admit he was feeling rather virile at the moment, and even his daughter's pained face wasn't enough to completely wash it away.

"She went towards the rose garden. She looked distraught, so I was coming to fetch you. God knows sobbing prepubescent girls are not my forte"

"Are they *anyone's* forte?" Gabriel muttered as he traipsed away across the grey cobbled path that wrapped around the topiaries and through Emma's garden.

***

Gabriel found Nora huddled beside a sprawling yellow rose bush, its fragrant buds partially opened to the sky and splayed between the elaborate scrolls of a wrought-iron bench. Her shoulders rose and fell rapidly as if she was trying to squelch impending tears, while the hands he had so often held, savagely ripped petals from a bud.

He sighed, his gaze travelling through the kaleidoscope of colour just beginning to come to life around him. It was a magical sort of garden, the kind you could disappear into and forget that the world still spun just outside the winding paths. Large, clumsy bees bumped into the flowers like drunken men stumbling from a pub. He could hear the fountain near the centre, trickling merrily in the distance.

"Poppet." He lowered himself to the ground beside her, and she scuttled several inches away. "Darling. Won't you talk to me?" She snapped the thorny stem in two with a resounding pop, slicing her finger against the thorns in the process. With a hiss of pain, she thrust her finger into her mouth and glared at him accusingly, as if he had stabbed her himself.

He extended his hand to reach for her, but her elbows tucked in, chin dropping to her chest like a roly-poly bug. Allowing his arm to fall helplessly to his side, he swallowed, then reached up to bend a rose stem back and forth until it became weak enough to give way, releasing its captive bloom.

He pressed the sunny yellow bud to his nose and inhaled deeply. "There are so many beautiful colours of roses, each special and unique in its own way. The yellows have always been close to my heart, but those soft pink blooms are really quite glorious as well. I enjoy when the gardener adds them to a bouquet, not only because I think they deserve to be appreciated in their own right, but because they're simply a different kind of stunning."

He extended his hand with the rose, entwined with an unspoken apology for the hurt she felt. "I know it must be hard to see me holding a lady who is not your mother."

She accepted the proffered rose and stroked the petals.

"I know you miss her. I miss her too. God, how I miss her. But Violet is my wife now." He rummaged through his thoughts, attempting to arrange his feelings in a way Nora could understand them. But they were all so mashed and mangled, a knot that refused to be untangled.

He took a breath and tried again. "Violet is my wife now, and she deserves to feel …" *Singular in my devotion, secure in my affection … loved.* He couldn't finish that sentence, so he just sat staring dumbly at his hands. The memory of Violet—patient, wonderful Violet—giving him the grace and understanding he could scarcely give to himself, made his heart kick to life with a rhythm that had fallen silent years before.

"She deserves to feel loved," Nora said. pulling the words right out of his heart. "And of course you love her. She is wonderful." She smiled up at him, a watery shimmer welling up in her eyes. She dashed them away with the back of her hand.

He considered himself at least passably fluent in the contrary and baffling language of women, but it was moments like these that left him dangling without direction and completely inside out in his assumptions. Like ordering a carriage in a foreign tongue and receiving a courtesan instead. Clearly, whatever he thought he understood was not what was actually occurring.

A honeybee landed on Gabriel's knee, and he watched as it ambled across his joint on thread-thin, quivering legs. "I don't understand, poppet. You were upset when you saw Vi and me … together." He stroked his hand down her mane of overzealous curls, twirling one tight ringlet around his finger. Relief swelled as she nuzzled into his touch.

"You said you were sleeping in separate beds." She sounded exhausted and cinched tight with worry. "When you were kissing her, it didn't look like…" She snagged him with a frustrated look, another errant tear escaping.

When had the last remnants of his little girl vanished from sight? The once rounded, cherubic cheeks and careless smile had melted away, leaving a thoughtful, intelligent young lady cuddled up against him in the place where his baby had been.

"I did say that. And we were in separate beds, or are … for the moment, at least in the way that you are insinuating. Or at least, that you seem to be …" He was not doing this well. *And how does she know what happens in a married couple's bed chamber? A question for another day.*

"But I don't want her to die!" Nora's head slumped into his chest and he felt her body shake with tears. *What in the hell was going on here?* He evidently lacked some critical piece of the puzzle, because no matter how many ways he examined and rearranged the facts of this conversation, they made absolutely no bloody sense.

"Why do you worry that Violet will die?"

For a while, the effort to breathe was too great to allow Nora to speak. He could feel her heart thumping like a startled sparrow.

And then, in a voice so quiet he almost didn't hear it, Nora spoke. "I know where babies come from, Papa."

Snap. The last puzzle piece suddenly clicked into place, allowing for a clear picture to come into focus. She wasn't jealous or angry at Violet's place in the family. She was terrified that Violet would become pregnant with his child. Terrified of losing Violet, exactly as they had lost Emma.

A Wildflower for a Duke

Chapter 34

Gabriel looked into Nora's eyes, and he could not hide from the truth when he saw his own terror reflecting back. Nora wanted Violet separated from him by bedroom walls, a physical barrier to prevent a child from ever taking Violet away. And, God help him, he had subconsciously wanted the same. He was the worst kind of coward.

While his barricade hadn't been as tangible as plaster and wood, it had been every bit as effective at keeping Violet far enough away to protect him from the soul-withering heartache of losing her. His had been constructed of memories held in such reverence that their very existence discouraged trespass. Each time Violet threatened to breach his defences with her whimsical curiosity and artless charm, the imaginary clock for the healing of his heart ticked louder between them. Of course his mourning for Emma had been a genuine consideration, as had Violet's past with her stepfather, but they hadn't been the only impediments. Grief over Emma had slowly transformed into fear that had held them hostage, long after their other struggles had been confronted.

He would always love Emma, but it wasn't the persistence of that love that had created, and now maintained, the unassailable barricade around his heart. It was the absolute certainty that he could not survive the loss of love a second time. Loving and losing Violet would categorically destroy him.

When Emma died, his heart beat only out of habit. Violet had made every beat feel purposeful again, and his cowardice was a betrayal to both women … and to love itself.

For a time, he could do nothing but squeeze Nora close, sprinkling light kisses across the crown of her head and wondering how in the hell he was going to make this better. Better for her. Better for him. Better for Violet. Because awareness of the fear did nothing to quell it, and he felt suddenly like a boat adrift at sea, with no hope of wind in his sails to guide him back to safe harbour.

"Carrying babies is harder for some women than it is for others. Your mother had a difficult time with each. We lost a child ... early on, when you were a mere pixie toddling around. Most women have uneventful confinements. There is no reason to assume Violet would have any trouble at all."

Even as he said the words, a stomach-churning picture of Violet struck him so vividly that he felt lightheaded from the force of it. Violet, blood pooled between her legs. Violet, as cold and white as snow. *No.*

"There's no reason to assume that she *wouldn't* either. Can't you just stay out of her bedroom? Can't *this* be enough?"

Can this be enough? A life of cautious affection. Of maintaining empty space between his heart and hers. But "empty" was an illusion. As fiercely as he worked to maintain it, all their feelings would permeate those boundaries, like the scent of roses perfusing the air around them now. The space would fill, if not with love, then with fear.

"Oh darling, it's not only about babies. Babies are merely the natural conclusion to the love between a man and his wife. There is always a risk, but I can't deny her that love." He left off the remainder of that sentence. That it wasn't something he could deny himself either, regardless of the panic that crept cold through his body.

"Sometimes we just have to love and have faith in the endurance of that love." She nodded into his shirtfront. If only he could comfort himself as he had comforted Nora.

"I love you so much. And I am sorry this is something that I cannot make better for you. Shall we go for a walk?" Movement seemed like a good idea.

***

Violet exchanged her wool riding habit for a lightweight day dress. Although it was from her new wardrobe, it still thumbed its nose at society's standards of beauty—devoid of even a single frill, soft as water, and rebelliously comfortable.

She could pinpoint the approximate location of the dowager based solely on the relative position of the scattered servants. Scanning each room as she passed, she paused before the door of the art studio. Violet took a steadying breath and crossed into the room.

Zachariah had been busy. With abundant supplies, he had unleashed his creativity with breathtaking results. No matter how many times she had seen and been captivated by his skill, the depth of his talent still rendered her awestruck. A nearly-completed painting was perched on a wooden easel in the corner … her and Gabriel the day they had built the goat loft.

In the picture, she faced away from Gabriel as she worked, oblivious to his gaze. She studied the expression on his face, the warmth of the sun highlighting the thickness of his eyelashes, his curls caught in the soft eastern breeze. She had never seen that look on his face before, as if she was everything he wanted and couldn't have. It was an expression of such intense, intimate longing that she had to look away. It felt intrusive, as if his soul was exposed for her casual perusal. Was this what Zachariah saw?

Across the room, the dowager studied a charcoal drawing of Nora sprawled out on her stomach in knee-high waves of grass. Her dress was tangled about her knobby knees, her chin resting in her palms as she studied the remnants of an animal being pecked clean by a buzzard some feet away. There was a stark contrast between her carefree youthful beauty and the unsightly bird sitting nearby, ravenously feeding on rotting flesh. Like the collision of dark and light, harmoniously entwined and accepting of one other. The dowager appeared equally entranced.

"Your son has remarkable talent." She paused, stroking the scavenging animal with one long, gnarled finger. "He sees things. Things that the rest of us can't until he spells them out letter by letter in swirls of colour on canvas."

Violet came to stand beside the dowager, whose face was as austere and remote as a weather-worn mountain.

"I saw him playing with Nora this morning," the dowager said. "She looked happy ... I don't think I was ever that happy." She wasn't seeking sympathy. In fact, Violet sensed that it would be unwelcome if offered. The statement was as dispassionate as a remark upon the weather.

"My son thinks I am hard, and I am, I suppose. My mother was strict, remote even, and her mother before her. Somehow Northam ... Gabriel," she amended, "knew to choose a wife that would send that course reeling off kilter. I look at these pictures..." Her eyes floated from one depiction of Nora to the next while she seemingly chose her words with care. "I look at these pictures, and I see a person that should be cherished and protected as she is. As I wish someone might have done for me." Some of the carefully manufactured stoicism slipped from her face, revealing a depth of regret that was startling. "I have spent a lifetime telling Gabriel that every choice in support of that was fundamentally wrong." She shook her head as if in surrender to the foreign conclusions assailing her. "I think I'd like to know the girl in this picture. And the young man who made her visible to me."

Violet gave a slow nod. "I think they would like that very much."

"I have no idea what kind of duchess you will be, but I suspect that if Gabriel chose you, you are exactly what he needs. However, I am right in saying that this dukedom still needs an heir, and I will harp on that relentlessly until I am cold in the ground ... or until this house overflows with young, strapping boys." The corners of her mouth lifted in a rusty attempt at an expression long lost, or perhaps never really learned. It was a smile nonetheless.

Violet felt her cheeks warm in response. "It's complicated. Emma was the love of his life. I've never met a man so intrinsically capable of giving his whole heart away to one person. He cares for me deeply, I know. And I think he's honestly happy to have been cast into this marriage. But that's not quite the same thing as love, is it? I am not sure that Emma left enough of him behind to gather up into a stronger sentiment. I believe he would freely give it if it were his to give."

How would it feel to be the recipient of all that love? Like sunshine that fills every corner of your soul, she imagined. She had lived her entire life in scattered light and dusky shadows, admiring the beams from just beyond the fringes of their glow. She had never expected to have more, never considered the possibility that she would be so close to love, and still somehow just beyond its reach. Like inhaling the rich savoury scents of someone else's dinner through an open window. To expect more than a life on the periphery of love felt like an inconceivable leap of faith.

There was a pleasant sort of silence between Violet and the dowager, each reorganising truths and assumptions while they wandered the room absorbing the magnificence of Zachariah's art. The silence stretched between them until Violet surmised that no response would be forthcoming, which was just as well because she'd said more than she had ever intended.

And then the dowager linked her arm with Violet's and squeezed her wrist. "I don't know the first thing about loving a husband, but I do know something of loving yourself enough to search for what you need … and what life looks like when you don't. Fear makes for a lonely friend, duchess."

The dowager kept her shoulders pulled regally straight, her expression devoid of the emotion that lurked beneath. Violet couldn't imagine the coldness of the life she must have lived, her statuesque exterior growing thick, multiplying in layer upon layer as a defence against the world and its cruelty. Over time, as that stone armour had hardened, it left no space for the presence of flesh and bone within. The same barriers that had served to protect her had nearly crushed her softness and humanity.

The dowager continued, "And love doesn't seem to be only available in finite quantities. Not in a man like my son. I saw the way he looked when you fled from the dining room. It was as if half his heart had just raced out the door." With that, the dowager patted Violet's hand with a few brisk strokes and walked away.

Fear makes for a lonely friend. Yes. But vulnerability and rejection sounded so much lonelier. Violet picked up one of Zach's sketchbooks and began flipping through the pages. On the very last page was a rough drawing of Nathan and Hamish, hands entwined, walking through a copse of cherry blossoms, the low-hanging branches forming a secret cave of blooms. Violet was in the foreground of the picture in profile, present but apart.

She felt an echo of that moment in the pit of her stomach. That resigned loneliness. She could see the passage of time that followed, when she would turn to her work to escape the sadness, immersing herself in the science of the world around her, cosseted by the comfort of its systematic predictability where she could elicit a reliable response. There was no such predictable pattern to be found in love.

***

Violet was absent from lunch. When she failed to arrive at the usual dinner hour, Gabriel excused himself and went in search of her. A quarter of an hour later, still unsuccessful, he changed his course to Keene, whom he knew would be taking his own dinner in the kitchens.

Present alongside Keene, Bennett, and a few other stragglers, was an unfamiliar face. A young woman who remained apart from the others, her posture unapproachable. She would have appeared entirely forbidding if not for a pair of inquisitive, moss-green eyes that swept the room, landing briefly on Keene before shifting direction to Gabriel.

"Miss Lioni, I presume? It is a pleasure to meet you. My duchess speaks very highly of you."

Despite the tidy twist to her chestnut brown hair, her index finger moved to sweep a non-existent tendril behind her ear, as if she had grown so accustomed to its disobedience that a habit had formed. She dipped into a curtsy. "The pleasure is mine, Your Grace. Your children are delightful." She slid back into the corner as if attempting to blend in with the walls that surrounded her on both sides.

Keene had stood respectfully upon Gabriel's entrance, with some prodding from Bennett, but he continued to shovel half of a ham sandwich into his mouth as he did so.

"Looking for someone?" he asked after swallowing.

"Violet."

"She doesn't generally take her meals with me, Your Grace." Gabriel lowered his chin and frowned. The other servants, long accustomed to the men's unorthodox relationship, paid the conversation no mind. Bennett, however, openly scowled.

"But I may know where she is," Keene added.

"You *may* know?"

Unable to contain his distaste for the valet's insubordination, Bennett quit the room with another parting look of disgust aimed at Keene, who appeared amused by the old man's ruffled feathers.

"He would fire me in an instant if you would allow it … gleefully."

"Yes, well, I may let him if you don't tell me where my wife has gone."

A footman coughed out a laugh, then buried his mirth behind his hand.

"I feel like the information you want is jostling around somewhere in my brain, but it lacks the proper glucose stimulant to break free. There is a treacle tart, you see, but Mrs Simmons smacked my hand when I went to take a slice. Hurt like the devil! That woman is feistier than a wild cat." He winced dramatically and rubbed at the back of his hand. Keene glanced at Miss Lioni, whose expression remained indifferent to his antics. "She informed me that there's only enough to serve the family for the evening meal. But it's a treacle tart, Gabriel. My favourite." His gaze floated wistfully towards the dessert, and then to Mrs Simmons, who guarded it with a dour expression.

"Oh give him the damn tart, Mrs Simmons," Gabriel said.

She huffed like a schoolgirl who had been asked to surrender a favourite toy, and plopped a slice in front of Keene with a shake of her head. "You should fire him, Your Grace. Troublesome little pest, he is." But there was no malice in her voice, and she tucked a napkin into his hand.

Keene beamed at the prize before him for a long moment, before he stood, carrying the plate tightly clutched in both hands. He stopped before Miss Lioni, who seemed to shrink smaller with every step Keene made in her direction. Keene looked between the proffered tart and the governess, an uncommonly wobbly smile tipping at the corners of his mouth.

Like a lioness awakening from slumber, she stretched to her full height, chin lifted at an angle that looked almost uncomfortable to maintain, and strode from the room.

The quiet that had descended upon the kitchen popped like a bubble, servants swiftly returning to the last of their meals.

Gabriel gave a low whistle. "She must really dislike you to have walked away from Mrs Simmons' treacle tart." The cook preened. Keene scowled.

He scratched his fingertips through his hair, his frown sliding into something like guilty bemusement. His expression was made more comical by his springy locks, which shot off in every conceivable direction. "It may have something to do with the fact that I told her that I was going to marry her. She didn't seem as excited about the prospect as I am."

Returning to his chair, Keene sank his fork into the slice, his unabashed exuberance instantly rebounding.

Gabriel tapped the toe of his boot impatiently while Keene chewed, swallowed, and groaned appreciatively.

"My wife?" he prodded.

"Art studio."

Gabriel started to leave, then circled back, scooped up a chunk of dessert from Keene's plate with a hooked index finger, and dropped it in his mouth.

"Hey! Savage!" Keene yelled. Gabriel exited with a chuckle.

***

Violet sat cross-legged on the floor with her back to the door. Gears and springs were scattered around her like flowers in a field. A few feathered locks of her hair cascaded down about her ears, but the majority was still restrained, artfully pinned at her nape, leaving her long slender neck exposed.

Her shoulders curled in as she concentrated on a task that was hidden from Gabriel's view.

"Just ... about ... there!" she exclaimed, winding some kind of tiny mechanical gadget with a key and setting it on the floor. Violet stared at it with rapt anticipation for a moment. When nothing happened, she flipped around in a mass of fluffy petticoats to lay on her stomach, flat on the carpet, eye to eye with the intricate invention.

She crooked one leg at the knee causing her skirts to slide to the ground, exposing her calf. Her chin rested in her palm. With one finger, she brushed along the garble of wheels and springs almost lovingly until the gadget jolted forward and began spinning in careless jerking directions, eventually flopping forward on its nose.

"Blast. The balance weight isn't quite right." She lifted the contraption and began to prod about the underside with a miniature, pointed tool.

She was enchanting. The mobile expressions on her face while she concentrated, her lower lip caught in her teeth as her mind worked at bounding speeds, her incandescent smile, glowing at every incremental success. He could have watched her for hours, caught in the trance she wove through the air, but his stomach growled noisily and her head jerked in search of the unexpected sound.

"I didn't see you there." She shuffled to a seated position, tucking her legs neatly beneath her skirts.

"I hate to interrupt, but I was beginning to worry you would starve without intervention. My stomach is protesting, and I ate a midday meal. Unlike some…" He raised his eyebrows, allowing them to complete the sentence for him.

"Nonsense. I couldn't have missed any meals. It's only …" She hopped to her feet before he could offer assistance, and glanced at the clock. "Well, there must be something wrong with the clock." She feigned seriousness only long enough to meet his knowing look, then melted into musical laughter. "I suppose my stomach thanks you, even though ladies aren't supposed to acknowledge the existence of their stomachs. How very improper of me."

"Well, I promise not to tell anyone that you have one … a stomach, that is." Reaching out, he found her hand hidden in the folds of her skirts, clutched tightly around her wind-up contraption. He slid it from her grasp, holding it up for closer examination.

"How very ingenious you are. Such a remarkable, clever mind." His index finger stroked the gears as he spoke. When he looked up again, he found her gaze, sensual and heavy lidded, trained to the path of his caressing finger. Her lips parted as if he had kissed her with his words.

Caught in the lure of her gaze, he cupped her cheek with his hand, tracing her lower lip with the pad of his thumb. Her tongue darted out, wet and warm, and touched the tip of his exploring digit before nipping it playfully. It was reminiscent of the day with the blueberry pie, only with vastly different results. How far they had come, he marvelled.

"Didn't you mention dinner?" Violet asked.

He cleared his throat and peeled his eyes away from her mouth. "Yes. Dinner. Right this way, Your Grace."

Chapter 35

Having grown tired of waiting on their parents, the children had finished their dinners and left to play in the nursery. Gabriel excused the footmen in favour of privacy.

"How is Nora?" Violet asked.

Gabriel studied his dinner for a moment, his previous joy subdued at the prospect of the complicated conversation, then shook his head. "Later. I want to hear about your day first."

She stared at him for a moment, as if combat
ting the urge to protest, then acquiesced with a nod.

"I met with your mother. She found her way into Zachariah's studio." Gabriel set down his fork, giving her his full attention.

"She saw something in his paintings, parts of you and Nora that she'd never been able to see before. Her exterior remains as dour as you've described, but somewhere inside, she's shifted a little. For that moment, at least, she saw Nora through Zach's eyes and recognized her value and beauty as a person, apart from the dukedom. A part of the dowager wants to protect that person. She even acknowledged the rightness of the choices you've made for Nora and the strength that it took to step away from the well-trodden path. I quite liked the woman I met today in that art studio, and I think we will get on just fine." All he could do was blink dumbly in response.

A delighted smile tugged at the corners of her mouth. In the dumbstruck silence that followed, she sliced her carrot into curiously uneven pieces and arranged the bits into the shape of a smiling face. Lightness bubbled inside him as he smiled back at the happy vegetables. He was grinning like an idiot at vegetable art, and he couldn't even bring himself to feel embarrassed.

"Your turn. Tell me about Nora. Is she all right?"

"She is. I misjudged her concerns." He took his time, slicing his meal into unnecessarily small pieces. "One would think that after eleven years parenting a young lady, I would stop trying to reach any conclusions on my own, as it appears I am consistently incorrect in my assumptions."

"Oh?" Violet prompted, popping a bite of venison into her mouth.

Gabriel flicked a carrot around his plate. "She is scared. Scared that you will die … in childbirth. Like Emma."

Violet choked on her food, coughing into her napkin. On his feet and beside her in a second, Gabriel laid one hand on her shoulder and offered her a glass of wine with the other. She nodded, taking a long gulp of wine and then clearing her throat.

He settled back into his chair. "Which served to further insinuate that concern to my mind as well. So much for level-headed parenting," he mumbled. "Now I am afraid you may have to contend with two anxious Ansons instead of one. Children have a way of voicing the fears that our adult minds would rather keep silent." He rubbed his forehead with his fingers, his meal forgotten. The grandfather clock ticked loudly through the room, counting off the seconds while Gabriel gathered his courage.

"I'm terrified, Violet." His voice was low and rough, like heavy-grained sandpaper pushed in long, punctuated swipes. He swallowed, trying to lighten his tone to something less desolate, but no sound would pass through his throat.

"Oh, Gabriel." Violet laid her hand on his leg beneath the table and squeezed.

He did his best to clear the emotions from his face; he didn't want her to see further evidence of how irrefutably damaged he was. Scarred not only by the death of Emma, but by the constant looming fear that loss would besiege him yet again. In his marriage

347

to Violet, he had doubled the size of his family, doubled the capacity for love, and, in doing so, doubled his chances for loss.

He couldn't look at her. He already felt too much. Too much grief. Too much fear. Too much frustration at the largeness of all these feelings and how they threatened to smother each fragile hope just as it began to feel sturdy and substantial. One look into those understanding blue eyes and all the emotions that tormented him would bleed out like ink into parchment.

He could feel her gaze on him. Not demanding or disparaging, only understanding and soothing. When they'd married, he told Violet he wanted to be unbroken for her. Never had he wanted that more than in this moment.

Then she whispered his name and he *did look*, because he could deny her nothing. And because the sheer magnitude of love that pounded in his chest felt large enough to decimate even the most indomitable fear. With a soul-weary sigh, he laid his worries at her feet, knowing that if there was a woman in this world strong enough to help him conquer them, it was Violet.

"I … I'm not sure I could survive losing my wife twice. I couldn't survive losing *you*. I never thought I would feel this way again. Hopeful. Alive. Bloody inside out at the sight of you."

I love her.

Of course he loved her, but he could barely form the words in his head without feeling like he was challenging fate. Like the universe would see the way his heart sped up every time she smiled at him and smite him right there on the spot.

It took him a moment to realise she was tracing the outline of a heart on the inside of his thigh with her index finger over and over.

Slowly, deliberately, he reached beneath the table, took her hand in his and turned it face up. There, he traced his own heart on the palm of her hand and closed each finger around it, as if to trap it there.

I love you. He couldn't say the words, but God, how he wanted to. They churned inside of him, gathering momentum until his chest throbbed with the strain of containing them, like a furnace with no pressure release. His body rebelled against his cowardice and inactivity, seeking connection with her through its own primitive means, with his mouth and his fingers, with his breath on her skin and his body covering hers. He wanted to lay her down and bury himself inside her. Wanted to show her that he loved her. Unequivocally.

She smiled warmly, oblivious to the sudden urgency laying waste to his reserve. It was one of a thousand smiles she'd given him, smiles that he had collected and held close to his heart. He had married her hoping to fill a void for Nora and to save Zachariah. He'd hoped for easy companionship and to offer care and protection. But she had found all his empty spaces and filled them with her smiles, and now he was glowing with the warmth of them.

"Have you had your fill of dinner then, or is Mr Smiley awaiting his sentence at the gallows?" Gabriel asked.

"Oh no. He's far too cheerful to be consumed."

He could feel her joy. It was thick and energetic in the air between them, absorbing into him like water on parched skin. "Good." He gave his muscles their freedom and they lurched into action, shoving the chair back, standing, and scooping her up in one fluid motion.

His lips were on hers before he made his way through the doorway. She squeaked then wrapped her arms about his neck like a scarf, meeting his mouth in ready, if surprised, reciprocation. With long, impatient strides, he made his way up the steps.

***

Gabriel reached clumsily for the door handle of his rooms with one hand, then kicked it closed behind them with a reverberating *thwomp*. His kisses rained down like countless snow flurries, leaving her lips only to feather against the dimples of her smiling cheeks, her jaw, her temple.

"My, you're like a little grey squirrel that can't decide where to bury his nuts for the winter." Her eyes twinkled despite the flicker of bewilderment.

Setting her on her feet, he pulled her into a fierce hug, struggling to bring order to his thoughts. His body couldn't decide how to proceed and which part of her to touch first. One of her hands stroked up and down his spine, rubbing away at the edges of his control.

"God, I want you. Every inch of me longs to be irrevocably and completely lost in you." He breathed the hoarse admission against the delicate shell of her ear, all warmth and rumbles. "Tell me I'm not scaring you, Violet."

She pulled back from his embrace enough to coax his eyes to hers. "Of course you're not."

And then she gave him one of the brilliant, trusting smiles that stole his breath and left him lightheaded in its wake.

There was nothing in her expression of shyness or fear. No indication of old wounds that doubtless still lingered from her past. Her expression communicated complete trust in the care and sweetness that his body would offer hers, and it was her faith that anchored him against the lust threatening to spur him in every direction at once.

"My love, I will try to make this good for you, but I am out of practice." He kissed her cheek then rubbed his lips back and forth against the skin there, breathing her in.

"Lucky you, then, that I have no measuring stick with which to compare."

He could feel her dimple peeking out again against his mouth. "True, but you will know what feels good to you, and you must tell me if you don't like something." His busy fingers worked the buttons free down the back of her gown. As the dress gaped open at the back, Gabriel strummed his fingers across the corset bones and teased the curve of her breast beneath. "And if you want more of something."

"More of that, please. I'll have more of that." The breathy catch in her voice ignited an answering pull of desire deep in his belly. Lifting his hand from her shoulder where it had been holding her gown in place, he watched as the fabric slithered to the floor in a heap.

"I would hate to see what *in practice* looks like if that is out of practice."

"If I was in practice, your corset would be on the floor with your gown by now." He nipped gently at the lobe of her ear then took her mouth in deep, drugging kisses.

Violet's hands worked beneath his coat from his shoulders down his biceps, sliding his evening coat to the floor. She entwined his hands with her own and gave a gentle squeeze, then released them to place the flat of her palms against his cloth-covered abdomen. His pulse seemed to centre on that single point of contact, his nerve endings sparking in cadence with the ticklish caress of her fingertips.

As a younger man, he'd been captivated by all the parts of Emma's body that differed from his own. But with maturity came an appreciation for the more subtle feminine treasures: the curve of her thigh, the tender pit of her elbow, the hazy, nearly translucent skin at the inside of her wrist. He wanted to worship every part of Violet and make every inch of her his own.

Violet broke away from his kiss, a coquettish smile curving her lips as her fingers trailed to the buttons of his waistcoat. She freed them each in turn and tossed the garment atop his coat on the floor. He remained still, allowing her to undress him at her leisure while every drop of his blood began a hasty downward descent.

For a woman with no experience in seduction, he felt utterly seduced. She stepped back, her eyes roaming over the cloth-covered muscles of his chest and stomach. Damned if she didn't wet her lips as her gaze dipped further.

He felt like a butterfly pinned to a corkboard, but instead of pain, there was only the delicious pleasure of anticipation. And he quivered with it. Embarrassingly, quite literally. Her breasts pressed into the unyielding corset with every quick inhalation.. She was not as tranquil as she appeared, and her carefully-guarded nervousness served to tame his voracious lust. What he needed, more than any pleasure Violet could give him, was the certainty that she felt safe, free to proceed in the direction and tempo she required with absolute confidence he would follow her lead.

So he waited.

She stepped back into easy reach and flicked open the top two buttons at his collar. Instead of continuing to the third button, she lifted her fingers and stroked the small triangle of skin revealed at the base of his throat. Lifting to her tippy toes, her warm lips tentatively pressed into the notch there. He filled his hands with the swell of her hips and gave a gentle squeeze of approval.

As she kissed in scattered constellations across the base of his throat, her fingers released three more buttons, opening his shirt in a wide "V" that fell just below his nipples. Again she pulled away, as if to enjoy the present she'd unwrapped in tiny, flirtatious fractions.

Her look of appreciation made him intensely glad he was not a sedentary man. While he would never have considered himself brawny in a traditional sense—certainly not beside men like Hamish—he was athletic and trim, fit for a man of thirty-seven years. Yes, he had a few more wrinkles about the corners of his eyes and a smattering of grey hidden in the curls of his hair, but he knew he was handsome. Violet stared at him like he was an icy glass of water and she'd been digging in the garden soil for hours in the sun. It made him feel quite like a god.

Her fingertips followed the slope of his clavicles, then drizzled down like beads of water along his chest, grazing his nipples before releasing the remaining buttons and discarding the starched linen to the floor. He stood still, watching her work.

Until this moment, she'd seemed decisive in her path, but now that she had him half-naked, her trepidation became apparent in her expression. She nibbled at her lower lip, the only movement in her otherwise frozen form.

"Would you like to know what I want you to do, Violet?" She nodded, her shoulders relaxing.

"Kiss me every place your fingers touched. Kiss me with your lips and your tongue and your breath. Love me with your mouth."

She nestled into the sparse hair of his chest, learning the texture of him. Then there was breath where her cheek had been, and soft moist lips. She tasted the skin of his collarbone, hesitant little kisses and timid nudges of her tongue at first, spurred on by the needy, appreciative noises that escaped the back of his throat. Then her mouth began a more deliberate course, her tongue sliding across one nipple. "What about here?"

"Definitely there," he said, low and sensual.

Heat and wetness closed around him with the gentle pulls of her mouth. Electric shudders of desire pulsed with the rhythmic friction of her tongue.

"Uhh, that feels … God you'll kill me, Violet. My turn, love. Let me loosen your corset." Violet groaned reluctantly, then her teeth gently grazed his nipple. Gabriel's head fell back and his hands came to her head, gently holding her in place. Violet was an eager student, sensitive to his responses, kindling his arousal with swirls of her tongue and long, teasing strokes until he was panting.

Gasping her name, he eased her away. "Vixen."

She grinned and turned obligingly, offering up her corset strings. When he didn't immediately approach or loosen the strings, she peeked over her shoulder, eliciting a chuckle.

"It's not a race, Violet. We have all night." Like him, she was an amalgamation of eagerness and anxiety, both inducing her to tumble along faster before her brain could settle on either emotion for too long. But experience offered Gabriel a perspective that Violet didn't yet possess; he knew the value of lingering on each incremental step before moving on to the next, rather than launching bodily up three at a time. He was too invested in her enjoyment to allow her inexperience to speed them along at a breakneck pace.

He drew her close, allowing the warmth of his body to surround hers, then rested his hands on her shoulders. With slow, penetrating strokes, he massaged a knot in her neck. After a few moments, she began to relax under his hands.

"Gabriel?"

"Yes, love?"

"Does it hurt a lot?" His fingers paused for a moment, then continued their attentive ministrations. "I don't know. The first time isn't the same for a man as it is for a woman. And it's been fifteen years since I made love with a virgin. My memories of the experience are faint. I only remember how clumsy I was, my good intentions pulverised by lust and inexperience. I can say very little about her body's reaction to my ungainly attempts beyond the fact that she was kind and forgiving, and that she gave me more chances to get it right later, thank God."

Gabriel had become accustomed to the ache that punctuated every memory of Emma. Like a chronic pain in his heart that flared as predictably as an injured knee during a cold rain. He closed his eyes, and he could see Emma, pink-cheeked and vibrant, and hear her shy reassurances to his fumbling exploration. He steadied himself for the onslaught of grief that would follow like a shadow. But for the first time since Emma's death, it did not come.

Every part of him remained here in this moment, with Violet.

She nodded, a worried, jerky little movement. His arms curled around her, an "X" across her chest, holding her in a snug cocoon while studiously avoiding her breasts. He could seduce her into forgetting the impending discomfort, could lull her into a lust-filled haze as easily as he could soothe a child to sleep with music, but there was no place in love for placating half-truths or distractions disguised as affectionate caresses. If she was scared, he would hold her and wait for her to find her courage. He would reassure her.

"But I'm not that same untried youth. I know how to make things easier for you, even if I can't prevent all the discomfort. I don't believe it will be unbearable or long-lasting. Your trust means everything to me, Violet."

He rested his cheek atop her head. "I hate that you're nervous, love. Tell me what I can do. Do you wish to stop for now? Slow down?"

She chuckled, and he was immediately soothed by the sound. "I don't want to stop, and three-legged turtles move at a swifter speed than you and I. Just kiss me." He dropped a quick peck on her cheek and grinned impishly.

"Not like that." She echoed his smile.

"No?" His forehead scrunched up in feigned confusion.

"No," she said in a huff.

"Consider it just recompense for comparing my sexual prowess to a disabled turtle."

Interrupting her giggling objections, he took her mouth with his in sensual, inflaming kisses, his tongue caressing hers in possessive sweeps as he worked the laces of her corset loose until only her thin white shift remained.

Gabriel removed the pins from her hair, watching the path of each wavy cluster as it tumbled down her back. He had seen her hair free plenty of times before, but tonight he found the sight overwhelmingly erotic. Crossing a few paces to the settee, he sat and gave his Hessians a resentful glare. "These blasted boots …"

Violet was there, kneeling at his feet and, with a determined heave, she removed both in turn. Setting the boots to the side, she laid a hand on each knee, her fingers plotting a strategic course up and down his thighs.

His legs drifted apart as her path traversed in bolder sweeps, her knuckles grazing his arousal with fleeting strokes. With a breath, he covered her hands with his, stood, and helped her to rise.

"Not good?"

"Too good."

His hands shook as he unfastened his falls and removed his trousers and small clothes. With his heartbeat loud in his ears, he steeled himself, raising his eyes from the pile of clothes on the floor until they collided with Violet's startlingly blue eyes. Nature had no match for that blue. They were wide. In terror? Anticipation? He didn't know, and not knowing was cutting away at his insides.

No matter how fervently she had protested that her fear of John and his heinous acts did not colour her view of other men, he had felt her panic under his hands before and never wanted her to experience that again. Least of all in his arms.

Her mouth was slightly open as she stared unblinkingly at his very naked body.

"If I'd been gentlemanly enough to wait until dark, I could offer to extinguish the candles." He pushed air in and out of his lungs. "It's not as bad as all that, is it?" He hoped she would take it as a light-hearted jest, but apprehension blazed through him, its sharp edges cracking open caverns of concern in his chest. He could feel his cheeks roasting.

"Violet, sweetheart. Say something." He was seconds away from retreating to wrap himself in a blanket when she reached down, grasped the hem of her shift, and lifted it over her head. Her drawers dropped to the floor. She didn't attempt to cover any part of her, only met his eyes and held them as she closed the distance between them in slow, even steps.

Chapter 36

“**I** wouldn't want it to be dark.” Violet's voice didn't quaver and her hands remained steady, which was more than he could say for himself.

She was stunning, brave, exquisite … like the brilliant colours of spring that fill your imagination through the winter, only to bloom more magnificently than you could possibly have imagined. Wrapping her fingers around his lean hips, she squeezed. He could only guess at what she saw when she looked into his eyes. He was utterly undone.

Lifting her up into his arms, he carried her to the bed, curling on his side next to her. She immediately crooked to face him, shimmying closer to touch her lips to his in a gentle, chaste kiss. It was achingly sweet, and he felt the effects of that softness all through his body.

Resting his lips against hers, he drew her closer, then closer still. He couldn't get near enough. Threading a leg between hers, he sought out the curve of her neck with his mouth, tentatively at first, then becoming less inhibited as gasps and soft moans fell from her lips. Her responsiveness and the almost unendurable friction of his length pressed against her thigh both relieved and aroused, and he burned for more.

“Christ, Violet, you feel so good against me. So warm and soft and perfect.” His hand crossed the silky plane of her abdomen, knuckles playing up and down the side of her breast. Seeking permission. Offering more.

Gabriel covered her breast with his hand, kneading gently before skating his thumb around her rosy-tipped peak. She arched off the bed with a moan. His mouth went dry, cock leaping in a rude, rowdy celebration. Reflexively, he thrust against her leg, his eyes squeezing shut at the momentary swell of ecstasy.

"Little love. Can I kiss you here, as you kissed me?" Arousal clouded her expression as she nodded, then squirmed when his breath blew across one turgid peak. The hazy orange glow of the low-hanging sun fell through the window in a blanket across her skin. He nuzzled her sun-warmed breast with his unshaven cheek, sighing at the unimaginable softness.

With meticulous attention, he nibbled and kissed slow patterns across her breast, patently avoiding her most sensitive places, allowing sensations to gradually intensify her arousal. Her toes were curling against his leg, synchronised with the gentle lapping of his tongue.

Teasing his lower lip back and forth across her nipple, he revelled in the texture of her.

"Gabriel." Her moan hovered somewhere between chastisement and plea. Then her fingers tunnelled in his hair, clasping with a demanding squeeze.

"Since you asked so nicely …"

If he wasn't so painfully aroused he would have smiled. Instead, he took her into his mouth, his tongue painting in hot, wet sweeps, responding to her every wordless request, every catch of her breath and quiver of her skin. She was magnificent.

"I need …" She gasped in response to a gentle nip.

"Yes, sweetheart? You need …"

She threw her head to the side and writhed against him. "More."

Moving lower, he kissed her navel, discovering a delightfully ticklish bit above her hip bone. He wanted to learn every sensitive place on her body, unearth every secret spot that made her flex against him, every kissable curve that would leave her keening his name.

Trailing his fingers down the roundness of her hip then between her legs, Gabriel teased through her soft curls. She was so slick, coating his fingers as he traced her petals and the seam of her sex.

"Come here." She pulled him up with a tug. The moment he was close enough, she threw her arms around his neck and kissed him hard. "That feels …" The rest of the sentence was lost in another kiss as he circled her clitoris in concert with the slow thrust of his tongue. They fell into a steady rhythm, her pelvis grinding against his hand. She whimpered in protest when his strokes gentled, moving away from that bundle of nerves and lower to the slick entrance of her sex.

"Shh, Violet. Trust me, love. I will take care of you," he crooned in her ear. He slid the tip of his finger inside, her silky inner flesh gripping and tightening around the unfamiliar invasion. Her hips jerked away, eyes connecting with his.

"Steady, love. This will make it better for you. You're so lovely. So perfect. Just try to relax your muscles here." As he murmured his encouragement, she softened again in his arms. He rocked his hand in a slow, careful rhythm, thumb whispering across her clitoris as his finger sank deeper into her sex. God, she was so tight around him, and when Gabriel felt the first twinges of her climax begin, he couldn't stifle his own groan.

"That's it, Vi." Her fingers dug into his shoulders, hips thrusting into his hand. When she cried out and clenched hard around his finger, his lust reached a point of crisis. As her last shutters receded, he rose up on his elbows and waited for her eyes to refocus on his.

"Love, you have to tell me if it hurts. If one way is too much we'll try another, but I need you to talk to me, Vi. Can you do that for me? Promise me."

"I promise."

He took his length in hand and slid it back and forth across the entrance of her swollen sex. His forehead dropped immediately to her shoulder, battered by sensation.

"This may be welcome news to you, but I won't last long once I'm inside of you." He nipped her shoulder. "I'm already wound so damn tightly, I almost spent just watching your climax." Arms shaking with restraint, he slid one inch inside and held himself motionless.

"All right?" His eyes remained closed ruthlessly tight.

"I'm all right. I'm fine." He felt her hand stroke his cheek. The breath he was holding slid out in a long sigh as he gingerly eased into her before retreating again.

"That feels quite … mmm …" With her breathy moan against his ear, his hips bucked reflexively.

"Ouch. Ouch ouch ouch!!" She didn't push him away but her expression was scrunched and her hands flew out to grip the blanket on either side. He pulled out immediately, gulping in a few shallow breaths.

"I'm sorry, Gabriel. I don't want you to stop. I just wasn't expecting … *that*. I'll be all right now that I know." She stroked his head as if *he* was the one in need of comfort. "It isn't unbearable."

His head jerked up. "No, Violet. That's not the way this is going to happen. I told you I wasn't willing to hurt you and that hasn't changed. We'll try one more thing, and if it's too much then I have a perfectly functional left hand and we can try again another night."

"Truly I'll be—"

"Hush." He kissed her soundly on the mouth. "Stop being stubborn and let me try to make this better for you."

In one quick movement, he wrapped his arms around her and rolled so she was on top of him. She frowned in confusion.

"Raise up on your knees, Vi, and take me in your hand. This way you control the depth and what feels best for you."

Gabriel felt her ribs expand under his hands on a long, deep breath, and then her eyes connected with his. It wasn't the starry-eyed gaze of youthful naivete that had been present on that first night with Emma. It was easy to be confident when you had no notion of fear or experience with pain or deceit. Instead, Violet's faith shone brightly in her eyes, in the way that she revealed every conflicting emotion that stirred inside her. There wasn't a complete absence of fear, but its sharp edges had been made inert by the trust they had built together.

"That's it, love. Guide me in." With his hands on her hips, he steadied her as she lowered a few inches onto him before rising up again. She repeated the movement gingerly, her hands pressed against his chest. It was a delicious brand of madness to hold himself motionless when every nerve in his body howled with the need to follow her hips with his own. For endless minutes she slid in slow, shallow thrusts.

"Kiss me, Vi. I need you here," he spoke through clenched teeth.

As Violet leaned forward to take his mouth with hers, she slid the remainder of the way down his shaft, and he was surrounded by her warmth. He groaned deep and long into her kiss.

With his concern for Violet ebbing to a simmer, he allowed himself to be carried away by the sounds she was making. The heaven of feeling her around him, covering him. Kissing him. No longer tentative, her hips circled, chasing the ecstasy that lingered just out of reach.

He could feel her need in every bunched muscle beneath his hands. In the grip of her fingertips, and the roughness of her kiss. She nipped at his bottom lip, sighing as she worked against his pelvis in short, jerky thrusts. Every sound she made pulled him into a freefall towards his own climax. Christ! He had to hold back just a few moments more. She was so close, he could feel it, but his body was screaming for release.

Reaching between them, he slid his thumb across her clitoris. She groaned his name into his mouth, her body racked by deep shudders as she clenched around his cock, squeezing him as if desperate to keep him deep inside of her. In two hard strokes, he relinquished his control and came with a guttural moan, her silky walls milking his release with little aftershocks.

Violet collapsed on top of him with a contented sigh. He locked his fingers around her back, holding her close, amazed and elated at the completeness he felt. After a few moments, he disengaged from her and left the bed to wet a square of flannel.

"Open your legs, sweetheart."

"I don't know if I can. I think you've done me in."

Kissing her bent knee, he opened her legs and cleaned her with soft, careful strokes. "It seems decidedly unfair that women have to suffer through their first sexual experience while men never feel the slightest physical discomfort."

She reached out to wrap her arms around his waist and pull him down beside her. "I can assure you with complete honesty that my suffering was short-lived and is already forgotten."

"You won't say that in the morning when you are sore. Let's get you into a nice soaking bath, and I will play some music for you. What would you like to hear?"

"Whatever comes to you."

***

When Violet sank into the massive steaming bath, her body and mind were at odds. While her muscles had fallen into a state of limp contentment, her mind was convinced she should never rest again. Incomplete thoughts overlapped one another, seeming to disintegrate the moment she tried to examine them closer. She would scarcely land upon one emotion before pitching forward into the next. Gabriel watched her as he played a lullaby. Dressed only in trousers, his body swaying slightly to the music he created, he had never looked more peaceful. Never appeared more present and content in the moment.

Everything had changed tonight. Their lovemaking, yes, but that was just one manifestation of a much larger transformation. Or perhaps the deeper connection she felt tonight wasn't new at all. Perhaps it had been this way for some time, waiting just beneath the surface for one of them to muster the bravery to tear away the last of what kept them apart. The last of what protected them from unadulterated vulnerability, yes, but also unadulterated love. And it *had* been lovemaking, not only in the pleasure they gave, but in the connection that was forged between them.

The entire course of her life had been a series of reactions to events that were beyond her control. She dodged and dove and made the best of where she landed. She would never have called her years with Nathan unhappy, but they had been colourless in so many ways. Ways that she never fully understood until Gabriel.

But Nathan had understood. There was often a sadness in his expression when he looked at her. When he talked about the sacrifice she had made when she took him as her husband. When he spoke of the possibility of love that she'd bartered in exchange for her safety and his. She prayed that, wherever he was, he could see her now. It would make him very happy indeed.

Gabriel filled the room with music until her racing mind slowed to a skip, then a plodding lope. She had rotated each moment around in her mind, examining it from every conceivable angle before her brain would allow her to tuck those moments into her memory. The process had felt endless but necessary, a long string of yarn that she needed to wind into a tidy skein before she could set it down. Finally, her eyes grew heavy. As if Gabriel had been waiting for her task to be complete, he rose and crossed the room, holding a massive, blissfully inviting bathing sheet. Instead of waiting for her to rise, he set the towel on a chair and plunged his arms into the water, lifting her. Cradling her close to his body, he kissed her nose, then placed her gingerly on her feet.

"Now your trousers are all wet," Violet chided.

"I wasn't planning to keep them on," he said with a smirk. "Did you have a pleasant bath?"

"I did." He lowered to his haunches, drying her toes, then the tops of her feet. He attended to her ankles, gliding up her body with exacting care and tenderness. With a satisfied nod, he wrapped the towel about her and carried her to bed, removing his saturated trousers and following immediately behind.

Gabriel had kept a candle burning on the table beside them, leaving half his face cast in shadows and the other half lit by a warm golden glow. This must be very much like Gabriel felt on the inside as well. It had only been two short years since he lost Emma, and while she didn't doubt that love for her had begun to flicker alight, that loss was still well and truly a part of him, and it always would be.

"You can talk to me about her, you know."

Gabriel rested his head on one breast as she played with the curls of his hair.

"She was your best friend. The mother of your children. Your lover for countless years. I am not trying to tear those pages out of your book, Gabriel. I only hope to add more chapters. It's all right to flip back when you need to remember, or to read aloud so I can come to know the woman who helped make you who you are today."

His hand paused where he had been tracing a pattern in the freckles across her shoulder. Easing up on one crooked arm, he took her chin between his thumb and index finger and brought her lips to his in a brief, tender kiss. Balancing his weight on his elbows, he looked down at her.

"She would have liked you very much. She'd like the way your infectious energy encouraged me to seek out the paltry spark that still flickered within me and let it flare back to life just so I could see what you would do next." He swallowed, and she watched his Adam's apple bob slowly with the movement. "When she died, I felt as if all the joy that the universe had promised me for a lifetime had been ripped away, and that I would have to survive on what was left behind, like crusts of bread. That I might learn to feel full on what was offered, but never be satisfied." He laid his forehead against her breastbone, puffs of warm air dancing across her skin. And then he raised his head, and the expression Zach had captured in his painting was there on his face. She realised in an instant that it wasn't longing. It was love. He loved her.

"And then you crashed into my world with your unquenchable curiosity and your mad goats, and instead of counting the days since I'd last held my wife, I found myself wiling away the time until I'd next see you again." He kissed her once, then punctuated each sentence with more, some soft and coaxing, others rich and slow and tender. "I found myself trying to figure out exactly how long it *would* take a porcupine to peel a potato or why you thought fish scales would make a functional rain jacket when there are already perfectly adequate slickers available. You filled my soul with the sounds of your laughter."

Violet's mind began to spin, intoxicated both by his words and the way he worshipped her with his mouth and tongue and lips. Her heart reacted enthusiastically to the love that was implied as he pulled out every example of her quirkiness, every flaw that had brought her shame, and embraced them as if they were the parts of her that he loved most.

"You scamper through the world finding compelling little miracles in ordinary things and bringing life to everything around you, even to a man who couldn't find the will to care much about living. I simply couldn't resist you. I will *never* be able to resist you, and surrendering has never felt so bloody good."

Violet broke away from the kiss that followed and smiled up at him. "I love you too, Gabriel Anson."

Gabriel threw his head back and laughed. "Wait. You're skipping ahead. I haven't even gotten to that part yet. "

"Yes, you have, and I love you too!" She kissed him again with awkward, smiling lips.

"Well, I am going to say it anyway, even though you've ruined my moment." He gave her a chastising frown. "I love you, Violet. I love your bravery and your strength, and I love the remarkable way you have seen the darkness of the world, but you've never let those shadows encroach upon your light. I love your softness and your dedication to raising Zachariah to be proud of his uniqueness." He paused to study his fingers as they ran back and forth across her stomach, and then his eyes returned to hers. When he continued, his voice was quieter. Almost a whisper.

"I love the way you accept my moments of sadness and give me the space to feel them." She was trapped in his gaze, ensnared by the intensity of emotions that swirled there and how he invited her to see each and every one.

"I love *all* of you."

The hand that had been painting trails across her stomach was quivering now, and she reached to cover it with her own.

"Quite desperately, Violet. When I think about the possibility of losing you, every breath burns in my lungs and my heart thrums uncontrollably in my chest. I break out in the most embarrassingly un-ducal sweat, and I can't seem to find my way out of the labyrinth of my own dark thoughts. But I am helpless to do anything but love you anyway because I am already yours." He smiled then. "You can say it now, Violet." He quirked an eyebrow and waited.

In one clumsy, energetic movement, Violet flipped on top of Gabriel and wrapped her arms fiercely about his neck.

"You *are* mine. And I will not give you back." He smiled into her shoulder.

"I love you, Gabriel Anson." She kissed him enthusiastically. He laughed against her lips and returned her ardour in equal measure.

"Again, please," he demanded between clumsy kisses.

"I love you," she said. "But I don't think I could say it half as beautifully as you did."

He rolled on top of her with a growl, kissing her soundly once more. "Then show me."

The intensity of his mouth against hers amidst all the joy left her body frantic for more contact. She mimicked his earlier kisses, greedy against the soft skin of his neck and to the shell of his ear. He panted in short, uneven bursts as she laved his earlobe.

"God Vi. We have to stop, or at least slow down. We can't again tonight. You'll be sore." She continued as if she hadn't heard him.

"Violet!" he pleaded in a laughing groan. "Have mercy on your husband! I'm not that strong a man, and the things you do to me! My God, you make me wild with wanting you. But we can't again tonight. Please, my sweet. I cannot hurt you."

She heard the desperation in his voice, and her body responded, gentling her kisses to soft nuzzles, and then eventually stilling against his warm muscular body. They lay there for several long moments wrapped around one another, waiting for passion to simmer and make space for quiet contentment.

Violet looked up with a sultry smile. "Ears. Who would have thought they would be so sensitive. That thing you did with your tongue …" a pleasant little shiver ran down her spine. "I finally know the reason why birds don't have external ears."

Gabriel rolled onto his back, taking her with him, then tucking her snugly in the crook of his arm. "Not all of our brains are capable of such massive leaps, Violet. I'm going to need you to find some stepping stones if you expect me to be able to follow you."

By means of an answer, Violet adjusted to position her mouth at his ear, her tongue circling the outer shell before taking his lobe in her mouth with a long, teasing pull. Then she whispered, "Avians have beaks. It's impossible to arouse their lover birds with those pointy things. Thus, no point in having external ears."

A single bark of laughter fell into a moan as Violet continued to make her point, toying lazily with his ear.

"And this epiphany came to you while we were making love?" Another soft hum of encouragement broke through his question. "Here I was aroused out of my head, and you were off considering bird anatomy." He turned into her mouth, kissing away her reply. "How I love you."

"You can't expect one hundred percent of my mind to remain on a single task. It's a busy place, my brain. But you captured at least ninety percent."

"Of this, I do not doubt. We will see if you relegate only ninety percent to me tomorrow; there are some other noteworthy places where I can use my tongue." His hand briefly caressed between her thighs before retreating. "I intend to make it my singular goal in life to arouse you into a state of such all-consuming ardour that there isn't space for a single scientific thought in your head." Gabriel looked smugly satisfied by her shocked silence.

She recovered.

"That sounds like an activity that might command ninety-*five* percent of my attention, but surely expecting one hundred percent is just greedy."

"Oh my duchess, I intend to be very greedy indeed."

Epilogue

Despite Gabriel's polite attention to every guest at the ball, there was an unwavering fraction of his awareness that never diverted from Violet. As diligently as he tried to maintain his complete focus on the conversations around him and his partners on the dance floor, the brilliance and gravity she exuded was impossible for him to evade. Both his mind and his body were continually pulled into her orbit. But more than just her beauty and irresistible charm were playing havoc with his self-control tonight. Concern rumbled through his soul with an instance and volume that was \
impossible to ignore.

Two months ago, she should have had a cycle that would have put a temporary pause to their nightly lovemaking … but no such pause had occurred. Anxiety had begun to claw at his insides.

Two weeks ago, Violet's appetite had vastly altered. She spurned bacon and kippers in favour of dry toast, which she proceeded to tear into tiny bits that littered her plate. On one occasion, apparently feeling the weight of his gaze, she had surreptitiously slipped half a slice inside of a napkin. Her normally boundless energy was resigned to painfully short spurts that fizzled out before they could even fully flare.

Two days ago, she had gone quiet.

She was carrying his child, and she knew it. He was as sure of that fact as he was certain that her consideration for his feelings was hurting her. Violet's reluctance to voice the truth that she believed would launch his terror was transforming a moment that should have been the happiest in her life into something dark and uncertain. He would not—could not—allow it to continue. And while her instincts about his gut reaction were correct, she had underestimated the capacity for his love to battle back that fear. Not destroy it entirely, but to subdue the terror well enough for joy and excitement to prevail.

That morning he could deny the obvious symptoms no longer. He rode Omen into the open fields for as long as he could and as fast as he could, until both he and his horse were sweaty and exhausted. Then, he circled around towards Emma's gravestone. There, he had unburdened himself of his grief and panic. The tears of past trauma watered the dreams of tomorrow until the visions of horror had cleared from his head, making way for a different sort of picture to emerge;: Violet's glowing smile as she looked down at an infant conceived of their love. When he walked away, his legs weak and mind exhausted, he was determined to nurture the seeds of that joy. To shine so brightly that only the good would grow. There would be no room for shadows or doubt.

A ball was the very last place he had wanted to be, but to please the dowager, Violet had worked tirelessly for this event. And in seeking his mother's happiness, she'd found much of it for herself as well. Despite the fatigue of her condition, she was incandescent. She danced with neighbouring tenant farmers, chatted animatedly with Hamish as they snuck away to the veranda to enjoy the cool air, and acted the charming and enthusiastic hostess.

The string quartet was about to begin the final dance of the evening—a waltz they would share—when he saw Violet slip into the great hall beyond the ballroom. He followed at a pace that would not garner notice, increasing his speed as he stepped beyond the double doors

He laid a hand on her shoulder. "Are you well, my love? You haven't overtired yourself with all that spirited country dancing, I hope." Gabriel gave her a glass of champagne and lifted her chin between his thumb and forefinger, noting her drooping eyelids and the pinched lines of her face. "I will claim my dance another time. Let's sit a while, and soon we can see our guests to the door and retire."

"No." She lowered her chin away from his assessing gaze and pressed her hand on his chest, just above his heart. "I want to dance with you. I haven't had the opportunity all evening, and how often will I have the chance to dazzle you with such a fabulous dress or spin around the floor in the arms of the most handsome man in the room?" She smiled, but like the rest of her body, it lacked the energy to remain steady for long.

He covered her hand with one of his own. "As often as you would like. We certainly aren't wanting for invitations, and I have been admiring you in that dress all evening. You are absolutely stunning." He lowered his head and kissed along the curve of her neck, hoping to coerce her with romance since logic was failing.

"Come, the waltz is beginning." She practically dragged him through the double doors and onto the dance floor, and they took their place amongst the couples. She must have summoned every ounce of her remaining fortitude, as the lightness of her steps showed nothing of the exhaustion that he knew was present.

"While I don't believe a ball packed with country gentry and tenant farmers was precisely what your mother had in mind, I am pleased with our debut ball," Violet said.

"I don't know that she's as displeased with the company as she would have us believe. I saw her strike up quite a lively debate with several other matrons." Gabriel eased her closer in his hold than propriety deemed acceptable. Given the assortment of colourful guests, however, no one would bat an eye. Many others had taken the opportunity offered by the waltz to hold their partners closer.

"We will have to pretend not to have noticed her newly acquired friendships." Violet winked.

"After the stragglers have been driven home, I wonder if you will join me for a walk under the stars. I find myself craving fresh air and the company of my favourite person." Her eyes flickered away.

"We won't go far, and I promise not to keep you out long. I know you're tired." She missed a step, and Gabriel pulled her close to counter her stumble. For a moment, he considered postponing the conversation. The night had taken its toll, but he was also certain that her anxiety was causing her every bit as much emotional strain, and he was eager to put an end to her worries. "Please?"

Violet nodded, and they fell into a silence that was not quite comfortable, finishing a sweeping turn as the musicians held out the final notes.

None of the attendants seemed eager to leave, and by the time Violet and Gabriel meandered out into the night, hand in hand, nearly an hour had passed. They moved together at a leisurely pace, Violet's pink satin gown trailing behind her through the clumps of wildflowers that puffed up from the meadow grass like rolling purple clouds in the breeze. They stopped at the base of a cliff face, hidden beneath thick climbing vines. Gabriel sat, reaching his arms up in invitation.

"It'll ruin my dress."

"I'll buy you ten more."

Violet sighed, plopped down gracelessly, and settled against his chest.

Then she released a different kind of sigh. One that escaped when words could not.

"My love, I have been a married man for more than half my life. I know about ladies' cycles. I know what it means when a happily married woman casts up her accounts like a rogue in his salad days." He paused, pulling her closer. "And I know my wife well enough to see when a secret she is holding to protect me is burning her on the inside." She slumped in his arms.

Gabriel had practised the start of this conversation in his head countless times, but he'd never thought beyond that. He'd assumed that once he announced he wasn't ignorant of her pregnancy that she would be relieved and she would pick up where he left off, talking and planning before eventually moving on to the kissing part of the evening. It had been far too long since her lips had been on his. Her silence had gone on for so long that he was beginning to wonder if he was wrong, if he had somehow misunderstood what he had thought were very clear symptoms.

"Violet? Did you fall asleep? Did I somehow misconstrue—"

"No. You didn't. I'm just … Gabriel, you don't have to put on a brave face for me. I know you must be—" He cut off her sentence with a kiss, using brutal pressure at first to halt her speech, as if allowing those words to escape would make them true. Then they grew softer, affectionate. Lovemaking relegated to hungry lips and entwining tongues, the exchange of gentle breaths and unspoken promises. When he ended the kiss, her lips were red, and her eyes were dazed and heavy lidded.

Gabriel exhaled a long breath. "You will have an uneventful, boring confinement, followed by the shortest labour in the history of Great Britain. A healthy baby will be born, pink and perfect and very much alive. She will scream so loudly and enthusiastically that the goats will hear her in the paddock and cover their ears with their hooves. You will comment that any fears that might have plagued me had been completely unfounded, as you were more physically taxed by sheep washing than by bringing our tiny child into the world. You will be healthy and vibrant and goddamned alive when you are finished. That is what is going to happen, Violet, and I will not even entertain the notion that anything less than blissful will occur.

"Gabriel. I've seen goat does in labour. Even the best circumstances are far from blissful." He cut her off with another demanding kiss then tore his mouth away. "BLISS-FUL. Do you hear me, Violet Anson?"

"All right. Blissful. May I just say one thing? Then I promise I will allow you to live in whatever cloud of rainbows you wish to reside for the next seven months."

He gave her a dubious look. "Very well, *one* thing. And then it's back to rainbows and kissing for me. I'm going to need a lot of kissing"

"All right." She gave him a peck. "I appreciate your valiant optimism, Gabriel, but it's all right if you're scared. I realise that it's in no way an indication of your happiness at growing our family further." She stroked her hand against the roughness of his cheek." I wanted to protect you from those feelings, even while I realised it was a ridiculously impossible thing to do. I am not going to be getting less pregnant anytime soon. I love you, Gabriel. I won't love you any less if you struggle your way through my confinement, counting the days until it's over."

Gabriel nestled his cheek into her hand and kissed the centre of her palm. "Thank you, sweetheart. But this is the only way I will be able to survive the next seven months. I need to hold onto those rainbows because the alternative is the kind of epic thunderstorm that will tear the heart right out of my chest. And I am going to need my heart to remain right where it is, because very soon I will have one more person to love. If I allow my fears to run rampant, I will drive you mad with my attempts to keep you safe … which I still may very well do." Their chests rose and fell together, gazes locked, wide and unblinking, connecting them with unspoken vows that were more eloquent than words could ever hope to be. And then Violet was on top of him, impatient hands tugging at everything that separated his skin from hers.

"Oh good. The kissing part of the evening. How I've missed you," Gabriel murmured into her lips.

"It hasn't even been twelve hours," she argued.

"No. You can't possibly be right. It's been forever."

She nipped his neck and he laughed.

"Easy with my dress, you'll tear it," Violet said

Gabriel pulled his mouth from hers, cocking his head to the side, palms out in front of him. I haven't done anything to your dress yet." There was another obvious tug and they both twisted to investigate. Apple Core had escaped her pen and was leisurely gnawing at the hem of Violet's ballgown.

"If she made it out, that means they have all escaped," Violet groaned. "We can call them back with some grain in the morning. Hopefully, the overnight mischief will be minimal and Emma's rose garden won't be any worse for the wear. I can't say as much for my gown, unfortunately."

Gabriel stood, half his buttons littering the ground and his hair mussed where her hands had been tugging. Reaching down, he helped Violet to her feet and wrapped an arm around her waist. "I've got a better idea. Let's go catch them together, or you can watch my ridiculousness if you're too fatigued. Come and be foolish with me Violet?"

Violet kicked off her shoes, hiked up her gown and ran after a very startled Apple Core.

Dawn slipped softly over the horizon, its subtle trickles of light glittering off the scattered dewdrops. Violet fell into bed, exhausted, smelling slightly of goats, and radiating happiness. Gabriel sat down at the piano.

"Come to bed, Gabriel. It can no longer even be called late. We are solidly into the category of early."

"One song. For the newest Anson."

From his heart, through his hands, a lullaby sweetly filled the upper floors of Northam Hall. *Berceuse* by Chopin.

The End

Printed in Great Britain
by Amazon

36180998R00219